HEAD HUNTERS

Also by Chris Ryan

Non-fiction
The One That Got Away
Chris Ryan's SAS Fitness Book
Chris Ryan's Ultimate Survival Guide
Fight to Win
Safe

Fiction
Stand By, Stand By
Zero Option
The Kremlin Device
Tenth Man Down
Hit List
The Watchman
Land of Fire
Greed
The Increment
Blackout
Ultimate Weapon
Strike Back
Firefight
Who Dares Wins
The Kill Zone
Killing for the Company
Osama

In the Danny Black Series
Masters of War
Hunter Killer
Hellfire
Bad Soldier
Warlord

In the Strikeback Series
Deathlist
Shadow Kill
Global Strike
Red Strike

Chris Ryan Extreme
Hard Target
Night Strike
Most Wanted
Silent Kill

CHRIS RYAN

HEAD HUNTERS

CORONET

First published in Great Britain in 2018 by Coronet
An imprint of Hodder & Stoughton
An Hachette UK company

This paperback edition published in 2019

1

A CIP catalogue record for this title is available from the British Library

B format ISBN 9781473668041
A format ISBN 978147366805
eBook ISBN 9781473668003

Typeset in Bembo Std by Hewer Text UK Ltd, Edinburgh
Printed and bound in Great Britain by Clays Ltd, Elcograf S.p.A.

Hodder & Stoughton policy is to use papers that are natural, renewable
and recyclable products and made from wood grown in sustainable
forests. The logging and manufacturing processes are expected to
conform to the environmental regulations of the country of origin.

Hodder & Stoughton Ltd
Carmelite House
50 Victoria Embankment
London EC4Y 0DZ

www.hodder.co.uk

1

In the secret world there are secret briefings.

They take place in unremarkable conference rooms that have been swept for listening devices. Or in secure Portakabins in cordoned-off sections of military bases. Windows are covered up. Military personnel guard the entrances. Clerical staff understand that *something* is being discussed, not for their ears.

They are, in other words, not secret at all.

And then there are briefings like this.

Secret briefings.

Nobody knows they are happening, apart from the people involved. They take place in safe houses, or public parks, or in the back of vehicles.

Or in rough pubs, where rough men can discuss rough business. Pubs like this one, the George and Crown, standing alone on a deserted roadside in a remote part of Cornwall, where a bored barman watches Arsenal vs Spurs on the overhead TV. An alcoholic stares into an almost empty pint glass at a table by the door. A group of five lads take turns at the pool table on the far side of the bar. Three of them are vaping. Nobody complains.

Danny Black had instinctively clocked each of his fellow drinkers as he entered the pub half an hour previously, leaving his BMW parked under the solitary street light outside. None of them had returned the favour and he liked it that way.

The message had come through five hours ago on his encrypted work phone. A set of GPS coordinates and an RV time: 20.00 hours BST. He'd arrived at 19.30, thirsty from the four-hour drive from Hereford but in a heightened state of awareness as he took a few minutes to check out the pub and its surroundings. Entry and exit points. Potential surveillance. Incidental weapons. He was hard-wired to do it.

He'd soon established that the only threat to his personal safety came from the out-of-date, curled-up sandwiches on the bar. And he'd put away a couple of pints of Fosters before his ops officer Major Ray Hammond walked into the pub, nodded at him and automatically walked to the bar to buy two fresh pints, before sitting opposite Danny.

Ray Hammond was the kind of soldier who only ever seemed at ease in camouflage gear. He looked uncomfortable in the civvies he was wearing – a pair of chinos and an open-necked shirt. Danny couldn't imagine what he did with his time when he was off duty, which he never seemed to be. Hammond commanded respect in the Regiment. He was a no-nonsense type, unwilling to take any shit from his men but always prepared to go the extra mile to look after them. Hammond would never admit that his men's well-being was always at the forefront of his mind, but it plainly was. He could be a grumpy old bastard, though. He had a hangdog expression and perpetual dark rings around his eyes. The darker the rings, the shorter his temper. Everyone in the Regiment knew that. Tonight they weren't so bad. Danny felt he could be reasonably at ease with the ops officer.

'We couldn't have done this in Hereford?' Danny said.

'If we could have done it in Hereford,' Hammond replied, 'we'd be in Hereford.' He looked at the two empty pint glasses on the table. 'And you'd have broken the two-pint rule.'

Danny took a deep swig from his third pint.

'Get it down you,' Hammond said. 'It'll be a dry old party where you're headed tomorrow.'

'Only place I'm headed tomorrow is the range.' But Danny already knew that this was unlikely to be true. His go-bag was in the back of the vehicle. He'd already made the call to the mother of his daughter that he was likely to be out of comms, maybe for days, maybe weeks.

'You thought I'd drag you down to this shithole because I like your company?' Hammond sniffed. 'You're deploying this evening. Afghanistan. After we've finished up here, we're going to head to a secret military operations base about ten miles away where you'll be briefed on a covert, deniable operation, codename Spearpoint. I just wanted to have a quiet word before you get the official line.'

Danny tried not to look surprised. 'I thought we weren't *in* Afghanistan, boss,' Danny said.

'We're not. Officially.'

'So why—'

'You're aware of the situation in Helmand Province?'

'Fucked up beyond all recognition?'

Hammond nodded. 'Pretty much. Since the NATO withdrawal, practically every square inch of the damn Province has reverted back into the hands of the Taliban.' Hammond looked around. Not that he needed to. The barman was still watching the football. The old drunk was still staring into his pint. Nobody was paying them any attention. And that, Danny realised, was exactly why they were here. 'It's hardly a surprise. There's nothing out there to stop the Taliban becoming dominant. We have a few hundred green army guys in the country, mostly providing security around the Kabul area. The Yanks have recently deployed several thousand. But the lion's share of security is down to the Afghan National Army. And frankly, I would trust those muppets to handle the security in this place.' He waved an arm to indicate the deserted pub. 'The top brass of the ANA are bent as three bob notes. Few months back, they had to put a general in prison for flogging fuel and supplies on the black market that were intended to get his men through the winter.'

'They should have let his men deal with him.'

Hammond shrugged. 'Half of those kids don't even know which end of a rifle goes bang. Not that it's really their fault. Afghanistan's still a war zone no matter what anybody says. Seven thousand ANA killed in the past twelve months alone. Trying to train kids up in the middle of that? It's like trying to build an airplane when it's in flight.'

'And the Taliban have taken their chance?'

'Not the only thing they've taken. Helmand Province is the biggest net exporter of heroin in the world. Just like it was before we went in. The Taliban control ninety per cent of the poppy fields.' Hammond drank from his pint. 'Put it this way: it's not a situation the Foreign Office is comfortable with.'

Danny said nothing. He'd been in enough briefings to know that Hammond was getting to the point.

'Operation Spearpoint has had a team embedded in Helmand for the last nine months. Two teams, in fact. For obvious reasons, their presence needs to be kept under the radar and separate from the Regiment. If the press find out about it . . .'

'What are they doing?'

Hammond took a moment to gather his thoughts. 'We've always had the same problem with the Taliban,' he said. 'One minute they're firing a rifle or digging in an IED, the next minute they're carrying no weapons, looking and acting like ordinary Afghan citizens. Our rules of engagement state that we can only engage a target if they're firing at us . . .'

'Thanks, boss, I seem to remember somebody telling me that.'

Hammond ignored his comment and carried on. 'It makes the Taliban difficult to identify, and even if we *do* identify them, there's not a whole lot a regular military unit can do about it. Killing an unarmed citizen is a war crime.'

'Good job *we* never do it, then.'

'Yeah, well . . .' Hammond tilted his head as if stretching out a tightness in his neck. 'Like I said, we have two teams out there. One of them is a reconnaissance unit embedded in an Afghan village. It's in the green zone just to the south of Sangin.'

Danny nodded. Anyone with a working knowledge of NATO operations in Afghanistan knew about Sangin. It had been the scene of some of the bloodiest fighting throughout the Herrick deployments, and countless International Security Assistance Force troops had lost their lives there. Holding Sangin had been a major military objective. To the British Army, its name was synonymous with hardship, warfare and death.

4

'Sangin reverted to Taliban control soon after the NATO with-drawal,' Hammond continued. 'It's crawling with them. But there are pockets of territory in the vicinity where the ANA have established forward operating bases to hold them back for now. Our team is running a hearts and minds mission in one of these areas, a large village called Panjika. Healthcare for the women, education for the kids, usual drill.'

'Very moving,' Danny said.

'In return, they're compiling information. Names and locations of active Taliban militants. It's mostly the women who supply the intel. The reconnaissance team pass it on to an ops centre in Cornwall, the one near here. They do what they can to confirm the sources, then they put together target packs for our second team.'

'The kill team.'

'Exactly. It's a four-man unit and it's been taking out Taliban operatives in Helmand for the past nine months.'

'How many?'

'Thirty-five, forty.'

'That's a lot of hits.'

'There's a lot of Taliban. If we don't keep on top of them, it'll be back to the bad old days. We lost nearly five hundred men in Afghanistan. If the Taliban take over again, people will start to wonder what for.'

'Do the Taliban know it's us?'

Hammond inclined his head again. 'They've probably put two and two together, but they're keeping quiet about it. Having their top guys taken out on a regular basis does their PR no good at all.' Hammond took a swig of his beer. 'Of course, it's not quite as simple as that. We've got the Special Investigation Branch of the Royal Military Police keeping an eye on the legality of the whole thing. They don't like it, but as long as we keep within certain parameters there's fuck all they can do. Each time we green light a target we have to present them with a document containing all the evidence. We have to show that we know that they're armed with pistols or Kalashnikovs, or they're in possession of bomb-making equipment. Trouble is, they aren't – not always. Too cute for that. So we sugarcoat it. Doctor the evidence. Plant weapons on the targets when we hit them and show those pictures to the police and the lawyers. It's all shit. Our intel is good, we know who these bastards are whether they're armed or not. We just want you to go out there, kill them and do it properly.'

'Why me? I thought you already had a team in-country.'

Hammond gave another precautionary glance around the room. 'You're right,' he said, his voice a little lower. 'Forty hits is a big deal. It can mess with a guy's head. Even one of us. The men we put on the kill team were specially selected. We were looking for guys who could keep up psychologically with that kind of hit rate.' He let the sentence trail off. 'You know Jimmy Murphy?'

'A Squadron?'

'Right. He flew back into the UK last night. He tried to OD on diazepam. The shrinks are dealing with him now. I'd be surprised if we see him back at Hereford any time soon. For now, we need to replace him.'

Hammond picked up his pint and gave Danny a 'that's where you come in' look as he took a swig.

'What makes you think I'm your guy?' Danny asked quietly.

'Syria, Yemen, Africa, Mexico, the Gulf. Your file speaks for itself. This isn't a job for a rookie. The Director Special Forces picked you out by name. To be blunt, I tried to talk him out of it.'

'Why?'

'Spud.'

Danny forced himself not to show any sign of emotion. Spud was his best mate, and he hadn't made it back from their last mission. When guys back at base had tried to offer him their condolences, he would blank them. Some things he just didn't want to think about.

'In my opinion,' Hammond said, 'you need time to get over your last op. We know the kind of mental stress this sort of outing puts on people. I don't think you're up to it yet. The DSF disagrees. That's why you're on tonight's flight out of Northolt. You'll hit the ground running, Black, and you'll need to keep your head.'

'Who else is on the team?' Danny asked.

An uncomfortable flicker crossed Hammond's face. 'I need a slash,' he said. He stood up and walked across the room to the gents.

Danny lifted his pint. He saw that his hand was shaking. He steadied it with a gulp of his beer and tried not to think about Spud. Easier said than done. His mind was still a welter of flames, rounds and screaming when Hammond sat down again.

'Who's on the team, Ray?'

'Some old friends of yours,' Hammond said. 'Most of the intel that we use to make up the target packs comes from the women's network. So we needed a female operative to be embedded with the reconnaissance unit. Caitlin Wallace has been out there since the start of the op.'

Danny nodded, once again forcing himself to stop any trace of emotion. Caitlin was an Aussie, seconded to the Regiment, who'd worked alongside Danny on a couple of jobs. She was an impressive operator, but last time he'd seen her she'd been in a bad way. If Danny hadn't made certain decisions, Caitlin would be a corpse rotting somewhere in the badlands of Iraq. That she was still operating at all was a miracle.

'Does the kill team have any direct contact with the recon unit?' he asked.

Hammond shook his head.

'You said "old friends",' Danny said. 'Who else?'

'That's another reason I wanted to meet you here first,' Hammond said. 'You know the kill team leader.' He fixed Danny with a direct gaze. 'It's Tony.'

Tony Wiseman. Put it this way: he and Danny had history.

If there was one Regiment guy who was known to everybody else in 22, it was Tony. He was a good soldier. A great soldier. Even Danny would have to admit that. But there were two sides to the coin that was Tony Wiseman. It was an open secret among the lads that he had links to organised crime in Hereford and beyond. Danny had seen him in action and knew it to be true. For some of the lads, it lent Tony an air of dangerous glamour, which he was very happy to take advantage of. Lots of the guys looked up to him. They'd do anything for a word of acknowledgement from Tony Wiseman. He was one of the cool kids.

But Danny? He had a very different take. If Tony walked into this pub right now, what would he do? Put the fucker on the floor? Worse? Truth was, he didn't know. Just the thought of him made Danny see red.

How much did Hammond know about Tony? Certainly the ops officer had fallen on Danny's side during previous confrontations between the two Regiment men. But did he know the depth of their enmity? Did he know what Tony had *done* to Danny? That he'd taken the glory for Danny's actions in the field? That he'd tried to kill Danny's best friend? That he had put his family at risk, just to get back at him?

Danny had no way of judging *what* Hammond knew or believed, and the ops officer wasn't going to hear it from him. The Regiment didn't work that way. You sorted out your own problems.

But Danny knew this: if he and Tony were in the same room together, there would be fireworks. Same team? Bad idea.

Seriously bad idea.

'Come off it, boss,' Danny said. 'You know me and Tony . . .'

Hammond's hangdog expression hardened. 'You're on that flight to Kandahar tonight, Danny. End of. Tony Wiseman's out there because we know he'll hit as many targets as we need without taking it too hard. *You're* going because you've shown yourself to be pretty damn adept at it yourself. I don't remember you ever having a crisis of conscience before. I'm not asking you to be Tony Wiseman's best buddy. You don't even have to be in the same room as the guy when you're not on ops. I'm asking you to do a job.' He paused. '*Telling* you to do a job. In case you hadn't noticed, this is me breaking the news nicely so you don't make a dick of yourself in front of people who matter. You have your orders.'

Hammond finished his pint.

'Who's in charge?' Danny said.

'Tony.' He raised one hand. 'Suck it up, Danny. The other guys on the team are Rees Dexter and Billy Cole. You know them?'

Danny clenched his jaw, but nodded.

'The Spearpoint base is ten miles north of here.' Hammond handed him a piece of paper with a fresh set of coordinates. 'It keeps things separate from Hereford, and deniable if the shit hits. The guy in charge is an MI6 officer called Cadogan. Military background, but he's a spook. Don't underestimate him. He comes across as a bumbling toff, but he's ruthless. He wants to meet you before you deploy. Look you in the eye, all that old-school kind of crap. Just don't be fooled by the Boris Johnson act. Understood?'

'Understood.'

'There's also a Special Investigation Branch RMP on site. His name's Holroyd. Bit of a twat. I did some digging. He used to be in the Royal Irish Regiment, but there was some business with his platoon in Iraq. He was the only one who walked away alive. There was some suggestion that he was at fault, but the paperwork's been buried. Came back to the UK, joined the RMPs and found God, believe it or not. I walked into his office the other day, saw him on his knees, praying. On the surface he sees it as his role to keep us bad lads on the straight and narrow, but deep down I think he's just your typical nosy policeman. Cripples him that he doesn't have sufficient vetting to get through the door into the main ops room. He'll probably make himself known to you, but just ignore him. We'll feed him whatever we need to feed him to keep everyone sweet.' Hammond narrowed his eyes at Danny, as though sizing him up. 'I'm heading down there now. I've got a few different people to see. Get yourself something to eat here, have another drink and meet me there in an hour. We'll get some face time with Cadogan, then we'll be on our way.'

Without another word, Hammond stood up and left. Danny didn't move for a full minute. When he did, it was to down his pint in one. He looked at the coordinates on the paper that

Hammond had left him. Then he looked up at the bar. The barman had dragged his attention from the football and was giving him the eye.

'Whisky,' Danny said. 'Double. Now.'

'Do I look like a fuckin' waitress?' the barman said in a thick Cornish accent. But he couldn't withstand the look Danny gave him for long. 'All right, all right,' he muttered, as he turned towards the optics behind the bar and started pouring Danny his fourth drink.

2

A full moon hung, startlingly bright, over the Helmand River. It silhouetted the Kajaki Dam in the north, and the stately mosque of Lashkar Gah further to the south. Between the two, it cast midnight shadows on the village of Panjika, where everything was silent.

Caitlin Wallace didn't like it when everything was silent.

Panjika was a village of two halves. A narrow riverbed – almost dry in summer – ran north-south, cutting it through the middle. Running parallel to the river on the eastern side was the main street, with ramshackle stalls and tumbledown shops. At the north end of that street was an open square with the village mosque on one side, which had been partially destroyed by an ordnance strike many years previously. There were perhaps fifty individual dwelling places on the western side of the river, and a further ten white-walled compounds – clusters of tiny buildings surrounded by square perimeter walls. On the eastern side of the river there were fewer individual dwelling places dotted around the main street, but more compounds – about twenty. The single room Caitlin had called home for the past six months was in one of these compounds, on the south-eastern side of the village about fifty metres from the river.

They called this area the green zone. Irrigated by the tributary of the Helmand River that cut through the village, it was lush and verdant. Here, the villagers could grow fruit and vegetables. And it was these that made it a potentially dangerous area.

Helmand was Taliban territory. Not all of it, and not this small village of no more than five hundred people. Panjika was protected

11

by three Afghan National Army forward operating bases – one to the north, one to the south and one to the east, with the river forming a natural barrier to the west. But if – when – the Taliban finally moved in, they would congregate around the green zone. Because militants need food too. The well-irrigated avocado trees that shaded Caitlin's compound attracted all manner of people: good, bad, and many whose loyalties were somewhere in between. In Helmand Province, it was often difficult to tell them apart.

Caitlin's room was half bedroom and half storeroom. A stubby candle provided the only light as their electrical generator was too noisy, and the fuel that ran it too precious, for it to be going all night. A rucksack was propped up in the corner. Under the bed, a small arsenal. She had an M4 and several boxes of 5.56 rounds. She had a Sig P226 handgun and its attendant 9mms. She hadn't fired either of these weapons on this deployment. But she was damned if she was going to stray very far from them.

Other items had proved more useful. Medical supplies. Clean bandages. Water purification tablets. Then of course there were the plain white boxes, piled up next to her rucksack, which contained her valued supplies: sanitary towels, paracetamol and ibuprofen. She had insisted on bringing substantial quantities of these items when she first arrived in-country. Whenever there was an opportunity for a re-supply, she insisted that Cornwall prioritised them as much as items such as MREs and ammunition. Cadogan queried it every time. Complained, even. He didn't realise that these items were helping achieve their objectives just as surely as Black Hawks, laser sights and night-vision capability. But that was men for you.

Caitlin lay on her bed, sweating in the appalling night-time heat. Damp, shoulder-length brown hair. Khaki trousers. A white T-shirt, damp across the back. Well-worn boots. Grey eyes open, listening to the silence. It made her nervous. She preferred the reassuring buzz of an ANA helicopter flying overhead. The noise of the locals in the street. Too often, silence meant people were scared. In Helmand Province, they frequently had good reason.

There was a banging noise. Caitlin started. She sat on the edge of her bed and reached underneath it for her Sig. Cocked and locked. The banging came again. She tucked the handgun into her khaki trousers and headed to the door. Opened it and peered out into the courtyard.

The courtyard itself was tiny. The size of a squash court. It was surrounded on three sides by rooms identical to Caitlin's. The fourth side was a whitewashed wall, five metres high, with a thick wooden entrance gate. A man and a woman had emerged from the other rooms. The woman was smaller than Caitlin. She was extremely petite, with a beautiful, dark-skinned face that had an almost childlike innocence to it. She wore plain black robes. The other was a beast of a man: six foot five and a beard so unruly that it concealed his white skin, and meant that even some of the locals mistook him for one of them. Gabina was an interpreter from Kabul who had moved to the UK in her early teens and offered her services to the military – a kind, thoughtful, precise young woman who helped Caitlin commune with the locals. Tommy Webster was Caitlin's SAS muscle, and a lump of a man. Caitlin wasn't sure an original thought had ever passed through his mind. He hardly ever seemed to speak. But Caitlin knew that Tommy had an eye for her and she wasn't above exploiting that. Not to mention that he would be useful in a fight.

They strode across the courtyard towards the gate. Gabina called something in Pashto. A voice came from the other side. Female. It sounded anxious. Gabina turned to Caitlin, clearly about to say something.

'It's okay,' Caitlin said, stepping out into the courtyard. 'Let them in.'

Gabina lifted the big metal bar that bolted the gate. It was a bit of a struggle for someone so small. Tommy positioned himself between Caitlin and the entrance. The moon cast his imposing shadow across the courtyard. As it swung open, Caitlin had to squint to make out who was standing there.

Two figures. Women, dressed in dark robes and headdresses. One old, one young. The older woman's face was deeply lined and weathered, with hard eyes and a hooked nose. Mother and daughter? Possible. People aged quickly in Helmand Province. But most likely, she thought, it was grandmother and grand-daughter. Gaps in the generations were common out here, where life was cheap. The older woman had one arm around the girl. They were both looking up at Tommy with apprehension.

Caitlin strode past him. 'Don't scare them,' she muttered as she hurried up to the new arrivals. She made a 'come in' sign with her hands and, when they gingerly entered, nodded at Gabina to close the gate again. Tommy stood still. Caitlin had to manoeuvre the newcomers round him towards her room. Gabina followed at a respectful distance. As they shuffled into the room, she stood in the doorway.

Caitlin offered them the edge of her bed to sit on. They sat close to each other. The young girl had one hand resting on her abdomen. The grandmother started to talk in Pashto the moment they sat. Gabina translated, but Caitlin held up one hand to silence her.

'It's okay,' she said.

Caitlin knew why they had come. She walked over to her supplies, took a box each of sanitary towels and paracetamol and handed them to the girl. Caitlin regularly distributed these items freely to the women and girls of the village. They only had to ask, but that was more difficult than it sounded. They were embarrassed – it was a cultural thing – and the Taliban disapproved of anything that made a woman's life easier. The older women remembered the punishments they received when those monsters were in charge, and the young women weren't stupid: they knew the situation was getting bad again. No wonder they crept up to Caitlin's compound, shamefaced and in the dead of night.

Caitlin popped a couple of paracetamol from the wrapper and handed the girl her beaker of water. The girl timidly swallowed the pills, avoiding Caitlin's gaze.

'Where do you live?' Caitlin asked the grandmother. The lines on her face seemed even deeper in the candlelight.

The grandmother replied with a nervous quaver in her voice. Gabina translated. 'At the edge of the village. By the poppy fields.'

'Her parents?' She indicated the girl.

The grandmother shook her head. 'Her father was in the army. He died six months ago. Her mother died when she was little.'

'I'm sorry.' Caitlin paused. 'I'm here to help in any way I can. You have a problem, come to me.'

The grandmother lowered her head. 'The wrong people would find out,' she said. 'The Imam . . .' Her eyes tightened a little. This wasn't the first time that Caitlin had seen women mention the village's Imam with a degree of apprehension. There were rumours that the old man who led the daily prayers in the nearby mosque was sympathetic to the Taliban. He commanded respect in the village, though. If Caitlin was to win hearts and minds, the Imam was off limits.

She turned her attention back to the grandmother, who said: 'I only came tonight because . . .' The old lady looked at her grand-daughter, who was also staring at the floor. 'It is her first time. The pain is bad. The men don't understand.'

'The medicine will help. If you need more, you come back and see me.' She crouched down and put one hand on the grand-mother's knee. 'Who do you mean by "the wrong people"? Can you give me a name? Tell me where they live?'

The grandmother shook her head vigorously. She stood, pulling her granddaughter up with her. 'We must go,' she said. 'If we are seen . . .'

Gabina's translation was interrupted by a distant bang. The old woman and her granddaughter started and looked frightened. Caitlin swore under her breath. She instantly grabbed a shoulder bag filled with medical supplies and a narrow torch. She hurried to the door, pushing the guests out of the way. 'Stay there,' she hissed. And when the older woman started to complain, she repeated herself more forcefully: '*Stay there!*'

Tommy was already at the gate, blocking it.

'We're going,' Caitlin told him. He shook his head. 'I said, *we're going!*' Caitlin knew that Tommy wouldn't resist her if she insisted. His face darkened with reluctance, but he stepped to one side and opened the gate. 'Gabina!' she called over her shoulder as she moved out into the village. 'We need you!'

Caitlin didn't wait for a reply as she sprinted out of the compound and into the village. She had been embedded in the region long enough to recognise the sound of a roadside bomb when she heard one. Maybe an IED had been dug into the road. Maybe explosives had been hidden inside the carcass of one of the many animals that were routinely left to rot on the side of the road – that was an increasingly common occurrence, Caitlin had noticed.

But the type of bomb was not of primary importance. Caitlin's reasons for getting to the blast site were at once humanitarian and tactical.

And for both reasons, she needed to get there fast.

Caitlin estimated that the explosion had been about a klick away. Although it was hard to tell the exact direction, she knew she had to head south-east. That was the direction of the only road in and out of the village. She had to take a circuitous route, however, along the main street that cut north-south through the centre of Panjika.

She emerged on to the street through a line of low, ramshackle buildings, Tommy at her shoulder. By day these were a bottle shop and a hardware stall of sorts. A couple of old bicycles were propped up against them, and some rusted steel oil drums littered the road in front. The village seemed completely deserted. No inhabitants were out at this time, nor any of the ANA soldiers who regularly patrolled by day. Opposite her was a line of rough stalls and shops, all bolted up and secured. A couple of stray goats were loitering by one of them, and a solitary old rickshaw had been left in the middle of the street. At the northern end of the street was the village mosque. It was a plain building: low, sand-coloured, much like any other in the village of Panjika. At some point in the past, its western corner at the rear had been destroyed in a munitions strike. The locals had tried to rebuild it using breeze blocks and concrete, but the job was still half done. Metal reinforcing rods pronged, porcupine-like, into the air, making the mosque look more like a building site than a place of prayer. It disappeared from Caitlin's peripheral vision as she ran south, her feet thumping against the hard ground as she curved round to the south-east, past another small grove of avocado trees and along the only road in and out of the village. There was danger here. She knew it. Whoever had set the IED might expect people to approach and help any casualties. She was aware of Tommy, just behind her, scanning the area with his weapon as he ran. Caitlin accepted his protection and sprinted straight ahead.

She could smell the plume of smoke before she saw it lit up by the moonlight on the far side of a parched field. This part of the village was dotted with tiny compounds, similar to the one in which Caitlin and her team had been living. The closest one was just twenty metres away, and from it she could hear a child wailing, woken by the noise. She knew from experience that very few people were likely to leave their compounds. It was safer for them to stay home.

The smoke was fifty metres away, but Caitlin couldn't risk heading directly across the field that separated her from it. Everyone knew that field was full of legacy mines and IEDs. The ANA were too stretched to clear it, and none of the locals had attempted to cultivate the land for years.

So she had to go round it. Her boots thumped against the hard-baked, red earth. Tommy was close behind her and Gabina trailed by ten or fifteen metres, her shorter legs unable to carry her as fast. It took a minute to get there. The acrid smell of explosives grew stronger. As Caitlin turned the corner of the field into the poorly made road, she knew that a terrible scene awaited her.

A vehicle had been hit. Not a military vehicle, most of which were properly armoured and reinforced against the threat of such devices. This was a civilian vehicle, but it was too much of a wreck for Caitlin to identify its model as she sprinted towards it. The chassis was twisted and gnarled. There was a glow of flames from the rear where the fuel tank had ignited. The smoke was coming from the smouldering tyres, and there was a huge crater in the side of the road.

And there was screaming. Caitlin identified two voices. They were screams of pain, not panic – she could tell the difference. And as she approached the vehicle she saw two figures on the road. They'd been thrown through the windscreen. They lay on their backs, surrounded by shattered glass. Caitlin shone her torch at them. A man and a woman. Their faces were bloodied from the impact of the glass. The man's forearm was jutting out at an angle. Caitlin could see that the ulna bone had broken away from the joint and pierced the skin around the elbow. The bleeding, however, was slow and the blood dark. It was not a catastrophic wound. Caitlin made a mental triage note: although the guy was making the most noise, his wounds were not life threatening. His screams were a good sign – they meant he was conscious and breathing.

The same went for the woman. She appeared to have twisted her foot. There were no obvious signs of major bleeding. She was in great pain, but she'd live.

Caitlin's immediate thought was for other passengers. She strode over to the smouldering shell of the vehicle and shone her torch into the rear seats.

She felt sick.

There were two children in the back. One of them was clearly dead. The heat of the explosion had peeled away the skin on the child's face. The flesh was cauterised in places, and still weeping in others. There was a glimpse of bone around the forehead, and what remained of the hair was still smoking. She couldn't tell if it was a little boy or a little girl.

A second child was next to the corpse. A girl. She was wearing traditional garb and couldn't have been more than fourteen. A twisted chunk of metal had embedded itself into the top of her forearm. She was staring at it, and her whole body was shaking. Caitlin shone her torch directly at the wound site. The girl's robes were black, so it took a moment for Caitlin to register the thick, gushing blood that was saturating them. She leaned in through the broken window of the rear door and touched one hand to the wet material. She looked at the blood on her fingers. Bright red. Arterial. The child was bleeding out. Fast.

Caitlin moved into autopilot. The rear door, misshapen from the explosion, was difficult to open. It took several yanks. Once it was open, she leaned in and, gripping the torch with her teeth, grabbed the sopping clothes around the wound and ripped them open. She winced when she saw the nature of the wound. The shard of metal had caused a gash at least three inches wide, and was deeply embedded just below the shoulder. Arterial blood was pumping out in waves to the rhythm of the girl's heart. If it carried on like that, she'd be dead in less than a minute.

The temptation was to remove the shard of metal from the girl's arm, but that would be a mistake. There was a chance it was partly stemming the arterial bleed. If she took it away, the blood loss could increase. There was only one other medical option. Caitlin opened up her shoulder bag. It took her less than five seconds to find the item she needed: a military tourniquet. She ripped it from its packaging and wrapped the sturdy elastic around the arm a couple of inches above the wound. Then she started twisting the windlass to tighten the tourniquet as hard as she could, and stem the bleeding from above.

Her hands were covered in blood. The windlass was slippery and sticky as she twisted it. The girl was shaking all over. There was no time to offer her any words of comfort. There was only time to stop the bleeding before she lost consciousness. It became hard to tighten the tourniquet any further. Suddenly the girl screamed in pain. Caitlin felt a moment of satisfaction. If the tourniquet hurt, it was doing its job. And if the girl was screaming, there was life in her.

Caitlin exited the burning vehicle. She looked around. There was no sign of anyone coming to help. She called over to Tommy, who was kneeling by the adults with Gabina, administering to them. Their screams had stopped. Caitlin didn't know if that was a good sign or a bad one. 'Carry this girl,' she shouted. 'Get her back to our quarters. We can come back for the others.'

Tommy rose. He moved swiftly to the back of the vehicle and, gently for someone of his great size, manhandled the girl out of the back seat. He held her very carefully, cocooned in his arms and started jogging back towards the village. Caitlin turned to Gabina. There were tears on her beautiful, petite face. 'Tell the parents we're going to do everything we can to keep the girl alive. We'll be back for them as quickly as possible.'

Gabina relayed this in urgent Pashto. The message seemed to get through, because the parents nodded vigorously. Caitlin and the interpreter sprinted after Tommy.

Cutting round the edge of the parched field, Caitlin saw that there was activity in the village up ahead. Several people had ventured out of their compounds. A man was shouting something. But nobody was heading in the direction of the road. Caitlin overtook Tommy and ignored the hard stares of the few locals outside the entrance to her compound as she raced inside to prepare some medical equipment. She had a checklist in her head of everything she'd need before she could get the girl taken to one of the nearby military hospitals for proper treatment. Morphine, a saline drip, clean bandages . . .

The old woman and her granddaughter were still in Caitlin's room, huddled on the bed. They stood up as soon as Caitlin entered and shrank into the shadows when Tommy arrived holding the girl. 'Lay her on the bed,' Caitlin said. Tommy silently did as he was told. Caitlin had her back turned to them as she rifled through her boxes of medical gear, looking for everything she needed, when she felt a tap on her shoulder.

She spun round. It was Tommy who had tapped her. Now he was pointing at the girl, and it was clear why. Caitlin's patient had her eyes shut. She wasn't moving. She didn't appear to be breathing. Caitlin swore under her breath, lurched over to the bed and felt for a pulse. Nothing. She swore again and started to administer CPR. Pressing the heel of her hand against the girl's chest, she pumped it vigorously thirty times before squeezing her nose and administering two rescue breaths. There was a dreadful silence in the room as Tommy, Gabina and the two Afghan women looked on. Caitlin repeated the process twice, three times, refusing to give up on the kid. As she leaned down to give her fourth set of rescue breaths she noticed warmth from the girl's mouth. She was breathing. Her pulse was back. She wasn't conscious, but she was alive.

'Get on the radio,' she told Tommy. 'We need to get her to the nearest hospital.'

Tommy nodded and ducked out of the room. Caitlin checked the girl's pulse again and became aware of the granddaughter standing behind her left shoulder. She said something in Pashto. Gabina, her face still tear-streaked, translated. 'She says she knows the casualty.'

'Right,' Caitlin said. She was more concerned with caring for her patient than with small talk.

'They are friends,' Gabina said.

Caitlin swallowed her irritation. She turned round. The girl was crying. She couldn't take her eyes off her friend, lying close to death on the bed. 'You need to go home now,' Caitlin said as kindly as she had patience for. 'I'll make sure she gets to a hospital.' She looked towards the door. 'Go carefully. Come and see me tomorrow, I'll let you know how she is.'

Once Gabina had translated, the two women shuffled towards the door. The young girl was clearly reluctant to leave her friend, but her grandmother hurried her out with a sharp word. Caitlin went back to her patient. There was still a pulse. She was still breathing. The bleed had almost stopped and the blood around the wound was beginning to congeal. She turned to find the saline bag she had retrieved from her stores, and it was only then that she saw the granddaughter standing in the doorway.

'What is it?' Caitlin asked.

The girl stepped inside and muttered something quietly in Pashto. Caitlin didn't understand her, but there was something in her tone that made her want to hear more. 'Gabina!' she called. 'Get in here.'

The interpreter hurried in. Caitlin nodded at the girl, who repeated herself.

Gabina hesitated. 'She says she knows who planted the roadside bomb,' she said.

Caitlin breathed deeply. She stood up, walked over to the girl, put one hand on her shoulder and smiled. 'Come and sit down,' she said.

The girl sat on the corner of the bed. Caitlin knelt next to her. The girl's eyes flickered between Caitlin and the patient. 'I think she's going to be okay,' Caitlin said, not entirely truthfully, and Gabina translated, her innocent eyes wide. The girl nodded. 'Who did it?' Caitlin said quietly. 'Can you give me a name?'

The girl swallowed hard. This was clearly difficult for her. She was scared.

'Nobody will know,' Caitlin said. 'I promise nobody will know it's you.'

The girl closed her eyes. She muttered two names. Gabina had to ask her to repeat herself. When she did, they were scarcely more audible.

'Abu Manza,' Gabina translated. 'And Abu Noor.'

'How do you know it was them?' Caitlin asked. 'Is it just a rumour?'

'I heard some men talking . . .' the girl said, and it was clear to Caitlin that she didn't want to elaborate.

'Do you know where they live?' she asked. 'Can you tell me that?'

The girl looked at the floor.

'I can stop them doing this,' Caitlin whispered. 'I can stop them from *ever* doing it again. But you *have* to tell me where they live.'

The girl closed her eyes. 'They both live in the village of Gareshk,' she said. 'Two compounds, on different sides of the village.' A sudden fierceness crossed her face. 'They have families,' she said. 'Young children.'

'The children will be fine,' Caitlin said. 'I promise you that.'

The grandmother appeared at the doorway. She wore a scowl. 'What has she been telling you?' she demanded through Gabina.

The girl gave Caitlin an urgent look, but it wasn't necessary. Caitlin collected another box of sanitary towels and handed them over. Then she walked up to the grandmother and grasped her hands. 'She's a good girl,' she said. 'Take her home. Look after her. Come to me if you need anything.'

Her words softened the grandmother's granite face. The old woman nodded and gestured at her granddaughter to leave. She walked out into the courtyard. The girl followed with a grateful look at Caitlin.

'Wait! What's your name?'

The girl blinked. 'Mina.'

Caitlin smiled at her. 'Thank you, Mina,' she said.

Gabina gently escorted them out of the compound and locked the main gate just as Tommy appeared from his room. 'Did you contact the hospital?' Caitlin asked.

Tommy nodded.

'Good.' She hurried back into her room, checked her patient's pulse once more, then retrieved an item from a flight case under her bed: an encrypted Iridium satellite phone. She powered it up and dialled a number. The call was answered in seconds. 'Go ahead.'

'This is asset Charlie Foxtrot Niner,' Caitlin said. 'Inform Spearpoint that we have two new targets for confirmation. Repeat, inform Spearpoint that we have two new targets for confirmation.'

'Roger that. Wait out.' The line went silent. Caitlin kept her eyes on the shallow rising of her patient's chest as she waited for Cornwall to come on the line.

It took approximately twenty seconds.

3

Danny was behind the wheel, his satnav directing him to the Spearpoint base. The booze did nothing to ease the thought of coming face to face with Tony Wiseman.

The roads were deserted. This was deep Cornwall. The needle tipped seventy as Danny expertly but subconsciously negotiated the winding country lanes. When the satnav announced that he was approaching his destination, he realised he'd been in something of a trance for the past ten minutes. He hit the brakes and brought the vehicle to a halt. He had just crested the brow of a hill. The road continued down towards a forest. Twenty metres away there was the corner of a high wire fence blocking off land to his right. He couldn't make out the extent of the cordoned-off area because it was dark, but the headlamps of his vehicle illuminated an entrance in the fence with a 'Danger' plaque warning against high-voltage electricity. As good a way as any, Danny thought, of keeping people out. On the near side of the fence he saw an armed soldier standing guard. He started up his vehicle again and wound down his window as he approached the soldier.

'They're expecting me,' he said.

The soldier peered into the vehicle, nodded abruptly and opened a gate in the fence. Danny entered the Spearpoint camp. The road took him through an inner perimeter fence, guarded by another armed soldier, and into a forested area. Thirty metres beyond the treeline was a clearing of a couple of acres. It housed a complex of low concrete buildings with a large white comms satellite dish on the roof. The headlamps of the vehicle illuminated the rain-stained walls. Danny had the sense that, although the satellite dish looked modern, the building was at least pre-war. There were no windows and just one door, which looked like a much more recent addition: metal, sturdy and very secure.

There were several vehicles parked in a line. Danny parked up alongside them and approached the door, aware of a camera covering the access. The door buzzed as he approached. He opened it and stepped inside.

Danny found himself in a small, brightly lit room. A soldier behind a desk stood up as he entered. He had a blond beard that attempted – not successfully – to mask a disfigurement of the right-hand side of his face. A burn, maybe. At the far side of the room was a secure metal door with an access keypad. To his left, two unsecured wooden doors. One of them had a sign: 'Mike Holroyd, Special Investigation Branch'. The other was unmarked. A briefing room, Danny guessed.

There were no pleasantries with the scar-faced desk jockey. 'I'll need an iris scan and a fingerprint please,' he said to Danny, indicating a small camera on a tripod next to him. Danny nodded, stepped up to the camera and allowed the soldier to scan his eye, before pressing his thumb on to a touch-screen sensor. There was a short pause as the soldier checked his laptop. 'You're Spearpoint cleared,' he said. 'I'll let them know you're here.'

The disfigured soldier tapped at his keyboard. Danny loitered for thirty seconds. A man entered the reception area from the room with the marked door. He wore a suit and tie. Danny instantly noticed a silver badge in the shape of a fish on his lapel. He was carrying a bit of weight and had something of a swagger. Straight black hair, thinning. Clean shaven. Maybe thirty years old. He had the unmistakable air of a policeman. *Nosy*, Hammond had said. *Cripples him that he doesn't have sufficient vetting to get through the door into the main ops room . . .*

He looked Danny up and down, then noticed that Danny was looking at the fish on his lapel. 'The sign of the fish,' he said. He had a very pronounced Ulster accent and there was a definite smugness in his voice. When Danny didn't reply, he seemed to feel the need to elaborate. 'Once a secret Christian symbol. Are you—?'

Danny gave him a 'you must be joking' look.

'Well,' the man said. 'We have no need for secrecy these days, do we?' A smile spread toadlike over his face as he realised this line of conversation wasn't going to get anything out of Danny. 'I'm Mike Holroyd,' he announced. 'Special Investigation Branch. You are?'

Danny didn't reply. He just looked back towards the secure door.

'Your name is?' Holroyd persisted.

'My own business,' Danny replied.

Another toadlike smile. 'Who is this, please?' he asked the soldier at reception.

The soldier looked flustered. 'Danny Black, sir,' he muttered. 'From Hereford. He's Spearpoint cleared.'

'Is that so?' Holroyd stepped round so that he was facing Danny again. He sniffed dramatically. 'You've been drinking,' he said.

Danny stared at him.

'I said, you've been drinking.'

'My hearing's pretty good.'

'Listen to me, soldier, you might be in the SAS, you might think that puts you above the law, but you're clearly over the limit, and we are none of us—'

The secure door opened, interrupting Holroyd. Hammond appeared. The rings around his eyes seemed to darken on the spot as he saw Danny talking to Holroyd. Holroyd turned to him. 'If this is one of yours, Ray . . .'

'Thanks, Mike,' Hammond cut him short. 'I'll take it from here.' He glanced into Holroyd's office. '*Songs of Praise* not on, Mike?' he said lightly.

Holroyd's face visibly flushed. Hammond turned and walked back through the secure doorway. Danny winked at Holroyd. 'Work to do, buddy,' he said. He followed his boss, closing the door on the RMP man who was fuming in the reception area, unable to follow where he had no clearance.

'Ignore him,' Hammond said. 'Puritanical twat's just there to tick boxes for the lawyers. Spearpoint know how to keep him quiet.' They walked along a corridor, past a couple of doors on the right. 'Signals,' Hammond said, pointing at them, 'plugged into the network in Afghanistan.' He indicated another door at the end of the corridor. 'This is the ops room,' he said.

It looked like a bomb shelter. Thick concrete walls. No windows. There were ten men here, and a huge array of wall-hung screens, laptops and comms equipment. The screens showed maps of Afghanistan, layouts of military bases and towns, satellite imagery and live footage through a NV lens of a cluster of boxy buildings, from what Danny assumed was a drone hovering above. Most of the men wore camo and headsets. Hammond indicated the room with a sweep of his arm. 'This is where we run Spearpoint. Completely separate from Hereford, and we provide all operational support—'

'This our new boy?' A man in civvies had stood up from his desk and was approaching. He was in his sixties, with floppy blond hair that was only now showing signs of grey. Hammond's previous comparison to Boris Johnson was well placed. He walked with a stick that helped him with a pronounced limp and blew his floppy hair off his forehead in an affected manner as he approached him.

'This is Danny Black,' Hammond said. 'Our kill team replacement.'

'My dear chap, your reputation precedes you. Marcus Cadogan. MI6. I'll be running you from here.'

Danny nodded and Cadogan gave a bland smile. 'Apologies for bringing you out of your way. One would rather be in the thick of it, but we can't run Spearpoint on the QT if our American cousins and the Afghans are sniffing around like truffle hounds. Hence these delightful environs. And I do think it's important to put a face to the name. We're going to be working hand in glove, as it were—'

Cadogan was interrupted by a soldier with bright ginger hair. 'Boss, we've just received a communication from our asset in Panjika.'

'That's Caitlin,' Hammond muttered to Danny.

'Go ahead, McLean,' Cadogan told the soldier.

'She has two potential targets. The names we have are Abu Manza and Abu Noor.'

Danny noticed an instant sharpness in Cadogan's eyes, quite at odds with his bumbling exterior. 'Splendid. Do they cross-reference with any other intelligence source?'

'Negative,' McLean said. 'It's the first we've heard of them.'

'Did our asset provide locations?'

'Roger that, sir. Two separate compounds in the village of Gareshk.'

'Do we have drones available?'

'Limited, sir. It'll take a couple of hours to fly one into the area, and that's if I can wrestle it off an SBS operation.'

'Make it happen, old thing. Get cameras above one of the targets at least. I'd like to know their movements in detail.'

'Roger that, sir.'

Cadogan looked over his shoulder at Danny. 'All hotting up here, as you can see. You've been fully briefed?' As he asked the question, he gave Hammond a meaningful look. Hammond nodded quietly. 'Excellent. Good. Well, best get on. Happy landings, Black.' Almost as an afterthought, he said: 'Oh, and do a fellow a favour, would you? It's a rum business, being on the Spearpoint team. It can mess with a chap's head. Any sign of that happening with the rest of the team, you'll let us know? All off the record, of course. Mum's the word. All right? Excellent. Now if you'll excuse me? With any luck, we'll have a target pack ready by the time you land.' He cocked his head, just as Danny heard the distant sound of a helicopter outside. 'Sounds like your lift's arrived.' He returned to his station.

'This way,' Hammond said. He looked at his watch. 'It's time.' He led Danny across the ops room to a secure door on the far side. As Hammond opened it, Danny looked back over his shoulder towards the ops room. He caught Cadogan leaning on his walking stick and staring at him, an intense but uncertain look on his face, as if he didn't quite trust Danny. But in a fraction of a second he'd turned away again and was looking at one of the big screens.

The door led directly to the exterior of the building, which was guarded by another soldier.

'Is that guy for real?' Danny jabbed one thumb over his shoulder to indicate Cadogan, but he had to raise his voice. Thirty metres from the building there was a helicopter landing pad and, accompanying the noise of the rotors, Danny saw the bright lights of a Sea King coming in to land.

'I told you. Don't be fooled. The posh idiot thing's an act.' He pointed at the chopper. 'Right on time!' he shouted.

They stayed clear as the Sea King touched down. Only once it had landed and one of the side doors had opened did the two Regiment men run towards it, heads down, approaching it from the front so they kept well clear of the tail. A loadie ushered them in and, as they took their places inside the chopper, closed the doors again. The Sea King rose. It couldn't have been on the ground for more than a minute.

'I don't think me and Holroyd will be going for a beer any time soon,' Danny shouted over the noise of the chopper.

'Holroyd doesn't go for a beer with anyone. Teetotal. He's suspicious of all of us, not just you. He's no different from the rest of the Special Investigation Branch in that respect. They'd love to get a piece of the Regiment. I don't need to tell you that.'

He didn't. It was well known that the modus operandi of the SAS was a constant challenge to the RMPs. The Regiment represented everything that the military police loathed. They made their own decisions. They called their own shots – literally. They were answerable only to themselves. It drove the Royal Military Police crazy that the Regiment considered themselves above the law, because as far as the RMPs were concerned, *nobody* was – except of course themselves.

'They'd have a fucking field day with Tony,' Danny said.

'They'd have a field day with any of us if we let them. Which we're not going to do. We can deal with Holroyd at this end. Just be aware that there are a few of the fuckers hanging around the

Stan. Tony and the team know to keep out of their way. Shame that the closest they'll ever get to a war zone is out there trying to nail the boys who are actually doing the work, but there we have it.'

Danny told himself to forget about Holroyd. He had bigger problems than that. In a few hours he'd be face to face with Tony Wiseman. Loathing brought a knot to his stomach.

But as Hammond had said: suck it up. It was what it was. Get used to it.

Danny rested his head against the webbing on the side of the chopper and closed his eyes. After several years with the Regiment he was used to resting in some uncomfortable shitholes, and he'd decided to get some sleep.

He had the feeling he was going to need it.

Spearpoint HQ was alive with activity. Radio operators were talking over their headsets in urgent tones. Interpreters were furiously translating documents at their laptops. A drone operator was barking instructions to unseen technicians thousands of miles away.

In the middle of it all stood Marcus Cadogan. He leaned heavily on his walking stick as he looked up at a large screen. It showed, through the rainbow colours of a thermal imaging drone camera, an Afghan compound somewhere in the heart of Helmand Province.

'Which one is this?' he asked McLean, the young soldier with ginger hair standing by his side.

'Abu Manza,' McLean said.

'Have we found anything on him?'

'He was subject to a full body search by members of the Afghan National Army approximately two months ago. The paperwork is a little vague. I'd say it's been doctored.'

'Our friend Abu Manza has been bribing the Afghan army?'

'I'd say so, sir.'

'Rather blots his copy book, wouldn't you say?'

'Yes, sir.'

There was movement on the screen. 'What's that?'

McLean went over to check with a drone operator. 'Movement of personnel, sir.'

'You sure about that, old thing? It's not a dog?'

'No, sir. Definitely a human signature.'

Cadogan checked a clock on the wall that showed the time in Afghanistan: 01.10 hours AFT. 'Switch to NV.'

The screen changed from the rainbow of thermal imaging to the green haze of NV. Cadogan watched carefully as their target exited the compound and climbed into a vehicle. 'Shall we follow him, sir?'

Cadogan gave that a moment's thought. This was Abu Manza's compound, but it wasn't necessarily Abu Manza they were watching. However, they were on the lookout for incriminating activity and that was unlikely to happen in the compound itself. So whoever it was, it made sense to follow them. 'Go ahead,' he instructed.

Cadogan and McLean watched the screen as the drone followed the vehicle south out of the village.

'How long before we get a drone up on target two? What was the fellow's name?'

'Abu Noor, sir. About an hour.'

Cadogan nodded. Without taking his eyes off the screen, he said: 'That Danny Black chap. What did you think?'

'Not much between the ears. But we don't really want brains on the kill team. We just want someone who'll follow orders and not ask too many questions.'

'Quite,' Cadogan muttered. 'Quite.' But although he'd met the other guys on the team and they were just as the int officer described, he wasn't so sure about Danny Black.

He rapped his walking stick on the floor to get the attention of everyone in the room, then pointed at the screen. 'Keep watching this fellow. I want to know his every movement. Understood?'

'Understood, sir,' said McLean without taking his eyes from the screen.

4

The Sea King touched down at Northolt at 23.00 hours BST. A uniformed RAF guy was waiting to escort Danny directly from the chopper to a Hercules stationed one hundred metres away across the tarmac.

'That thing Cadogan said,' Hammond shouted over the roar of chopper's rotors as they took their leave of each other. 'About keeping an eye on the others. That wasn't a blank cheque for you to get Tony sent home, you get that, right?'

Danny didn't reply.

'We have skeleton personnel at Kandahar,' Hammond continued. 'A handful of green army guys to guard the Spearpoint cordon. Your watchkeeper is Harry Isherwood. He's your liaison between the unit and any regular forces in the area.'

Harry had never worked with Isherwood before, but knew him by sight. He'd come up through the ranks in the Regiment and was on his way to a commission. He'd recently done his knife and fork course, where NCOs were taught how to eat, talk and behave like an officer. A posting like this was the standard next stage on his career path.

'Yeah,' Danny said. 'I've seen him around.' He glanced towards the Hercules, whose tailgate was lowering. 'Anything else?'

'Nothing. Get going.'

Danny gave the ops officer a curt nod and followed the RAF guy towards the Hercules. Danny boarded and made his way to the flight deck, where he introduced himself to the 47 Squadron crew.

'I'm going to sling my hammock and get my head down after I've had some food,' he told the pilot, before returning to the main cabin. Within five minutes, he was airborne again. He got some food and hot coffee into his system, then tried to sleep as the lights of western Europe slowly gave way to the oil fields of the Middle East.

But his mind was filled with images of Tony Wiseman. He saw Tony's sweat-covered face on a burning oil rig in the Gulf. On a migrant boat in the Med. In the forests of Norfolk, holding his gun to the head of a terrorist who had information that Danny wanted. *Needed.* It was that image that stuck with Danny most of all. It made his throat hot with bile. A voice in his head told him he needed to put his anger in a box for another time. Other guys in the Regiment looked up to Tony. No doubt the rest of the unit out in Helmand would be the same. Danny needed to take a chill pill. But another voice wondered whether he would ever be able to do that. Danny genuinely did not know what would happen when he saw Tony in just a few hours.

Flight time Northolt to Kandahar: 8 hours 30 minutes. It seemed to pass in a quarter of that time. Danny felt he'd only just boarded when he realised they were catching up with the sun. Dawn was breaking over the familiar desert landscape of the Middle East, staining the sky and the sand the colour of blood. Danny expected a steep descent into Kandahar. Low-flying aircraft were well within the range of militants with ground-to-air missiles. Better to stay high as long as possible, and start your descent close to the military base at the last minute. He felt his stomach lurch as the Herc suddenly lost height. The aircraft banked sharply to the right, and Danny caught a glimpse through the window of Kandahar base in the distance: a huge, sprawling military city, surrounded by miles of flat, parched desert. There were mountains on the horizon: bleak, imposing cliffs that Danny knew had been, and probably still were, the hideouts of all manner of militants, and the scene of fierce fighting. The sky was cloudless and, as they swooped in to land on the runway that cut through the centre of the air base, a shimmering haze across the parched landscape told him it was furnace hot outside. As the wheels touched down, he saw dust billowing up through the window: a reminder that Afghanistan was a hard place to operate.

As the Herc taxied off the runway, Danny saw a khaki Land Rover pulling up and figured that was his escort. He was right. Stepping down on to the tarmac, where he was almost knocked back by the brutal heat, a British soldier with a familiar face approached, hand outstretched.

'Harry Isherwood,' he shouted over the noise of the Hercules's engines powering down. 'I'm your watchkeeper. I'll be looking after you while you're here, providing liaison with ANA and NATO troops in the area. Good to meet you properly.'

Danny nodded at him, then followed as Isherwood led him towards the khaki Land Rover. He took the passenger seat, and Isherwood swung the vehicle round in a semicircle that kicked up more dust from the airfield, then accelerated hard.

'You won't have much time to get settled in, I'm afraid,' Isherwood said. 'I've had word from Cornwall. They're compiling target packs as we speak.'

'I'll be ready,' Danny said. He was sweating heavily as they sped through a car-parking area only half full of old, dust-covered vehicles. They passed a line of aircraft hangars that contained a varied collection of fast air and workhorses. To their left was a vast area of living quarters – khaki-coloured tents arranged with military geometry, enough to house a couple of thousand men. But these were Afghan quarters. He knew the Spearpoint unit would be located well away from them, so it was no surprise that his driver was now weaving his way past sanitary blocks and a line of shops for the troops in camp, past refuelling stations and engineering units. A couple of mechanics had a sand-coloured Husky tactical support vehicle raised above the ground. It had clearly been hit by an IED: the massive front wheels were blown off and the chassis mangled. The mechanics were removing the axle, perhaps in an attempt to get the vehicle running again. Good luck with that, Danny thought, as they continued to an area on what Danny judged to be the eastern side of the base.

This area was cordoned off by a four-metre high wall constructed of sand-filled crates – opaque, impenetrable and sturdy enough to withstand small arms fire. An armed British soldier, his hair already damp with sweat, guarded the entrance. Isherwood pulled up in front of him, but made no attempt to alight. He just leaned out of his open window and called to the guard: 'This is our new Spearpoint package. He has full access.' He turned to Danny. 'I'm late for a sit-down with the Afghan camp commander,' he said. 'Make yourself at home.'

Danny glanced at the grim, military cordon of the Spearpoint base. How could he do anything but? He climbed out of the Land Rover. Isherwood was driving off almost before Danny had shut the door behind him. The green army guy was already opening the gate for him.

'The rest of the unit here?' Danny asked before stepping inside.

'Roger that,' said the soldier. 'Sleeping, I wouldn't wonder.' He sniffed. 'Them lot have sleeping pills in the day and ephedrine at night. Keep different hours, if you know what I mean.'

Yeah. Danny knew exactly what he meant. 'Thanks, buddy,' he said. He entered the cordon, and the soldier closed the gate behind him.

There was nothing about Spearpoint's Kandahar ops centre that gave any clue as to the true nature of its occupants' business. It comprised four grey Portakabins, set in a line, whose windows were covered with steel sheeting. Beyond them was a comms satellite and a concrete sanitary block. The block was thirty metres away, but Danny could still smell it. And beyond that, two larger breeze-block buildings. A couple of sand-coloured MWMIK Jackal armoured vehicles were parked up by the gate, and by one of the walls there was an electricity generator with a thick black cable snaking into one of the rear breeze-block buildings. There was no sign of personnel.

Danny stood for a moment. On the edge of his hearing was the sound of another aircraft coming in to land, but he wasn't really paying attention. He was wondering which of these Portakabins contained Tony.

His question was answered thirty seconds later.

The door to one of them opened. A figure stepped out. He wore khaki trousers. No top, no shoes. Aviator shades. His arms and torso were muscular, his hair dishevelled. He walked to the end of the adjacent Portakabin, stood with his back to Danny, and pissed thunderously against the bleak, grey structure. A puddle of urine dribbled between his feet across the hard-baked sand as he made a big show of shaking himself off. The liquid steamed in the heat. With his back still turned to Danny, he rapped on the exterior wall of the Portakabin. And only then did he speak. 'This is yours,' he said.

Danny forced himself to breathe deeply. He knew Tony's ways. He knew he was only trying to get him to rise. He wasn't going to give him the satisfaction.

Tony turned, his bare feet slapping in the puddle as he walked towards Danny. His shades glinted in the early morning sunlight. He had several days' stubble and a distinct sneer on his lips. He stopped when he was a metre away, then removed his sunglasses.

Danny was shocked by what he saw. In appearance, at least, this was not the Tony he remembered. His eyes were bloodshot. Raw. There were deep bags that almost looked as if they had been painted on.

They stood, face to face, for several seconds. Tony put his sunglasses back on. Danny saw his own reflection in the mirrored glass. He looked tired. Older than he expected. Worn.

'I heard Spud got what was coming to him,' Tony said.

Danny felt his jaw setting.

'He was a fucking spare part,' Tony continued. 'Always amazed me that the cunt lasted as long as he—'

It happened like lightning. Danny raised his right hand, the middle knuckle protruding, and went for the soft flesh of Tony's bare neck. But Tony knew it was coming. His left arm shot up and grabbed Danny's wrist. There was no difference in strength between the two men. Their arms locked. Their muscles strained. But the explosion of violence was quelled, for a moment.

'If we're not on ops, I don't want to speak to you,' Tony breathed. 'I don't even want to *see* you. The guys on the team?

They're my guys. They're not your guys. I've warned them about you and they know what to expect. We sent the last one home because he wasn't up to the job. I don't expect a pussy like you to last more than a week.'

He released Danny's grip. Danny let his hand fall.

'The hut on the far side of the shitters is the armoury. Get yourself sorted. You can zero in on the range in the north-western corner of the base – I don't want you fucking things up by not being on target. We operate at night, and we need to be ready to deploy with thirty minutes' notice. I'm going back to bed.'

He turned his back on Danny and started walking back towards his Portakabin.

'Tony,' Danny called.

Tony stopped but didn't turn.

'Any shit, I'll nail you and be happy to do it.'

Tony looked over his shoulder. He moved his sunglasses so they were resting on the top of his head. Once more Danny saw the raw, bloodshot look in his eyes. 'Don't make me laugh,' he said.

He turned again, continued walking and this time reached and entered his quarters, leaving Danny sweating in the Afghan sun, his throat dry and a vein throbbing noticeably in his temple.

5

'What do you have, chaps?'

Marcus Cadogan had allowed himself a couple of hours' sleep. He showed no sign that he'd been woken up just five minutes ago. His clothes were not wrinkled, his eyes were not tired. He blew his floppy blond hair off his forehead, then rapped the floor with his walking stick as he spoke.

The ginger-haired soldier McLean, by contrast, looked exhausted and he didn't smell too fresh. When he spoke, his voice had a hard edge. 'I think we can green light them, sir.'

'I'll be the judge of that, old chap,' Cadogan said. 'Go ahead.'

McLean frowned slightly at the put-down, but quickly regained his composure. 'To recap,' he said, 'our targets are known locally as Abu Manza and Abu Noor. We've managed to commandeer drones to follow them for the past eight hours. It's captured enough imagery for us to cross-reference their identities. They've been operating together.'

McLean turned to one of the tech guys and nodded. The tech guy tapped on his keyboard. Photographs appeared on two side-by-side screens, six on the left-hand screen, five on the right-hand screen. They were blurred and distant, but obviously the same two people. 'The guy on the left,' McLean said, 'is Abu Manza.' The photographs on the left-hand screen disappeared, to be replaced by a single, much clearer, image of an Afghan man. 'Also known as Hassan al-Din. He's on the FBI watch list and is wanted in Saudi Arabia on terrorism charges.'

McLean turned his attention to the second screen. 'Abu Noor is a real piece of work. We think his real name is Khalid al-Din. Thought to have been a protégé of Bin Laden's, list of terrorist activity as long as your arm. Previously believed to be hiding in Lebanon, quite the surprise to find him here.' The drone pictures disappeared to show a single black and white image, clearly of the same man.

'These are good targets,' Cadogan said. 'How did our asset come by them?'

'A teenage Afghan girl, sir. She seems to have a way with them.'

Cadogan smiled. '*Affidamento*,' he said.

'Sir?'

'Where on earth did you go to school, McLean?'

'Not Eton, sir.'

'Obviously. *Affidamento*. It's an Italian term. It means a relationship of trust between women.'

'Sir, if we could—'

'This isn't enough to green light the targets,' Cadogan said. 'Those chaps at the Foreign Office will want more than that.'

'Bear with me, sir,' McLean said, with a note of impatience in his voice. 'There *is* more. Our drones followed these characters and we got lucky. I'll give you the edited highlights. At 03.00 local time they met at this road junction ten miles north of Gareshk.' A map appeared on the screen. A red dot indicated a crossroads. 'You'll see that this road heads north-west. There's an ANA forward operating base about three kilometres along the road, so I think we can safely assume there will be a high volume of troop movement in that direction.' He nodded at the tech guy and the picture changed to an NV camera view of a vehicle from above. 'We'll scrub forward,' McLean said. The camera footage moved into fast forward. The vehicle sped along the road moving north-west. When it came to a halt, the tech guy slowed the footage down. They watched as two figures emerged and opened up the trunk of the vehicle. It was hard to see exactly what they removed from it, but a few seconds later they were plainly digging a hole in the centre of the road. It took them no more than two minutes. They returned to the trunk of the vehicle, then removed something else. Whatever this object was, they placed it in the hole they'd just dug and refilled it with the displaced earth. They hurried back to the car, reversed back up the road, made a three-point turn and returned the way they'd come.

The footage stopped and the screen went blank.

'It's rather crude, isn't it?' Cadogan said quietly.

'Effective though,' McLean said. 'Our guys estimate that IED is enough to take out a truck full of ten to twelve soldiers with about fifty per cent loss of life. If a civilian vehicle hits it, all the occupants will be killed.'

'We can't identify the targets by this footage?'

'No, sir. But we know it's them.'

'Do tell me you haven't warned the Afghans about this one,' Cadogan said.

McLean frowned. 'No, sir.' He paused for a moment, before quickly adding: 'But I do think we can arrange a convincing reason for that road to be closed off . . .'

'Absolutely not,' Cadogan said.

'Sir, if we—'

'If we give the targets any indication that we're on to them, they'll go to ground. The IED stays where it is. But for heaven's sake don't put that in Holroyd's report. Where is our pious investigative friend, by the way?'

'He was called back to London last night, sir.'

'Well, that's something to be thankful for. Is this everything you have?'

'No, sir. Abu Manza and Abu Noor are high-value targets. We have their DNA on file. If the Foreign Office decide to green light the hit, we can take samples once they're dead to confirm their identities. Should ease things with the RMPs if we need it to.'

'I do hope you didn't get their DNA from the Americans, old chap.'

'The Australians, sir.'

Cadogan thought for a moment. Then he nodded. 'Get me the Foreign Office,' he said.

The Portakabin that would be serving as Danny's quarters was devoid of luxury. A low military cot. A chest of drawers. A table and a chair. Nothing more. The insane Afghan heat had penetrated its flimsy walls and it was hotter inside than out. Danny could still smell the body odour of the room's previous occupant. He presumed that was Jimmy Murphy, who'd tried to top himself and been sent home.

Danny dumped his shoulder bag on his bed. Looked around. There was nothing keeping him in here, so he decided to go and investigate the armoury. He stepped back outside, wincing, into the bright sunlight, then entered the Portakabin Tony had indicated. He had to walk past the sanitary block, which smelled even worse up close.

The armoury was twice the size of Danny's accommodation. Along the far wall were two racks, one above the other: handguns and sub-machine guns on one, assault rifles on the other. There were boxes of ammunition. Fragmentation grenades. Flashbangs. Optics – laser sights, torches, night sights. There were clothes racks packed with ops gear – tactical vests, body armour, Crye Precision digital camouflage combat apparel. A metal shelf contained a line of NV helmets, each with four individual NV tubes spread out to give an extra wide field of vision. There were freefall rigs and HALO gear. There were packages of C-4 plastic explosives. Tucked away in one corner was a crate filled with attack dog paraphernalia: a canine freefall harness, a canine tactical vest, bite sleeves, GoPro harness attachments and several types of lead.

This was a well-stocked room. It was almost as if the Regiment's armoury had been lifted from Hereford and dumped here in the middle of the desert. It was the storeroom of a team that meant business.

Danny approached the weapons rack. He selected an M4, suppressed. Like all the other weapons, it had been spray painted in brown and khaki desert colours. Danny took it down from the rack and instinctively checked that it was made safe and there was no ammunition. A loose round in here could be like a fag end in a petrol station. He slung it over his shoulder and picked out a Sig P226 handgun. Then he bent down to select a box of 5.56 for the rifle and 9mms for the handgun. He reckoned that just this once he'd take Tony's advice and go spend some time on the range.

He turned. And stopped.

He had left the doorway to the armoury open. Now it was blocked. Silhouetted against the bright sunlight outside was the outline of a dog. It was standing and its back was arched. Danny recognised the distinctive outline of a Malinois and he could immediately sense – both from the dog's position and from the low growl that came from its throat – that the beast was consciously restraining itself, but ready to attack at the same time. Like a rock being stretched back in a catapult.

Danny didn't move. He made no eye contact with the dog, because he knew it could take that as a threat. Instead he glanced over to the crate in the corner where the dog gear was stashed. Nobody had told him that the team was using an attack dog, but it made sense.

A human figure appeared behind the dog. Broad shouldered. Scruffy hair. Danny couldn't quite make out his face. His presence didn't seem to worry the Malinois, who continued to growl.

'Baron, at ease.'

The voice was deep, with a very pronounced Northern Irish accent. It spoke to the dog with quiet authority, and the dog itself responded immediately. It sat. The growling stopped. It cocked its head at a slight angle, as though patiently listening for its next command. It didn't, however, take its gaze off Danny.

The man entered. His scruffy hair and beard were a red-blond colour, and his skin was also blasted red by the sand and the sun. There was something boyish about his appearance. He wore camo trousers and no top, which showed off not only his muscular, sunburned torso, but also the full sleeve of tattoos from his right forearm up to his shoulder. Nothing military, of course, that might identify him, but there was barely an exposed patch of skin. The muscles in his arms were well defined, and his non-tattooed arm was grimy, like he'd just been out on ops and hadn't cleaned up yet. Ray-Bans, which he'd propped up on his forehead. A full beard, if anything a little redder than his hair. A rugged watch on his left wrist. He stepped inside, past the dog, stroking its head as he did so and making a clicking noise in the back of his throat, which seemed to calm the Malinois a bit more.

'Danny Black,' he said, without much enthusiasm.

'Rees Dexter.' Danny recognised the A Squadron man, but they'd never spoken. He was well known for being one of Tony's yes men, and for being considerably fonder of his dogs than of people.

Dexter gestured over his shoulder with one thumb. 'That's Baron. Do yourself a favour and steer clear of him. I'm his handler. He answers to nobody else. His teeth are steel capped, his jaws are strong and he's got a taste for fresh blood.'

'Shouldn't he be properly housed when he's not on ops?' Danny said.

Dexter didn't answer immediately. He looked distracted. Like he was staring at a point somewhere beyond Danny. After a few seconds, he said: 'What about you, Black? You got a taste for fresh blood, too? Because you'll need it, out here.'

'You didn't answer my question.'

'Ah, don't you worry about Baron. As long as I'm nearby, he's as happy as a pig in shit.' He pointed at the weapons Danny was carrying. 'You want me to show you where the range is? Zero those bad boys in?'

Danny nodded.

'Sure, Baron could do with stretching his legs. C'mon, I'll show you the ropes.'

Dexter put his Ray-Bans on properly and led the way out of the armoury and across the enclosure to the exit. Baron walked obediently at his side. The dog gave no sign of its former aggressive self, but Danny kept his distance anyway. There was something about Dexter that put him on edge. He seemed somehow different to most of the Regiment guys he knew. There was no camaraderie in his manner. And Danny knew about dogs and their handlers. If Dexter lost his cool, nobody could vouch for the behaviour of the Malinois.

'It's not far,' Dexter said. 'Best hope you don't have to share it with those fuckin' ANA jokers. That's kindergarten time.'

'How long have you been out here?' Danny asked as they walked past a line of low, brick buildings that housed sand-coloured armoured vehicles.

Dexter moistened his lips. He didn't answer.

'Hammond said Spearpoint has been running for about nine months,' Danny prompted him.

'Aye, nine months.' Dexter sounded uncertain. 'The days kind of run into each other,' he said. 'And the nights, of course. We work at night.' He stopped suddenly, and looked around. A few Afghan soldiers were milling about, but none of them were paying them any attention. 'A word to the wise, Black. This is Tony's patch. He calls the shots.' He moistened his lips again. 'He said you and he had some history.'

'Which way is the range?'

Dexter removed his Ray-Bans. For a moment, Danny saw the same dead expression in his eyes that he'd seen in Tony's. 'Good man, Tony,' Dexter said. 'Good man.' Dexter sniffed and the strange look in his eyes faded. 'This way,' he said.

The range was a cordoned-off patch of sand at the edge of the air base, with three body-shaped targets positioned in front of a large bank of earth, which was there to stop any loose rounds. A bored Afghan soldier was manning the place, but he stayed in a small concrete hut out of the sun. There were sandbags lying here and there on the ground.

Danny left Dexter with his dog and pulled out a thirty-round magazine of 5.56s. He checked that the lip was smooth. Too often, guys rammed these magazines into the weapon, dinging the lip, which would eventually cause a stoppage. Satisfied that the mag was good, Danny loaded it up. He positioned a sandbag 150 metres from the central target. He lay down in a prone position, supporting his right arm on the sandbag, and aimed for the central mass of the target's chest. He released five aimed, deliberate shots. Immediately he could tell that his grouping was good – the shots had all fallen within an inch of each other. But when he walked up to the target to examine the position of the group, he saw that it was a good couple of inches to the right of centre. He adjusted the weapon's sight a couple of clicks before returning to his prone position at the sandbag and releasing a further five rounds. Bang on.

He approached the target again. Fifty metres out, and still walking forward, he raised his weapon and released two rounds. Direct head shots. Still walking, he lowered the weapon then raised it again. Two rounds. Directly on target. He switched the weapon to automatic, emptied the magazine, loaded a new one and put another thirty rounds through the weapon. All sweet. Danny's rifle was zeroed and working as he expected it to.

He removed his Sig. Stood five metres from the target and emptied the handgun. The 9mm rounds fell exactly as he was expecting.

Danny was sweating as he retrieved his shredded target from its hanger. He'd only been in-country for less than two hours and already his skin felt grimy and sandblasted. He turned. Through the haze of heat, he saw Dexter cross-legged on the sand giving Baron commands and rewarding him with treats from the pocket of his camo trousers. If he had any interest in Danny's skill with a weapon, he didn't show it.

Danny started trudging back towards his firing point. As he did so, he saw an armoured truck speeding towards the range, a cloud of dust billowing up around it. It scraped to a halt twenty metres from the range and a man jumped out whom Danny recognised as Billy Cole, also A Squadron. Cole had a bald head, a scraggly black beard and very tanned, leathery skin. He was dressed similarly to Dexter – Crye camo trousers, boots and a tactical vest over his bare torso. Precisely the same sunglasses. He left the truck turning over and ran towards Dexter. From a distance of thirty metres, Danny saw the two men in conversation, occasionally looking over towards him. And as he drew nearer, Danny saw Cole glance at him with a flat, unfriendly look.

'We need to get back,' he said in a low voice as Danny approached. Very hoarse, like he'd been shouting a lot, or had damaged his throat.

'Why?' Danny said.

Dexter flicked Baron another treat, and the dog jumped up to get it.

Cole gave Danny a 'what are you, stupid?' look. 'Because we've got a green light,' he said.

6

Cole had the wheel. Danny was in the front passenger seat while Dexter and the dog sat in the back.

'Is it tonight?' Dexter asked from the back.

'Roger that. A double hit. The Watchman wants us in the ops room now.'

It took a minute to get to the cordon. The crap hat at the gate had seen them coming and was already opening up. Cole skidded to a halt and the three team members alighted quickly. Cole led the way past the accommodation cabins to the concrete building next to the armoury. Dexter issued a single instruction to the dog: 'Wait.' Baron sat by the entrance to the building as the men filed in.

Tony was already there. He had a black T-shirt on now, his aviators clipped to the neck. He was standing at a table that was covered with maps, papers and a couple of sturdy, scuffed laptops. Isherwood was standing next to him, examining photographs. He waved the rest of the unit in without even looking at them. It was, Danny noted, the slightly superior gesture of an officer. That knife and fork course had served him well, but it was obvious from the way that Tony nodded his agreement that Dexter and Cole were more in thrall to him than to Isherwood. Danny made a mental note to watch his back around those two.

'Let's get the headshed on the line,' Isherwood said.

Tony positioned himself in front of one of the laptops. He tapped at the keyboard. A few seconds later, as clear as if he was in the same room, Danny heard Marcus Cadogan's voice. 'Can you hear me, chaps?'

'Roger that,' Tony said, rolling his eyes at Dexter. Dexter grinned. It was a strangely obsequious gesture, like a kid sucking up to the school bully. It seemed to please Tony.

'Roger that,' came Ray Hammond's voice over the line.

Tony manoeuvred the laptop so the unit could see the screen. Half of it was taken up with a close-up of Cadogan with his unruly blond hair. The other half showed Ray Hammond.

'Splendid,' Cadogan said. 'We have two targets green lit by the Foreign Office. They have been awarded the imaginative monikers Target Red and Target Blue. Target Red is Khalid Al-Din, pseudonym Abu Noor. He lives in the village of Gareshk, in a compound with his wife and two children. Target Blue is his brother, Hassan Al-Din, pseudonym Abu Manza. He lives in the same village, also with his wife, but three children. Surveillance footage suggests the targets are in situ, so the hits will have to be tonight and in close succession. If we only get one, the other will go to ground. Tell me what you need.'

Tony answered without even looking at the others. 'Distance to target?'

'A hundred and fifty kilometres.'

'Terrain between here and there?'

'Partly mountainous. High risk of IEDs.'

'So we freefall in,' Tony said. 'Four of us.'

'Plus the dog,' Dexter added.

Danny had no argument with that.

'The Herc is on standby,' Hammond said. 'Flight crew is being briefed at the moment.'

'Do we have a Met report?' Danny asked.

'I've got it here,' Isherwood said, holding up a tablet in a rugged case. 'We have cloud cover coming this afternoon. It's going to be a dark night. No moon. But dry.'

'Can we stop talking about the fucking weather for just one minute?' Tony said.

There was silence in the room and on the line. Cole and Dexter looked like they were enjoying Tony's interruption. Tony himself glared dangerously at everyone before continuing. 'And if it's okay with everyone else, the new boy can keep his pie hole shut, since he doesn't know what the fuck we're dealing with.' He glared at Danny. 'The last three hits we've done, these fuckers have been tooled up. *Properly* tooled up.' He strode over to the back of the briefing room where there was a line of metal shelving full of bits of military gear. He picked up a laser sight. 'AN/PEQ-2 laser,' Tony said, holding it up. 'Fitted to the rifle of that kid we nailed outside Musa Qala three nights ago.' He returned the laser sight to the shelf and picked up a compact radio handset. 'Encrypted,' he said. 'So much for the Taliban communicating on walkie-talkies that my granny could hack into with her hearing aid. We picked this up last week when we nailed those two targets south of Lashkar Gah. Cunt had used it, too. We had to dodge three of his fucking raghead mates on the way to the pickup zone.' He chucked the radio back on the shelf. 'This is SF gear. Our targets are better equipped than we've been expecting. Fuck knows where they're getting this stuff, but someone's arming them properly. We don't up our game, we're going to get burned.'

A brief silence followed Tony's outburst. Then Cadogan spoke. 'Have you quite finished, my dear chap?' he said quietly.

'No I fucking haven't, my dear chap.' Tony returned to the table. 'First things first. I want a fast-air strafing run over the target to mask the noise of our aircraft when we deploy. These guys aren't stupid. They know the sound of a Hercules when they hear it.'

'You'll be HALO-ing in from twenty-two thousand feet,' Hammond said. 'It's not necessary. No one's going to hear you at that height.'

Tony's eyes went flinty. He didn't like being told no.

'You'll tell the ANA and any NATO forces to stay clear of the target area?' Cadogan asked. 'One would rather avoid a blue on blue.'

'Of course,' Isherwood said. 'I've already made the calls. There's a four kilometre no-go zone around each target location. There'll be no military operations getting in your way.'

'That's the least I'd expect, pal,' Tony insisted. Danny could tell this was now a matter of pride. 'I want a patrol making some noise on the south side of this highway here.' He pointed at a map on the table for Isherwood's benefit. 'Everything goes quiet, our targets will know something's up. If we have a few green army boys laying down rounds, it'll just be another normal night in Helmand and the targets will be looking the other way.'

Isherwood inclined his head. 'I'll do what I can.'

'You'll fucking do more than that. You'll make it happen.'

Isherwood straightened up to his full height. 'I'll do what I can.'

'I'm not finished,' Tony said. 'I want full drone support throughout the op.'

There was a moment of silence as Cadogan consulted someone back at the Cornwall control room. 'Not possible, I fear,' he said finally. 'We have limited drone assets available to us. They're needed elsewhere.'

'Fine,' Tony said. 'Then we'll just put our boots up and call in a few hookers. Because if you're not giving us the backup we need, we're staying home.'

Danny had to hand it to Tony. He was up himself, but he knew how to get what he wanted. And deep down, Danny didn't disagree with anything he was saying.

There was another pause at the Cornwall end of the line. Cadogan's eyes narrowed and Danny recognised the sharp expression he'd seen back at Spearpoint HQ. 'Very well,' Cadogan said finally. 'We can follow you for the first hit, then get you on target for the second. But as soon as you breach Target Blue's compound, we have no option but to pull them off. They're needed 200 miles to the south for another operation.'

'That's not good enough—' Tony started to say.

'Deal with it, Wiseman,' Hammond cut in. His voice had an edge. 'Otherwise I'm pulling *you* out.'

Tony jutted out his chin, but didn't reply.

'If there's nothing else, gentlemen,' Isherwood announced, 'I have some calls to make.'

'Wait,' Tony said. He nodded in Danny's direction. 'I've been with this cunt on ops before. Like I said, he's a liability.'

'Give it a fucking break, Tony,' Danny muttered.

Tony ignored him. 'The three of us have been on the ground for six months now. We know the ropes. I want it understood that he takes his orders from me.'

Silence.

'Agreed,' Hammond said. Danny felt his blood run hot, but knew there was no point arguing. He stared carefully at the screen, ignoring the looks he knew the others were giving him. 'We'll make the drop at 23.20 hours local time,' Hammond continued. 'We'll speak again at 19.00. Get ready.'

The video feed on the laptop died.

Tony turned to Dexter and Cole. 'Posh twat,' he said, clearly referring to Cadogan. 'You two, get the gear packed up.' He nodded at Danny. 'He can help you with the donkey work.'

'Let's go, Black,' Dexter said.

Danny stood his ground. 'Not yet,' he said. He turned to Tony. 'Do you have visuals for the targets?'

'We'll do that when the gear's packed,' Tony said.

'We'll do it now,' Danny replied.

There was silence in the room. Danny and Tony faced off across the table. The other three men watched them carefully. It felt like everyone was holding their breath.

'Sort the gear out,' Isherwood said. 'Be back here in an hour. We'll continue our briefing then.'

Dexter smiled. Cole looked slightly anxiously between Danny and Tony. Tony inclined his head and gave Danny both barrels of his most insulting look.

'Show him the ropes, fellas,' Tony said.

Cole and Dexter headed out of the ops room. Danny had no option but to follow.

The safest time to be outside her compound, Caitlin had learned, was between 13.00 and 15.00 hours. Midday prayers were over and the temperature was almost intolerable. It was intolerable for everyone. At this time of day, she could move around without attracting too much attention.

But the streets were not deserted. Members of the Afghan National Army, based at one of the FOBs to the north, east and south of Panjika, were patrolling in groups of three or four. They were clad in standard camo gear, although some had bandanas over their faces even in this heat, to hide their identity. In Helmand Province, it wasn't always wise to let it be known you were on the side of the authorities. Aside from the ANA patrols, the streets were full of women. Caitlin had made an observation. While the men of the village took shelter in their homes during the hottest parts of the day, the women were more likely to be out. It was a cultural thing. The women were the hardest workers. Or maybe, she thought to herself grimly, it wasn't a cultural thing at all. Maybe it was the same everywhere.

She wore traditional Afghan clothes: a blue burqa, complete with headdress that covered her face. Her presence in this village was hardly a secret, but she liked to keep a low profile in front of the ANA. Underneath her robes she wore body armour and had her handgun holstered at her side. She didn't expect any trouble, but that was no reason not to be careful.

Caitlin took this walk a couple of times a week. She avoided any kind of schedule – it was hardwired in her to mix things up a bit so that she didn't present an open target if she was under surveillance. But the women of the village knew there was a chance that she might be walking the streets at this time of day. They could recognise her by the shoulder bag she carried, which contained her medical gear. Those who were too shy, or scared, to come to her compound could approach her in the street. She insisted that Tommy stay home. He didn't like it, but his alarming presence would make these midday walks entirely useless. He was a scary-looking guy – and it wasn't like Caitlin couldn't take care of herself. Gabina, on the other hand, was a necessity. Without her, Caitlin couldn't talk to anyone. The petite, pretty young translator walked alongside her, similarly dressed, head down.

Ordinarily, Caitlin would loiter on corners, or outside the ramshackle stalls that made up the main street, waiting for women to come to her, talk to her and – hopefully – give up nuggets of intelligence that she could report back to Cornwall. Today, she had a different objective. She strode with purpose, past the stalls with their corrugated iron roofs and pitiful collection of wares for sale, past rickshaws and bicycles and the occasional stray goat. When groups of two or three women watched her pass, she didn't stop to talk as she normally would. Today, she had a destination.

She continued to the end of the main street, past the plain arch at the front of the mosque – all closed up now – and turned left where eight or nine old motorbikes were parked. From here she could see the derelict building site at the back of the mosque, where reconstruction of its bomb-damaged north-western corner had stalled. Beyond that, a number of trees were dotted around, behind which the dried-out riverbed ran parallel to the main street. On the other side of the river was a collection of low compounds and other dwellings. This area was normally deserted. She ignored a lean, hungry-looking dog that watched her intently as she approached one of the very few two-storey buildings in the village. The ground floor comprised a garage with heavily bolted shutters. This was where the only mechanic in the village worked. But of course he was not there today, because the previous night he had been thrown through the windscreen of his car, along with his wife, while his little boy had been burned to death and his daughter had suffered a massive arterial bleed, and only survived thanks to Caitlin's swift intervention at the scene of the car bomb.

The mechanic and his daughter were now in an ANA medical facility thirty klicks from here. Caitlin didn't even know if they were alive. The little boy – whose burned, peeled face Caitlin would never forget – would be buried before sundown at the edge of the village, as was the custom.

The mother, however, was here.

Her wounds – lacerations on her face from the windscreen and a broken ankle – had not been considered severe enough for an emergency medical evacuation. Word was that the Afghan soldiers had brought her home, given her some rudimentary care and basic pain relief, and then left.

A rough staircase was carved into the side of the house by the garage, leading to the first floor. Caitlin and Gabina climbed it together. Caitlin knocked on the wooden door at the top of the stairs. There was no answer, but the door wasn't locked. She let herself in.

It was a poor place. Just one room with two old double mattresses in opposite corners. A rickety metal table with four chairs. An old gas stove with a scuffed propane canister next to it. An ancient wooden cupboard. No sign of a sink or a toilet.

The woman was lying on one of the mattresses. The skin on her face was closed up here and there with steristrips and her ankle was bandaged. She was wrapped in an old blanket but despite the heat was still shivering. She was also crying: a desperate, repetitive mew. Caitlin could tell she was in pain, but she could also tell that she knew about her son. It was that kind of cry.

It was very gloomy in here. The one window in the room was covered with a shutter. Caitlin and Gabina left the door open to give them a bit of light. Even so, the woman didn't appear to notice that she had guests until they were practically by her bedside. When that happened, her anguished face became suddenly fearful. She tried to push herself up on to her elbows, but couldn't. She collapsed on her back again, her eyes shut, her whole body racking with sobs.

'Tell her I'm going to give her some medicine for the pain,' Caitlin told Gabina.

Gabina translated, her eyes wide with sympathy. The woman gave no indication that she even heard her. Caitlin kneeled by her side and opened up her shoulder bag. She removed a sealed packet containing a pencil-shaped auto-injector. The lettering on the side read 'Morphine Sulfate 10mg'.

Caitlin administered the morphine shot through the woman's clothes and into the flesh of her left thigh in a matter of seconds. The impact was almost immediate. The woman stopped crying.

Her breathing became more regular. Caitlin could sense her patient's whole body relaxing. The drug wouldn't have taken away the pain of the trauma, but it would have softened her body's harsh response to it.

Caitlin was honest enough with herself to admit that the morphine also had a secondary effect, besides giving the woman comfort. It would have loosened her tongue.

She looked up at Gabina and nodded. 'Tell her I'm the one who helped her daughter,' she said.

Gabina translated. The woman spoke weakly in Pashto. Her words were slightly slurred.

'She wants to know where her husband and daughter are,' Gabina said.

'In the hospital,' Caitlin said. 'As soon as I hear anything I'll tell you. But for now they're safe.'

Gabina translated. The woman closed her eyes.

'I want to ask you a question,' Caitlin said. She knew she had to be careful with her words. Say the wrong thing and her potential source would clam shut, morphine or no morphine. 'Do you want to help me stop this happening again?'

The woman didn't respond.

Caitlin gave it a moment. 'The more I know,' she said, 'about the people doing these things, the more I can help.'

Silence.

Caitlin and Gabina exchanged a look. 'Tell her we'll come back this afternoon,' Caitlin said quietly. 'If she wants some help getting to the burial, we can sort that.'

Gabina translated. The woman gave no indication that she'd heard.

Caitlin knew not to push it. She packed her things and stood up again. She nodded at Gabina and they turned to leave.

They were halfway to the door when the woman spoke.

Caitlin and Gabina stopped and turned. The woman still had her eyes closed. 'What did she say?' Caitlin breathed.

'She said: "The Imam knows."'

'The Imam knows what?'

Gabina made a 'I don't know' gesture.

They returned to the woman's bedside. 'Is he involved with the Taliban?' Caitlin asked. Gabina asked the question in a low, reassuring voice. The woman started to speak again, and the interpreter translated.

'My daughter told me. She is friends with the Imam's granddaughter. They live together in a compound on the other side of the river, with the rest of the Imam's family. She told my daughter that someone visits him at night. For religious comfort. Someone important in the Taliban.'

'Who?' Caitlin said. 'Does she have a name?'

Gabina asked the question, and Caitlin didn't need to translate the answer. 'Al-Zafawi,' said the woman.

Caitlin found herself breathing very deeply. Al-Zafawi was a name that needed no introduction to her. He was reputed to be the mastermind behind several of the Taliban's worst atrocities in recent times. A school massacre in Pakistan that killed more than 100 children. A wave of suicide and gun attacks in Kabul that killed 200 in a single day. An attack on a hospital in Jalalabad that killed as many medical staff as it did patients. It was even rumoured that he was behind a number of attacks in the UK. He certainly had the contacts, having been a student at the University of Bradford in the eighties.

Now, though, he had reinvented himself. He was reputed to be the leader of what the Helmand Taliban considered to be their own special forces. The Red Unit. That, along with the rap sheet from hell, made him just about the most high-value target in the province. And also the most difficult to locate.

'How do you know this?' Caitlin said.

Gabina spoke her translated response extra slowly, as though she was taking great care not to make any errors. Her voice wavered slightly. She clearly knew that this was dangerous information. 'The Imam is old. He knew Al-Zafawi when he was younger. From time to time Al-Zafawi wishes to speak to him about spiritual matters. He is his ...' Gabina took a moment to search for the right word. 'His confessor.'

The woman's eyes suddenly opened. She appeared more alert and she spoke more quickly. 'You cannot harm the Imam,' she said. 'People will be angry.'

'I'm not going to hurt anyone,' Caitlin said. 'If you need anything, get someone to come and find me. I'll be back later to see how you are, and I'll bring news about your family.'

She muttered something in a sleepy voice. 'You can't hurt him,' Gabina translated. 'She says: you can't hurt him.'

'I know,' Caitlin muttered. But she thought to herself: *We'll see*.

The sunlight outside the house hurt her eyes, even under the burka, as they emerged from the shadowy room. Caitlin strode purposefully back along the main street towards the compound. She felt the gaze of a group of ANA soldiers standing outside the bottle shop, but they didn't interrupt her. She could also sense that Gabina wanted to talk about this new piece of intelligence. But Caitlin didn't need a discussion. She needed to get on the radio to Cornwall. A lead on Al-Zafawi was big, but her brief was very distinct: hearts and minds. If she wanted to do what she was planning, she needed clearance from Spearpoint first.

Tommy was cleaning his weapon in the shade of the tree branches that overhung their compound wall. As soon as they entered, he stood up, but he didn't say anything.

'I need the sat phone,' Caitlin announced.

Tommy nodded and opened the door to his quarters where the comms equipment was kept. Caitlin ducked inside. Tommy's quarters had a soldier's neatness, but there was no denying the ripe, male smell that hung in the air. Caitlin ignored it and headed straight for the table opposite Tommy's bed. There was a sat phone, but also a laptop and various boxes of comms-boosting equipment. She powered up the sat phone, connected it to the laptop and typed in the access codes that would log her on to the encrypted VPN connection to Cornwall.

All this took less than a minute. A face appeared on the screen. A red-haired soldier in camo gear. He looked tired and a bit harassed.

'McLean,' Caitlin said. 'Do you copy?'

'Roger that,' McLean said.

'I need the boss.'

'Wait out figures two.'

The screen went blank. Two minutes later, Cadogan appeared.

'Caitlin,' he said, a slight edge to his voice. 'How delightful to hear from you.'

'Spare me the smarm,' Caitlin said. 'I have a lead on Al-Zafawi.'

There was no reply. Maybe there was a problem with the connection. 'Repeat: I have a lead on Al-Zafawi.'

'I heard you the first time, my dear,' Cadogan said.

'He's in charge of the Red Unit. He's—'

'I know who he is.'

'My source tells me that the local Imam acts as his confessor. He's known him for years. They have regular contact. I think I need to speak to the Imam. Find out what he knows.' She paused. 'He'll need a bit of persuasion.'

No reply.

'Cadogan, can you hear me?'

'I can hear you. Now listen carefully. You're to go nowhere near the Imam.'

Caitlin felt a surge of frustration. 'He's a Taliban sympathiser and associate,' she flared. 'If he can give me something on Al-Zafawi, we could break up the Red Unit in one—'

'Absolutely not,' Cadogan said. 'You're there to make friends. If you start interfering with the local Imam, you'll do the precise opposite.'

'But—'

'Must I repeat myself?' Cadogan said. 'You're forbidden from making contact with the Imam. If you do, you'll be on the first plane out of there. Am I understood?'

Caitlin took a deep breath to smother her anger. 'Understood,' she said, even though she didn't understand. Why *wouldn't* Spearpoint want intel on a target as valuable as this. It wasn't as though she couldn't deal with the Imam discreetly. She might not even have to resort to violence. She'd learned long ago that the flutter of the eyelashes and an implied promise of something more could be as effective as a gun to the bollocks, when it came to guys.

'Keep a low profile for twenty-four hours, my dear,' Cadogan said. 'The team's going in tonight. By the way, there's a new chap. Old chum of yours, I'm told. Does the name Danny Black ring any bells?'

Caitlin blinked. 'Sure,' she said. 'It rings some bells. You've put him on the same team as Tony Wiseman?'

'Is that a problem?'

Caitlin paused. 'No,' she said a moment later. 'No problem.'

Because Spearpoint clearly weren't in the mood to listen to her. And she was sure Danny wouldn't want her interfering in his affairs anyway.

In any case, she had other things to think about. Cadogan seemed shifty. His refusal to allow Caitlin to follow the Al-Zafawi lead didn't add up. There was more to this than he was letting on.

She killed the line and stared at the blank screen, thinking deeply.

Maybe she couldn't make contact with the Imam, but that didn't mean she couldn't keep an eye on the old boy.

She decided to do just that.

7

The pre-op briefings were complete.

At 15.00 hours they'd conducted a weapons and equipment check. Danny had loaded his rucksack and ops waistcoat with everything he needed for the op: ammunition, optics, med pack, mapping, torch, 24-hour ration pack and drinking water.

At 16.30 hours they'd performed a radio check, established working comms codes and given their boom mikes and earpieces a once-over. Each man's radio was fitted with a GPS tracker that meant Cornwall could keep tabs on their location at any point. Danny had memorised emergency access numbers into the Kandahar and Spearpoint bases.

At 17.30 hours they'd given their Ram Air freefall rigs a dedicated check. The plan was to jump from 22,000 feet so the Herc could fly high enough to avoid suspicion. Ordinarily, anything above 14,000 required the use of oxygen. The extra gear involved could slow them down on the ground, however. If it was just a quick blast up to 22k you could plug into the aircraft's oxygen supply, take a couple of deep gulps before you jumped, and you'd get away with it. Danny asked Dexter if the dog would be okay with that.

'Baron's a better freefaller than you and me put together, Black,' was the reply. And as Dexter continued to check over his rig, he said: 'Fucking drones have a couple of Hellfire missiles hanging underneath. Don't know why they don't just wipe the whole fucking village.'

'Small matter of civilian casualties,' Danny said.

'Ah well, Black. You can't make an omelette without breaking some eggs, hey?' And he looked at his other two unit mates. Tony grinned. Cole looked uncomfortable.

At 18.00 hours, as dusk arrived, they met with the pilot. He didn't ask any questions about what the team would be doing once they'd inserted. He was just businesslike and to the point about the drop.

'I'm going to keep it high,' he said. 'We'll be flying over several areas in full Taliban control. It's unlikely they'll take a pot shot, but the extra altitude will make us less obvious to them. Your drop zone will be three klicks from your target. Is there anything else you need from me?'

There was nothing. The unit traipsed back through the air base towards the Spearpoint cordon. The sun was sinking large behind the mountains in the distance. It saturated everything with a dusty red colour. The military personnel and apparatus all around wavered in the heat haze. Danny felt the bite of excitement and anxiety that always preceded an op. A sharpening of the mind, a focusing of energy. Even the antagonism between him and Tony seemed to have dissipated over the past few hours. There wasn't time for that on an operation. Once they were loaded up into the belly of that Hercules, they were no longer individuals. They were part of a unit, with a common purpose: to take out two militants, and stay alive in the process.

The final briefing back in the Spearpoint ops room was terse but frictionless. Isherwood took the lead. They were given their operation call sign: Delta Bravo Niner. Then a rundown of the geography. 'The village of Gareshk is situated on a tributary of the Helmand River. It's just a trickle this time of year, but there's a very lush green zone fifty metres either side. A forested area to the north and a central field fed by an irrigation ditch which we believe to be IED-free. There are extensive poppy fields to the west of the village.'

He brought up a satellite map and pointed out all these features on the map of Gareshk.

'The village itself mostly comprises high-walled compounds, each with approximately three or four buildings within. There are a few individual houses dotted around, if you want to call them that. It's a pretty poor place. Population approximately five hundred. You can see that the most densely inhabited area is here to the east of the tributary and to the south of the central field. There is a Taliban curfew in force after dark, so the locals are likely to be tucked up. Assume any movement of personnel is a threat.'

'Roger that,' Cole muttered.

'Targets Red and Blue both have compounds on the edge of the village. Target Red is on the eastern edge, Target Blue is on the western edge. You'll hit the eastern compound first, then cut around the northern edge of the village to the western compound, which you'll hit second. Your drop zone is two klicks to the east of Gareshk. You'll follow this wadi west – ' Isherwood indicated the path of a dried-out riverbed on the satellite map ' – until you reach this area of high ground here. At this point you'll be fifty metres from Target Red's compound. You'll have drone support from this point on, so we'll be able to confirm movement of potential threats in the area, but you'll need to keep eyes on the target as you approach . . .'

'Thanks for the advice,' Tony muttered.

Isherwood ignored his sarcasm. 'Estimated arrival time at Target Red's location: zero hundred hours. As you can see, like most of the compounds in the village, it's square, thirty metres by thirty. Walls are between three and four metres high. Scalable, in other words. The main door is on the eastern side. You know what to do when you're in there. We need DNA and photographs. Once Target Red is neutralised, you'll need to follow this bearing towards the forested area that extends from the northern perimeter of the village. We'll have you plugged in to the drone, so you'll have advance warning of movement ahead.'

'And we'll have Baron,' Dexter said, glancing towards the door that was being guarded by the Malinois.

'Of course,' Isherwood said. 'You'll need to move west through the trees, using them as cover, cross the tributary here, and skirt round the north of Target Blue's compound. It's bigger, and rectangular. Thirty by sixty. Two entrances, here on the north-western side, here on the southern side. There's an east–west dividing wall bisecting the compound, which we believe has a door in it. Surveillance footage suggests that the target will be in the northern section of the compound, his family in the southern section. The drone operator will get you to Target Blue's location, but then you're on your own ... forget it, Tony, it's the best we're going to get.' Tony gave him a sour look, but didn't complain. 'We've requested a withdrawal of all friendly troops within four klicks of the target zone, with one exception. We'll have some tame Afghan forces putting down rounds here ...' He tapped a map, indicating an area about three klicks to the north-east of the target. 'They'll make their noise at about 23.15 hours. Everyone's attention should be in that direction, not yours. Any questions about the approach?'

No questions.

'Your extraction location is here, two klicks to the south-west of Target Blue's compound. As I said, the area's full of poppy fields. We suggest that you don't move directly through them as the crop is high and you'll leave a trail. There's an irrigation ditch here, heading west, that you can follow for a klick before turning south here. We've arranged for a farm vehicle with a full tank of juice to be waiting for you at this location here. You're to use it to advance to Camp Shorabak, formerly Camp Bastion. We'll extract you from that location when we have the assets available.'

'How the hell long will that be?' Tony demanded.

'A few hours. A day, max. Just keep your heads down.'

Isherwood handed round photographs. Two men. Target Red and Target Blue.

'All look the fucking same to me,' Dexter said as they examined the photographs.

'We have some further identifying features. Turns out Target Red spent some time as a guest of the Americans in Basra as a young man. Still has something to show for it: electrical scarring around the genital area. Target Blue has a bullet wound to the left shoulder. Positive IDs shouldn't be a problem, but we'll still need DNA samples. Any questions about ID-ing the targets?'

No questions.

'It's now 18.27 hours. Fuel up. Get ready.'

Danny loitered by the maps. He identified the village of Panjika, approximately twenty-five klicks from the targets, where he knew Caitlin was embedded. He sensed Tony at his shoulder.

'Been there, done that,' Tony muttered. 'You're welcome to my cast-offs.'

Danny ignored him, and followed the others to get some food. There were ration packs and hot sweet tea waiting for them.

'Better this than the shit the local slop jockeys serve up in camp,' Cole said.

Danny picked up a foil pack of chicken curry and was about to rip it open when it was snatched from his hands by Dexter. Tony and Cole grinned like a couple of playground bullies.

'Chicken curry's mine, Black,' Dexter said. 'I've been known to put a guy's lights out for taking the chicken curry.' He ripped open the foil MRE and started squeezing the contents into his mouth without taking his eyes off Danny. When he'd swallowed a few mouthfuls, he squeezed some of the food into one hand and fed it to the dog, who was sitting expectantly at his side. 'It's Baron's favourite and all,' Dexter said.

Danny shrugged and grabbed another foil pack at random. Vegetable pasta. Whatever. The shit all tasted the same to him.

Each man made his way separately to the sanitary block to evacuate themselves before the op was a go, then returned to the armoury block for their final preparations. Danny put on his base layer and plate hangers, then his digital camouflage trousers and ops waistcoat, fully prepped and loaded. He selected a pair of tactical gloves. He stashed two magazines of 5.56s and one of 9mm into his ops vest, found himself a roll of duct tape, then set several sets of plasticuffs in double loops, ready to be tightened around wrists or ankles. He clipped his altimeter and GPS dial to his left wrist, fitted his helmet, complete with NV tubes, then gave the laser sights on his rifle a final check. He holstered his Sig – suppressed – across his chest, before slinging his rucksack over one shoulder and picking up his freefall rig.

He was the first to be ready. Dexter had the dog to deal with. As Danny headed to the exit he was clipping on Baron's freefall harness, talking to him calmly and quietly. The dog itself was sitting obediently with no sign of anxiety. The animal clearly knew the routine. He'd done this before.

Cole was strapping on his plate hangers. Danny went to give him a hand. He had the vague sense that Cole was not quite in Tony's pocket as much as Dexter was. But when Danny offered to help, he got a sour look in return. 'I don't need a personal fuckin' dresser, Black,' he said, and Danny backed off.

Tony was selecting some weaponry from the rifle rack. These were not for him. His own suppressed M4 was propped up against his rucksack, and in any case the weapons he was choosing were pistols: two Makarov 9mms. Danny knew that they would be unmarked and unattributable. They were not intended for firing. They were props, nothing more. 'Proof' for the RMPs and lawyers back home that their targets were armed and dangerous.

'Hey, Tony,' Dexter said, 'don't forget the Tipp-Ex.' He laughed at his own joke and pointed to Tony's M4. Along the stock there were fifteen or twenty tiny white dots. 'One dot per kill,' Dexter said. 'Amazing how they add up, hey, Blacky?'

'You should scrape them off,' Danny said. 'They identify you.'

Tony didn't respond. He just carried on with his work.

Outside, it was now fully dark and the temperature had dropped slightly. The cloud cover that the Met report had promised had swept in. There was no moon, no stars. A dark night for dark business. Outside the Spearpoint cordon, the shouts and mechanical noises of a working military base were ongoing. Inside, it was very quiet. Danny took a moment to breathe deeply and gather his thoughts.

The others joined him. 'Let's go, Black,' Dexter said in his broad Irish accent. Cole said nothing. Tony just gave him a serious look. There was no friendship in it. Just an unspoken acknowledgement that whatever beef was between them, it would wait for another day. Tonight they had work to do.

'Roger that,' Danny said, and the unit headed to the exit.

An unmarked van was waiting for them. They climbed inside with all their gear and sat in silence for the two minutes it took to transport them to the airfield. As they passed the engineering sheds, Danny saw the same mechanics from earlier working on a different IED-blasted vehicle, this time with the help of bright portable floodlights to illuminate their working space. He had the impression there was a never-ending supply of wrecked chassis and twisted wheel axles for them to fix.

The Hercules's engines were turning over as they arrived at the airfield. The van deposited them at the bottom of the tailgate. They carried their gear up into the aircraft. The noise of the engines blocked out any other sound, and the stench of fuel caught the back of Danny's throat. Inside the Herc, they took their places at benches facing each other. Danny was opposite Dexter and the Malinois, which sat quietly and calmly at his handler's feet. To Danny's left was Cole, silent and brooding.

Each of the Regiment men removed their helmets and rested them on their laps before strapping themselves in, unhooking sets of headphones from the side of the aircraft and putting them on. The headphones cancelled out some of the ambient noise and put them in contact with the flight deck, though there was no commentary from the pilot at the moment. An RAF loadie, wearing heavy cans and a boom mike and carrying a clipboard, trotted up the tailgate and nodded curtly at the unit, who barely responded. The loadie checked some instrument readings on the side of the plane, then spoke into his boom mike. His voice came over Danny's headsets. 'We've got a full house. Ready to fly when you are.'

Immediately, the tailgate started to rise. The engines of the Hercules increased in pitch. Dexter picked up the Malinois and allowed him to sprawl out on his lap. Danny didn't know why. Maybe the dog got spooked by take-offs. Whatever, it was clear his handler was in full control of his charge as he fitted a muzzle to the dog's snout. The tailgate sealed closed. Almost immediately the Herc juddered into movement. It noticeably vibrated as it taxied towards the runway. It came to a halt for a few seconds as the engines started screaming. A minute later, Danny was airborne for the third time in less than twenty-four hours. He could feel the aircraft gaining height very quickly. As soon as it levelled off, the captain's voice came over the cans.

'Okay, gentlemen, we've levelled out at about sixteen thousand. We'll be popping her up to 22k in about twenty minutes, and we'll be above the drop zone five minutes after that.'

The guys removed their cans, unclipped themselves and stood up. Each of them picked up their freefall harnesses and clipped them on securely, before strapping their weapons across their bodies and attaching their rucksacks to the back of their legs. Sitting down again, Danny watched Dexter securing the dog's harness to the carabiners on the front of his own rig while he put his own headphones back on. Within a couple of minutes they were ready to jump.

The time passed quickly. It seemed only a couple of minutes before Danny felt the aircraft gaining altitude again. Each guy had a mask connected to a tank of oxygen. Danny reached out, grabbed his mask, fitted it to his face and continued to breathe normally. A few minutes of this would keep his blood oxygen saturation levels up, ready for the jump.

The captain's voice came over the cans. 'Five minutes out, repeat, five minutes out.'

As he spoke, the tailgate started to lower. Danny looked outside and immediately saw that they were above the cloud line. Thousands of pinprick stars dotted the sky and although there was no sign of the moon from this angle, there was a silver haze that told Danny it would be full and bright when he jumped. He checked the altimeter on his wrist. The dial was hovering between 20 and 21.

On the back of Danny's helmet was a light with an infrared filter. Invisible to the naked eye, but a useful beacon to anyone wearing NV. Danny flicked it on, and he saw the other guys doing the same.

The loadie stood up and gave them a thumbs-up sign.

Danny took another few deep breaths of oxygen, then removed the mask. He got to his feet and, along with the others, started shuffling towards the tailgate. His altimeter was nudging 22,000 feet as they lined up two abreast – Tony and Cole first, Danny and Dexter second. Dexter was holding the Malinois in his arms, close to his chest. The dog showed no sign of anxiety. Like the guys, he was ready for the jump.

A red light appeared on the side of the aircraft. Danny felt his pulse quicken. The loadie raised one arm. Ten seconds later the light turned green. The loadie lowered his arm. Tony and Cole tumbled out. Danny, Dexter and the dog immediately followed.

All the sounds changed. The constant drone of the Hercules' interior disappeared. There was a boom as the aircraft burst away from them, then the familiar rushing in the ears that accompanied a freefall jump whether it took place in Helmand or Hereford. Here above the cloud line the stars were like clouds and the waxing moon lit up the cloud bank 10,000 feet below him like a soft, silver blanket. The moon itself was visible now, and would hurt your eyes if you stared at it too long.

Which Danny didn't. He was concentrating on falling stable, his arms and legs spread out, his core rigid. Only when he knew he was in the correct position to fall safely did he look at the GPS and altimeter strapped to his wrist. The GPS told him they were roughly on target – they were aiming for the bank of a deep wadi where they could stash the parachute gear – and the altimeter indicated that they were already at 18,000 feet.

Fifteen thousand.

Twelve thousand.

Danny looked to his right and saw Dexter falling at the same height about twenty metres away. The attack dog was still harnessed to his handler's chest, as calm as he had been on the aircraft . . .

Ten thousand.

Eight thousand.

He looked down and could already see two chutes deploying. At 4,000 feet he deployed his own rig. Seconds later his rate of fall suddenly decreased. He, and the rest of the unit, were drifting towards the earth.

He engaged the NV goggles on his helmet. The atmosphere turned into a haze of green. The stars and moon became astonishingly bright, but Danny focused on the space below him. He could see the infrared light on the back of Tony's and Cole's helmets.

Then: blackness. Danny had entered the cloud line. The air was thick and humid, but he could still just make out the helmet lights, hazy through the fog, guiding him down.

It wasn't a thick cloud bank. In seconds he was through it. The temperature suddenly increased, the hot air radiating from the parched earth below trapped by the cloud line. Helmand Province opened up beneath him. The grainy green of the winding Helmand River was just visible on this dark night, demarcated by the bright clusters of lights that indicated inhabited areas.

Tony's voice came over his earpiece. 'You fuckers still with me?'

'Roger that,' from Dexter and Cole.

'Black?'

'I'm here,' Danny said into his boom mike.

'Stack up behind me,' Tony instructed.

Guided by the IR lights on the back of their helmets, Danny adjusted his position so that he was banking up in a line above Tony and Cole. He found himself trying to identify certain features that he should recognise from his intense study of maps of the area earlier in the day. The village of Gareshk, where their targets lived, lay three kilometres to the north-east. Beyond that, along the line of the river, was another village. Danny knew that this was Panjika, where Caitlin Wallace and her team were embedded.

Below he saw Tony make landfall, then Cole. Only now could he make out the line of the wadi they were aiming for: the other two had landed twenty to thirty metres to its north. Danny unclipped his rucksack and let it dangle by a lanyard beneath him. The rucksack hit the ground. Twenty seconds later Danny did the same. He immediately started gathering up his chute. The billowing fabric made only a whisper of a noise in the silent Afghan desert. They were on parched, flat, cracked ground. Danny knew there was a main highway 200 metres to the north, but it was as dark as they'd expected, the cloud obscuring the moon, and he couldn't see more than thirty metres in any direction. This meant he could only just make out the edge of the wadi that they'd been aiming for, off to his south. Once he'd collected in his chute, he saw Dexter on the ground unclipping the dog from his harness. The dog sat obediently by his handler's side while Dexter removed its muzzle then gathered up his own chute. It didn't move as the four men congregated with armfuls of parachute.

'Black,' Tony said, 'find somewhere to stash the chutes.'

Danny didn't argue. The others dropped their bundles of fabric and spread out in a semicircle, down on one knee in the firing positions, their weapons engaged as they scanned the area. The dog sat by Dexter's side, its nose in the air, its ears pointed, its senses on high alert.

Danny bundled up the chutes and ran to the edge of the wadi. The dried-out riverbed was about ten metres deep and fifteen wide. Danny instantly saw a small cave on the far side that would be suitable for hiding their gear. He clambered down a nearby gulley and had weighted down the chutes under some loose rocks within a minute. They were write-offs now. Rejoining his unit mates he fell to one knee like them. 'Anything?' he breathed over the comms as he disengaged his NV goggles before scanning the surrounding area through the night sight on his rifle. He saw nothing but featureless desert terrain in the green tinge of NV. Sparse patches of brush sprouted from the dry ground. Apart from that, nothing.

Nobody answered his question directly. 'Patrol formation,' Tony said. 'Dexter, Black, me, Cole. Eyes on Dexter. He gets any sign from the dog that there's trouble up ahead, we hit the ground.'

The men didn't need to reply. Having shouldered their rucksacks, they slung their weapons across their chests and once more pulled their NV tubes forward on their helmets, then adopted the straight line of their patrol formation. Danny was seven metres behind Dexter, who now had the dog on a short leash. The others were spaced out a similar distance behind him.

Time check: 23.31 hours.

They moved at a steady pace, keeping their formation. Danny's NV capability gave him a wider field of vision than unaided sight, so he was able to scan a full 180-degree vista as he moved. There was nothing. Even the highway, when they hit it, was deserted. The unit jogged across the rough road and continued north-east towards the village.

Dexter suddenly raised his left hand. The dog had stopped. Danny saw that it was holding its front right paw up in the air. Its nose was raised somewhat. Dexter made a 'down' gesture with his hand. The unit members hit the ground. Danny arranged his rifle so it was aiming forward. He saw the dog crouching, head close to the desert floor. It was very still, but Danny sensed that it was waiting for a command to lurch forward and attack.

But attack what? Danny didn't know. Whatever the dog had sensed up ahead, Danny himself couldn't see it. He raised his NV tubes and scanned the terrain up ahead through his rifle sights, panning left and right. It was a full minute before he spotted movement, and another minute before he could clearly make out what the dog had seen long before the humans. It was a single man. He was dressed in traditional robes and headdress and was surrounded by a flock of goats, perhaps eight of them. Distance 150 metres. He was heading directly towards them.

'Where the fuck's he going with those goats at this time of night?' Dexter spoke into the comms.

'Who cares?' came Tony's voice. 'Keep the dog close. If he spooks the goats, they'll make too much noise.'

'Roger that.'

'If he comes within fifty metres, let the dog do him. Better to make it look like a wild animal attack than leave a trail of rounds.'

Silence.

Danny could see the dog shaking a little. Its instinct was clearly to go into attack mode, but his handler hadn't given the word so it stayed pressed to the ground, like a cocked round in a high velocity weapon. Danny focused back on the newcomer. He was only a hundred metres away now and, surrounded by his goats, seemed to have difficulty walking in a straight line. Danny wondered if he'd been partaking of the product of local poppies.

Seventy-five metres. Danny could hear the dull clunk of bells round the goats' necks. The guy was still heading directly towards their position, unaware of the danger he was in.

The dog's left hind was twitching. It was desperate to do what it was trained for.

Sixty metres. The Afghan man stopped.

Had he seen them? Danny didn't think so. He was drinking from a water canteen. When he had finished, he tucked the canteen back into his robes. When he started walking again, it was in a different direction. South-westerly.

The dog followed with his head as the man and his goats passed to the west of the unit, but he didn't move his body. Ten minutes later, the clunk of the goats' bells faded from earshot. The unit gave it a couple of minutes. Then, on Tony's order, they got to their feet again and continued their advance towards the village, the dog sniffing and scouting the way as before.

They covered another kilometre. There was no distinct line that marked the boundary of the village. The landscape simply became less sparse. They passed an old farm vehicle, burned out and neglected. Several buildings were not only run down but practically turned to rubble. An old yellow camper van lay across their path, its wheels removed and stolen, its rusted doors hanging off and holes in the roof. It emitted a pungent, organic smell that told Danny an animal had likely died sheltering in it not too many hours or days ago.

The terrain started to slope upwards. Danny knew they were approaching the raised ground Isherwood had pointed out in the briefing. When they reached the upper contour, they'd have eyes on Target Red's compound.

Dexter raised his left hand again. The dog crouched. Dexter hit the ground and Danny followed suit. He was aware of Tony and Cole doing the same behind him. The unit crawled to the brow of the raised ground and looked out.

Target Red's compound was directly ahead of them. Danny

recognised it from the satellite map at the briefing: it was the easternmost compound of the village. Distance: fifty metres as expected. Clear open ground between the unit's OP and the wooden door set in the four-metre-high wall facing them. No sign of movement. No sound. Beyond the compound, Danny could make out a few other buildings, but the unit was too far away and too low to the ground to have a visual on the Helmand tributary that bisected the village north to south.

They remained static for thirty seconds. Danny checked the time: 23.59. Bang on schedule. An unfamiliar voice crackled in Danny's earpiece. 'This is Eagle One control. Do you copy?'

Tony's voice replied to the drone operator: 'Delta Bravo Niner to Eagle One, loud and clear.'

'We have your position marked. Currently eyes on your first location. We've just seen a single male enter the north-eastern room of the compound.'

'Expect that to be Target Red,' Tony said. 'If his family are there, they'll be in a separate room. They always are.'

'That'll be the south-western room,' said the drone operator. 'We think there are personnel inside – there's a heat signature coming from the door. We also have two human signatures thirty metres beyond the target compound, but your approach is clear, repeat, your approach is clear.'

'Black, Dexter, get over there,' Tony said. 'We'll cover.'

Danny hesitated. Crossing the open ground towards the compound was hazardous. Did he trust Tony to cover him properly if there was a problem?

He didn't have a choice.

'Let's move, Black,' Dexter said. He made a clicking sound in the back of his throat as he got to his feet. The dog started moving forward, nose up, ears pricked. Danny followed, his weapon slung across his front.

8

Danny and Dexter moved across the open ground at a jog. Danny's every sense was heightened. The four NV tubes on his headgear gave him an extended field of vision, and he was aware of a jumbled layout of houses and compounds further into the village, but his principal focus was on the wall of the compound up ahead. It would only take a moment for someone to appear above the parapet and open up. If Tony and Cole weren't on the money, Danny and Dexter would be goners.

Thirty metres.

Fifteen.

They safely reached the compound wall and positioned themselves on either side of the wooden door. It looked like a couple of decent kicks would knock it in, but they didn't want to alert their target. They raised their weapons and aimed them towards the top of the exterior wall. The dog remained on all fours. Danny could sense its prickling canine awareness as it listened for movement.

'In position,' Dexter said over the radio. 'That's a go.'

Silence. Danny didn't look across the open ground to check Tony and Cole were approaching. His job was to make sure the drone operators hadn't given them dodgy intel about the position of the personnel inside the compound.

A whole minute passed. Tony and Cole reached the compound. Tony removed a set of bolt cutters from his pack. He pointed at Danny, then pointed up. His instruction was clear: you're going over.

Scaling the wall would be a risky moment. No surprise that Tony was telling him to do it. Whatever. Danny knew the drone operator would warn him if there were any immediate threats waiting for him on the other side. He grabbed the bolt cutters before approaching Cole, who was crouching by the wall ready to give a leg up. He put one foot in his unit mate's hands, launched himself up on to Cole's shoulders and grappled for the top edge of the wall. Seconds later, he was over and down.

He raised his weapon and scanned the interior of the compound. The central courtyard was sparse: a few old tyres and a beaten-up motorbike against the far wall. One room to Danny's right – that was where they expected the target to be – and another room to his eleven o'clock. The compound's external door was two metres to his left. It was locked from the inside with a sturdy iron padlock on a chain. Danny lowered his weapon, took the bolt cutters and cut through the padlock. Quietly, he unbolted the door and opened it.

The rest of the unit entered in complete silence, the dog keeping to Dexter's heel. Tony turned to the team. Danny was waiting to be given the lesser job of dealing with the family. But no: Tony jabbed one finger at Cole then pointed in the direction of the south-western room where they expected the family to be located. Cole made no complaint: he crossed the courtyard and took up position by the door of the room. Tony led Dexter towards the target's room, the dog following. They positioned themselves on either side of the entrance, while Danny got down on one knee four metres from the door itself, weapon engaged, ready to put down rounds if necessary.

Tony held up three fingers.

Two fingers.

One.

Dexter kicked the door open with a solid blow from his heel. The Malinois didn't need a command. It shot forward into the dark room. A fraction of a second later there was a scream: a male voice, in pain.

Everyone moved. Cole took the scream as a sign to enter the other room and restrain the family members. Tony and Dexter followed the dog into the target's room. Danny did the same, his weapon still engaged, his NV goggles giving him a perfect, wide-angled vista on to the scene inside.

The room was a mess. There was a low bed up against one corner and piles of clothes dotted around. A bad smell of stale sweat: this was obviously a guy's room. The guy in question was on the ground just next to the bed. The Malinois had its jaws clamped round the target's forearm and had sunk its teeth into his flesh – Danny could see the dark stain of blood. The screaming had stopped. The target was staring blindly into the darkness, but he clearly knew there were men approaching him. His fear of them appeared to have overwhelmed the pain of the dog's bite.

Tony reached the target first. He put one foot on the man's chest as Dexter made a clicking sound that instructed the dog to release his jaws. Tony removed a torch from his ops waistcoat and shone it directly in the target's face. The target winced, but even at a distance of a couple of metres, Danny recognised his face from the photographs at the briefing. This was their guy. No question.

Tony looked back over his shoulder at Danny. 'You can check his bollocks, Black,' he said. 'Try not to feel him up, eh?'

Danny almost smiled. He knew Tony, and he knew now why he hadn't been told to guard the family. But he wouldn't give Tony the satisfaction of thinking he felt humiliated by this job. He approached the target as Dexter stuffed a rag into his mouth to keep him quiet and Tony kept his boot on the guy's chest to keep him pinned down. He was wearing loose trousers with a cord at the top to tighten them. Danny yanked them down to expose his genitals. The target squirmed violently, forcing Tony to jab into his breastbone with the heel of his boot. Danny shone his own torch between the target's legs.

The Yanks had clearly done a job on him back in the day. The skin on his inner thigh was scarred white and there were piebald patches where no hair grew. There was a stench from his crotch that made Danny want to retch, but the scarring gave them the positive ID they needed.

'It's him,' Danny said.

'Get the biometrics,' Tony said.

This was Dexter's job. As the target writhed on the floor, he removed a cylindrical iris scanner and a hard plastic DNA sample kit from his ops vest. He knelt down, placed his left hand over the target's face and held his right eyelid open. He placed the tube-shaped scanner over the eyeball. The scan took a fraction of a second. Dexter yanked a hair from the target's head and deposited it into the sample kit, then took his utility knife and, since the blood from the target's forearm was potentially contaminated by the dog's saliva, deftly slashed the target's cheek for a blood sample. The target squealed impotently, but couldn't shout out because of the rag in his mouth. Dexter swabbed the blood, stashed the sample and stood up again.

'Done,' he announced.

Tony turned to Danny again. 'You're the new boy,' he said. 'You do it.'

Power play again. Danny didn't care. He removed his Sig and stepped up to the prone man. Target Red could evidently see a little better than when they'd first burst into his room, thanks to the open door. As Danny straightened his arm and aimed the suppressed handgun at his face, it was clear that he knew what was coming. His writhing became more vigorous, the animal-like squealing from behind the rag more desperate. Danny had to do it quickly. Any more noise from the target and there was a risk that he would alert others in the village to their presence.

Danny released a single round. The suppressed weapon made a dull, knocking sound. The 9mm round slammed into Target Red's forehead. There was a burst of brain matter from the skull. The body flopped suddenly still. The squealing stopped.

'One more,' Tony said, his foot still on the target's chest.

'He's dead,' Danny replied.

'I said, one more,' Tony growled.

Danny inclined his head. He released a second round into the face of the target, whose features split and melted with the impact. Almost before the round had hit, Danny was holstering his weapon and turning towards the exit. 'Let's get out of here.'

'Not yet,' Tony said. He removed one of the two Makarovs, propped it up against the wall just beyond Target Red's corpse and took his NV camera. He made a ten-second film of the weapon – doctored evidence, since there were no other weapons in the room, that their target had militant tendencies – then handed the camera to Cole. 'Upload it,' he said, then he went to retrieve the pistol. He turned to the others with a grin. 'Anyone up for a medal tonight?'

Dexter returned the grin. 'I'll have a piece of that,' he said.

'Take your plate hanger off,' he said.

Dexter did just that. He held up his body armour. Tony released a single round into it. 'Okay,' he said. 'Put them back on. Your firefight with this cunt will make good reading in dispatches.'

'You kidding me?' Danny breathed.

'Shut your pie hole, Black,' Tony said. He crouched down by the target and pressed the corpse's fingers around the Makarov to capture his prints, then dropped the weapon into an evidence bag and stashed it in his rucksack.

'Tony.' Dexter's voice was quiet. He had moved to the far side of the room as he put his body armour back on. Here there was a wardrobe and a table. He had lifted something off the table and was holding it up. It was a military helmet, almost indistinguishable from the type the unit members themselves were wearing.

Tony and Danny stared at it for a moment. Danny remembered the SF gear Tony had shown them back at camp. Nobody picked a helmet like this off the shelf. They cost serious money. They were too expensive for regular troops.

'Fat fucking lot of good it did this muppet,' Tony said. Danny, who knew him well, could tell he was trying to sound unconcerned, but he wasn't managing it. 'What's that next to it?' Tony walked up to the table. 'Bomb-making gear. We didn't even need to fuck around with the Makarov.' He held up a bunch of wires with a nine-volt battery attached – clearly a blasting cap. A small handheld detonator. Two blocks of military grade C-4 in black wrappers. A plastic medical syringe and small phial, which he examined closely. 'Mercury,' he said. He made a short film of the bomb-making gear, then stowed the objects in his ops vest. 'You never know,' he muttered, and turned to Dexter. 'Leave the helmet,' he said. 'It's no good to us and we're carrying too much gear as it is.' He strode to the exit.

Danny, Dexter and the dog followed him out into the court-yard. Danny took a moment to stop and listen. He couldn't determine any sounds outside the compound. No indication that anyone had heard them at their work. There was some light spill from a moving torch in the family quarters, however. He raised his NV tubes and approached the door without their benefit, following Tony in.

Cole had been efficient. As expected, there were three other figures in the room. A woman, a little boy and a little girl. They were lying face down on a threadbare rug. Their wrists were plasticuffed behind their backs, and their ankles were also bound. Danny couldn't see their mouths, but he knew they were stuffed with rags because they were all crying and the sound was muffled. Cole stood over them, pointing the Maglite torch attached to his weapon in their direction to make it clear to them that they were under surveillance.

Tony raised his weapon. For a moment, Danny thought he was going to nail the woman and kids and stepped forward to stop him. Mindless butchery was not part of their remit. But Tony didn't fire. He spoke. 'Did you find a key?'

'In the door,' Cole said.

'We'll lock them in. We can tip off the ANA to free them when we're out of here. Get moving.'

Cole killed his Maglite. Danny re-engaged his NV as they turned their back on the prisoners and exited. Cole locked the room from the outside.

Time check: 00.13 hours. They'd been in Target Red's compound for approximately eleven minutes.

'Eagle One, this is Delta Bravo Niner. Target Red is down. Awaiting your green light to advance on Target Blue.'

'Delta Bravo Niner, that's a go. Repeat, Target Blue is a go.'

The unit moved in patrol formation towards the exit. Danny had the layout of the village, and their route to its western side, fixed in his head. But he was glad to know they had guidance from above. Something about finding that SF helmet had unnerved him. There was something about their enemy that they didn't fully understand, and he didn't like the idea of them being properly equipped. The Regiment's strategy was to dominate completely. Harder to do that, when the other guy has the same gear as you. So as the unit turned left out of the compound, it was good to hear the drone operator's voice over the earpiece.

'This is Eagle One. Continue on your bearing for one hundred metres. You'll pass two buildings on your left then hit the irrigation ditch by the forested area that extends from the north of the village. Remember, you're using that forested area as cover to skirt west around the village to the next target.'

'Any movement of personnel in the vicinity?' Danny said.

'Negative. You're good to go.'

They moved with purpose, Dexter and the dog taking the lead, the dog sniffing and scanning. The only sound was the regular crunch of the unit's footfall. The two buildings that they passed were a bombed-out compound covered in weeds and an empty barn that smelled strongly of goat shit. The wide field of view of Danny's NV goggles illuminated the featureless desert to their east, but he kept his attention on what was straight ahead.

It took a minute to reach the irrigation ditch. It was a narrow trench, just a metre and a half wide and a metre deep. The treeline was three metres beyond it. The unit crossed the ditch and penetrated the treeline by just a couple of metres.

'This is Eagle One. Follow the treeline in a north-westerly bearing for 250 metres.'

The drone operator was merely confirming the route the unit was already taking. Now that the ground was softer underfoot, they moved ghost-silently through the forested area, the trees deeper in the forest passing the edge of Danny's vision in a blur.

'*Go static! Go static!*'

They had moved a hundred metres on their north-westerly bearing when the drone operator's voice crackled in their ears. Danny immediately hit the ground. The rest of the guys did the same. Danny could hear the tense breathing of the Malinois, and could smell its pungent breath, as he looked towards the treeline, listening hard.

Nothing.

Then . . .

'We have two heat signatures thirty metres to your south,' the drone operator said. 'Moving towards your position.'

Danny adjusted his orientation fractionally. He was in a prone position, his rifle stretched out ahead of him. He made use of his rifle's night sight to penetrate the darkness.

Was it voices he could hear?

He held his breath. Definitely voices. One male, one female. There was a giggle. Twenty metres away. Nothing more.

'If they see us,' Tony breathed over the comms, 'we nail them.'

Ten seconds passed. 'They're fifteen metres from your position,' the drone operator said. And as the voice crackled in Danny's ear, he saw movement towards the irrigation ditch. He aligned his weapon.

'Is the dog ready?' Tony said.

'Roger that,' Dexter replied.

'Ten metres,' said the drone operator.

Danny kept his breathing shallow.

Sudden silence.

'They've changed their bearing,' said the drone operator. 'Moving away. Remain static.'

'Did they see us?' Tony asked. His voice had a cold edge.

'Negative,' Danny breathed.

'They're moving south-east along the irrigation ditch,' the drone operator reported. 'You'll be good to move in sixty seconds.'

It felt like twice that long as Danny remained in the prone position. Complete silence surrounded them again.

'That's a go,' said the drone operator.

As one, the unit rose and continued moving north-west through the trees.

A minute later they emerged beyond the treeline at the edge of the Helmand tributary. Danny could hear the faint trickle of water running along the riverbed. The tributary itself was only a metre deep and maybe ten metres wide.

'You're good to cross,' came the instruction from the drone operator.

The unit forded the tributary in patrol formation, their boots splashing on the thin trickle of liquid as they passed the central point. After that, they returned to the treeline, now heading in a south-westerly direction for a further 200 metres, the drone operator occasionally confirming that their way ahead was clear.

Target Blue's compound came into view even before the drone guy told them to halt. The north-eastern corner of the compound butted up against the forested area. Each member of the unit knelt down in the firing position, their weapons fanning out in a semicircle formation as they waited for a further update.

'This is Eagle One, we have a similar set-up in the Target Blue compound. A woman and child have just entered the south-western building. Expect the target to be in the north-eastern one.'

Danny pictured the rectangular compound that they'd examined on the satellite maps. It was divided in the middle by a central wall running east-west. The northern half of the compound had a door in the western wall, the southern half in the southern wall.

'Any movement of personnel?' Tony asked.

'Negative,' said the drone operator. 'Gentlemen, I can give you another two minutes.'

'We'll enter through the southern entrance,' Tony said. 'That's the furthest away from where our guy is sleeping. Black, we've got no bollocks for you to feel up, so once we're in the compound you're on kid duty. Make sure the fuckers don't squeal. Gag them up if you have to. Let's move.'

They emerged from the treeline at 00.44 hours in patrol formation and skirted along the western edge of the compound. To their right was a poppy field. A hundred metres up ahead was another irrigation ditch and, beyond that, more fields. The unit kept close to the western wall of the compound, making almost no noise as they headed to the south, turned a corner and approached the door on the southern wall.

'This is Eagle One,' said the drone operator. 'Time to fly. You're on your own. Goodnight, gentlemen.'

Nobody replied. They were too focused on the job. Danny knew he was going to be sent over the wall as before. He grabbed a roll of duct tape from his pack before that happened. He looped it on to his right arm for quick access.

Their method of entry was the same as for Target Red. Danny scaled the wall with the bolt cutters, then checked the courtyard for threats. This compound was more littered with the stuff of everyday living. There was a fire pit in the centre and several bicycles up against one wall. A tree grew up in the middle of the courtyard, under which there was some welding equipment. Beyond it, the wall bisecting the compound. The door in the middle was slightly ajar. A long, low room ran along the eastern side of the courtyard, with a ramshackle external staircase leading up on to the roof. Danny knew that his personal targets – the wife and three kids – were in the room directly to the left of the door.

He silently cut through the padlock to let the others in. There were no instructions. Tony, Dexter and Cole headed straight across the courtyard towards the open door in the bisecting wall, the dog prowling by their side. Danny turned his attention to the room on his left. Access was via a wooden door with peeling paint – impossible to tell the colour through his NV goggles. As the others disappeared from view into the northern half of the compound, Danny felt for the looped plasticuffs in his ops vest, then removed his suppressed Sig and approached the door. He pushed it open with one foot and carefully entered, weapon engaged.

He immediately saw that the room was tidier than the quarters where they'd nailed Target Red. Robes hung on the wall, and there was a smell of soap. Four low beds sat in a line against the far wall, each of them a metre apart. Three of the beds contained small, sleeping figures, each under a sheet. But the one on the right contained an adult woman. She was sitting up, eyes wide but staring blindly in the darkness, a sheet pulled up to cover her nakedness. Through the green haze of NV, Danny could tell she was terrified.

And that she was about to scream.

His instinct was to fire. He suppressed it. Instead he surged forward, covering the five metres between them in as many strides. He couldn't stop the beginnings of the scream – it cut through the air for a fraction of a second – but he soon curtailed it with one large hand pressed firmly over the woman's mouth and nose. She wriggled with the fury of a mother who knew that her children were under threat.

The kids were stirring. Danny cursed himself for having allowed the woman to make even the slightest noise. With his free hand he holstered his Sig, then removed the roll of duct tape from his arm. He peeled off a strip and stuck it firmly over the woman's mouth before winding the tape twice round her head.

'What the fuck's going on in there?' Tony's voice came over Danny's earpiece.

'It's under control,' Danny said. He quickly bound the wriggling woman's arms, then her ankles, before turning his attention to the kids. They were a lot easier to subdue: a short strip of duct tape over each mouth, plasticuffs round the wrists and ankles. In under a minute he had four figures face down on their beds. They were squealing and crying behind the duct tape, but the noise was subdued. The mother was the problem. She kept trying to sit up and wriggle her way off her bed. Danny had no option. He took the butt of his Sig and cracked it against the side of her head. The woman collapsed. Danny twirled the Sig and pressed the barrel against her face, as if daring her to make any noise. She got the message and fell silent, although she continued to tremble with fear and rage.

Maintaining that position, Danny listened hard for any sound of the rest of the unit going about their work. There was nothing. All he could do was watch over his four prisoners until he got the word to extract. He found himself concentrating on his next move. Their pickup point was two kilometres to the south-west. Without the benefit of the drone overhead to keep surveillance on their route, they needed to get away from the village as quickly as possible. It was only a matter of time before someone discovered evidence of the two hits. When that happened, distance was the unit's best friend. Danny was impatient to leave.

Time check. 00.55 hours. The others had been dealing with Target Blue for nearly five minutes and there had been no word. What the hell was taking so long?

The woman started squirming again. Danny bent over and once more pressed his weapon into the side of her head. She fell still.

'Update,' Danny said into his comms.

'Hold your position,' Tony said.

Was it Danny's imagination, or did he sound more on edge?

'What's your status?'

'I said, hold your position.'

Danny glanced towards the door. It was a couple of inches ajar and a thin slice of light fell into the room. He felt his skin going clammy. A sixth sense, that something wasn't right.

He looked back towards the prisoners. Face down on the bed, they were sobbing silently, their bodies limp with terror. They weren't going anywhere.

Holstering his Sig, Danny raised his assault rifle. Stock firmly into his shoulder. Barrel towards the door.

He advanced. When he reached the door itself, he hooked it open with his right foot. Listened hard.

No sound.

He stepped out into the courtyard, swinging immediately left and scanning the area.

Everything was just as before. The tree. The welding gear. The bicycles against the wall. The only difference was that the door in the bisecting wall was now fully shut.

'What's your status?' Danny repeated into the comms.

Silence.

'*Repeat: what's your status?*' He took a few steps towards the closed door, his weapon pointing directly at it, his eyes scanning up and from side to side.

Silence.

Danny's mouth was dry. Sweat beaded on his face and down his neck. He had a call to make: stay with the prisoners, or advance on the target and find out what the hell was going on in the northern half of the compound.

Whatever it was, it didn't feel good.

He breathed deeply. Then he moved towards the door.

Danny was halfway across the courtyard when his earpiece burst into life. Tony's voice. Urgent. Aggressive. '*Exit by the south side and proceed to the pickup point. Repeat, exit by the south side.*'

Danny felt his eyes narrowing. 'Confirm Target Blue is down,' he said.

'*Do what I tell you, Black. Exit by the south side and proceed to the pickup point. That's a fucking order!*'

'What are you doing?' Danny hissed back. 'Confirm your movements. Is Target Blue down?'

A different voice over the earpiece. Dexter. '*I shot him in the fucking head, Black. Normally does the trick. Just do what you're told, will you? We think there's explosives between you and us. We're exiting by the west door. Leave the compound and get to the pickup point . . .*'

Danny remained immobile, weapon still engaged, eyes still scanning. Explosives between here and the northern edge of the compound. He didn't buy it. Why would Target Blue booby-trap his own gaff? His every instinct told him to advance. To find out what was going on behind that door. He even took a step forward . . .

But then he stopped. If the rest of the unit were right, he'd be an idiot to ignore them.

He turned a hundred and eighty degrees. Strode to the south side of the compound and the door that would lead him back outside, into the outskirts of the village of Gareshk. To his right, he could hear the whimpering of the woman and her three kids. It didn't matter now. Their father was a corpse and the unit was extracting. They'd done what they came to do.

Outside the compound, with his back to it, Danny took a moment to get his bearings. The pickup point was south-west of their position, two klicks distance. He knew he was currently facing directly south. An irrigation ditch was approximately twenty metres ahead of him and, beyond that, poppy fields as far as he could see. Their intended route was to follow the irrigation ditch west for a klick, before turning south towards the pickup point. Danny cut across at a diagonal towards it, moving at a steady jog. He was acutely aware of the sound of his footfall, and his heavy breathing.

When he hit the irrigation ditch, he altered his trajectory so that he was moving along its north side. But then he stopped.

'This is bullshit,' he muttered.

The situation wasn't right. They shouldn't be splitting up. He should be waiting for his unit mates.

He turned and looked back towards the compound.

The north-western door from which the others were supposed to be leaving was 150 metres away, maybe a little more. A poppy field covered the intervening ground. There was no sign of the rest of his unit.

He spoke into his comms. 'State your location.'

No reply.

He raised his weapon. Aimed directly towards the compound. 'Talk to me, guys. What the hell's happening?'

Silence.

'I'm moving . . .'

Danny didn't get the chance to finish. As he was speaking, he felt the unmistakable rush of air displacement as a round whizzed past his right shoulder.

Almost by instinct, he fell to one knee in the firing position. Even as he scanned the ground up ahead for the shooter, his mind was analysing what had just happened. The round had been fired from a suppressed weapon. Otherwise he'd have heard the retort of the rifle that fired it. He found himself picturing the night sight Dexter had found in Target Red's compound. The helmet and encrypted radio Tony had shown them back at base. Whoever had just taken a shot at him was well equipped. Danny couldn't even get him in his sights.

He scanned left.. Right. 'Contact,' he hissed into his comms. 'I'm drawing f—'

The second round was as quiet as the first.

And this time it was on target.

The round slammed into Danny's left shoulder. It felt, at first, like a punch. He lost control of the weapon as he slammed backwards on to the ground. Only then did the pain kick in: a biting, cold agony spreading from the entry wound. Warm, sticky blood pulsed from the wound in time with the beating of his heart. It saturated his front.

He tried to breathe. It was difficult: as though his lungs couldn't inflate sufficiently. He realised he was gasping. His eyes were rolling. He was light-headed . . .

Danny pressed his right hand against the bleeding entry wound. Direct pressure: he wanted to howl with the pain. But he kept quiet and managed to roll over on to his front. The irrigation ditch was five metres away. It was the only cover he had. He couldn't risk getting to his feet. He had to crawl there.

But he was weak. He realised his body was going into shock, which was potentially more dangerous than the bullet wound. His pack and weapon weighed him down. Five metres felt like five miles. He crawled, painfully slowly, a cold sweat breaking out over his body, the whole world seeming to spin.

A voice in his headset. Danny couldn't tell who it was. Tony? Dexter? Cole? '*Where are you, Black? State your location . . .*' Danny couldn't reply. All his energy was focused on getting to the irrigation ditch, out of the line of fire. When he finally reached its edge, he rolled over the lip of the ditch and landed at the bottom with a heavy thump that seemed, momentarily, to make the blood pump more thickly from both the entry and exit wound. He tried to suck in a lungful of air, but it felt like there was no room in his chest cavity to inhale sufficient oxygen.

He tried to speak into the comms. 'Taken a round . . . losing blood . . . shock . . .'

He used his good arm to unholster his Sig, which he pointed towards the top of the irrigation ditch. His hand was shaking badly. His eyes were rolling.

'Cover . . .' He wasn't sure whether he'd actually formulated the word, so he tried again. 'Cover . . . irrigation ditch.'

His gun hand dropped. He tried to raise it again. The weapon felt as heavy as a boulder.

The green haze of his NV was growing cloudy. Blotches appeared in front of his eyes. *Don't close them*, he told himself. *Stay awake . . . do not close your eyes . . .* But he couldn't help it. It was as if he had no control. And in any case, maybe it would be good to sleep. Maybe the pain would go away. He let his eyelids fall . . .

Footsteps. He forced his eyes open again. He became half aware of a figure standing over the edge of the irrigation ditch, but he couldn't make out the face. He tried to lift his weapon again, but there was simply no strength left in him.

This is it, he thought. *This is the moment I die.*

The world went black.

Seconds later – or maybe it was minutes, or hours – he slipped back into consciousness.

He was still lying on his back, but was no longer wearing his NV headset. He was half aware that his clothes had been ripped open to gain access to the entry wound. A figure was bending over him, applying pressure to the wound. He could smell sweat and dirt but his sight was still blurred. He was aware of the pain, but it didn't bother him. In some corner of his mind, he knew he'd been given a morphine shot. The person giving him medical aid was talking. A male voice. But Danny was too weak and too woozy to understand who it was, or what he was saying.

He felt someone removing his tactical gloves. He didn't understand why.

He blacked out again.

Noise.

A regular, pulsing pattern. Danny thought he was dreaming at first, but then realised that the sound of twin rotary blades was quite real. Even on the edge of consciousness, Danny recognised the sound of a Chinook in action.

He tried to force his eyes open.

Lights.

Bright, stabbing beams. Even the morphine couldn't stop him instinctively clamping his eye shut. Even then, the light was visible through his lids.

Shouting.

Male voices. Many of them. Danny tried to force himself to listen to what they were saying. He couldn't make it out. Either his brain wasn't functioning, or they weren't speaking English. The latter, he decided.

Wind.

Not natural wind. Not on this hot, humid Afghan night. This was the downdraft of the Chinook, and it was getting stronger. Danny realised he was moving. No longer was he lying on the hard ground. He was swaying slightly. He was on a stretcher, being casevac'd into the Chinook.

As the casualty evacuation personnel jogged on to the tailgate to move up into the belly of the Chinook, the stretcher tipped up at a slight angle. Dizziness overcame Danny. Once again, he lost consciousness.

When he regained it, he could tell that he was airborne. There was an oxygen mask clamped to his face. A drip in his right arm. Somebody was shouting instructions, so urgently that he could hear it over the deafening noise of the Chinook. The pain had returned. It was all encompassing and he found himself shivering.

Even worse than the pain, however, was the storm in his mind.

What had happened?

Why had he been alone?

Who had shot him?

Where was the rest of the unit?

Despite everything, he tried to push himself up on his elbows, but that made the pain so bad he almost vomited.

Danny groaned. A figure leaned over him. Danny felt the unmistakable prick of a needle in his right arm. He half wanted to shout out: *don't fucking sedate me!* But then, a blissful feeling of almost-euphoria seeped through his body as more morphine hit his bloodstream.

The shivering stopped.

The storm in his mind abated.

His breathing regulated.

He slept.

9

For Doctor Hussein Karim, a good day was when he only lost one man on the operating table. On a bad day, he could lose three or four.

Today had been a bad day. A vehicle containing eight members of the Afghan National Army had hit an IED returning to their forward operating base near Musa Qala. Two men had been killed outright. A further five had been airlifted to the hospital here at Camp Shorabak military base for emergency surgery. Of these, two died on the chopper, three under the knife. They had been moved to the mortuary. The attendants had been obliged to shuffle corpses around to make room for them. There was a backlog.

Yes. Today had been a very bad day. Doctor Karim had been on his feet for more than twenty-four hours before collapsing into bed. So when a soldier woke him from a disturbed sleep at 01.20 hours to say that another casualty evacuation would be landing in approximately ten minutes, he was so exhausted that he found it hard to stir. But then the soldier said a single word that got the doctor moving: 'British'.

It was all back to front, of course, but if a foreign soldier needed medical care, the pressure was increased. Nobody cared about another dead Afghan soldier, he thought bitterly. But a dead *British* soldier? That would make international headlines, and the politicians would look bad. The doctor's superiors would consider this unacceptable and he would know about it. In seconds, Doctor Karim was splashing water on his face, issuing instructions in Pashto and pulling on his clothes. 'Is the theatre free?'

'They're scrubbing it down now.'

'Do we know what the injury is?'

'A bullet wound to the left shoulder.'

'Do we have a blood group?'

'The disc around his neck says O positive.'

'Go to theatre. Tell the nurse to have bloods ready. I'm on my way.'

The soldier turned and ran. Doctor Karim put his shoes on and followed, jogging out of his quarters in Accommodation Block A towards the medical centre.

Even now, in the small hours of the morning, Camp Shorabak was buzzing with activity. Nothing like it had been ten years ago, when the camp was named Bastion and it was home to the occupying British force. Doctor Karim had been a medical assistant in those days, and had learned his trade on the job. He had no true qualifications, but he'd removed more shrapnel, and amputated more limbs, than he could even count. Come to him with the flu, he wouldn't be able to help you, but in the field of military medicine he was an expert.

'Something happening, doctor?'

Doctor Karim was hurrying down the alleyway between Accommodation Blocks A and B when a figure lurking in an entrance called out the question in English. He stopped to see who it was. The figure stepped a little closer. Doctor Karim recognised him. He was a member of the British military, but he had a bit more weight to him than most soldiers, as well as a neatly trimmed goatee beard flecked with grey. Doctor Karim had noticed that, whenever British military personnel were in camp, they avoided this man. Their suspicion had rubbed off on the doctor. 'Excuse me,' he said in his best English. 'I cannot stop.'

He ran past the British man and across the open ground that separated the accommodation blocks from the medical centre. A stationary Afghan National Police vehicle stood halfway between the two, its lights flashing and seven or eight ANP guys hanging around it. None of them paid him any attention. A medic rushed off his feet was nothing new at Camp Shorabak.

Once, this fifty-bed medical unit had been a crisp, white, state-of-the-art facility. As well equipped as any hospital in Britain or

America, they used to say. Now it was looking tired. Paint was peeling. Equipment was showing its age. There was a lack of specialised staff. As Doctor Karim swept aside a mosquito net to gain access to the trauma unit, there were already six tired-looking medical staff in green overalls in the reception area, along with two casualties attached to drips and machines monitoring their vital signs. The casualties shouldn't really have been there, but there was nowhere else for them.

In an adjoining room, the doctor approached a ceramic sink stained with watermarks and started scrubbing up. As he was rubbing antibacterial gel on to his hands and arms, he heard the distinctive sound of a Chinook passing overhead and he knew that must be his patient arriving. He finished cleaning himself up and grabbed some green overalls, mask and hat before striding back through the reception room and out towards the operating theatre.

Three theatre nurses were waiting for him – two male, one female – and a male anaesthetist, all masked and overalled.

'Bullet wound,' the doctor announced in Pashto. 'Left shoulder. Arrival any minute now. Do we have bloods?'

'Yes,' said the female nurse.

The doctor approached the operating table and took a moment to check that all his instruments were there. He felt he barely had time to do that before the commotion out in the corridor became apparent. Thirty seconds later, the casualty was being wheeled in by two ANA soldiers, with a third holding a drip up and an Afghan army medic striding alongside.

There were no formalities. The anaesthetist immediately asked the army medic what pain relief the casualty had received, and went about his business while Dr Karim took a closer look. The casualty was a big man with a grim face and dark hair. A day or two's stubble. He was still wearing body armour and a fully laden ops vest. His clothes had been torn away around the wound, which had been stuffed full of haemostatic dressing to stem the bleeding. Dr Karim's eyes were drawn to the patient's tactical gloves. They were drenched with blood. He frowned momentarily. So far as he could tell, there was no reason for that. The wound was on the patient's shoulder.

'Cut away the body armour,' he said as he turned to his instruments and selected some long, pointed tweezers with which to remove the dressing. 'Okay?' he asked the anaesthetist.

The anaesthetist nodded.

Dr Karim got to work.

Train, advise, assist.

This was the mantra of NATO's current mission to Afghanistan. The mantra of Western doctors who were there to support and educate the Afghan medical teams. Of the specialist units giving tactical advice to the Afghan National Army and Police. There were NATO personnel dotted all around Helmand Province and Afghanistan in general.

Training. Advising. Assisting.

And spying.

Some were spying on the Afghans. Some were spying on their own people: on British military personnel.

Jacko McGuigan had applied to join the Royal Military Police when it had become clear that his career in the Scots Guards was leading precisely nowhere. He was ambitious, and joining the military police gave him options. Sure, it meant that none of his former army mates wanted anything to do with him. But that was an occupational hazard. He'd soon learned to keep his distance from regular army guys. You didn't want to get too friendly with someone you might have to put behind bars. Not that there were many British Army guys here in camp. Jacko was an anomaly, only here because he knew there were operations occurring in the region that certain members of the British Army wanted to keep tightly under wraps. To a member of the Royal Military Police, that was a red rag.

As he watched Doctor Karim sprint towards the medical centre, Jacko knew something interesting was happening. There was an anxious buzz about the place. He had learned to read the atmospherics. When, ten minutes later, a Chinook banked over Camp Shorabak towards the landing zone, the anxious buzz heightened. He watched from the shadows as an ambulance, lights flashing, siren blaring, stormed from the LZ towards the medical centre, and four men removed a casualty on a stretcher and carried him in. The urgency and efficiency of it all told him that this was not an Afghan casualty. This was a Brit or a Yank. Jacko would find out soon enough.

He looked at his watch. 01.35 hours. He needed to sleep. He was just turning to head back to his accommodation block when his phone rang.

'McGuigan,' he answered.

'It's me, boss.' An Afghan voice.

'Yeah.'

'We have another one. The ones you're interested in.'

McGuigan stopped. Looked around to check he wasn't being overheard.

'You're sure?'

'Sure, boss.'

'Go ahead,' he said. And he felt a little bit of excitement.

Regular squaddies scrapping and smuggling hooch into camp were not Jacko McGuigan's quarry. That would be like a top detective nicking drivers for parking violations. No. Jacko was RMP through and through. He knew that the way to impress his superiors was to go after bigger game. Marines. Paras. And of course special forces. SBS would be a good catch. But the scalp everybody wanted was 22 SAS. Those guys were out of control, and all the RMP knew it.

But damn, it was like catching smoke. Jacko had been embedded in Helmand Province for four months now and he knew that a Regiment kill team was active here. The Special Investigation Branch was aware of their activities, but the crime scenes did not always match up with the reports that were being fed through to the RMPs. The SAS were acting illegally and not admitting to the full extent of their activities. Jacko knew it. His boss Mike Holroyd knew it, although even Jacko had to admit that Holroyd's vendetta against the SAS was bordering on the obsessive. Less a criminal investigation, more a religious crusade.

Be that as it may, the Regiment's behaviour had to stop. And Jacko was not above hanging on to Holroyd's coat-tails. If he managed to help Holroyd nail the Regiment, he'd be fast-tracked to the top of the tree.

So he listened hard to what his contact had to say. He was an officer in the Afghan National Police. The ANP were an improving law enforcement outfit, but they were not above accepting a backhander. Not strictly legal, of course, and Jacko wasn't stupid enough to think his guy wasn't also taking bribes from the Taliban and any other groups that wanted his services. But for the reasonably modest sum of fifty pounds a week, the officer provided Jacko with regular updates of any crimes that ticked certain boxes. And as the officer spoke, Jacko agreed that this one might. A night-time hit? Check. High-value Taliban target? Check. No evidence of the perpetrators within several miles of the crime scene?

'The army, they sent in Chinook.' Said the ANP officer down the line to Jacko in his serviceable but patchy English. 'Wounded soldier, British. They airlift him to Camp Shorabak. And boss, this one, it's messy. Even my men, they can't look at it.'

'What do you mean?' Jacko said, glancing back in the direction of the medical centre.

'The family, boss. They killed the family too.'

Jacko felt his expression harden. 'Where is it?'

'Gareshk, boss. Ten miles south of Shorabak.'

'I need to see it.'

'You must hurry, boss. I cannot keep the Taliban away for long.'

'Can you arrange transport? Protection?'

A pause as the officer hesitated at the end of the line.

'I'll make it worth your while,' Jacko said.

'Meet my men at the south entrance of the camp in ten minutes,' the officer said. 'They will drive you here.'

'I'll be there.'

Jacko killed the line and sprinted back to his room where he pulled on his body armour and ops vest and checked his handgun – a Glock 17. Then he jogged out of his quarters and ran towards the area behind Accommodation Block B where the rusted old Toyota that he used to drive about the camp was parked. He floored it past the satellite dishes of the comms centre towards the southern entrance to the camp. It took him two minutes to get there. Out of the corner of his eye through the passenger window, he saw the Chinook rising from the ground in a storm of dust, and he ran past the memorial wall, lit up to commemorate the dead soldiers of Helmand Province and largely ignored by everyone. At the south gate, an ANP Land Rover was waiting for him, headlamps burning in the darkness, one rear door open. He ditched his Toyota in an open area near the guardhouse, alighted and clambered inside the Land Rover.

There were three Afghan police officers waiting for him in the vehicle. They were plainly not impressed at being called out at this time of night, for this type of job. A night-time journey, in an un-armoured vehicle, into Taliban-held territory was nobody's idea of a good night out. None of them attempted any pleasantries, and Jacko was too out of breath to talk as they trundled towards the outer cordon of the camp and were waved through the barrier by one of five armed ANA guys. Three months previously a group of Taliban militia had gained access to the camp and planted an explosive device. Fifteen men dead meant that the guards were a lot more diligent about checking the identities of those entering the camp than those leaving it.

As the lights of the military base disappeared behind them, Jacko and his ANP guards drove in silence through the desert. Jacko watched the dark terrain pass through the side window. He found that was easier on the nerves than looking straight ahead, trying to pick out pressure plates or IEDs on the illuminated road. The ANP patrolled these areas all the time, he told himself. They knew what they were doing.

And so it turned out. It took forty-five minutes on the rough desert roads to reach the village of Gareshk, but they arrived without incident at 02.31 hours. As they hit the northern edge of the village, the ANP driver took them off road and slowly negotiated the eastern perimeter of the village, coming to a halt on the northern side of an irrigation ditch that the Land Rover couldn't negotiate. Jacko and the ANP guys exited the vehicle.

'You,' Jacko said to one of them, 'lead the way. You two, stay on either side of me.'

The ANP seemed to understand his command, although they looked unimpressed. Jacko didn't care. They were there to protect him, not the other way round.

They moved past an empty barn on their right that stank of goats, then a bombed-out building covered in weeds. Jacko's contact was waiting for them at the entrance to a compound fifty metres beyond that. An ANP vehicle was parked outside and several police officers were guarding the entrance. Jacko's contact stood by an open wooden gate. He wore ANP uniform, had a full black beard and carried a rifle. As always, he looked at Jacko's goatee with undisguised amusement. 'You have something for me?'

Jacko handed over two hundred American dollars. His contact counted them, shoved them in a pocket then inclined his head towards the compound. 'There were two hits. The first one was here. This way.'

Jacko removed a torch from his ops vest and followed him in. He observed that the padlock on the inside of the gate had been cut with bolt cutters. His contact led him to a room on the far side of the compound, guarded by another ANP guy. There was no light inside. When Jacko peered in with his torch, he saw a woman and two children huddled up together on a bed. They looked terrified and had clearly been crying, and they shrank back from the light of Jacko's torch. Then his contact led him to another room on the north-eastern side of the compound.

The only occupant of this room was dead.

He was almost naked, his trousers in a tangle around his ankles. As Jacko shone his torch up the length of his body he saw that his genitals were scarred and hairless from some previous trauma. There were dog bite marks on his right forearm, and he had been shot twice. Once in the head, once in the face. Jacko felt sick. He couldn't look at it for more than a couple of seconds, and was glad his contact seemed to be in a hurry.

'We should go, boss. Follow me.'

A team of five ANP guys escorted him across the village. It was clear the inhabitants knew something was happening – Jacko could hear voices and see lights – but nobody ventured out of their houses or compounds. Jacko's contact led them across a dried-out tributary of the Helmand River and in ten minutes they had come to a second compound, this one guarded on the south side by three ANP. They stepped aside from the gate to let Jacko and his contact through.

The compound was divided into two: up ahead, Jacko saw a dividing wall with a door in it. In this southern half of the compound there was a tree in the middle with some welding equipment underneath it. Jacko pointed towards the door. 'That way?'

Jacko's contact shook his head. 'There is nothing that way, boss. The sign of a struggle, but just empty rooms. But here . . .' He pointed to a room on the south-west corner of the compound. Its door was open, but it was dark inside. He looked Jacko up and down, as though uncertain that he was up to witnessing the scene that awaited them. Then he shrugged. 'Go and look,' he said.

Jacko hesitated. He was still feeling nauseous from witnessing the corpse in the other compound. His skin went clammy and he almost decided not to look at what was in the room. But his contact was staring at him, and this was what he'd come for after all. He raised his torch and entered.

Jacko McGuigan would never forget what he saw.

There were four people in this room. A woman and three children. They were all dead, but Jacko had been expecting that.

It was the manner of their death that turned his core to ice.

They were lying, face up, on the floor. Their mouths were covered in duct tape. Each of them had been shot in the head, clearly at a range of no more than a few inches. The children had a third of their skulls blown away, the adult about a quarter. But even these catastrophic injuries were not the worst of it.

Each corpse was naked. Their night attire – plain robes – had been split down the middle. So had their abdomens. Each body was sliced from the neck down to the groin. The innards were bulging grotesquely out. They were still slightly glistening in the torchlight and there was a terrible stench of faecal matter and urine.

Jacko emptied the contents of his stomach noisily on the floor. He continued to retch even when there was nothing more to bring up. He sensed the silhouette of his contact standing in the doorway. 'Get out!' he shouted, embarrassed. The silhouette ebbed away into the night.

Get a grip, Jacko told himself. You've seen bodies before. Dead is dead. You need to see those bodies for what they are. Promotion. Advancement. He straightened up, wiped the phlegm from his mouth and removed a camera from his ops vest. He went about the grim work of photographing the bodies, and felt dizzy from the flash of the camera and the grimness of the work. When he was done, he stood in the darkness for a moment, wondering what his next move should be. This was an atrocity. A war crime of massive proportions. Jacko had truly lucked out. But he was alone in this part of the world, the only RMP representative at Camp Shorabak, and for all he knew in Helmand Province at large.

He needed backup.

He took out his phone and dialled a number. It rang three times before a male voice answered.

'Holroyd.'

'It's me, boss. McGuigan.'

'What time is it there?'

'Just after three in the morning.' He glanced at the shadowy forms of the bodies lying in the darkness. 'You need to get out here,' he said.

He told his superior what he had just seen.

Then he turned on his heel and strode out of the room. 'Get me back to Camp Shorabak,' he told his contact. 'Now.'

10

It was the opinion of Doctor Karim that his patient had been extremely lucky.

A couple of inches either way and the bullet would have hit a major artery. He would have bled to death within minutes. As it was, a speedy casualty evacuation and some skilful surgery meant that the patient would be up and about in a couple of days. Blood and fluids had been replaced. The wound had been neatly stitched. It would hurt, of course. There was a risk of infection. The soldier – Doctor Karim didn't know his name – would be scarred for life in the shoulder area. But he'd live.

However, as his medical team cleaned down the operating theatre and wheeled the patient into a recovery ward, Doctor Karim found himself contemplating some things that didn't quite add up. Those bits of the casualty's clothes and body armour that the medics had removed or cut from his person had been placed on a metal trolley. He stepped over to it and examined the tactical gloves. The palm and the back were stained with blood. It would make sense that the palm of one of the gloves would be stained, if the casualty had used it to press against his bleeding wound. But both sides of each hand? After a bullet wound to the shoulder.

And there was something else. He had placed the bullet, which he had excavated from the patient's shoulder, in a petri dish. Doctor Karim knew something about ballistics. This was a 5.56. It had probably clipped the edge of the patient's body armour before entering his shoulder, fractionally reducing its velocity. He picked it out of the petri dish with a pair of forceps and carried it over to the sink at the side of the operating theatre, where he ran it under the water and scrubbed off some of the blood that still remained. There was no doubt about it. Definitely a 5.56. But almost without exception, ANA, ANP and Taliban forces fired 7.62s. Only the British and Americans fired 5.56s.

A wave of tiredness overcame him. He dropped the round into a pocket, then went to clean up. Twenty minutes later he was back at his quarters in Accommodation Block A. Lying on his bed he tried to sleep, but despite his exhaustion sleep wouldn't come. He pulled out the round, held it up and continued to examine it.

Time passed. He didn't know how long. He was snapped out of his daze by a knock on the door.

Please, he muttered to himself in Pashto. Not another one. He walked across the room and opened the door.

The last time he had seen the British soldier with the goatee beard flecked with grey had only been a few hours ago. How different he looked now. His face was dirty and sweat-streaked. His goatee beard was matted. He smelled of vomit.

'We need to talk,' he said.

Ordinarily, Doctor Karim would have asked him to leave. He neither liked nor trusted the man. But the haunted look on his face echoed the doctor's own uncertainty about the night's events. He stepped aside.

'Come in,' he said. 'It's Captain McGuigan, isn't it?'

McGuigan nodded as he entered. At Doctor Karim's invitation he sat on a hard-backed chair.

'The casualty evacuation you received into the medical centre tonight,' he said. 'That was a British soldier?'

'I believe so.'

'Will he live?'

'Oh yes. He's lucky, but he'll be fine.'

'Was there anything unusual about him?'

'Apart from a bullet in his shoulder?' Doctor Karim endured McGuigan's unimpressed stare for a few seconds before inclining his head and handing him the round. 'He was shot with a 5.56. I am almost certain it would have come from a British or American weapon.'

McGuigan examined it, his face expressionless. 'Anything else?' he said.

Doctor Karim nodded. 'His gloves,' he said.

'What about them?'

'They were blood stained. I don't believe it was all his blood.'

McGuigan stared into the middle distance. He looked like he was remembering something. 'In your opinion,' he said, 'had the man you treated been in close contact with other casualties?'

'Yes,' said Doctor Karim. '*Extremely* close contact.'

McGuigan's eyes gleamed. It was a very unpleasant expression, Doctor Karim thought, given the circumstances.

'May I keep this?' McGuigan asked, holding up the spent round.

'If you must,' said the doctor. 'Now if you will excuse me, it has been a long night. I must rest.' He walked to the door and held it open.

McGuigan left.

Dawn was arriving as Jacko walked back to his own accommodation unit, a steely grey creeping through the camp as a terrible night gave way to an uncertain day. At the far southern end of the camp, he could see a plume of smoke rising from the burn pit where the refuse created by the camp's inhabitants had been smouldering all night, but it didn't look as grim to him as it normally did. His criteria for unpleasantness had been reset.

Jacko's phone rang before he reached the accommodation unit.

'It's me,' said Holroyd's voice at the other end. 'Where are you?'

'Shorabak. I've just interviewed the medic who worked—'

'The casualty's name is Danny Black,' said the voice. 'I came across him a couple of days ago. He's a troublemaker. 22 SAS. He was on an operation with three more SAS members. Tony Wiseman, Rees Dexter and Billy Cole. They're approaching Shorabak from the south as we speak.'

'How do you know?' Jacko said.

'It doesn't matter how I know. Intercept them as soon as they're in camp. Debrief them fully. Find out what happened and make them squirm. Is that understood?'

'Understood, sir. Are you—'

'I'm on my way to Brize. I land at Shorabak at 15.30 local time.'

The line was dead.

Jacko drew a deep breath, fortifying his aching limbs. Then he ran to his Toyota, turned the engine over and headed once again through the slowly rising dawn to the southern entrance of the camp. Here he dumped his vehicle by the guardhouse as before, nodded to the guards who recognised him, and looked through the barriers out across the desert. To his right, mountains. To his left, the sun was nudging its way above the horizon. Jacko looked straight ahead, scanning the desert in front of him from left to right and back again, as he'd been taught in basic training. The terrain was parched, empty and featureless. He could see nothing.

The sun rose a few more inches above the horizon, flooding the desert red. The terrain shimmered in the heat haze so that anything more than a couple of hundred metres distant was blurry.

Jacko had been standing there for fifteen minutes before he saw it: a solitary vehicle, indistinct, but definitely approaching.

He checked his watch. 05.31 hours.

As it grew nearer, Jacko could make out more features. It was a small, open-top truck, but not a military vehicle. It looked more like it had been taken from a local farm. It kicked up a cloud of dust as it approached, and it was clearly making the five Afghan guards at the guardhouse nervous. Four of them stood in a line at the entrance barrier, their weapons engaged, while the fifth remained in the guardhouse itself.

The vehicle stopped thirty metres from the barrier. Nobody exited. The guards kept their rifles raised.

A minute passed. The fifth guard shouted something in Pashto from the guardhouse. The others looked nervously at each other, but then they lowered their weapons and opened the barrier.

The vehicle advanced. Jacko jogged from the fence and positioned himself so that he was standing in the vehicle's path. It drove past the guards, into the camp and came to a halt just a couple of metres from where Jacko was standing.

There was only one person in the cab. He was wearing full camo gear, tactical helmet and sunglasses. Even if Jacko hadn't been expecting an SF unit, he'd have recognised the personnel immediately. The driver just had that look. He stared straight through the windscreen as if Jacko wasn't even there, and occasionally revved the engine.

'Tony Wiseman?' Jacko shouted. His voice was as dry as the terrain.

Silence.

Then, from the back of the vehicle: 'Who the fuck wants to know?'

'Captain McGuigan,' Jacko shouted. 'Royal Military Police.'

Another silence.

'Praise the fucking Lord,' said the voice. 'A long day at the office, we rock up here for a little R and R, and what do we get?'

There was a clattering sound. Two soldiers appeared from the back, one walking round either side of the vehicle as they approached Jacko. They were both dressed like the driver: full desert ops gear. They looked dirty, tired and they didn't smell very good. A dog, wearing its own battle gear, trotted alongside one of them.

The other man stopped directly in front of Jacko and removed his sunglasses. He was much taller than the RMP, and he had to look down to lock gazes with him. 'We get a fucking rat, lads,' he said quietly. 'That's what we get.'

His companions said nothing. The dog let out a low growl from the back of its throat. Jacko made a conscious effort not to stare at the animal. He locked gazes with the soldier who had just spoken to him instead.

'Are you Tony Wiseman?'

The soldier looked down at him. Then he nodded almost imperceptibly. 'I want to speak to my CO.'

'Not a chance. You're to follow me. We're going to a debriefing room for an informal chat. No lawyers, off the record. But you don't deviate, and you don't speak to anyone else. I don't *want* to put you under arrest, but if I have to, I will. Am I clear?'

Wiseman didn't answer. He just continued to stare down at Jacko for a full ten seconds. Then he turned and headed to the cab of the vehicle. His mate did the same, and the driver revved threateningly. 'We're not signing any fucking autographs,' Wiseman shouted as he climbed in beside the driver and slammed the door closed.

Jacko didn't know if they were going to follow him. Sweat was running down the nape of his neck. Wiseman had unnerved him. He jogged back to his vehicle and got behind the wheel. As he turned the engine over, he could see that the three SAS men were in conversation. He started driving back towards the centre of the camp. To his relief, the farm vehicle followed him.

The building to which he led them had once been an ammo store, squat and thick walled. These days it was seldom used for anything: a bleak, empty space set apart from the medical centre and the accommodation blocks, at least a kilometre from the helicopter landing zone and runway. It was a place Jacko knew they wouldn't be interrupted. He gathered three chairs from different corners of the room and was arranging them in a line as the three SAS men entered.

'Sit down please, gentlemen,' Jacko said, trying to avoid eye contact.

The three men stood in the doorway. They didn't move. The Malinois dog sat to one side. It was staring at Jacko.

'I said—'

'What is this?' Wiseman said. 'Musical fucking chairs?' He stepped a little further into the room, flanked by the two others. 'We'll stand,' he said.

They were an imposing sight with their battle gear, their helmets and their rifles spray-painted in the colours of the desert. But it wasn't the way they were dressed that made Jacko nervous. It was the look in their eyes. Steely. Determined. But also . . . tense.

Like they could snap at any minute, and you wouldn't want to be there when it happened.

'You were operating last night in the village of Gareshk.' Jacko framed it as a statement not a question. Nobody contradicted him, which gave him a little more confidence to continue. 'I've just returned from there.'

'Glad to hear it,' Wiseman muttered. 'Does you good to get out once in a while.'

'Be careful what you say,' Jacko replied. 'If the things I saw last night are the responsibility of a member of the British Army, it's enough to put them in prison for life. Is that understood?'

No reply.

'Did you assassinate a single male target in a compound to the south-east of Gareshk?'

Wiseman remained completely expressionless. So did the guy with the dog. The third soldier licked his lips and glanced momentarily at the floor.

'Yes,' said Wiseman.

Jacko felt a small thrill. He was close to something. He tried to keep cool.

'Did you kill and mutilate the bodies of a woman and three children in a compound to the west of Gareshk?'

'No.'

'You're certain?'

'It's been a long night, fella. I don't want to answer your questions more than once.'

'Fine,' Jacko said. He nodded at Wiseman's rifle. 'Are you carrying spare magazines for that.'

'Of course.'

'Show me.'

A flicker of annoyance crossed Wiseman's face. He took a magazine from his ops vest and handed it to Jacko. Jacko removed one of the rounds and held it up. 'A 5.56,' he said. He handed the magazine back to Wiseman, then took from his pocket the spent round that the doctor had given him. 'This is also a 5.56,' he said. 'It was retrieved from the shoulder of a fourth member of your team, one Danny Black, who is currently extremely lucky to be alive. Do you have any idea how this round might have got there?'

'Sure,' said Wiseman.

'How?'

'I shot him,' he said.

Jacko found himself breathing very deeply. He looked from Wiseman to the others. The dog guy looked completely unconcerned. The third man, not so much. He was looking into the middle distance and there was a tightness around the eyes. Jacko moved his attention back to Wiseman, the self-appointed spokesman of the trio. 'Go on,' he said.

'Black went berserk.'

'What do you mean?'

Wiseman sniffed. 'We had instructions to take out two targets and plant weapons on them to prove they were an active threat. The first one went smoothly. Black made the hit while Cole here watched the family. They were all alive when we left the eastern compound.'

'They still are,' Jacko breathed.

Wiseman inclined his head. He clearly didn't much care either way. 'We moved on to the second compound. I told Black to watch the family. He didn't like it. Wanted to be in on the hit. I told him tough shit. Left him to deal with the missus and the kids while we went after the target in another part of the compound.'

'Go on.'

'The target must have heard us coming. He'd left by a different exit. Door was still open. We heard him starting up a vehicle outside the compound. Ran out. Saw him leaving to the northwest. Decided to go after him, but we needed to find a vehicle first. Dexter and Cole here went car shopping. I headed back to get Black and make sure he'd secured the family.'

'And?'

'He'd secured them all right. Permanently. Had his fun with them, too.' Wiseman frowned. 'It was bad shit.'

Jacko remembered the butchered family. Bad shit didn't do it justice. 'Where was Black?' he asked quietly.

'Gone. Left the same way that we entered. I went after him. Saw him running away along the irrigation ditch to the west.' Wiseman shrugged. 'Knew I had to put him down, didn't I? Fucker was out of control, simple as that.'

'So you shot him?'

'No, I used a fucking lasso. Of course I shot him.'

'In the back?'

'No. He turned round to check if he was being followed.'

'At what range did you shoot him?'

'Seventy-five metres. A little more.'

'Are you trying to tell me that a member of 22 SAS couldn't kill a man at that distance?'

Wiseman sneered. 'Kill him? I wasn't trying to kill him, mate.'

'Why not? You said he was out of control.'

'What's your parent regiment, pal?'

'I'm asking the questions, Wiseman.'

'What is it?'

Jacko hesitated. 'Scots Guards,' he said.

'And I'm guessing,' Wiseman said, 'that since you've thrown your hat in with the RMPs, you wouldn't think twice about shopping one of your former mates?'

'If they'd stepped out of line I'd know what my duty was,' Jacko said.

'Well it's not like that in the Regiment, sunshine. Me and Danny Black? Not friends. Far fucking from it. But on ops, that doesn't matter. I put Black down because it was the right operational call, not because I wanted to. I aimed for the front of his shoulder. Then I called in a casualty evacuation to make sure he got out of theatre safely.'

'And the rest of you?'

'We went after the target.'

'Did you get him?'

A grim smile crossed Wiseman's face. 'Yeah,' he said quietly. 'We got him.'

Silence.

Jacko turned his back on the others. Walked to the far end of the room. His mind was turning over. Everything Tony Wiseman had just told him was gold dust. Holroyd had been saying it for months: that the SAS was out of control. That they were performing illegal operations in Afghanistan. That the Royal Military Police had a duty to investigate, and prosecute if they found evidence. Jacko had better than that. He had a full confession from an SAS operator. He had a smoking gun. These three meatheads might be good fighters, but they were stupid. They shouldn't have said a word to Jacko. They could have kept silent, waited for Hereford to get them lawyered up.

But they hadn't, and Jacko had the mind of an investigator. He realised that he needed these three on his side. An off-the-record confession was one thing. Getting them to repeat their story in front of other witnesses? Quite another. That would only happen if they knew they were safe from prosecution. They would each need to testify against their unit mate, and they were only likely to do that if they thought it was the only way they could save their own skins.

Jacko turned to face them again. 'You're all confined to camp,' he said, 'pending further investigations. Your commanding officers will be informed. You're not to speak to anybody about this matter. Is that understood?'

No reply.

'*Is that understood?*'

'You want my advice, Colombo?' Wiseman said quietly. 'Put some guys on Danny Black's guard detail. He won't want to talk to you and even if he's injured, there aren't many men who'll stop him. It'll be a numbers game, if you want to keep him where he is.'

Jacko felt his eyes tightening. The horrific scene at the village flashed in front of his eyes again. Once more he felt nauseous. He put it from his mind and focused on what this case could do for his career.

'You're damn right I want to keep him where he is,' he said.

He strode past the SAS unit, ignoring the growl from the Malinois as he passed, and exited swiftly into the bright morning sunlight of Helmand Province. He felt excited. Sure, Holroyd would take the lion's share of the glory, but Jacko would surely be moving up the ranks with him. He'd be known as the guy who revealed the Regiment for what they really were. As a guy who was going places. His superiors in the Scots Guards who'd refused him promotion would soon understand how mistaken they'd been.

He looked at his watch. 06.03 hours. Holroyd would be landing in just under ten hours' time. Then the fun would really begin.

Until then, he was going to follow Tony Wiseman's advice. Bullet wound or no bullet wound, he was going to make sure there was no chance of Danny Black going anywhere.

The three SAS men watched the royal military policeman leave.

'You think he bought it?' Dexter said quietly, scratching the Malinois' ears as he spoke.

'I dunno . . .' Cole started to say. 'What if . . .'

'He bought it,' Wiseman said. 'All we need to do is stick to the fucking script. You muppets think you can do that?'

'Course,' said Dexter.

'Cole?'

Cole looked uncertain. 'What if they do a DNA test?' he said.

'Fuck's sake,' Wiseman replied. 'Out here? They'll have the bodies in the ground before sunset. No one's doing any DNA tests.' He looked Cole up and down. 'Your hands are fucking shaking,' he said. 'What's the problem? You not up to it? You know there's no way back, right?'

'I'm up to it,' Cole said.

'Good. Because the only way this goes wrong is if one of us fucks it up.'

'It's not a problem,' Cole said.

'It had better not be. Let's find our digs.' Wiseman nodded towards the door to indicate that they should all leave.

Dexter exited first, with the Malinois walking obediently to heel. Cole went next. He had his back to Wiseman, so he had no way of noticing how his unit leader looked at him, his jaw set, his eyes hollow, his expression calculating and cold.

11

'For goodness sake! Will one of you please tell me what's going on!'

The ops room at Cornwall had been a shit storm ever since the operation had gone south. They'd lost voice contact with the team at approximately 01.00 Afghanistan time, fifteen minutes after they'd lost drone support. Everything they knew about the unit's movements they'd had to piece together from scraps.

There was a casualty. That much was certain. Radio intercepts had confirmed that a British soldier had been evacuated to Camp Shorabak for medical treatment. Nobody in the ops room had been able to confirm that the casualty was Danny Black, but since his was the only GPS tracker that was not showing up on their systems, the analysts at Cornwall had joined the dots. The remaining three GPS trackers – they were fitted to the unit's radio packs – had shown that the rest of the unit had headed north from the village of Gareshk. Their speed of travel indicated that they were in a vehicle – presumably the farm vehicle that had been left for them as an extraction tool. They had continued for five miles and come to a halt at an area that the ops room's mapping indicated was a steep slope in the foothills of a small mountain range. The team had remained there for approximately thirty minutes before returning – by vehicle again – to Camp Shorabak.

All that time, they'd been out of contact. 'We had no communication from Tony or the guys,' McLean had explained.

'Don't we have any assets at Shorabak?' Cadogan shouted across the ops room to nobody in particular. He sighed huffily: 'Ten years ago we had thousands of men there.'

'It's an outpost now, sir,' said one of the ops room guys. 'A forward operating base for the ANA, a medical centre ... we've no reason to have anybody there ...'

'Sir,' McLean interrupted. He had a phone to his ear, and he'd turned pale. 'We've got a problem.'

'I'd noticed,' Cadogan muttered.

'A bigger problem.' McLean killed the phone. 'That was a contact of mine at Brize Norton. He keeps his ear to the ground for me. He just arrived at work and—'

'What's the problem, McLean?' Cadogan snapped. 'Spit it out, man.'

'A specially commissioned Hercules left Brize for Camp Shorabak at 07.30 BST. Only one passenger. Mike Holroyd. Royal Military Police.'

Cadogan stared at him. 'Is that so?' he said, very quietly. He thought for a moment. 'Can we get a legal team out there? When does our devout friend land?'

McLean looked at his watch. 'It's too late, sir. Wheels down in ten minutes.'

Cadogan closed his eyes. 'The lord is clearly with him,' he muttered. He opened his eyes again. 'I need to know what's happening,' he said. 'Do whatever it takes.' He opened his eyes again and waved an arm to indicate everyone in the room. 'Gentlemen, be under no illusion. If the RMP get their teeth into this, every single one of you is compromised. Make contact with the unit. On no account are our chaps to speak to *anybody*. And find out about Danny Black. What happened? How badly is he hurt? Is the fellow even alive?'

He collapsed into a chair, swept his hair back from his forehead in a way that only made it more untidy and surveyed the industrious scene of the operations room. He had a nasty feeling he'd just been outmanoeuvred by Mike Holroyd. He had no intention of staying outmanoeuvred for long.

Danny Black drifted into consciousness.

He kept his eyes closed. To open them was too massive an effort. He felt nauseous. Every limb was too heavy to move and there was a deep, pounding pain in his left shoulder. Somewhere – maybe it was close, maybe it was far away – he could hear the regular beep of a pulse monitor. Elsewhere, shouting and clattering. None of the voices he heard were speaking English.

His brain was a fog. He tried to clear it. Where was he? What had happened? It hurt to think. He saw himself, as if from outside, lying in a ditch. A figure standing over him. He tried to make out the features, but couldn't. Flashes of recollection pierced his consciousness. Freefalling through the cloud line. The first hit. Moving through the village to the second compound. The terrified family it was his job to secure . . .

Nausea again. The beep of the pulse monitor grew faster. He tried to take a deep breath. It made his shoulder hurt even more.

He drifted back into unconsciousness.

When he woke again the pain was still there but the nausea had subsided a little. He was aware of a commotion nearby. An argument. He couldn't make out the words. He winced as a shock of pain cut down his abdomen from his shoulder.

He heard a lock click. A door open. Footsteps. Approaching. He sensed somebody close and tried to force his eyes open.

An opaque blur. Vaguely, he was able to discern the outline of a figure standing by his bedside. But, just as when he'd been lying in the irrigation ditch, he couldn't make out the face.

'Black?' said a voice. 'Are you awake?'

Danny recognised the voice. He tried to place it but couldn't. He felt himself squinting, trying to discern the features. But the effort was too much. He closed his eyes and slept again.

When he woke for the third time it was easier – a little – to open his eyes, and his vision was fractionally less blurred. The figure was still standing by his bedside. Danny didn't know how long he'd been out. He felt a moment of panic. Who was this person? A doctor wouldn't just be standing there.

'Black?' the voice said again. As he spoke, the fog cleared a little more. The figure's features became visible. Black hair, thinning. Slightly overweight. Thin lips, which he was brushing with his forefingers. A silver fish on his lapel.

'Holroyd,' Danny breathed. His voice was cracked and weak.

Holroyd leaned over. '"You restored me to health and let me live",' he said in his thick Ulster accent. 'Isaiah, chapter thirty-eight. But you'll have plenty of time to be reading the good book where you're going.'

'What are you doing here?'

'Flew out specially to have a little chat with you, didn't I? A little chat between friends.'

Danny tried to take in some more of his surroundings. He appeared to be in a single room. One exit. Distance, seven metres. Door closed. He was lying in a hospital bed, surrounded by drip stands and machines monitoring his vital signs. Bright strip lighting on the ceiling. A clock on the far wall told him it was just after five in the afternoon. No windows. There was a low buzz from an air-conditioning unit. Against one wall was a trolley containing medical supplies – tablets, swabs, blue plastic bowls, sample pots. Danny glanced down at himself. His wound was swabbed and padded. Cannulas had been inserted on the back of both hands. Tubes emerged up to the drip stands. An uncomfortable feeling in his dick told him he was wearing a catheter. There was a background smell of antiseptic, but it was overpowered by a rank stench from Danny's own body.

He closed his eyes. 'Get out of here,' he breathed.

'Sounds like you've been a busy boy, Black. I turn my back on you for seventy-two hours and what happens?'

'I said, get out of here.'

'You know, I can't stop myself wondering which one you did first. The little girl, was it? No? Probably the mum then. Get the adults out of the way before you deal with the kiddies.'

Danny exhaled slowly. Holroyd wasn't making any sense – or was it just that Danny was confused? 'What kids?' he said.

'You know what I'm talking about. I've got the pictures. Your team have confessed. Tony Wiseman's explained why he had to put you down. Under normal circumstances, those three would be looking at the wrong end of a ten-year stretch. As it happens,

I'm sure we can forgive them their trespasses, in the light of what you did to that family.'

Silence.

'What pictures?' Danny said. 'What did Tony tell you?'

'Everything, Black.' He lowered his voice. 'I knew you were a wrong 'un the moment I saw you. I didn't predict you'd go berserk, granted, butcher a whole family. But it's no less than I expected of your lot. Rules of engagement are there for a reason. As soon as we let heathens like you think they don't apply, this is what happens. Dead women and children. You, my friend, are going down – and you're going to bring your nasty little regiment of bully boys down with you.' His toadlike smile spread across his face. 'And when you've answered to me, you'll answer to a higher power.'

It still made no sense to Danny. He screwed up his face, trying to keep focused, trying to remember what happened. 'Tony's lying,' he whispered. 'The wife and kids were fine. I tied them up . . . that was all . . .'

'That was all, hey?' Holroyd said. 'Well, it doesn't look like all.'

He held up a photograph, colour printed on to a piece of A4 paper. The picture was overexposed – a flash in a dark room – but the image was clear. Four bodies: one adult, three children. Duct tape round their heads. Wrists and ankles bound. But Danny's eyes were immediately drawn to the horror. The bodies had been split along their torsos. Their guts were bulging out. Danny, who was no stranger to such sights, turned his head away.

'Tony's playing you,' he breathed.

Holroyd smiled. 'Tony Wiseman,' he said, 'is following the right path for once in his life and blowing the whistle. Going the full Snowden, as we say. You, Danny Black, are the worst of everything your regiment represents. I'm making preparations to have you flown back to the UK. Once we're on home turf, I'm going to throw the book at you.' Holroyd straightened up. He looked Danny up and down, then placed the gruesome photograph on his bedside table. 'I'll leave that picture with you, so you can think carefully about your misdemeanours,' he said. 'You're not in a position to go anywhere by yourself, but I'm putting security on your door anyway. Tony Wiseman seems to have a grudging respect for your abilities. I can't say I share it.'

He turned and walked to the exit.

'Holroyd,' Danny said.

The RMP man turned. 'What?'

'Did they get him?'

'Who?'

'The target.'

Holroyd's face twitched. 'No thanks to you. After they'd called in your casualty evacuation, they chased the target north across dangerous ground. They got him in the end.' He touched his lips with his fingertips again. 'No doubt somebody at Spearpoint will manage to provide me with incontrovertible evidence that he was about to commit a terrible atrocity. But his family? That's another matter entirely. You, soldier, will answer for this. In this world and the next. Believe me.'

He turned again. As he left, Danny caught sight of an Afghan guy in uniform outside. Holroyd started talking to him, but the door swung shut so Danny couldn't hear the conversation.

Not that he needed to. Holroyd was plainly giving his guards their instructions.

He heard the lock click shut.

Danny told himself to keep calm. A sense of panic was rising in his gut. He forced himself to master it. He needed to clear his head. To work out what the hell was going on.

His memory of the op was more concrete now. Everything had been going according to plan, right up until the point that Tony and the others had instructed him to leave the compound and head to the RV point. At that moment, he'd been suspicious of something going down. But what?

And how had those innocent family members ended up not only dead but butchered? Had Tony and his guys done that? They had spun a web of lies. About Danny committing that atrocity, sure. But also about nailing the target. During the op, Dexter had said he'd shot Target Blue in the head while Danny was still in the compound. Tony had told Holroyd they'd gone after the target once they'd called for a casualty evacuation. One of those claims wasn't true. Maybe both. But for the life of him, Danny couldn't understand what advantage those lies handed his unit mates.

Had it all been just to set Danny up? To frame him? Tony hated him; that was no secret. But would he really go to such lengths to fuck Danny over? Would he take such risks? Danny didn't think so.

But he knew this: whatever Tony was up to, he had Holroyd eating out of his hand. What was more, the RMP had made his decision about Danny before Danny had even been deployed. It was almost a crusade, as if Holroyd saw him, Danny, as the devil incarnate. As soon as he got airlifted back to the UK, his chances of changing anybody's mind about what had happened were practically zero.

He looked towards the door. Then down at the bandage on his shoulder. He tried to lift his left arm and winced with the pain. Movement was going to be difficult. But he *did* have to move. If he stayed here, he was fucked.

A noise from the lock. The door opened. A doctor entered. He was wearing green overalls and carrying a clipboard.

'Good evening,' he said in decent English. 'I'm Doctor Karim. I removed the bullet from your shoulder. How are you feeling?'

'The catheter hurts,' Danny said. 'Can you take it out for me?' Danny knew it wasn't a job for unskilled hands.

'Really it should stay—'

'Please, doc. I'll use a bottle or whatever.'

The doctor inclined his head. He stood at the side of the bed, lifted the sheets and did what was necessary. 'I'll ask someone to remove the bag.' He walked over to the trolley containing medical equipment and held up a plastic urine bottle to indicate that he would have to use that if necessary. 'You are lucky. A couple of inches either way, the bullet would have . . .' He left it hanging.

'Thanks for fixing me up.' Danny nodded towards the door. 'They seem a bit nervous about having me here. I'm beginning to get a complex.'

Doctor Karim forced a humourless smile and avoided Danny's eyes. Danny knew, immediately, that he had suspicions about him. He knew there was no point trying to deny whatever fake news Holroyd and Tony had been spreading about him. All he could do was to make himself appear relaxed, to gather as much intel as he could, and maybe spread a little misinformation of his own. 'Guess I'm not going anywhere,' Danny said as the doctor examined the data on the machine next to his bed, 'with an armed guard at my door.'

'Two armed guards, sir,' the doctor corrected.

'Right,' Danny said, noting that information. 'Two armed guards. I guess I'll be out of your hair soon, anyway. Seems they want me back in the UK when I'm fit to travel.'

'That is correct.'

'So, when do you think that will be?'

'Tomorrow morning,' the doctor said. 'I have to keep you under observation for one more night.'

'It'll be good to get back,' Danny said. 'See the family.'

The word 'family' had an effect on the doctor. Yeah, he knew.

'Do you need anything for the pain?' the doctor asked stiffly.

'I'll take whatever you're offering,' Danny said. 'Just no morphine. I prefer to keep my system clean of that stuff.'

The doctor nodded and walked over to the trolley against the far wall that contained the medical equipment. He selected a white box of tablets, placed two in a plastic bowl and poured a glass of water. He brought the pills over to Danny and helped him to take them. 'If you need anything,' he said, 'press that button.' He indicated a button to the left of the bed. 'I'll have someone check on you in the night and administer more pain relief if necessary. Is there anything else you require?'

'I guess a hot flannel and a pretty nurse is out of the question?'

The doctor didn't look amused. 'I'll be here in the morning to discharge you,' he said.

'Right,' Danny said. 'Thanks, doc. I appreciate it.'

The doctor nodded curtly and left the room. The moment the door locked shut, Danny's fake smile faded. He screwed his face up in pain.

Time check: 18.29 hours. Danny watched the second hand of the clock on the wall tick a full revolution as he worked out his next move.

He needed the cover of darkness. That much was sure. And he needed to wait until the medical facility was quiet. The doctor had told him that somebody would check on him in the night. He had to wait until that had happened. Between now and then, he needed to rest up. The painkillers were kicking in, but he was drained and exhausted. He needed as much vigour as possible if he was going to attempt to escape from a military base. There was no room for error: if he was caught trying to get away, Holroyd would take it as further proof that Tony was right.

No fuck-ups, Danny, he told himself.

There was a light switch by his bed. He reached over and hit it. The room descended into darkness. He decided that he would feign sleep, to lull his guards into security. In reality, he knew as he lay in the darkness that sleep would be impossible. His active mind, and the pain in his shoulder, would see to that.

He listened to the clock ticking in the silent room.

Minutes passed.

Hours.

He lay very still, breathing deeply.

The door opened. A man entered. Behind him, through half-closed eyes, Danny saw his two armed guards. They were seated on either side of the door, legs stretched out. The position of their bodies told Danny they had a low level of awareness.

The hospital guy switched the light on and leaned over Danny, who groaned. He caught sight of the clock: 23.00 hours exactly. The hospital guy said something in Pashto that Danny didn't understand, then made a note of the readings on the monitor by his bed. He gave Danny some more painkillers, replaced one of the saline drips and then, wordlessly, switched the light off and left the room. Danny heard the click of the lock.

He gave himself a couple of minutes for his eyes to get used to the darkness. When he had sufficient NV, he raised his right arm, peeled off the tape that kept the cannula pressed to the skin on the back of his hand, then gently slid the needle out of his body. He closed off the valve to stop the tube leaking, then repeated the process on his left hand, where it was more difficult because of the pain of his wound.

Free of the tubes leading to the drip stands, he lay back again, clutching the two cannulas so that any unexpected visitors wouldn't have their suspicions raised by the sight of unattached tubes. He would let half an hour pass. Time for things to settle down for the night in the medical facility.

The second hands of the clock sounded improbably loud as he waited.

When he had estimated that half an hour had passed, he drew a deep breath. 'Hey,' he called out. 'Hey, I need some help in here.'

Silence.

'Hey, can you hear me?'

The lock clicked. The door opened. One of the guards was silhouetted in the doorway. Danny could just make out the other one, still sitting, head back against the wall as though sleeping.

The guard in the doorway grunted. A 'what do you want?' noise.

'I need to take a piss, mate. You know? A piss? Can you help me out?'

No reply. The guard stood stupidly in the doorway. Danny leaned over to switch the light on. Checked the time: 23.36. He nodded down at his groin area, made a pissing sound, then nodded towards the plastic bottle that the doctor had left on the trolley for that purpose.

The guard looked disgusted.

'Please, mate,' Danny said. 'I'm fucking desperate. I'll do it myself.'

Whether the guard understood him or not, Danny couldn't tell. But he stepped inside the room, let the door shut behind him and walked over to the trolley. Danny checked him out as did so.

He was a big guy, and young – no more than twenty – with a black beard, neatly trimmed. He was wearing standard camouflage gear and desert boots. There was no overt sign of a weapon, but the bulge under the right-hand side of his camo jacket told Danny that he was carrying a handgun there. His gait was relaxed and sloppy. He clearly didn't see the wounded man lying in a hospital bed surrounded by drips and machines as a threat.

That was his first mistake.

His second mistake was getting too close.

He took the urine bottle from the trolley, holding it between his fingertips like it was a disgusting object. Then he walked it over to Danny. When he was close, Danny reached out his good right hand to take it. The ANA guy's eyes widened slightly as he saw the cannula fall from Danny's palm, but by that time it was too late. Danny didn't grab the urine bottle. He grabbed the guy's wrist, then yanked him violently towards him.

Speed was key. If Danny gave his opponent the chance to shout out, it would be game over. But his left arm was out of action. He had to put his man down one-handed. He released his grip, shaped his hand into a hammer fist and cracked it down against the side of his head with all the force he could muster. Danny inhaled sharply as the twisting of his body sent a shock of pain down from his wound. He did what he could to ignore it and delivered a second blow to the guard's head. Not that it was necessary. The guy was already unconscious and sliding down to the floor.

The scuffle had been noisier than Danny wanted it to be. He quickly slung his legs over the side of the bed and moved over to the door, his hospital robe flapping around his ankles, ready to attack the second guy if he came in to investigate. Breathing deeply to steady his pulse rate, he listened hard. There was no sound from the other side of the door. He didn't seem to have alerted the second guard.

Danny moved over to where the first guard was slumped on the floor. He bent down and felt inside his jacket pocket for his handgun – an old Glock 9mm. He withdrew it, cracked his guy over the head with the stock to ensure that he remained unconscious, then returned to the door. He felt momentarily dizzy, so he breathed deeply again to steady himself. Then he tapped the barrel of the gun gently against the closed door.

Silence.

He tapped again.

The guard on the other side of the door called out. Danny couldn't distinguish the word, but he sounded like he was calling for his mate. He also sounded sleepy. Danny raised his weapon to head level, and waited.

The guard called again. When there was no reply, Danny heard him approach the door.

It opened. The guard stepped in. Within a second, Danny had the weapon pressed up against the side of his skull. The guard froze.

Danny made a shushing sound, then nodded his head to indicate that the guard should enter.

He did as he was told. The door closed. Danny looked the guy up and down. He was nearer to Danny's size and build than the other guard, which would make his next job easier.

'Get your clothes off, pal,' Danny said.

The guard narrowed his eyes, not understanding. Danny approached, pressed the gun up against the guard's head again, and with his bad arm started unbuttoning the guard's clothes. The guard soon got the message. Danny stepped back and watched him undress to his underpants. Danny indicated that he should remove those too. The guard obeyed, then stood with his hands covering his crotch, terror in his face. Danny approached and quickly slammed the butt of his handgun into the side of the guard's head. He collapsed to the floor like his mate.

Danny knew he had to move fast. Killing the guards, of course, was out of the question. But they could wake up at any moment. The guard's clothes were in a pile on the floor. Changing into them was a painful business because of his wound, but he put that from his mind and in less than a minute he was wearing the standard ANA camo gear. He found a peaked camouflage cap in the guy's jacket pocket, which he crammed on to his head, and removed the watch from his wrist to put on his own. Then he moved over to the trolley containing the medical gear. He took a couple of packets of painkillers and some sterile swabs and shoved them in his pocket. The first guard started to stir. Danny cracked him in the head for a second time. He grabbed the gruesome picture of the butchered family that Holroyd had left for him, put it into a pocket and killed the lights in the hospital room. The key was in the lock on the outside. He closed the door and locked it from the outside, pocketing the key to make it more difficult for anyone to gain access when the guards inevitably raised the alarm. He made his weapon safe and pocketed it in his camo jacket.

Time check: 23.41. He headed out.

The medical unit was mercifully understaffed. Nobody challenged him as he walked, head down, along the sterile, slightly tired corridors. He didn't know the way to the exit but he walked with purpose. An air of uncertainty would attract more attention than not being recognised – Danny had been on enough military bases to realise that nobody knew everybody. He took a couple of wrong turns, but in under two minutes he was stepping out of the medical centre and into the open air.

It was much hotter outside than in. Danny's wound throbbed in time with the heightened beating of his heart. He estimated that he had a maximum of five minutes before the guards woke up, five minutes before they raised the alarm and five minutes before Holroyd learned that his prize catch had got away. Fifteen minutes to exit the base. It was almost no time at all, especially in his weakened state.

He scanned the area around him. Even now, in the middle of the night, the base was busy. Accommodation blocks a couple of hundred metres to his one o'clock. Would Holroyd, and the rest of the unit, be sleeping? Danny thought they would, but didn't want to make any assumptions. A low profile was essential. To his nine o'clock, in the distance, a chopper was landing. Several vehicles were moving around the base, headlamps shining. And a vehicle was what he needed. Leaving the base and trying to cross Helmand Province on foot was not an option.

He evaluated his potential strategies. Back in the med centre, he'd been able to confront the two guards individually. Two on one, in his state, he'd have had no chance. If he wasn't carrying a wound, he would have taken his chances with the drivers and passengers of one of these vehicles. But not tonight. He moved quickly across fifty metres of open ground to a low building which, from the smell of it, was the cookhouse. He stood in the shadow of a wall and watched the various vehicles criss-crossing the base. It took him a couple of minutes to identify his target. It was driving towards him. The glare of the headlamps in the darkness stopped him from identifying the type of vehicle, but it was indicating to the left and drawing to a halt alongside the cookhouse. Distance: thirty metres. The headlamps died. Danny thought he could discern the outline of a Hilux. Two soldiers emerged, slammed the doors shut and walked round the back of the cookhouse.

Danny advanced. He knew there was a good chance that they'd have left the keys in the ignition – on military bases like this, it was standard practice. He kept his head down but his eyes forward and reached the vehicle in about twenty seconds. No sign of the soldiers. He quickly got behind the wheel. Checked the transmission: automatic – easier for one-handed driving. The keys were there. He turned the engine over and resisted his temptation to floor the accelerator. He moved gently, unobtrusively, away from his position, constantly checking his mirrors for any sign of the two soldiers he'd just robbed. There was none as he became just another vehicle driving across the base.

Danny didn't know where the nearest exit was, but he did know that he'd find it by following the perimeter. One hand on the wheel, he cut in a straight line across the base in the opposite direction from where he'd seen the chopper landing. He checked his stolen watch. It was 23.52 hours. Eleven minutes since he'd left the hospital room. He had four minutes left of his self-imposed deadline. It was going to be tight.

He had cut through to an open area with no vehicles, and could just about see the perimeter 300 metres up ahead – a solid concrete wall topped with razor wire. Off to the north, smoke obscured his view of the moon. He assumed it came from an incinerator or burn pit. He allowed himself to accelerate and, when he reached the fence, swung round to the left. He calculated that a vehicle circling the perimeter would not raise suspicion: it would be a regular security measure in a place like this. With the speedometer tipping 60 kph, he followed the fence.

Time check: 23.54. He had two minutes.

Up ahead, the perimeter wall curved round to the left. Danny could see an exit point: a guardhouse, a barrier and armed personnel. He slowed down and drew away from the perimeter, so he could approach the exit head on.

Time check: 23.55. One minute.

The exit was a hundred metres ahead of him. Now was the moment of his biggest gamble. Security for those entering the camp would be massive. But for those exiting? He hoped not.

Seventy-five metres. Something caught Danny's eye in the rear-view mirror. A flashing light, about 300 metres behind him, approaching from the heart of the camp.

He swore under his breath, and fixed his concentration on the exit. Painfully holding the wheel with his bad hand, he took the stolen handgun from his pocket and laid it on his lap.

He slowed down. Distance to the barrier, fifteen metres. Ten metres. Five. Danny came to a halt. There was only one guard. He was carrying an assault rifle and his bearded chin was jutting out aggressively. He approached the driver's side window.

Danny glanced in his rear-view mirror. The flashing light was closer. Two hundred metres.

He wound down the window. 'Open up, pal. I haven't got all night.' He jabbed the index finger of his good hand towards the barrier.

The guard looked him up and down. It was dark, so Danny hoped the standard Afghan camo gear would look like any other. Danny forced himself not to look in the rear-view mirror.

The guard straightened up. Nodded. Walked to the barrier and opened it. Danny accelerated. He burst out of the camp with a spin of wheels. In the rear-view mirror he saw the guard closing the barrier. Beyond that, the flashing lights approaching fast. Danny accelerated hard. It bumped and rumbled over the rough road and the jolting caused a lot of pain in his wound. He didn't slow down. Looking back, he saw the vehicle with the flashing lights stationary on the far side of the barrier. A figure emerged from the vehicle and stood, silhouetted, in front of one of the headlamps. Light radiated from behind him like a halo. It was Holroyd. Danny knew it.

Up ahead, there was a fork in the road. Danny killed his lights to make himself more difficult to see, and took the left fork. A brief glance at the stars had told him this road would take him south. That was the direction he needed to travel if he was to head back to the village of Gareshk.

Because as far as Danny could tell, he only had one course of action. Tony and the others were trying to frame him for an atrocity he hadn't committed. He had to return to the scene and find out why.

12

Holroyd slammed the brakes of the one ANP police vehicles in camp that he'd managed to appropriate. He stopped five metres from the southern exit barrier to Camp Shorabak. He jumped out of the car, his face flooded with anger, and stood by the flashing neon light of the police car. Beyond the perimeter of the camp, he saw the vehicle that had cleared the barriers thirty seconds previously. It was speeding out into the darkness of the Helmand desert. A moment later, the driver killed his vehicle's lights. And a moment after that, the moonlit silhouette disappeared.

Holroyd stared. Then he stormed up to the ANA guard who had just left the vehicle through the barrier. 'Who was it?' he demanded. 'Was he English?'

The guard clearly didn't understand him.

'English?' Holroyd shouted. He pinched the white skin of his own cheek. 'Like me? English?'

The guard shrugged, then nodded.

Holroyd spun round, marched back up to the vehicle and, unable to restrain himself, kicked the tyre as hard as he could.

The Afghan guard was looking at him in bemusement. It made Holroyd even angrier. 'How dare you look at me like that!' he shouted, even though he had no jurisdiction over this man. He thumped the chassis of the vehicle with a clenched fist, climbed back behind the wheel, reversed a half circle with a screaming engine, then floored it back towards the centre of the base. 'Danny Black,' he growled to himself as he drove. Just saying the name made him want to slam the steering wheel in frustration.

What could he do? Holroyd was damned if he was going to go after him. That would mean setting foot outside the camp, exposing himself to the danger of roadside bombs and ungodly Taliban patrols. There was a good chance one of the two would put Danny Black in a shallow grave before a couple of days were out. He was weak. Injured. He couldn't survive the Afghan desert for long. Black could answer to a higher power. Holroyd didn't have the resources to send anybody after him.

No. Holroyd's priority had to be the remainder of the SAS unit. So far, they were on side. They were willing to shop Danny Black, to testify to the details of his obscene atrocity, in return for Holroyd's personal protection when he went after the SAS at large for their illegal activities.

He screamed to a halt outside the accommodation block where the unit was quartered. It was a separate building, set about thirty metres away from the regular ANA accommodation. Holroyd's deputy Jacko McGuigan – an ambitions little worm with no thought for anything but his own advancement – had installed them here, and it was here that Holroyd himself had debriefed the unit, and come to a mutual understanding with them that they could barely refuse. He killed the engine and sat quietly for a moment, his head bowed, one fist to his chest. He exited the vehicle and looked up to the heavens. Strengthened, he entered the block and strode down the corridor to the room where he knew they were bunking down. He burst in without knocking.

It was dark in the room, but light spilled in from the corridor. The three SAS men were lying on their bunks. Fully clad – camo trousers, T-shirts, boots – and staring at the ceiling. The dog, however, was staring at Holroyd. It launched itself forward, stopping less than half a metre from the door frame where Holroyd was standing, baring its teeth and growling. Holroyd froze, too scared to step back and certainly too scared to step forward.

'Will someone,' he breathed, 'get this cursed dog into isolation. There are kennels in the camp.'

'He doesn't like kennels,' his handler growled. Rees Dexter's Irish accent was very pronounced. 'So unless you want to take him there . . .'

'Then will you at least get him on a leash?'

Dexter gave a clicking sound. The dog visibly relaxed and curled its way back to its handler. Dexter himself was sitting on the edge of his bunk. 'Word of advice, pal,' he said quietly in his broad Irish accent, softer than Holroyd's Ulster twang. 'Don't give this little fella the heebie-jeebies.'

By now the others were sitting up. They winced as Holroyd switched on the main light. 'We've got a problem. Black's escaped.'

Tony Wiseman – the man Holroyd understood to be the leader of this unpleasant trio – stood up. 'I told you to put some fucking guards on his door,' he said.

'I did. He dealt with them.'

Tony's scowl was poisonous. 'Useless frickin' choggas,' he muttered. He bent down and picked something up from the floor. Holroyd saw that it was a holstered pistol, which Tony started to strap to his torso.

'What are you doing?'

'He won't get far with his arm hanging off. I'm going to go find him.'

'No,' Holroyd said.

Tony gave him a dangerous look. 'What?'

'You're staying here. In camp. That was the deal. We'll find Black, somehow. Right now, I want you three where I can see you.'

'Fuck that,' Dexter muttered. 'Black's a liability.'

'I'm telling you now,' Holroyd said, 'if any of you leave this military base without my direct permission, the deal is off. You go down with Danny Black and the rest of the Regiment. You'll have plenty of time behind bars to think about what a stupid idea it was to disobey me.'

He glared at them. They glared back. All except Cole who was, Holroyd noticed, staring awkwardly at the floor. It looked like his hands were shaking. 'What's wrong with you?' he said. Cole didn't reply.

Tony looked between Holroyd and Cole. Then he sat on the edge of his bed again. Dexter did the same.

'You're right,' Tony said. He pinched his brow. 'You're right, buddy. Sorry. I spoke out of turn.' He breathed deeply. 'We're on edge,' he said. 'I'm not going to lie. Six months of this kind of work, it gets to you.' He looked directly into Holroyd's eyes. 'It's not good for the soul. I was out of line. We appreciate what you're doing. It won't happen again.'

Holroyd looked from one to the other. Tony had closed his eyes and was breathing deeply, apparently calming himself down. Dexter was scratching the dog's ears. Cole hadn't moved. His hands were still shaking.

'Right you are,' the RMP man said. 'We'll talk in the morning. Black will probably be limping back into camp by then anyway. If he hasn't met his maker.'

He turned and left, closing the door behind him.

The three SAS men kept their silence for a full minute after Holroyd left. It was Cole who broke it.

'What now?' There was an edge of panic in his voice.

'Fuck's sake, Cole, keep a lid on it,' Tony said quietly.

'Yeah, but what now?'

'Nothing. We do nothing. It doesn't matter if Holroyd has Black in custody or not. Nobody's going to believe him.'

Cole shook his head. 'I don't know,' he said.

'What do you mean?'

'I don't trust Holroyd.'

'You don't have to trust him. Without us, he's got nothing. If we refuse to go on the record—'

'What about the Regiment?' Cole said.

'Fuck the Regiment,' Tony said. 'Those cunts in Hereford wouldn't give us the steam off their piss. If we get slotted out here, what do they give us? A plot in St Martin's churchyard and a piss-up in the squadron hangar? Bollocks to that. This way, we get a proper payday. But only ...' He swung his legs over the edge of his bunk again and looked from Dexter to Cole. '*Only* if we're all singing from the same hymn sheet. If the three of us stick to our story, we're made. One of us gets cold feet, we're fucked. Understood?'

Dexter nodded. So did Cole, but less enthusiastically. He stared at the floor for a few seconds. His hands trembled. He clenched them. Then he stood up. 'I'm going to get some air,' he said.

Tony and Dexter watched him leave. They both had blunt, dead-eyed expressions.

'You think he's losing his nerve?' Dexter said quietly.

Tony stared at the door. He nodded.

'So what do we do?'

Tony sniffed. 'I mean it, mucker. If he squeals, we're fucked. Only one thing we can do, if we want to make sure he keeps his mouth shut.' He looked at his unit mate. 'You in?'

Dexter looked over at the door, then back at Tony, then down at his dog. 'I'm in,' he said. He continued to scratch the Malinois' ears, and the dog whimpered with pleasure.

13

Danny navigated by memory, instinct and skill.

He had instant recall for the mapping the unit had examined back in Kandahar. A crescent moon was high in the sky: he followed the line joining its horns down to the horizon to approximate a southerly bearing. And once he was out of sight of the military base, he turned his headlamps back on and carefully studied the road ahead, searching for fresh earth that might indicate the presence of a newly dug-in IED. The risk of a roadside bomb was at least as significant as the risk of meeting a roving Taliban patrol or an ANA unit.

He estimated that it would take forty minutes to return to the village. He tried to work out what kind of response Holroyd could muster in that time. He was almost certain the RMP man wouldn't venture after Danny by himself. Would he get Tony and the guys to accompany him? Probably not. Holroyd was out to nail the Regiment and he seemed to think he was doing God's work. It would be too big a blow to his pride to ask for their help. If he wanted ANA support, he would probably have to wait until morning. Any NATO troops active in the area would need to be pulled off whatever ops they were engaged in. Chances of them doing that at the request of the RMP? Not good. But possible. Danny couldn't be complacent, even if it was unlikely anyone would expect him to return to the scene of the crime. In any case, he reckoned he had to be in and out before daybreak. That gave him approximately five hours.

He'd been driving for twenty minutes when the last batch of painkillers started to wear off. The pain was sinister. Cold. It felt like it was spreading from his wound all the way down his arm and torso. He stopped to neck a couple more of the pills he had taken from the med centre. They took another twenty minutes to kick in, by which time Danny was shivering hot and cold. He was also approaching the outskirts of a village, which, if his memory of the maps was correct, had to be Gareshk.

Turning the vehicle off road, he juddered over a patch of stony ground towards a line of trees. He drove the Hilux into the treeline and killed the lights. He figured that this must be the wooded area at the north of the village. He exited the vehicle and took a moment to search it for anything that might be of use. There was a jerrycan of fuel in the back, and a torch in the glove compartment. He pocketed the torch and then, clutching his stolen Glock, crouched down by the front wheel and listened hard for a full minute. There was every chance that the village would be on high alert in the wake of their attack the previous night, but Danny heard no sound to indicate that his arrival had been noted. He breathed deeply, wiped some sweat from his brow and advanced silently through the trees in a southerly direction. Fifty metres later he came to the edge of the forested area and realised that he was looking out on to the northern edge of Target Blue's compound, from the same position as he'd viewed it the night before with the rest of the unit.

He took a moment to watch and listen. Somewhere in the distance a dog was barking. Apart from that, nothing. The occupants of Gareshk had clearly decided that it was safest not to be outside. Clutching his weapon in his good hand, Danny advanced.

The previous night, he had entered through the southern entrance of the compound. But as he skirted round the perimeter, he saw that the entrance in the western wall – the one through which the rest of the unit had said they were leaving – was ajar. Danny approached it carefully, his handgun raised.

He listened hard.

Nothing.

He stepped through the doorway.

This northern half of the compound was unfamiliar to him. Last night he'd been confined to the southern section. They looked similar, however. A low-roofed room spanned the wall directly opposite the entrance, with a door to Danny's ten o'clock. Three metres to the right of the door, hanging from the wall, was the exterior fan of an old air-conditioning system, not currently working. The courtyard itself was littered with junk – rusted oil barrels, a metal trench against one wall for feeding animals, an old motorcycle propped up next to it. An ancient electrical generator was propped against one wall. It was switched off, but a greasy stench of fuel hung in the air. There was nothing to indicate that this had been the scene of a hit, or a police investigation, just the previous night. However, the door to the low-roofed room was half open, suggesting to Danny that the place was deserted.

But he was not going to take that for granted.

He crossed the courtyard silently. The crescent moon was bright enough to cast a short shadow on the ground as he moved. When he reached the open door, however, he realised he'd have to make use of the torch he'd found in the Hilux. He didn't like doing it: holding an illuminated torch made him a target if there was anyone inside. But his options were limited. He painfully raised the torch in his bad hand, held it firmly under his handgun, then swung round, entered the room and switched on the torch. He pointed the beam to the four corners of the room, directing the pistol's barrel with it, his finger resting lightly on the trigger, ready to fire at the first indication of a threat. Only when he was satisfied that the room was unoccupied did he examine it more carefully.

There was no immediate evidence that an execution had taken place in here. There was an unmade bed against the left-hand wall. Danny examined the sheets, looking for blood. There was a little, but not enough to indicate a bullet wound. There was a prayer mat rolled up on the floor next to the bed. It was pristine. Danny wasn't surprised. Tony had told Holroyd that he and the others had chased the target north. Maybe that was true. But if it wasn't, the unit wouldn't have been stupid enough to leave obvious evidence of the hit here.

So what was Danny looking for? What kind of evidence did he expect to find? He didn't really know.

He carefully shone the torch around the room. There was an old wooden table, empty. A rucksack propped against the wall. The interior mechanism of the old air-conditioning system with its vents half open. Opposite it, an ancient, heavy wardrobe, its doors open and evidence that a locking latch had been tampered with. Inside, the wardrobe was empty.

Danny swore. Without a SOCO team, what chance did he have of working out what had really happened in this room?

He turned to leave, but as he swung round, something caught his eye: a security camera, above the door.

It looked completely out of place – too modern for this Afghan compound that felt as if it hadn't changed much for a hundred years. Danny examined the camera closer. Someone had tampered with it. The power cable had been cut and a compartment on the side of the housing was open. This was clearly where a digital tape was supposed to be, but someone had removed it. Danny could hazard a pretty good guess who that had been. Standard operating procedure, Tony would have told anybody who'd asked. Unacceptable to have hostile documentary evidence of our operation.

But why was the camera there in the first place?

Danny checked which way it was pointing. Directly at the old wardrobe that looked as if it had been broken into. Why, he wondered, would anybody want to keep surveillance on a wardrobe, unless it contained something important?

He walked back over to the camera, wincing as a sharp pain ran through his left shoulder. Examined it again. Inside. Underneath. On top. Shone his torch behind. It was empty. There was nothing. He looked back to the camera.

Something wasn't right.

The camera was too blatant. Too obvious. Easy to disable, should anybody want to. Tony and the others had shown that.

What would Danny do, if he wanted to put in surveillance on a location like this? There was no question. He'd use the double camera trick.

He raised his torch again. Shone it round the room, looking for secondary hiding places. Almost immediately, his beam fell on the air-conditioning unit opposite the wardrobe. He narrowed his eyes. If the air conditioning wasn't on, why were the vents half open? One handed, Danny dragged the little table across the room, climbed up on to it and examined the unit. Shining the torch into the vents, he immediately saw what he was looking for. A second camera.

He examined the fascia of the air con unit. It was old, and the screws on either side were loose. He had it off in under a minute and immediately saw that the hidden camera was of a different order of sophistication to the one above the door. It was wireless – no tapes or hard drives – and had night-vision capability. It was not, as far as he could see, switched on. But it was a serious piece of kit. A high-end, covert surveillance device capable of uploading a live feed to a remote server.

Danny carefully replaced the air-con fascia. Moved the table back to its original place. Killed the torch beam and, standing in the darkness, analysed what he'd just discovered. There had been something of interest in this room, most likely in the wardrobe as the second camera was also pointing towards it. He didn't know what, but he was certain that Tony and the others had found it. He was equally certain that, in their haste, they'd failed to consider the possibility of the double camera trick. Which meant that someone, somewhere, had footage of them in this room last night.

But who? And where? Danny had no idea, and his leads had run dry.

Other thoughts crept into his mind. Had they put Danny out of action because they didn't want him to know what they'd found? Had they made that decision independently, or was it an officially sanctioned operational move? Either way, he knew he had to stay dark. He had no evidence. Only suspicions. And suspicions would never be enough to get Holroyd off his back.

Danny froze. There was a noise. Outside. It sounded like the entrance gate creaking.

Slowly, and in complete silence, Danny moved to the door. Weapon raised, barrel pointing up, he stood by the door frame, back to the wall. Listened hard. There was definitely movement in the courtyard outside.

Scuffling.

Then silence.

Danny gave it thirty seconds. The sound had definitely stopped. He carefully swung round the door frame, aiming his weapon out into the courtyard.

He had company. But it wasn't human.

A dog stood between Danny and the exit. For a horrible moment he thought it was Dexter's Malinois. But it was clearly a wild animal: lean and unkempt, its haunches bony, its hackles raised. Danny was a dog guy and he knew an aggressive beast when he saw it. This was one.

He directed his weapon at the dog. Stepped forward. The dog gave a low growl and flattened its back.

Danny didn't want to fire. The Glock he'd taken from the Afghan guard was not suppressed. If he released a round, he'd announce his presence to everybody in the village. But he was in no state to fight a wild dog with his bare hands.

He glanced to his left. The door leading to the southern half of the compound where Danny had been the previous night was open. He edged towards it. The dog followed, keeping low. Its eyes glinted in the moonlight. Danny couldn't turn his back on the animal. If it pounced he would have to shoot. So he moved backwards through the door that divided the compound, checking over his shoulder that nobody was waiting for him.

The courtyard was empty and silent. The welding gear was still propped up the tree that grew in the middle of the courtyard. The fire pit looked untouched. The bicycles were still leaning against the wall. It looked exactly the same as the previous night.

The dog was still following him. Prowling, but keeping a distance of five metres. Danny could smell it: a rank stench of God knows what.

It was baring its teeth. Danny continued to step back, heading towards the room in the south-western corner where he had stood guard over the wife and kids. The door was a few inches open.

This was where the atrocity had taken place.

He was five metres from the door when the dog suddenly stopped. It raised its nose and sniffed. It had clearly caught a new scent and its focus was no longer on Danny. It loped towards the room, poking its nose into the gap between the door and the door frame, and slinking inside.

Danny knew he should leave. Get out of there. Now. But something drew him to the room. He removed his torch, raised it along with his weapon, then advanced to the door. Standing in the door frame, he switched the torch on.

The bodies were no longer there, of course. The only living thing was the dog. It had pulled a bloodstained sheet from one of the beds and was gnawing hungrily at it. Momentarily, it looked towards Danny, its eyes shining in the torchlight. But the morsel in its mouth was too tempting. After a couple of seconds, it returned to its feast. A quick glance of the other bloodstained sheets told Danny that there would be no shortage of nutrition for the dog.

Danny hurried back to the northern half of the compound and exited the same way he had entered. He ran back through the treeline towards his stolen vehicle. Here, he swallowed down a couple more painkillers – the wound was throbbing – and gave himself a moment to consider his next move.

Making contact with Cornwall was out of the question, even if he had the equipment to do it. Tony had been spreading fake news about Danny, and Danny had no idea how widely that disinformation was being believed. Which left him with two options.

Option one: go into hiding. His Regiment training meant he could go off grid and stay dark for as long as was necessary.

Option two: find out who was at the other end of that covert camera. If he could do that, he could work out what Tony and the others were up to.

But how? He was alone in Helmand Province. Wounded. Under-equipped. Hunted. Friendless.

With one exception.

Danny Black got behind the wheel of the Hilux, turned over the engine, reversed out of the treeline and hit the road.

14

'What do you *mean* you've lost him?' Marcus Cadogan's voice was incredulous and the six other members of the Spearpoint personnel in the ops room were silent. 'He was fresh out of surgery and under armed guard. How the devil can you *lose* him?'

The three-way video link between Spearpoint HQ, Hereford and Camp Shorabak was grainy.

'This isn't a wet-behind-the-ears green army squaddie we're talking about,' Ray Hammond said from Hereford. The rings around his eyes were noticeably a shade darker than the last time Cadogan had seen him. 'If they'd wanted to keep Danny Black incarcerated, they should have upped their game.'

'It doesn't matter.' Holroyd's voice was scratchy over the line. 'We have enough evidence of his activities to start legal proceedings whether we have him in custody or not.'

'Legal proceedings?' Hammond asked lightly.

'Against Black, against Spearpoint and against 22 SAS.'

'You're quite a piece of work, Mike. When are you going to understand that the work of the Regiment is above your pay grade?'

'Don't talk to me like that, Hammond.'

'I'll talk to you how the hell I want. Is it not enough for you that you walked away when those men in your platoon died in Iraq. On your watch, wasn't it? Now you want to fuck things up for the rest of us?'

'How dare you—'

'Give it a break, Mike. You're on a damn crusade against my men. Jesus.'

'I'll thank you not to blaspheme when you're talking to me. And if I'm on a crusade against your men, it's no more than they deserve.'

Hammond's lugubrious eyes flashed. 'You don't know what you're talking about. You have no idea of the conditions, the expectations, the pressures—'

'*They're sin*—' Holroyd stopped himself and the word 'sinners' died on his lips.

There was a silence. Hammond looked away, shaking his head, muttering something. Holroyd's nostrils flared – he plainly knew he'd gone too far. Cadogan forced himself to remain expressionless. 'Gentlemen,' he said. 'May I suggest we do our best to keep calm in what are, after all, very difficult—'

'Don't tell me to keep calm!' Holroyd cut in. 'My duty is clear. You people have considered yourselves above the law for far too long now. Atrocities like these are the natural conclusion of that kind of attitude—'

'You're simply prejudiced against Danny Black,' Hammond said.

'Prejudiced? I certainly am prejudiced. I've seen what he did.'

'I want to speak to the rest of the unit,' Hammond said.

'That's not going to happen. They're my witnesses and they're prepared to go on the record in return for immunity.'

'Each one of those men has signed the Official Secrets Act,' Hammond said.

'Like I said,' Holroyd countered. 'Immunity. I'm informing you about Danny Black's disappearance as a matter of courtesy and because I do things by the book. But make no mistake, if he's still alive he's going down and he's taking the rest of you with him. Now if there's nothing else . . .'

The screen showing Holroyd went blank.

There was silence in the Spearpoint ops room. The eyes of all personnel were on Cadogan.

'Options?' Cadogan said.

'Limited,' Hammond replied.

'My dear chap, you do realise that if the press get hold of this, the SAS go from being the heroes of the Iranian Embassy to the villains of—'

'I understand the implications.' Hammond was not charmed by Cadogan's flowery speech.

'This Danny Black,' Cadogan said. 'I only met the fellow for a few minutes. Hard to make a judgement, but . . . he didn't strike me as the type?'

'He's not. There's more to this than meets the eye.'

'Be that as it may,' Cadogan said, 'our best course of action may well be to . . . how should one put it . . . let him take the rap. A one-off. A rogue element. Swiftly dealt with.'

'You're suggesting we get into bed with the RMPs?'

'I'm suggesting that sometimes one must take a pragmatic approach. Our pious friend seems very determined.'

Hammond shook his head. 'Black has a family. He's one of us. I need to speak to him before we make any decisions.'

'Not easy, old boy,' Cadogan said quietly. 'We don't know where the fellow is.'

'We'll find him,' Hammond said.

'How?'

'We have a unit operating north of Kabul. I'm going to give the order for them to redeploy to Helmand. They'll start the search. If Black leaves a trail, they'll find him.'

'And if he doesn't?'

'Then they'll be there to provide support if and when he puts his head above the parapet. Can everyone in the ops room hear me?'

'They can.'

'Then understand this. If Holroyd gets his way, every single person at Spearpoint is implicated. What you hear within those four walls goes no further if any of you want to stay in a job.' He nodded at Cadogan. 'I have arrangements to make,' he said. 'Let me know immediately if the situation changes.'

Cadogan's eyes narrowed as Hammond's screen went blank.

★   ★   ★

Dawn.

The unit's body clock was all messed up, so they had risen before the sun. Not that any of them had fully been asleep. Cole's dozing had been restless, occasionally muttering something in his disturbed half-slumber. Tony and Dexter had been wide awake, eyes pinned open, staring at the ceiling.

Waiting.

Cole had sat up suddenly. Stared around the room, as if momentarily unsure where he was. 'I need a piss,' he muttered, and staggered sleepily towards the door and out.

Tony and Dexter sat up. Tony switched the light on. He looked askance at Dexter, who nodded. Dexter pulled off his T-shirt to reveal his muscular torso and full sleeve of tattoos. He removed his boots, then made a clicking sound to Baron and opened the door. The dog understood the unspoken instruction perfectly: it stood up from where it was curled at Dexter's bed still wearing its ops vest, and took up position in the corridor. Dexter rummaged around in his pack and pulled out a pair of plastic SOCO gloves, which he folded carefully and put into the pocket of his camo trousers. Then he removed a spare pair of trousers, which he slung over his shoulder.

'You know what to do?' Tony said.

'Yeah.'

Dexter left, leaving the door slightly ajar. Tony heard him tell Baron to stay before he turned left down the corridor towards the washrooms.

Tony's Sig was holstered on a small table by his bunk. He sat on the edge of his bed, took the weapon out of its holster and removed the magazine. He cocked the empty weapon. Fired it. The mechanism felt perfect. He cocked it again just as the door opened and Cole entered.

Cole stood in the doorway. Stared at Tony, who was holding the weapon up at him. Hesitated.

Tony smiled. 'Relax, buddy. What you think I'm going to do? Nail you?'

He squeezed the trigger. The mechanism fired with an empty click.

As Cole entered the room, Tony lowered the weapon again. Examined it. 'Fucking thing doesn't feel right,' he said.

'What do you mean?' Cole said, sitting on the edge of his bunk.

'Ah, I dunno. Sticky. Here.' He handed it by the barrel over to Cole. 'You're the firearms guy. What do you think?'

Cole didn't take it for a moment. Then he shrugged and grabbed the handle. He cocked and discharged the weapon several times. 'Feels okay to me,' he said. 'Chuck us the magazine.'

Tony did exactly that. He watched silently as Cole examined the lip of the mag for dents, then loaded it into the Sig. He cocked and released the handgun another couple of times. 'Sweet as,' he said. He cocked it for a final time, made it safe and then handed it back to Tony, who had just stood up and was walking to the far side of the room.

'Thanks, mucker. Stick it on the bedside table, will you?'

Cole gave him an evil look, clearly unimpressed at being spoken to like a lackey. But he did as Tony asked.

'Nice one,' Tony said. He was standing by the door now, and he could see Dexter waiting just outside. The SOCO gloves were on, but he was no longer carrying the spare camo trousers.

They locked gazes. Tony nodded.

It happened in seconds. Any longer and Cole would have had the opportunity to fight back. Dexter entered the room. Marched straight up to the bedside table. Took the weapon in one gloved hand. Checked that it was cocked. Clicked off the safety. Closed in on Cole who was still sitting on the edge of his bed. Put the gun to his unit mate's right temple. Fired.

There was no suppressor. The weapon gave a full retort as the slug slammed into Cole's head. The result was catastrophic. At least a third of the skull blew away, scattering a gruesome cocktail of hair, bone and brain matter over his bunk and the wall against which it sat. Cole crumpled sideways on to the bed in an instant, his death sudden, heavy and mundane. Dexter immediately dropped the weapon, fresh with his victim's prints, on the ground where it would have naturally fallen had Cole administered the shot himself.

Blood poured heavily from Cole's skull and soaked quickly into the mattress on his bunk. The splashback had been limited but not non-existent: there were spots of red on Dexter's SOCO gloves and spattered on his torso and camo trousers.

'Get in the shower,' Tony said. 'Hide the camo trousers and the gloves. We'll get rid of them when we can.'

Dexter gave him a 'don't tell me what to do' look, then marched out of the room. As he left, he gave Baron a single instruction: 'Noise.' The dog responded immediately with several sharp barks.

Tony checked his clothes. Having moved across the room before Dexter entered, he was entirely free of blood spatter. But his work was only just beginning. He needed to get out of here. The unit was accommodated about thirty metres from the nearest ANA accommodation block. They'd have heard the gunshot in there, and would be able to hear the Malinois barking right now. But Tony estimated it would be approximately ninety seconds before anybody got to the scene. That gave him another forty-five seconds or so.

He ran ten metres down the corridor. The toilets were on the right, the showers on the left. He turned into the toilets. Entered. Unbuckled his belt. Undid the button on his camo trousers. Paused, listening at the door. The dog was still barking.

He only had to wait about twenty seconds before he heard footsteps and shouting. He stepped into one of the line of three cubicles and flushed the chain. Then stepped out into the corridor, doing up his button, the noise of the flush ongoing as the door shut behind him. There were four ANA soldiers approaching the bunk room. Two of them were carrying pistols. To Tony's trained eye, they looked like a bunch of amateurs. But they were here, and that was what mattered. They were evidently apprehensive about approaching the barking Malinois, but one of them was braver than the others and got close enough to the open door to look in. He started shouting dramatically in Pashto. The others crowded round him.

'Hey!' Tony shouted above the chaotic noise of the dog barking and the soldiers talking anxiously to each other. He did up his belt as he strode towards them. 'What the hell's going on?' As he reached the congregation around the door, he pushed through them to look into the bunk room.

He stared, as if in shock. The ANA guys fell silent, although the dog was still barking. The animal was clearly on edge. Its teeth were bared, and it was looking around for its handler.

'Jesus ...' Tony stepped back, shaking his head. 'Dexter,' he breathed. Then he shouted: 'Dexter, get here, now!'

Dexter was already emerging into the corridor from the shower rooms opposite the toilets. His hair and beard were wet. He was wearing the new camo trousers. Beads of water dripped down his torso. 'What the fuck's going on?' he said.

'Get Holroyd.'

'Why? What the fuck—'

'Cole's done himself in. Get him *now*!'

But there was no need. Holroyd was running down the corridor, red-faced. He pushed through the ANA soldiers. They complained loudly in Pashto and the area around the door was chaos again. '*Can't you stop this dog barking?*' Holroyd shouted.

Something seemed to flip in the dog's behaviour. It lurched forward, clearly disturbed, and bit one of the ANA soldiers around the ankle, an aggressive growl emanating from its throat. The ANA soldier screamed in pain and the crowd around the door was suddenly twice as noisy. Dexter shouted a command at the Malinois and the dog released its bite. The soldier staggered back, then crouched down to grab his bleeding ankle while the other soldiers fell silent again. He gave Dexter a poisonous look as the SAS man bent down to calm the dog, who was still snarling and baring his teeth.

As he did this, Holroyd was standing in the doorway, staring silently into the room. He swore under his breath.

Tony turned his back on the room. Pinched his forehead. He felt Holroyd's hand on his shoulder. 'You okay?' the RMP man said.

'I was just having a shit,' Tony said. 'Dexter was in the shower.' He exhaled heavily. 'I shouldn't have fucking left him on his own.

I knew he wasn't right. He'd been up all night, talking. Couldn't shut him up. I didn't think he'd . . .' He left it hanging as he looked over his shoulder into the room again. 'Jesus, he used my fucking gun . . .'

Holroyd grabbed him by both shoulders. 'Listen to me. It's not your fault, okay? If somebody wants to top themselves on an army base, there's a million opportunities. This isn't on you.'

'We should have kept an eye on him.'

'*Will you stay out of there!*' Holroyd barked at one of the ANA guys who had just set foot inside the room. Dexter was looking, ashen-faced, into the room, shaking his head. 'Listen,' Holroyd said. 'You're my guys, okay? You understand that? Stuff like this . . .' He pointed into the room. 'This is why we need to lift the lid on what's going on.'

They stared at him, dumbly.

'From now on, you're with the good guys, okay? The Regiment needs its wings clipping, and the three of us, we're going to do that. Okay?' He looked from one to the other. '*Okay?*'

Tony and Dexter nodded. Dexter clicked his fingers and Baron was immediately by his side. He knelt down to stroke the dog while Holroyd stepped up to the room and firmly closed the door. 'Nobody enters,' he told the ANA guys. They seemed to understand the gist of his instructions because they stepped back from the door.

'I'll get the medical boys here immediately,' Holroyd told Tony and Dexter. 'I'll inform Hereford and we'll get him repatriated as soon as possible. You don't talk. Anybody tries to tap you up about what happened, you let me know. Understood?'

Tony and Dexter nodded.

Holroyd pointed at the dog. 'That animal needs to be isolated.' When Dexter looked like he was going to complain, Holroyd interrupted him. 'Don't tell me he doesn't like kennels. I don't want to hear it. The Afghans won't tolerate it attacking their men. It's for the animal's own safety.'

'Safety my arse,' Dexter said. 'He's more vulnerable where they can—'

'He's right,' Tony interrupted, and when Dexter looked like arguing, he repeated himself. 'He's right.' Dexter didn't look happy, but he backed down.

'Come on,' Holroyd said. 'Let's get you two out of here.'

He turned on his heel and marched down the corridor. Tony and Dexter followed, the Malinois trotting obediently behind. It showed no sign of its former aggression. At one point, the two SAS men glanced at each other. But they didn't hold their gaze for long. They had an appearance of shock and mourning to keep up, after all.

There were times when the four walls of Caitlin Wallace's tiny room inside her compound started to close in on her. Times when she needed to get outside, without being shadowed by Tommy or by her interpreter. This was one of them.

The night had been long, and she'd slept poorly. There were too many questions going round in her head. Why had Spearpoint blocked her from questioning the local Imam about Al-Zafawi, the Taliban leader? Surely that was exactly the kind of intel she was on the ground to gather. She could have seen to it that the Imam wasn't in a state to tip Al-Zafawi off, and if she wasn't allowed to follow up her leads, what was the point of being here in the first place? These were the questions that circled in her brain, and which continued to circle as, in the quiet darkness of the half hour before dawn, she strapped on her handgun, covered her camo gear, boots and T-shirt with blue robes, wrapped a head-dress around her head so only her eyes were showing, and stepped out into the street.

It was deserted. The call to prayer had not yet been sounded, nor had the inhabitants of the small town of Panjika emerged from their houses. Caitlin had only walked a few paces before admitting to herself that this was not a random pre-dawn walk. She had a destination this morning. She kept to the shadows as she hurried past compounds and individual dwellings, along the ramshackle main street of the village and past the pitiful shops that were all shuttered up. She arrived at the mosque in about five minutes and stood, for a moment, in the shadow of a single tree about thirty metres from the building, watching its entrance.

It was not an impressive-looking place, although the cover of darkness made it look less like a building site, despite the silhouettes of steel reinforcing rods from the reconstructed corner sprouting up into the sky. Caitlin stared at the entrance for a couple of minutes, before swearing under her breath. She didn't even know why she was here. What the hell did she think was going to happen? That Al–Zafawi would stroll up to the mosque while she was watching and waiting? In any case, the implication from her source had been that Al–Zafawi visited the Imam at the family compound on the other side of the dried–up riverbed behind the mosque. And even if she saw him, what would Caitlin do? Her instructions from Spearpoint were clear: don't follow that line of inquiry.

But why? Five minutes passed and the questions started circling her head again.

So much so that she almost missed it.

The movement had come from the eastern corner of the mosque, to Caitlin's two o'clock. For a moment she thought she'd imagined it. But then a bird, clearly disturbed by something, flew up from the same position. There had definitely been somebody there.

Caitlin pressed herself up against the tree trunk. Her pulse had suddenly accelerated. She had the unnerving feeling that somebody had been watching her.

Get back to the compound, she told herself. *You don't need a confrontation now . . .*

She glanced back the way she came. And the voice in her head that had just advised caution instantly acknowledged that she was going to do nothing of the sort.

Caitlin slipped her right hand into a slit in her robes and loosened her pistol in its holster. She kept it hidden, but held it firmly as she stepped out from beneath the tree and crossed the open ground towards the mosque, scanning left and right. She moved silently and reached the front of the mosque in under thirty seconds. There she stopped and listened. It was almost unnaturally silent. She crept towards the corner of the mosque. She removed her handgun. Held it head height, barrel up. She quickly turned the corner and scanned the ground in front of her.

Nothing.

Only then did she feel the unmistakable pressure of a gun barrel against the back of her head.

She froze.

Very slowly, she lowered her weapon. Made it safe, then dropped it on the ground.

A male voice spoke. 'Desert boots under your robes. A Sig nine millimetre. Call me cynical, but I'm thinking you're not quite who you seem.'

Caitlin blinked heavily. That voice seemed out of place, here in the humid darkness of a Helmand dawn. But there was no doubt that she recognised it.

Slowly, she removed her headdress. Turned round to face the gunman.

He didn't look good. He had scruffy black hair. Several days' stubble. His face was pale and although his pistol was still raised in his right hand, he held his left as if it was broken.

'Call *me* cynical,' Caitlin said, 'but I'm thinking that *you*, arriving *here*, right *now* – that's probably not good news. Am I right, Danny Black, or am I right?'

15

Danny lowered his weapon. Looked around the deserted area. 'You should put your headdress back on,' he said. 'Women don't walk the streets of—'

'You're really going to mansplain to *me* what the women of this village do and don't do?' Caitlin bit back in her spiky Australian accent. But she did put the headdress back on.

Danny allowed himself a smile. He liked Caitlin. Maybe a little too much. She'd made it pretty clear on a previous op that she was interested in him. He'd turned her down and she'd embarked on a short-lived fling with Tony, of all people. But there was always that frisson between them whenever they saw each other.

'Jesus, Danny,' she said, 'you scared the living crap out of me there. What the fuck are you doing here? Last I heard you were on Tony's team.'

'Didn't work out,' Danny said.

'How did you get here?'

'Stole a vehicle. It's in a ditch on the north side of the village.' He looked around. 'Where can we talk?'

'Back at my compound.'

'Who else is there?'

'My interpreter. And Tommy – you know, D squadron.'

Danny shook his head. He had his doubts about making contact even with Caitlin. If he was to stay dark, he needed to keep his location a secret from anyone else with the ability to report it back to Hereford. 'Anywhere else? We need to get off the street. It's going to get light any minute.'

Caitlin thought for a moment. 'Follow me,' she said.

She led Danny further up the main street, turning left by a line of old motorbikes, up to a two-storey building with heavy shutters on the ground floor. 'I know the woman who lives here,' Caitlin said. 'Her old man and daughter are in hospital. Little boy died in a road bomb a couple of nights back. I've been helping her out. She doesn't speak any English.'

Caitlin led them up a rough external staircase to the first floor. She knocked lightly, then let herself in through the unlocked door and removed her headdress. Danny found himself in a poor living space. The only light came from a flickering gas lamp whose yellow flame illuminated mattresses in two corners, a rickety table with four chairs and an ancient gas stove. A woman lay on one of the mattresses. Her ankle was bandaged and her face covered with steristrips. She was muttering deliriously to herself and didn't seem to register Danny and Caitlin's arrival.

'She was hurt by the IED,' Caitlin murmured. 'I think she'll pull through, but for now ...' She waved one arm around the room as if to indicate that this was now their domain. 'What the hell are you doing here, Danny? What's happening?'

Danny closed his eyes. Took a deep breath. Then he started talking. He told Caitlin everything. The details of the hit on Target Red. What happened when they made a move on Target Blue. His injury. Holroyd. The atrocity. Escaping from Camp Shorabak. The hidden camera he'd found in the compound. Everything. And as he spoke, he became increasingly unsure of himself, and of the wisdom of tracking Caitlin down. Would she believe him? Would Danny, in her shoes? He wasn't sure. Danny's trump card was that Caitlin had been on ops with Tony before. That, and her ill-advised relationship, meant she knew what he was like. She knew what he was capable of.

Danny finished his explanation. He fell silent. Caitlin would have questions. She would try to pick holes in his account. He gave her the space to do just that.

'The gear,' she said.

Danny was momentarily wrong-footed. 'What gear?'

'The gear that Tony and the others found on the Taliban targets they've been hitting. The laser sights. The encrypted radios. What was it you found at Target Red's compound – an SF helmet?'

Danny nodded.

'Did Tony relay that stuff back to Spearpoint?'

'It came up in the briefing. It's not that important. What matters is—'

'It is important,' Caitlin cut in. As she spoke, there was a wailing from outside. It made Danny momentarily start, until he realised what it was: the call to prayer from the nearby mosque. Dawn must have arrived. Caitlin moved to the door, checked there was nobody outside, then returned to Danny. 'Does the "Red Unit" mean anything to you?'

Danny shook his head. 'I just need to get to the bottom of why Tony—'

'Will you shut the fuck up, Danny? You came to me for intel, right? Well let me lay it on you.'

Danny made a 'go ahead' gesture. Caitlin paused for a moment while she formulated her thoughts. 'I hear things, you understand? I'm in thick with the women of the village. They know more than their husbands and the tribal elders think. The guys, they reckon just because they can keep the women silent, they can stop them listening, using their brains. It's a pretty dumb mistake. In the last six months, I must have identified fifteen high-value Taliban targets, just by talking to the women. Spearpoint has been confirming my intel, then green-lighting targets for Tony and his kill team. The only thing is, they've started getting picky about which bits of intel they act on, and which bits they sit on.'

'What do you mean?'

'There's one name that keeps coming up. Mohammad Al-Zafawi. He's a Taliban commander. He lived in the UK back in the day, just one of your regular student extremist crazies. Now he has a list of atrocities as long as your arm – kids, hospitals, you name it, he's blown it up. The word is that he's putting together a team of Taliban fighters trained to SF level. That's what the Red Unit is. Taliban special forces.'

'It'll never happen,' Danny said. 'You know what SF training involves. Expertise, time, money. What does it cost to train up one SAS guy? A couple of million? Doesn't matter what they call themselves, they'll still be amateurs.'

Caitlin gave him a sceptical look. 'Amateurs with laser sights, encrypted radios and SF helmets?' she said. 'Jeez, Danny, you don't strike me as the type to underestimate the other guy. Trust me, the Red Unit's a thing, and Al-Zafawi's at the head of it.'

'I'll take your word for it,' Danny said.

'You do that.' Caitlin looked over at the woman lying deliriously on her bed. 'That woman gave me a solid lead on Al-Zafawi. I phoned it through to Spearpoint, asked their permission to follow it up. They weren't interested. Stamped me down immediately.'

'Did they give a reason?'

'Oh, sure, they said—'

Caitlin was interrupted by a groan from the woman on the mattress. She moved over to check on her. The woman fell silent and lay there breathing heavily. Caitlin returned to Danny. 'There's this Imam at the mosque. I've seen him a few times. Even spoke to him once. He's a frail old guy. Looks like your regular village elder – beard, robes, you get the picture. He's a Taliban sympathiser, but he commands respect in the village. There's a rumour that Al-Zafawi has contact with him. Consults the old boy pretty regular, or that's what I've heard. I asked Spearpoint for permission to interrogate him.' She shrugged. 'Look, he's not going to give up the location of one of his congregation just because I ask him to, so there's a chance the interrogation might get a bit spicy. Spearpoint said no. I'm here to win hearts and minds. Squeeze my intel out of the locals the softly softly way. If I start roughing up their precious Imam, I might lose a few of them.' She made a disgusted snort. 'Like I'd even let anyone know it was me,' she said.

'Panjika's not a big place. People would put two and two together. Maybe Spearpoint's on the level. Maybe that *is* the reason they don't want you near him.'

'Don't make me laugh. Every Western intelligence service in the world wants to put their hands on him, and you weren't in on the conversation. They were cutting me short with a bullshit excuse. There's a reason they don't want me going after Al-Zafawi—'

'Hang on,' Danny interrupted. 'You said you spoke to him?'

'Sure.'

'He speaks English?'

'Yeah, pretty well.'

'Why would some back-country Helmand Province Imam speak English?'

'I don't know,' Caitlin said. 'I guess I just—'

'You said Al-Zafawi was a student in the UK?'

She nodded.

The call to prayer was still continuing and there was a steely grey light spilling in under the door. Danny considered what Caitlin had just said. It was true that something didn't quite add up. The whole point of the Spearpoint operation was to take out high-value Taliban targets. Why would they be resistant to taking out one of the highest? And if they both spoke English, had they *met* in the UK? Had the Imam radicalised Al-Zafawi in the first place? Was he now Al-Zafawi's guy, embedded in this village?

'Fuck it,' Caitlin said. 'If they want to ignore a lead that could take them to the head of the Red Unit, that's their lookout. But if I was you, I know who *my* next call would be.'

Danny nodded. Whatever the Imam's history, he knew what she was driving at. The targets the kill team had been hitting had been in possession of expensive military gear that would only normally be in the possession of well-funded special forces. They didn't come from nowhere. If what Caitlin was telling him about the Red Unit was true, the presence of that equipment suggested a direct link between Target Blue and Al-Zafawi.

'What do we have on this Imam?' Danny said. 'Leverage-wise.'

'There's the family. They live on the other side of the village.'

Danny gave that a moment's thought, but quickly rejected it. He was out to prove that he hadn't butchered one Taliban family.

It wouldn't help his cause if he went about it by turning the screw on another without official sanction.

'I think I need to have a little face to face with our Imam,' he said. 'Want to join me?'

Caitlin stared at him. 'Spearpoint are right about one thing,' she said. 'If the locals think I've hurt the old guy, my cred will be blown.'

'It doesn't matter,' Danny said. 'Spearpoint's dead in the water. Holroyd will see to that if Tony blows the whistle for him. We don't get to the bottom of this, you'll get dragged into the shit storm too.'

Caitlin gave a grim smile. 'If he finds out I've been helping you, I *definitely* will.'

'So you want to get into bed with Tony and Holroyd?'

'Maybe I don't want to get into bed with any of you,' Caitlin said. 'Maybe I don't want to get in the crossfire of a bunch of alpha males who won't stop shooting till one of them's out of the game.'

Danny stared her down. 'Maybe,' he said. 'I wouldn't blame you.' He looked around the room. 'You heard about Spud?'

She nodded. 'I'm sorry. He was a good mate of yours.'

'Helped you out of a fix or two and all.' And Danny refrained from saying what didn't need to be said: that he himself had been instrumental in saving Caitlin's life on ops before now.

'More than I can say for Tony,' Caitlin said. 'What's he up to, Danny? What really happened the other night?'

'That's what I'm going to find out. Are you with me?'

Caitlin sniffed. 'Of course I'm with you,' she said. 'We'll go find our Imam after midday prayers. That's when things are at their quietest round here. Too hot for anyone to be active. ANA patrols keep to the shade.'

'And you don't mention this to Tommy or your interpreter. For all I know, Holroyd's got half the British army out looking for me.'

'Noted,' Caitlin said. 'You can hide out here. Nobody wants anything to do with this one.' She pointed at the woman on the mattress. 'Now take your shirt off. Relax, Danny Black, I think I can just about manage to keep my hands off you. But that wound is going to need cleaning out and I need to take a look at it first.'

Danny had been running on adrenaline. Now that he had a moment to rest, alone with the delirious Afghan woman, his exhaustion and hunger caught up with him. His gun wound was pulsating and a cold pain crept down his arm and across his torso. Caitlin had returned to her compound to get some supplies. Danny had positioned himself in a seated position, his back to the wall facing the entrance. He kept his stolen handgun by his side, gripping it with his good hand. The delirious woman presented no real threat, but he couldn't be sure, despite Caitlin's reassurances, that an unexpected guest wouldn't arrive. He felt almost naked with only a single clip of ammo, but it was what it was. He did what he could to stay awake and alert.

Without success. He was woken by Caitlin gently shaking his good shoulder. He started and felt for his gun, but Caitlin had moved it away. 'Let's not have a negligent discharge when I'm in the line of fire, eh?' she said.

Danny cursed himself for falling asleep. He felt worse for it, not better. 'How long—' he started to say.

'Relax. Twenty minutes, max. Here, get this down you.' Caitlin ripped open a foil-packed MRE. Danny wolfed down the cold sludge straight from the packet, then gulped down a canteen full of water, which had the faintly chlorinated taste of purification tablets. He felt his body soaking up the liquid. 'Okay, Rambo,' Caitlin said. 'Let's have a look at that wound.'

Danny removed his stolen camo jacket and winced as Caitlin peeled off the dirty dressing covering the wound. 'Okay,' she said calmly. 'They've closed it up pretty good. I'm just going to give it a clean, then we'll pad it up again.'

She worked efficiently, filling a syringe from a sealed pack of sterile water and using that to flood the wound, before cleaning the area with antibacterial gauze and applying a fresh dressing. It hurt, but Danny waited until she was done before necking another couple of painkillers.

'Okay, fella,' Caitlin said. 'You need to get some shut-eye.'

'No way,' Danny said. 'Someone's got to keep stag—'

As he spoke, Caitlin removed a Sig 9mm. 'You're telling me I'm not up to the gig?'

Danny smiled. 'No,' he said. 'Nothing like.'

'You've got about five hours,' she said. 'Then we move on the Imam.'

'Roger that,' Danny said.

He lay down on the hard floor. Almost immediately, he was asleep.

Camp Shorabak was no longer home to military dogs. But this had not always been the case. In the days of the ISAF occupation, working dogs had been commonplace, and a dedicated area set aside for their accommodation. Holroyd's insistence that the Malinois be confined meant that as the sun rose over the desert, Tony and Dexter found themselves heading to that seldom-visited section of the camp – much to Dexter's annoyance.

'That twat doesn't know what he's talking about,' he muttered. 'I understand Baron. He's more comfortable with human company. He gets edgy if he's separated from me.'

'Mate, he just bit one of the camel jockeys,' Tony observed. It hadn't escaped his notice that Dexter was a lot more upset at having to put the dog into confinement than at Cole's death.

'Course he did. He was stressing him out.'

'Well, let's put him somewhere there's *no* ANA to stress him out, okay?' And when Dexter looked like he was going to continue arguing, Tony stopped and grabbed him by one arm. 'Listen to me,' he said in a low voice. 'We've got Holroyd eating out of our hands right now. We're going to be on a plane out of here in the next twenty-four hours – you, me, the dog. For now, we do what he says. Let him think he's in charge. Got it?'

Dexter gave him a dark look. 'That ANA cunt was lucky Baron didn't go for his throat,' he said, but he didn't argue any more.

The working dog accommodation was in the north-western corner of the camp. There was a high-fenced enclosure about the size of a tennis court – an exercise yard where handlers could throw balls and perform training routines with their animals. The ground inside the enclosure was dusty and littered with debris and stones. It plainly hadn't been used for a very long time. The gate in the fence was unlocked. Tony and Dexter walked across the exercise yard towards a line of man-high, steel-barred dog crates with enclosed kennels at the rear. Dexter had to drag the reluctant Malinois towards one of them: the dog clearly knew what the kennels were and had no desire to be cooped up inside one. Tony loitered in the exercise yard while Dexter entered one of the kennels with the dog. He looked around. There was a handful of military vehicles driving west–east across the camp about 150 metres away. A chopper was coming in to land from the south. But this section of the camp was deserted, apart from them. He had the impression that this was normally so.

A strategy began to form in his mind.

'He'll need water,' he called to Dexter over his shoulder. 'It's going to get hot in there.' But he couldn't see either the dog or its handler – both were inside the covered kennel area. He could hear Dexter talking soothingly to the animal. When he emerged a minute later, he was tightening the lid of an empty water canteen. He exited the crate and closed the door latch behind him. There was no sight or sound of the Malinois. It had remained in the kennel.

'Maybe you should take its ops vest off,' Tony said.

'He's more comfortable with it on.'

'Hot though.'

'Look, who's his fucking handler, Tony? You or me?'

'Just a thought.'

'A stupid one.'

Dexter was stony faced as they walked back across the exercise yard. Tony kept quiet until they'd left the enclosure. 'We need to get back to Holroyd,' he said. 'He wants to debrief us about Cole. You got it all straight in your head.'

Dexter stopped walking. 'You need to stop talking to me like I'm a fucking child.'

Tony stared at him. Then he raised both hands. 'Buddy,' he said, 'take a chill pill.'

'Don't tell me to fucking chill. Cole was our mate. I didn't see you putting a gun to his frickin' skull.' Strain was telling around Dexter's eyes.

'Mate, I just want to make sure we're singing from the same hymn sheet. Holroyd's a dickhead, but if our stories don't add up—'

'I'm fucking watching you, Tony. Don't think you can do me the way you did Cole.'

'*You* did him, buddy. Remember that. *You* did him.'

Dexter gave him an evil look, then spat on the dusty ground. 'Let's get back,' he said.

He strode off towards the centre of the base. Tony watched him go. He glanced back towards the dog enclosure, taking a mental snapshot to confirm the geography of the area. Then he jogged towards Dexter and fell in beside him. His unit mate clearly wasn't in the mood to talk, and that suited Tony just fine.

Danny's sleep was uncomfortable and disturbed. He kept reliving the moment he was hit and the gruesome sight of the butchered bodies. And he kept seeing Tony's face: ruthless, calculating. More than once he woke suddenly, half expecting to see Tony standing over him. But all he saw was the outline of Caitlin, still in her robes but crouching down with her 9mm pointing at the door.

He was dragged out of sleep for a final time by the sound of the midday call to prayer echoing across the village.

'Hey, sleeping beauty,' Caitlin said as Danny sat up, sweating heavily. 'You stink like a dingo's ball sack. No offence.'

'None taken. Is there any more water?' His throat was sandpaper, his limbs lead.

Caitlin chucked him another canteen. 'Go easy,' she said. 'It's all we have left.'

Danny used a couple of mouthfuls to get some more painkillers down his throat. Then he stood up. 'Let's go.'

'Hold your horses,' Caitlin said. 'You can't go walking around like that in the middle of the day. The villagers are used to seeing Tommy, but not you. You'll freak them out. Here, put these on.'

She threw him a bundle of blue material: another set of women's robes. Whoever had supplied them had been a big girl, because they looked like they would fit Danny well.

'I brought you some bits and bobs,' she added. She handed Danny an M4, a couple of full clips and a lanyard. An ops vest filled with a couple of fragmentation grenades and a flashbang. A night sight. Danny silently accepted the gear. He put the ops vest on, slung the assault rifle by the lanyard down his side and then pulled on the robes. She handed him a headdress, which Danny put on. He didn't like the way it limited his peripheral vision, but Caitlin was right: stealth was crucial. He made his handgun safe and plunged it into a slot in the robes.

Caitlin had done the same. Fully robed up, she was now leaning over the delirious woman. 'Asleep,' Caitlin said. 'She'll be okay.' She straightened herself up. 'We'll give it ten minutes,' she said.

'How old is our guy?'

'Hard to tell. Looks pretty ancient, the way some of these Afghan guys can. I'd say he's in his seventies.'

'I might have to get rough with him. You got a problem with that?'

'What do you think I am, some kind of fucking snowflake?'

'No, but if he's an old fella—'

'Listen, if he's thick with Al-Zafawi, he deserves everything he gets. The things those Taliban guys do to women and children? One of his hits in Pakistan killed a hundred kids. Do what you have to do. If it turns your stomach, ask me and I'll do it for you.'

'You've got the layout of the mosque's exterior in your head?' she said.

'Remind me,' Danny said. It had been dark that morning and he'd been preoccupied with locating Caitlin.

'The front is a low, single-storey building with a concrete dome and an arched entrance. No good for us – men only – but that's where most of the guys will be going in and out for prayers. No women, of course. Adjoining that, at the rear, there's a two-storey building. Shuttered windows on three sides, but I've never seen them open. The back of that building was damaged several years ago. Reconstruction has stalled so it's a building site out back. There's a single exit. If we want to get into the mosque, that's the one to use.'

'Is it locked?'

'I don't know.'

'Any suitable OP?'

'Sure. About thirty metres from the building site out back there's the shell of an old armoured lorry. It's been completely stripped down and it's not going anywhere without a pickup. The riverbed is about twenty metres beyond it, but it's set at an angle – we'd be out of sight of the compounds on the western side of the river, and it'll give us eyes on the rear of the mosque.'

'Not both of us,' Danny said. 'One of us needs to keep eyes on the front, in case he leaves that way.'

'That's your call,' Caitlin said. 'But I've been watching him for the past couple of days. I've never seen him use that front entrance. It's quicker for him to use the rear entrance to get across the river and back to his family compound. I suggest we either put in surveillance from the rear of the old lorry, or we enter the mosque from the back.'

Danny gave that a moment's consideration. Caitlin knew the ground. He should listen to her. 'Okay,' he said. 'Surveillance first. If it doesn't look like he's coming out, we'll move in. When it happens, we want him on his own. I don't want this to be noisy, and I don't want to leave a string of bodies that will make anyone looking for me start sniffing around here. If he's got company, we hold off. Wait till he's alone. Got it?'

'Understood.'

Danny took up position by the door and waited. They stood in silence for ten minutes. 'Let's do it,' he said.

Danny lowered his head and hunched his shoulders to make himself look less imposing as Caitlin led the way out of the dwelling, down the stone steps and into the street. It was insanely hot. Within seconds, the cloth of Danny's robes was scorching his skin. They walked side by side towards the top of the main street. It was practically deserted: the handful of people Danny saw seemed to be hurrying to get out of the heat. He scanned left and right as they headed south towards the mosque. Here, a few Afghan men were leaving by the arched front entrance. The men paid Danny and Caitlin no attention as they turned right to skirt along the side of the mosque towards the rear of the building.

A heat haze shimmered from the unmade breeze blocks piled up around the unreconstructed area around the back of the mosque. A black bird of some description sat on one of these piles, silently watching them as they passed. Thirty metres up ahead, Danny saw the derelict armoured lorry Caitlin had mentioned. He looked around to check they weren't being observed. There was nobody in the vicinity and the shutters of the mosque's first floor windows were closed, just as Caitlin had predicted. They advanced swiftly towards the vehicle.

It truly was a husk. The tyres had been removed, the windows were long gone and the metal panels of the chassis were corroded. But it afforded good cover, especially now that the sun was high and their shadows short. Danny crouched behind the front end of the lorry. The open desert around him was a featureless expanse of shimmering brown earth meeting piercing blue sky, with a mountain range off to Danny's ten o'clock. There was no cover in that direction: anyone approaching would be visible from miles off. Turning towards the village, he peered round the corner of the lorry and had direct line of sight over the thirty metres of open ground, the rubble at the back of the mosque, and the rear entrance that also shimmered in the heat haze. Caitlin took up position at the opposite end of the vehicle.

'Eyes on?' Danny asked.

'You bet.'

Time check: 12.23 hours. Danny kept a constant watch on the back of the mosque – not only the entrance, but also the shuttered windows on the first floor, checking for movement or any other

164

indication of counter-surveillance. The movement of a shutter. The glint of an optical device. There was none. If anybody had seen two apparently female robed figures setting up an OP, and were watching them, they were making a good job of not being seen.

'Hey, Danny,' Caitlin said after they'd been watching for a couple of minutes. 'Tony mention me at all?'

'Don't tell me you've still got your sights on him.'

'Give me a break,' Caitlin said, her voice contemptuous. 'I'm just curious is all.'

'He didn't mention you.'

A pause.

'Good,' Caitlin said. 'I prefer it that—'

'Movement,' Danny cut in.

The door at the rear of the mosque had opened. Danny squinted, trying to see through the heat haze. Three people were exiting. As they picked their way through the building site at the back of the mosque, Danny identified their features. Two of them were young men, probably in their twenties. They looked almost identical: short-cropped hair and long black beards. Plain Afghan robes. One of them had a rucksack slung over his right shoulder. The third man was much older. His beard was grey but short-cropped, his shoulders somewhat stooped. His face was very dark and deeply lined, but to Danny's eye he looked surprisingly like an Afghan Jeremy Corbyn.

'Is that our guy?' Danny said quietly.

'That's our guy,' Caitlin replied.

The Imam held his hands behind his back and was talking as he walked. The two younger men listened intently. When they reached the edge of the building site, the older man stopped talking. He reached inside his robes, looked around to check he wasn't being observed, then removed a handgun. He looked at it, nodded approvingly, and handed it to the young man who dropped it rather carelessly into his rucksack. He and his companion nodded respectfully at the Imam, then turned and walked along the side of the mosque, back towards the main street. The Imam watched them go.

He suddenly turned and stared directly towards the lorry, squinting. Danny froze. He knew that the slightest movement from either of them would reveal their location. The Imam kept his gaze on the vehicle for almost ten seconds, before shaking his head, turning and, still stooped, walking back towards the mosque's rear entrance.

'You reckon he was giving those two lads spiritual guidance as well as live firearms?' Danny asked.

'I guess there's only one way to find out. If Spearpoint saw that little exchange, I don't reckon they'd feel so bad about knocking the old boy around a bit.'

Danny watched him disappear through the door. Scanned the surrounding area again. The two younger men were out of sight. There was nobody around to see them. 'Let's go,' he said.

They crossed the open ground between the lorry and the mosque side by side, heads bowed. When they reached the building site, Danny checked their surroundings again. Nothing, so they picked their way across the building rubble towards the old wooden door set in the back wall of the building.

The mortar on the wall surrounding the door was coming away in large patches. Danny also picked out a line of bullet marks forming an arc a couple of metres above the door. There was a heavy iron latch, which he lifted. The door creaked open. A blast of cooler air emerged, but it was dark inside and Danny's visibility was less than a metre.

He stepped inside, followed by Caitlin. They gave themselves a moment to adjust to the relative interior darkness. They were in an almost empty back room. There were robes hanging on hooks along one wall, and another door opposite them. This one looked sturdier, but only a little. They approached it quickly and quietly. Danny listened at the door frame. Silence at first. Then –

'Footsteps,' Danny breathed. 'Step back from the door.'

Caitlin positioned herself three metres from the door while Danny stood with his back to the wall, a metre from the door frame. He removed his handgun and raised it.

Breathed slowly as he waited.

The door clicked open. A dusty light from inside the mosque flooded out. The Imam appeared in the doorway. He stopped, his eyes fixed on the robed and hooded figure of Caitlin standing in the darkness in front of him. The old man started – he was clearly nervous about something – then his expression changed from one of surprise to one of annoyance. He started to speak. Danny didn't understand his words but he sure understood the harsh nature of them as he reprimanded Caitlin in an aggressive and patronising way.

But he fell silent a few seconds later when he felt the barrel of Danny's handgun hard against the side of his skull.

'Next time you speak without my permission,' Danny said, 'I'll kill you. If you understand, nod.'

The Imam nodded.

'Is there anybody else in the mosque? Say yes or no.'

'This is an outrage!'

'Yes or no?'

'No.'

'You understand that if you're lying, you'll be dead within a minute? Say yes or no.'

The Imam looked like he was going to argue, but thought better of it. 'Yes.'

'Take three steps forward, then get to your knees.'

The Imam did as he was told. Danny moved forward with him. He jutted his chin out at Danny, refusing to kneel. So Danny put his gun to the old man's head. That got him to the ground. He looked up at Caitlin. 'Check it,' he said.

Caitlin entered the mosque without speaking.

'Many people will come,' the Imam said. 'In one minute, they will be here.'

Danny said nothing.

'They will drag you into the village and shoot you.'

Danny's continued silence had the desired effect: the Imam started to tremble, and his trembling got worse, quickly. By the time Caitlin returned, a minute later, Danny was pretty sure from a waft of urine that the old boy had pissed himself.

'It's clear,' Caitlin said. 'Front entrance is locked from the inside.'

Danny bent down and pulled the Imam up by the scruff of his robes. The old man wriggled vigorously. Danny kept his grip and pushed him through the door back into the mosque. Only then did he remove his headdress so the Imam could see his face. The old man looked at him like he was looking at the devil. That was fine by Danny. He wanted his target to think the very worst of him. He looked around the interior of the mosque. It was plain. No frills. The room itself was square, twenty metres by twenty. To Danny's right there was a raised area, like a plain altar, where he assumed the Imam would ordinarily stand. Against the front wall was the arched door Danny had identified from outside. To either side of it were wooden racks for shoes. The walls were covered in brushed Arabic script, although the plaster on which it had been painted was crumbling away in places. Along one wall was a bookcase with perhaps twenty or thirty old books. And in the far left corner there was a circular stone font, about three metres in diameter, surrounded by a couple of wooden benches. Danny pointed towards it. 'What's that?' he asked Caitlin.

'It's where they wash before prayers,' Caitlin said. She removed her headdress. The Imam looked outraged at the sight of a woman speaking to a man in his prayer room. His expression changed quickly to one of recognition – he clearly knew who Caitlin was.

'You!' he said. 'A woman?'

'Count the tits, darling,' Caitlin said. She pointed back the way they came. 'I'll watch the exit.'

Danny nodded.

'Hey,' Caitlin said. 'If there's any chance of anyone seeing him, he needs to be intact.'

'Don't worry about that,' Danny said. He turned to the Imam. 'Why don't you have a little wash,' he said.

He used his weapon to prod the old man in the direction of the font. The Imam had bare feet, so he made no noise as he stumbled towards it. Danny's booted footsteps echoed around the prayer room as he followed close behind. When they reached the font, Danny saw that the water inside was about five inches deep, and stagnant. Deep enough for his purposes, and its cleanliness didn't matter.

Danny swapped his gun over to his bad hand, then grabbed the Imam by the back of the neck and, ignoring a sudden sharp pain from his wound, forced him to bend over the edge of the font. Danny plunged the old man's face into the shallow water. The Imam flailed his bony arms and kicked his feet. But he wasn't a strong man. Danny easily kept his face in the water with one arm. The Imam tried to shout under the water, but there was just a muted, gurgling protestation. Danny kept him under.

He counted to twenty, then pulled the Imam out of the font. The Iman inhaled deeply and noisily, his beard dripping wet and his eyes wild. Danny thrust his face back into the water even before he'd finished inhaling. He held it there for another twenty seconds, then pulled him out again.

This time he let the old man recover his breath. But he still held him by the neck, and he pressed the handgun into his forehead in case he should be tempted to cry out. 'Are you listening to me?' he said.

The Imam nodded desperately.

'I've got some good news for you,' Danny said. 'I'm going to let you live. But only if you give me some information. Do you understand?'

Another nod.

'There is a man called Mohammed Al-Zafawi. You know him?'

This time the Imam shook his head.

Danny smiled. 'That's a shame,' he said. And he plunged the old man's face back into the water.

This time he held him down for thirty seconds. He paid close attention to the flailing of the man's arms. Only when the strength started to leave him did Danny pull him back out. 'You know him?' he repeated, his voice quiet and twice as dangerous.

The old man's eyes were rolling as he gasped desperately for a lungful of air. He coughed up a mouthful of stagnant water, then nodded.

'Now we're getting somewhere,' Danny said. 'Your English is pretty good. You used to live in the UK?'

The Imam nodded again.

'That where you met him? You were the one who radicalised him?'

'Why do you care?'

'I'm asking the questions, pal. You're not just here to pray with him. You're not just a provincial Imam. He's put you in this village for a reason. To distribute weapons to your Taliban cronies?'

The Imam didn't have to answer. Danny could tell from the Imam's expression that he was on the money. 'Okay, pal. Sorted. Now listen carefully: the next words that leave your mouth are going to be Al-Zafawi's location.'

The Imam made a harsh, hacking sound in the back of his throat. He drew breath again. Then he spoke. 'I would rather die,' he whispered.

'Well in that case, my friend, you're talking to the right person.' And for a fourth time, he thrust the old man's head under the water.

Danny knew he was playing a dangerous game. Experience of field interrogation told him that no matter how brave the Imam's words, he would likely change his mind when the prospect of death became an immediate reality. He needed the Imam to be sufficiently convinced that Danny was on the verge of killing him, but cogent enough to provide the intel and to be moved if necessary. He watched his target's fist carefully. It was clenched, the nails digging into the palm. But after another thirty seconds of drowning, the fingers gradually loosened as the Imam started to lose control of himself. That was Danny's sign to pull him out again.

For a moment he thought he'd gone too far. The old man was limp, his eyes closed. Danny thumped him between the shoulder blades. Another substantial volume of water spewed out and when the Imam inhaled this time, it was with a much more sinister hoarseness. He was on the edge.

'Where is Al-Zafawi?' Danny demanded.

The Imam gabbled something in Pashto. Danny pressed his weapon into his damp cheek. 'English,' he said.

'The cave . . .'

'Which cave? Where is it?'

'The cave . . .' the Imam repeated. His eyes rolled again and he reverted to jabbering Pashto. Danny started to push him back down to the water. 'North-east!' the Imam gasped. 'In the mountains range. I can take you there.' He went almost completely limp again. 'I can take you there,' he repeated. 'Thirty kilometres . . .'

Danny knew he had pushed the old man far enough. He let go of his neck and let him fall to his knees next to the font. He marched across the prayer room to the exit where Caitlin was standing, Sig in hand, facing outside.

'What took you so damn long?' she asked without turning to look at him.

Danny ignored that. 'Al-Zafawi's hiding out in a cave thirty klicks north-east of here.'

'He'll have guys,' Caitlin said. 'And there's ANA forward operating bases north and east of here. They patrol the area at night, sometimes during the day.'

'I know. I'll need your help. I won't be able to get to him alone.'

'We should bring Tommy.'

'No. I don't know the guy. I can't trust him not to contact the head shed.'

'How do you know you can trust me?' She looked at him and they locked gazes for a moment before Caitlin lowered her eyes. 'When do we go?'

'Soon as. We need to be out of the village by afternoon prayers – that's when people will start to miss this guy. And if word gets to Al-Zafawi that something's happened to his precious Imam, he's likely to get spooked and move position. We need to get to this cave by tonight at the latest.'

'How?'

'I told you – my vehicle's in a ditch on the northern edge of the village. I can get it here in ten or fifteen minutes, but we need to bundle him in and get out of the village as soon as I do that.'

He closed his eyes for a moment. Breathed deeply to stop a wave of pain and nausea emanating from his wound.

'Are you okay?' Caitlin asked.

Danny ignored her. 'I need to get moving,' he said.

'Not yet.'

'We can't fuck around,' Danny said.

'I can't just leave without telling the others,' Caitlin said. 'If I'm AWOL for more than an hour, they'll call it in.'

'What are you going to tell them?'

'I'm following up a lead. Woman to woman. Some shit like that. Leave it to me.'

Danny nodded. 'What gear do you have back at your digs?'

'Mostly medical,' Caitlin said.

'Any more grenades? Ammo?'

'I'll get what I can.'

'Do it now and quickly,' Danny said. He looked back over his shoulder at the Imam who was crouched down and retching. 'I'll keep him under control. When you get back, we'll swap and I'll get the vehicle. Then we'll go find this Al-Zafawi. See what he's got to say for himself.'

Caitlin nodded. Seconds later she was gone.

16

The morning had passed slowly in Camp Shorabak. Once they'd kennelled the dog, Holroyd had taken individual statements from Tony and Dexter in neat handwriting using a fountain pen and a leather-bound notebook. The debrief had happened in the privacy of a sweltering Portakabin set aside for their use. It was empty apart from a table and four chairs. A couple of minutes after they'd arrived, Holroyd's number two, Jacko McGuigan, had brought them their rucksacks – but not, Tony noted, their personal weapons – which he propped up in one corner before inclining his head obsequiously to Holroyd as he laid their ops vests over them. The vests had been emptied out.

Holroyd obviously wanted to keep Tony and Dexter on side. His overly friendly manner had been transparent. When he'd finished taking their statements, he'd gone out of his way to act like their best mate.

'Look lads,' he'd said. 'You know I've got to confine you to camp. Not that you'd exactly want to go sightseeing anyway.' He laughed at his own joke, while Tony and Dexter smiled politely. 'Seriously, I don't want to put you on total lockdown. Like I told you, move around the camp by all means, visit your dog if you need to – just stay inside the perimeter. My advice is that you keep away from the ANA boys. You'll eat and sleep in this Portakabin. I'll have someone bring you some ration packs and water. I'm hoping to get us out of here and back to the UK tomorrow evening at the latest.'

'Roger that,' Tony had said.

Dexter had maintained a surly silence while Holroyd was

present. 'I'm staying here,' he said as soon as the RMP man had left. 'Everyone on the base will know about Cole by now. And they'll know about Baron going for that ANA guy. I don't want to be the centre of attention.'

Tony nodded his agreement. They remained in the Portakabin, away from the general population of the base, with a thick silence between them. Neither of them felt any need to discuss what they'd done that morning and their argument outside the dog enclosure still hung in the air. Dexter took a rubber ball with teeth marks from his rucksack, propped the pack against one wall, sat with his back to it and bounced the ball repetitively against the opposite wall. Minute after minute, hour after hour, the thud-thud of the ball was the only noise in the Portakabin. He continued throwing it when McGuigan arrived and dumped some ration packs on the table. When Tony returned after going for a piss he was still at it.

'You going for an Olympic gold in bouncy ball?' he said.

Dexter gave him a foul look. Tony shrugged and didn't say anything else. He slumped on a chair in the opposite corner and feigned sleep.

Thud-thud.

Thud-thud.

Tony inhaled slowly. Kept his calm. He was going to need it.

At 13.30 hours, the thud of the ball suddenly stopped.

'I'm going to check on Baron,' Dexter said. He stood up and stomped out of the room.

Tony stood up the moment the Portakabin door closed. Headed for his rucksack that was still propped up in one corner. It was neatly packed and he found what he was looking for in less than ten seconds: a small foil packet of tranquillisers. Diazepam. Ten milligrams. Two would do it, he reckoned. He pricked them out and put the remaining tablets back in his rucksack.

The ration packs that McGuigan had supplied were in a box on the table. Tony rummaged through them. There were two foil packs of chicken curry. Tony took one of them and stashed it in his rucksack. He opened the second one and pressed the two tablets of diazepam into the cold, sludgy curry. He left it on the table, then took another MRE at random, ripped it open and got it down his neck. He left the empty packet next to the full chicken curry and took his seat again.

Dexter returned after half an hour. His face was a thunder-cloud. 'It's too fucking hot for him in that kennel.'

'Take it easy,' Tony said. 'This time tomorrow, we'll all be back home.' He pointed at the MRE on the table. 'I opened the chicken curry by mistake,' he said. 'All yours.'

'I don't see why I can't just bring him back here.'

'Because right now, the smart move is to do what Holroyd says.' Tony sniffed. 'Get some scoff down you. And do me a favour, mate. Give it a rest with the ball. It's like the frickin' Chinese water torture in here.'

Dexter gave him another dark look, but didn't reply. He grabbed the foil-packed chicken curry and started squeezing it into his mouth. A minute later, he chucked the empty wrapper on to the table and returned to his position by the wall, lean-ing against his rucksack. He started up with the rubber ball again.

But not for long. Ten minutes later he was asleep.

Once Caitlin had left, Danny returned to the Imam, pulled him to his feet and dragged him to the rear entrance. While it was easier to keep the Imam hidden inside, there was only a single exit point. If anyone came looking for the old boy, Danny had only one escape route. Outside, of course, there was a danger of being seen, but his escape options were less limited. So he forced the Imam towards the exit.

But something stopped him before he hit the exterior. He remembered how the Imam had handed over the firearm to the two young men just minutes earlier. If this guy was a friend of Al-Zafawi, did that mean he was sitting on more weaponry?

'Wait,' he told the Imam.

The old man's eyes darted towards the exit.

'Where is it?'

'Where is what?' the breathless Imam managed to say.

'Al-Zafawi's cache. His weapons. You just handed over a hand-gun to one of his goons. I'm thinking there's more like that hidden here.'

'You are wrong,' the Imam said. 'There is nothing.'

But as he spoke, his eyes flickered towards the raised area against the southern wall of the prayer room. Danny bustled the Imam towards it, threw him on to the wooden platform and examined it a little more closely. He immediately saw that there was a trap-door, about a metre square, with a lock flush to the wooden plat-form. Danny kicked the Imam towards it.

'Get it open,' he said.

At first the Imam shook his head, but then he caught sight of the look on Danny's face and it was enough. With trembling hands, he removed a key on a cord round his neck and fumbled the lock open. Danny pulled the trapdoor up and looked into the space below the platform.

'Bingo,' he muttered.

It was an arsenal. Three AK-47s lay side by side. Two rocket launchers, and a stash of RPGs. A couple of helmets with fourth generation night sights – equivalent to the one Tony had shown them back at Kandahar. There were boxes of C-4 plastic explo-sive. There were remote detonators. It was a terrorist's wish list. And now it was Danny's.

He closed the trapdoor. The gear wasn't going anywhere. He turned to the Imam. 'Get outside,' he said. Pulling him to his feet, he forced the old man to the exit. They needed to hide while they waited for Caitlin to return.

After the dim interior of the prayer room, the exterior bright-ness hurt Danny's eyes. He squinted as he dragged the old man across the rubble-strewn building site at the back of the mosque towards a pile of old breeze blocks through which a few hardy weeds were trying to grow. The Imam struggled surprisingly forcefully. Danny kept a firm grip on him with his good arm, bundling him to the far side of the blocks. He cried out, earning himself a blow to the pit of his stomach. Danny forced him down on to his front, then kneeled on his back so it was difficult for him to fill his lungs with air and shout any more. And in case he was tempted to try it, he pressed his weapon into the back of his prisoner's head. 'If you try to alert anyone,' Danny whispered, 'I'll kill you first, then I'll kill them.'

The Imam kept quiet.

It wasn't true that Danny had everything he needed. The Imam's directions were vague, and in any case he and Caitlin couldn't just walk up to Al-Zafawi's cave and ask for a friendly chat. A strategy was forming in Danny's mind, to which the old man was central.

Danny's wound felt wet – he didn't know if it was sweat or if it had started to weep. It certainly hurt. He did what he could to put that from his mind. Instead he concentrated on keeping the Imam silent. He was able to keep surveillance on the area to the back of the mosque through some gaps in the pile of breeze blocks. He also listened hard for the sound of anyone approaching.

Every few minutes, the Imam would wriggle in a futile attempt to push Danny off. He was persistent if nothing else. But Danny kept his full weight on the old man. The Imam wasn't going anywhere.

Danny heard footsteps after half an hour. Looking through the blocks, he saw a figure in blue robes and headdress. He recognised Caitlin by her purposeful gait. He gave a low whistle. Caitlin stopped and looked round. Danny held his weapon up above the pile. Recognising it, Caitlin came to join him.

'Catching some rays, mate?' she said as she removed a heavy rucksack from where it was secreted underneath her robes and crouched down.

'Anyone follow you?'

'Not that I could see. I doubled back a couple of times.'

'Keep him quiet. I found us some toys.'

It took Danny three journeys to fetch the rocket launchers, RPGs, NV helmets, C-4 and detonators from the cache. Caitlin looked surprised to start with. When Danny had finished piling up the gear behind the rubble mound, she was grinning. 'I'm guessing you stumbled on one of the Red Unit's caches.'

'I'm guessing I did,' Danny said. 'I'm going to get the vehicle. We need to load it up as soon as I get here.'

'ETA?'

'Fifteen minutes.'

Caitlin took his position kneeling on the Imam's back. The old man made a sudden struggle and pathetic attempt to shout out, but fell silent again when Caitlin rapped him on the back of the skull with her own handgun. 'Jeez, he doesn't get the message, this one.' She looked back at Danny. 'The only road comes in from the south-east,' she said. 'You'll be conspicuous if you use it.'

'I'll stay off-road,' Danny said. He pointed off to the north-west. 'From that direction.'

Danny emerged from the rubble, his handgun secreted under his robes. He walked with purpose, knowing that nothing was more likely to make him appear conspicuous than being hesitant. He cut across the deserted building site, along the side of the mosque, past the dwelling where they'd hidden out for the morning and emerged at the top of the main street.

There were only a few locals out in the heat of the middle of the day. None of them seemed to be paying Danny any attention as he crossed the street and veered to the north, past a few derelict houses where a couple of meagre goats were scratching around looking for food. The ditch where he'd left the Hilux was approximately a hundred metres to his north-east, across an expanse of parched, scrubby ground. Danny could just see it: a dip in the ground, slightly obscured by the shimmering of heat off the hard-baked earth. The intervening ground afforded no cover. If anybody was watching from the direction of the village, they'd see him. His only option was speed and, for that, the women's robes he was wearing were a hindrance. He hid behind the walls of one of the derelict buildings and removed them. Knowing that they might come in useful later, he slung them over his right shoulder while he fixed his assault rifle across his chest. He scanned the area back towards the village to check nobody had eyes on it. His only company was the goats, so he made a run for it.

Danny could tell his strength was down. The sprint across open ground was unusually difficult and running caused a jolting pain in his left shoulder. Every few paces he looked back to check he wasn't observed – there was no sign of anyone – but it was only when he reached the ditch and was looking down at the secreted vehicle that he realised he had a problem.

Two problems, in fact.

A couple of kids in dirty robes, boys, no more than ten years of age, standing in the ditch, looking at Danny's Hilux as if they'd found hidden treasure. They looked up at Danny – heavily armed, dirty, stinking and threatening – as though he was the devil himself.

Danny stared at them, silently cursing.

The very fact that these kids had seen him meant that he was compromised.

He pulled his handgun. Aimed it at one of the kids. The boy froze. His mate shrank back against the far side of the ditch.

Danny had a split second to make the call. Did he take the kids out and get rid of the immediate problem? The retort of two rounds from the pistol – which would easily be heard back in the village – would make matters worse for him. And the last thing he wanted was a trail of dead bodies.

Or was it just that he didn't want to kill two kids in cold blood?

He jumped down into the ditch. The kids flinched. Danny flung his robes into the open back of the Hilux and strode round to the driver's side. In the side mirror he saw the kids scampering back along the ditch. He swore under his breath – it was unthinkable that they wouldn't tell an adult they'd just seen a white-skinned soldier climbing into a hidden car. He had to leave immediately. Turning the engine over, he knocked the Hilux into gear and accelerated. The terrain moved at an upward incline, out of the ditch and on to the flat desert plain surrounding the village. Even at a relatively modest speed, the tyres kicked up a cloud of dust as Danny sped anticlockwise around the northern perimeter of Panjika. From his left window he could see, above the rooftops, the two-storey tower at the back of the mosque that marked Caitlin's position. The speedometer hovered around twenty mph. At this rate it would take a good two minutes to get to Caitlin. The temptation was to floor the vehicle, but that would make more noise and potentially attract more attention. So he kept a steady speed.

Time check: 14.25 hours. He cursed. He'd been more than fifteen minutes. The Hilux jolted over the uneven ground as he swung it round the edge of the village. Fifty metres up ahead he saw the derelict vehicle they'd used as an OP. Beyond that, the back of the mosque. He tried to pick out Caitlin and the Imam, but they were both hidden. As he continued to head to the rear of the mosque, he looked along its side towards the top of the main street. He saw four figures. Two children. Two men. Distance: 150 metres. One of the children was pointing in his direction.

He swore again and pressed the accelerator. The tyres kicked up even more dust. He reached the back of the mosque in approximately fifteen seconds. Caitlin and the Imam were exactly where he'd left them, only now Caitlin was standing up and pulling the Imam to his feet. The old man's arms were flailing wildly and he looked like he was shouting out. Danny came to a halt ten metres from their position and left the engine running as he jumped out. He grabbed the headdress from the back of the Hilux and ran towards them.

'Could you make any more frickin' noise?' Caitlin said as Danny approached.

'We're blown. Two kids found the vehicle. I just saw them talking to two adults at the top of the main street.'

'Jeez, and you couldn't do something to keep them quiet?'

'Just get him in the fucking car,' Danny said, covering the wriggling Imam's head with the headdress so that he couldn't be easily identified. He thrust the old man towards Caitlin and started loading up armfuls of the stolen weaponry into the back of the Hilux. 'You take the wheel,' he barked. 'Head north to put anyone watching off the scent.'

'There's an ANA forward operating base directly north,' Caitlin said. 'Five klicks.'

'We'll change bearing when we're out of sight of the village. I'm going to get in the back to supply covering fire. *Move!*'

Caitlin didn't argue. As Danny continued to load up the hardware, she dragged the Imam towards the vehicle and bundled him into the passenger seat before slamming the door closed and slinging her rucksack into the back. While she got behind the wheel, Danny loaded up the last batch of hardware, jumped into the back of the Hilux, unslung his assault rifle and crouched in the firing position, using the raised sides of the vehicle as cover.

'Go!' he shouted. '*Go!*'

Caitlin floored it, turning the vehicle in a full circle to head back the way Danny had arrived. Danny half closed his eyes to stop the cloud of dust compromising his vision, but he remained firmly in the firing position, aiming out of the right-hand side of the Hilux so that his weapon would be pointing across the ground that led to the top of the main street when it came into view.

Which it did in five seconds. And a second after that, they were under fire.

There was no sign of the kids. But the two adult figures were still there and they were closer. Thirty metres, maximum. The instant he saw them at that proximity, Danny recognised them as the two young men he'd seen speaking to the Imam. One of them was holding up the pistol, presumably the same one the Imam had given them. He fired it.

He was clearly not a marksman. His arm was locked straight and it flew up to the left as soon as he released the round. But the shot was almost lucky. It slammed into the side of the moving Hilux, its ricochet sparking just a few inches to the right of Danny's position.

Danny's response was instinctive, ruthless and executed within a fraction of a second. He couldn't risk the gunman releasing a second round. It wasn't just that Danny risked taking a direct hit. If they blew a tyre, their whole operation would be fucked. Both these guys knew the Imam. Both of them had militant tendencies.

It could also mean they were in contact with Al-Zafawi. If so, Danny couldn't risk them tipping off the Taliban leader.

He had to put them down.

He did it with a single short burst. He hadn't zeroed the weapon, and the speeding Hilux was jolting violently. But Danny was well trained in firing from a moving platform, and his aim was accurate enough as he moved the weapon left to right with the trigger squeezed. The rounds cut into the abdomens of the two men, mowing them down instantly, but not immediately killing them. Danny was aware of figures appearing behind them – crowds gathering. As the retort of the assault rifle subsided, and the two young men collapsed, he could hear their agonised screams above the noise of the engine.

The screams soon faded as the Hilux headed north over hard-baked, bumpy terrain. In the absence of any further threats, Danny crouched below the sides of the vehicle. He made his weapon safe and clutched his wounded shoulder – firing the weapon had made it more painful and he had to quell a wave of nausea. The Hilux swerved to the right as Caitlin continued to speed across the hard-baked, uneven ground. Peering over the edge of the vehicle Danny saw the village of Panjika diminish into a haze. Only then did he start to swear beneath his breath.

He hadn't wanted to leave a trail of corpses. Corpses meant questions. Local army. Local police. Word might even get back to Holroyd.

He looked out of the back of the Hilux. The heavy wheels were leaving a trail on the terrain. He shuffled up to the front end of the vehicle and hammered on the back of the cab with a flat fist. The Hilux skidded to a sudden halt leaving an even more pronounced mark on the ground. He sprinted round to the driver's side and opened the door.

'Move up,' he told Caitlin. 'I'll take the wheel.' And when it looked like Caitlin was about to protest, he said: 'A woman driving is going to stick out. Now move up.'

Caitlin did so, forcing the hooded Imam further up against the passenger door.

Danny took the wheel. 'We're leaving a trail. We need to get to the road.'

'North-east,' Caitlin said, pointing to their two o'clock.

Danny accelerated in that direction. He paid as much attention to his rear and side mirrors as he did to the way ahead. If anyone was following, they needed early warning. But so far, all he saw was the parched terrain. Danny glanced at Caitlin. 'We need directions,' he said.

Caitlin nodded. She removed her handgun and roughly pulled off the Imam's headdress. He winced in the sudden brightness, then started gabbling in Pashto. 'What a fucking pain in the arse,' Caitlin said as she pressed her gun into the side of his head. 'How do we get to the cave?' she shouted over the noise of the engine and the Imam's frenzied shouting.

'I do not know,' the Imam spat.

'Oh, shame,' Caitlin said. She grabbed him by his hair and slammed his face against the dashboard. 'Can you remember now?' she asked.

The Imam looked dazed. 'T . . . take the road heading east. You will come to a shrine. That is where you must come off the road and go north towards the mountain.'

'What's the ground like?'

The Imam gave her an uncomprehending look.

'The ground,' she repeated. 'The terrain. Flat? Bumpy? Mountainous?'

'Yes,' he nodded. 'Very bumpy.'

'Does Al-Zafawi have guards with him?'

'I do not know. I am just a humble Imam—'

'Shoot him in the leg,' Danny said.

'*No!*' the Imam said, as Caitlin pressed her gun into his knee. 'I will tell you, I will tell you!'

'Do it fast.'

'There are four people, plus him. Sometimes three, if one of them is going for supplies. There are always two of them awake.'

Danny nodded. 'Cover his head,' he said.

Caitlin complied. As she pulled the headdress over the Imam's head, Danny looked left. He could just see, shimmering on the horizon, what he presumed was the perimeter fence of the ANA forward operating base to the north of Panjika. Distance, two to three klicks. No sign of patrols on the intervening terrain. He fixed his eyes on the open ground ahead and floored the Hilux as fast as he dared on this rough ground. They needed to get to the road as quickly as possible.

It took ten minutes of mute driving to achieve this. When the road appeared up ahead, it was on raised ground. Danny slowed as they approached, easing the Hilux on to the poorly laid highway and turning east. In his rear-view mirror he saw a farm vehicle disappearing into the distance. Up ahead, a rickety Transit van was travelling in the same direction, about fifty metres distant.

'We need somewhere to stop,' Caitlin said, speaking quietly so it would be difficult for the Imam to understand them.

Danny only nodded in reply. He fixed his eyes on the road ahead and drove.

It took another five minutes before a suitable stopping point presented itself: a solitary, derelict building set back about twenty metres on the southern side of the highway. Danny couldn't just head off road: there were now at least five other cars in view. Instead he pulled over and waited a couple of minutes until there were no passing vehicles to spot his movements. Then he sped across the rough terrain towards the derelict building and pulled up behind it, hidden from the highway. He killed the engine.

'Leave him there,' he said, pointing at the hooded Imam. 'We'll talk outside.'

The afternoon heat was brutal as he exited the Hilux and walked round to the back. When they spoke, it was in low voices.

'We need leverage,' Danny said. 'If Al-Zafawi and his goons are holed up in a cave and armed, we can't just walk in there. They'll mince us. Fragmentation grenades are no good because they'll kill Al-Zafawi. We need to use the Imam to lure them all outside.'

'Send him in first?' Caitlin said. 'Are you crazy. He'll just tell them what's going on.'

'Which is why we need leverage. You said his family's back in the village?'

'Sure, but if we were going to get to them, we should have done it before.'

Danny looked out across the parched desert. 'How many villages like that do you reckon have been wiped out by a British or American bomb strike?' he said. 'Tens? Hundreds?'

Caitlin looked at him like he was crazy. 'We can't exactly call in fast air,' she said.

'Course not,' Danny said. 'But he doesn't know that. And if I was him, and two British soldiers told me they were about to order a Hellfire strike on the village where my family are living, I think I'd listen up.'

Caitlin stared at him. Then she shook her head and smiled. 'In another life, Danny Black, you and Tony could have been friends.'

'I seriously doubt that,' Danny said. 'What did you bring from your digs?'

Caitlin grabbed her rucksack from the back of the Hilux. She rummaged inside. 'Nine millimetre rounds,' she said. 'Morphine shots. Sterile dressings.' She looked meaningfully at Danny's bad shoulder. 'Sat phone.'

'Tell me it's switched off.'

'Relax, Danny. No one's tracking us.'

'Anything else.'

'Duct tape. MREs. Women's things – help yourself to those.' She held up a fistful of tampons.

'Very fucking useful.'

'You'd be surprised,' Caitlin muttered.

'Let's move our guy out,' Danny said. 'I want to talk to him.'

He walked round to the passenger side, opened the door and roughly pulled the Imam out of the vehicle, before dragging him round to the back. He ripped off the hood, then forced the old man to his knees, handgun to head. The Imam was more subdued now. He closed his eyes and trembled. He clearly had a good idea of what normally happened to people in this position.

'Do you know who we are?' he asked the Imam.

The Imam kept his eyes shut and shook his head fervently.

'Have a guess. I said, *have a guess.*'

'British soldiers,' the Imam said, his voice cracked and dry.

'Got it in one. Do you know what would happen if I told my bosses that I'd just shot the guy who I think was responsible for radicalising Al-Zafawi in the first place? They'd give me a medal. So my advice is to do what I say.' He mouthed the words 'sat phone' to Caitlin, who delved into her rucksack and handed it over. 'Open your eyes.'

The Imam did as he was told.

'Know what this is?'

The Imam nodded.

'Good. It takes one call from me, and twenty minutes later a British or American aircraft flies over Panjika and delivers a payload of Hellfire missiles into the area to the west of the river. Remind me where your family lives.'

He didn't reply. Danny cracked him over the head with the handle of his pistol. 'To the west of the river.'

'Children? Grandchildren?'

He nodded.

'We're going to fuck them up, my friend, unless you do exactly what I tell you. You want to see what happens when people get fucked-up by British soldiers?' He pulled the crumpled A4 photograph of the butchered family from his pocket and held it in front of the Imam's face. For a moment he thought the old man was going to puke. He let the image sink in for a moment before shoving the picture back into his pocket. Then he knelt down so he was face to face with the Imam. 'This is what's going to happen,' he said. 'I hope you're listening carefully, because if you mess this up, those kiddies back at your compound don't get to see another day. You're going to guide us to the place where Al-Zafawi is hiding. When we get there, you are going to approach the cave. We'll be watching every single step you make. When you get there, you're going to tell Al-Zafawi that two British soldiers came to your mosque asking questions. You'll tell him that you put them off the scent – you understand what that means?'

The Imam nodded again.

'How do you normally travel to see him?'

'He sends people. They drive me.'

'Tonight it's going to be different. You'll tell him that you made the journey by yourself because you wanted to warn him that people are looking for him. Then, when the time is right, you're going to lead him and his guys outside the cave for prayers.'

The Imam stared at him. 'And then?' he said.

'We'll be very careful to make sure that you're not hit.'

'What about Al-Zafawi?'

'We need him alive.'

'And the others.'

Danny didn't answer. He just gave the Imam a meaningful stare.

'You screw this up, I'll make the call. Your family will be dead by midnight. Do you understand?'

The Imam bowed his head. 'You are a monster,' he said.

'I haven't even got started yet. *Do you understand*?'

'I understand.'

Danny looked up at Caitlin. 'Put him back in the vehicle.'

Caitlin pulled the Imam up to his feet. Dragged him round to the passenger door again and shoved him into the cab. She returned to where Danny was still standing at the rear of the Hilux. 'You're a real hearts and minds guy, you know that?'

Danny gave her a dangerous look. 'Just get in the car,' he said.

'This isn't watertight, Danny. He might make the call to keep Al-Zafawi in the cave. Tell him everything. Then we're forced to go in blind. We don't have the gear or the personnel to make a success of that.'

'I'm not done with him yet,' Danny stated. 'Just get in the car. We haven't got time to fuck around.'

17

The two diazepam would keep Dexter under for at least eight hours. Tony needed to make good use of that time.

At no point during their debriefs had anyone mentioned the bomb-making gear in Target Red's compound. It was still safely stowed away in Tony's pack. Two blocks of military grade C-4 plastic explosive. A blasting cap and remote detonator. A nine-volt battery. A syringe. A small phial of mercury. Enough here to make a substantial roadside IED. Take out a vehicle and kill a few of its occupants.

Tony glanced over at Dexter. He was clearly in a deep sleep. But Tony could still be interrupted. Holroyd or McGuigan could walk in unannounced at any time. So he put on his ops waistcoat, stowed the items in its empty pouches, along with a small roll of duct tape and a penknife that he always kept at the bottom of his pack, and stepped outside.

It was the hottest time of day. Anyone who had the opportunity had retreated inside. A few military vehicles were moving across the base. Wherever ANA soldiers had congregated, they did so in whatever shade they could find: accommodation blocks, vehicle hangars, the med centre, briefing units. Tony glanced across the camp in the direction of the dog enclosure. Nobody had ventured in that direction. Nor did Tony. Instead, he hurried past the med centre and moved north, towards a tendril of smoke drifting lazily up to the sky.

The smoke had been ever-present since his arrival in camp. Tony knew that it had to come from some kind of burn pit, where waste products from the camp were disposed of. As he approached, he saw a rough structure made of metal posts and a pitched corrugated iron roof, maybe forty metres wide. No walls. Up close, he saw that it was a sprawling, industrial mess. Four metal chimneys emerged from the roof and the interior was covered with scaffolding units and yellow iron ladders. Directly beneath each chimney were a cylindrical incinerator and a once-white control cabinet. An old forklift was parked up to one side of the building, but this refuse unit was derelict, the incinerators unused. Instead, the Afghans had reverted to the time-honoured method of digging a big hole in the ground and incinerating any waste in the open air. The area around the burn pit stank of charred debris, the air was thick with toxic smoke and of course it was hot. Refuse would be tipped into the burn pit morning and evening. During the day, it was unpleasant, a health hazard and deserted.

A place where a man could work unseen.

He took up position behind a mound of charred waste on the very northern edge of the burn pit. There was nothing between him and the perimeter fence, thirty metres distant. He crouched on the hard ground, keeping as low as possible between the choking fumes, and removed the individual items from his ops vest.

The blocks of C-4 were soft in the heat, but the plastic explosive would be entirely stable if kept separate from a detonating charge. He put them to one side and examined the rest of the gear. Demolitions were Tony's thing. He knew the importance of understanding your equipment. Checking it for faults. He examined the blasting cap closely. Two cylindrical metallic prongs connected by a length of blue and green wire to a plastic red junction box with terminals for the battery. He cracked open the junction box. Examined the wiring inside. Got to work.

It was fiddly. He had no wire cutters so he had to rely on his penknife to ease the cables out of the junction box, strip them down and re-circuit them. It took a careful half hour to complete the job, sweaty in the direct heat and keeping his breathing shallow because of the toxic fumes. When he'd finished, the syringe had been cut down to a simple cylinder, blocked at either end with a strip of duct tape. A bare wire pierced each piece of duct tape and the syringe was half-filled with mercury. Held vertically, the mercury covered only one terminal. Moved to the horizontal, it touched both. A basic trip switch. The bare wires led from the syringe to two prongs of the blasting cap and the terminal for the nine-volt battery. The battery was not attached, nor were the prongs of the blasting cap inserted into the C-4. But the device was ready. The IRA would have been proud of him, he thought to himself with a grim smile.

He carefully stowed the re-wired gear back into his ops waistcoat. Stood up and skirted back round the burn pit and past the derelict incineration units. He headed back to the med centre and as he crossed over to the Portakabin he felt the stare of a small group of ANA soldiers standing in the shade of the centre's entrance. He ignored them.

Dexter was still asleep, his breathing steady. Tony removed his ops waistcoat and carefully stowed it behind his rucksack. He was just straightening up when the door opened. Holroyd entered. He looked around the Portakabin and his eyes fell on Dexter.

'Been a long couple of days,' Tony said. 'He's shagged. We all are. I mean ... both of us.'

Holroyd nodded curtly.

'Just went for a slash,' Tony said. 'Those ANA boys by the med centre gave me the eye. Nasty atmospherics. They didn't like one of their boys getting done by the dog. Sooner we're out of here, the better.'

'It's in hand,' Holroyd said. 'Don't you worry about it.' His former chumminess had slipped. He seemed to realise this and gave Tony a fake smile. 'I'll catch up with you boys later.'

He turned his back on Tony and left the Portakabin, closing the door firmly behind him.

The Imam had told them that they needed to head north when they came to a roadside shrine. Danny had imagined some kind of religious statue. In fact, it was an ugly structure made up of old truck tyres, bound together with rags and sticks that poked up randomly into the air. A pile of sand had drifted up against one side. Danny pulled up alongside it and checked the time: 15.26 hours. Two and a half hours until sunset, when the Imam would ordinarily make the call to prayer. Everything had to be set up by then.

The road was busier now. Rickety trucks and ancient saloon cars were passing in either direction. A full ten minutes passed before Danny could knock the engine back into gear and take the Hilux off road in the direction the terrified Imam indicated. The three occupants of the car spent that time in relative silence: the Imam muttering inaudibly under his breath, Danny and Caitlin examining the terrain to the north. It was undulating, which meant that once they had left the road, they would be reasonably well camouflaged. The ground was hard and cracked in places, but with patches of stone and boulder that Danny would have to negotiate. Principally, however, his attention was the low mountain range towards which they were heading. It formed a featureless brown ridge, approximately five miles distant. It wasn't very high – a couple of thousand feet, max. Certainly not high enough to be snow-capped. But even from this distance Danny could see that the foothills were extensive and rocky. This was easy terrain to hide in, but difficult to cross.

When, for a brief moment, there were no vehicles in sight, Danny headed north. By the time they were thirty metres from the road, they were camouflaged from it by a dip in the terrain. He soon established that he wouldn't need regular directions from the Imam because there was a faint trail of vehicle marks on the ground ahead. He figured they were only headed one place. And they served a dual purpose: if he followed fresh tracks, he almost eliminated the risk of encountering IEDs.

Danny drove slowly. Carefully. A mile from the road, he stopped. His fuel gauge had hit the red. He got out of the car and took the spare jerrycan of fuel from the back of the Hilux. The can was hot, and the stench of evaporating fumes was nauseating as he unscrewed the cap and poured the fuel into the Hilux tank. Caitlin joined him.

'Spearpoint might be looking for us. They could have drones up . . . anything.'

'I know.'

'What if Al-Zafawi's not there?' she said.

'Then we wait for him.'

She wiped some sweat from her brow. 'You realise he'll have spent the last forty-five minutes working out what he's going to do when he gets to this damn cave? He's thinking: does Al-Zafawi have comms? Can he contact anyone in Panjika to get his family evacuated?'

'I know.' Danny drained the last of the fuel into the tank and slung the jerrycan into the back of the Hilux, where it clattered noisily.

'So why don't we just use him to get us on target? We've got NV. We can move into the cave after dark and pick them off.'

'Lots of reasons,' Danny said. 'For a start, those cave systems can go on for miles. Soon as we're inside, we're at a disadvantage because they'll know the terrain better than us. Second, we know Al-Zafawi and his Red Unit guys are well equipped. This is some of their gear we're using, right? So if they also have NV, that neutralises the one advantage we would otherwise have. Third, we don't even know which one is Al-Zafawi. We need a positive ID so we know who to keep alive . . .'

'Okay, Danny. Jeez, I get the message. All I'm saying is, what's the plan?'

Danny closed his eyes. Inhaled deeply. The pain in his left shoulder was bad. A distraction. It was all he could do to keep his eye on the road ahead. But Caitlin was right. She needed to understand what Danny had in mind before they reached the target. 'Get him,' he said.

Once again, Caitlin dragged the Imam to the back of the Hilux. Danny held him at gunpoint again. 'Can you drive?' he said.

The Imam blinked. Then nodded. 'Yes,' he breathed.

Danny moved to the back of the Hilux. He grabbed the pack of C-4 plastic explosive that he'd confiscated from the arsenal in the mosque. He unwrapped it and held it up to the Imam. 'You know what this is?'

The Imam swallowed nervously, and nodded.

'Good,' Danny said. 'Take your robes off.'

The Imam stared at him.

'You *really* want to make me ask you again?'

The Imam glanced at Caitlin. To disrobe in front of an unfamiliar woman was obviously a big deal for him. That was fine by Danny. The more uncomfortable he felt, the more pliant he was likely to be. Danny stared him down, and after a few seconds the old boy reluctantly pulled his robes over his head. His body was thin, bony and almost hairless. He wore sandals and a pair of yellowing underpants that looked too big for him. Danny pointed at them, and made a 'take them down' gesture.

The Imam looked almost more outraged about this than he had about the prospect of a Hellfire strike on his family. But one look at Danny told him this wasn't open for negotiation. He shuffled out of his underwear to reveal his genitals.

'Get him on his back,' Danny said. While she did this, he took Caitlin's rucksack from the back of the vehicle, placed it on the ground alongside the Imam and pulled out the roll of black duct tape. Kneeling down by the side of the Imam, he pulled a handful of the plastic explosive and moulded it into a sausage shape. He pressed the C-4 along the Imam's penis, then wrapped duct tape around both. 'They won't touch his dick if they pat him down,' Danny said quietly to Caitlin. 'Cultural thing.' Then, in a slightly louder voice: 'Pass me the remote detonator.'

It came in two sections. A handset with a simple switch, and a slave unit with two metal prongs to insert into the C-4. With the Imam still lying on his back, Danny used the prongs to pierce the tape surrounding the plastic explosive, then taped the slave unit to the left-hand side of the Imam's perineum.

The old man had his eyes closed. Good. Danny covertly removed one of Caitlin's tampons, bent it in the middle and taped it to the right-hand side of the Imam's genitals. 'That's a remote microphone,' he said. 'We'll be able to hear every word you say. I'm going to patch it through to my command centre, who will translate it in real time. Do you understand?'

The Imam nodded his hooded head.

Danny covered the genital area with more tape. Then he pulled the Imam's pants back on and removed his hood. The Imam looked down his torso towards his crotch with undisguised terror. Danny leaned in. 'You want my advice, champ?' he said. 'Don't piss yourself.'

The Imam looked at him in horror.

'We hear you say *anything* that makes us nervous . . .' Danny said. He held up the detonating unit and made a clicking sound. 'You're carrying enough explosive to blast your bollocks back to Panjika.' The Imam looked as if he understood the sentiment, even if not the exact words. 'Put your robes back on.'

The Imam gingerly complied. When Caitlin ushered him back into the cab, he stepped awkwardly.

'Walk properly,' Danny told him. 'It won't blow unless I detonate.'

The Imam looked round at him as if he was mad, but then continued his path to the passenger door in a slightly less awkward fashion.

'Get the idea?' Danny said.

'You know,' Caitlin said, 'I almost feel sorry for the old git.' Caitlin looked towards the mountain range. 'How much further do you reckon?'

'We'll lie up in a couple of klicks. I'll do a recce, see what we're dealing with, you watch our guy.' He checked his watch. 15.58 hours. 'Two hours till sunset. We need to move.'

They returned to their vehicle and continued their slow, careful way north. The terrain became rockier and more boulder-strewn. The vehicle trails that Danny was following wound in and out of the obstacles ahead. At one stage he was obliged to head west for half a klick before doubling back on himself to avoid a deep trench in the desert floor. When he double-checked with the Imam that they were heading in the right direction, the terrified old man nodded with a wild-eyed expression, before looking down nervously at his groin area.

'Don't do that,' Caitlin told him. 'Seriously, mate, you give anything away to Al-Zafawi and his boys, we won't have much option but to blow it.'

From that point on, the Imam looked straight ahead.

They came to another halt twenty minutes later. They were in a dip between two mounds of raised ground, the crests thirty metres apart. About twenty metres to their left was a boulder-strewn area that afforded a little cover for the vehicle. As Danny stepped outside, he felt that the sun's heat was dissipating a little. Time check: 16.25 hours. The mountain range loomed over them. Danny estimated that its foothills were about 750 metres away. 'Watch him,' he told Caitlin as he checked over his handgun and his rifle, now slung across his chest. 'Any problems, release two rounds in succession.'

Caitlin nodded, pulled the Imam from the cab of the Hilux and forced him down to his knees, hands behind his back, before putting herself in the firing position facing up the incline towards the mountain range. Danny located the tyre trails again, and started to follow them. The incline led to a hill brow, which he negotiated on all fours. He followed the trail downhill, round a patch of rough desert scrub and up towards the brow of another incline. He negotiated this, then stopped.

It was immediately clear to Danny that they were on target. A hundred and fifty metres of open ground presented itself, moving down at a shallow incline before levelling out a hundred metres or so from the mountain face, and broken up by rocky patches and more areas of rough gorse. Beyond the open ground was a sudden slab of exposed mountain face, a deep red sandstone colour, rising almost vertically from the desert floor. The face itself was deeply fissured and the sun sinking behind Danny rendered it at once glowing and intricately shadowed. Under normal circumstances it would have been impossible, from this distance, to identify one single cave in the mountain face. However, Danny didn't even need to follow the line of the tyre trails: two Land Rovers were parked, broad side on, at the front of a fissure in the rock that he estimated to be at least ten metres wide and thirty metres high. On top of the right-hand-side Land Rover there was a communications satellite receiver. And standing between the vehicles was a solitary man, looking out almost directly in Danny's direction.

Danny froze. He knew he was well hidden in his ANA camo gear as long as he lay on the brow of the incline. Twenty metres to his right there was a patch of high rock sitting atop the brow that he instantly identified as a potential firing point. A smaller patch lay ten metres to his left – less ideal because reaching it would mean moving several metres down the incline. From this distance, Danny himself was just another shapeless blip on the uneven landscape. But if the guard noticed him moving, he would cease to be invisible.

As he lay there watching, he calculated. From the firing position he had identified, the distance to target was 150 metres. With a properly zeroed rifle, that would present no problem. Un-zeroed, Danny still liked his chances, but he'd have to go for body shots rather than head shots. The Land Rovers were a potential problem: they provided cover for the targets if they came under fire. They would have to take those vehicles into account when they planned their assault. He checked the position of the sun and the way it was sinking into the west, then consulted a mental map of the Near and Middle East. When praying, Al-Zafawi and the Imam would kneel towards Mecca. From this point of the globe, that was in a south-west-westerly direction. They would need to emerge further than the mouth of the cave in order to stop their path to the holy city being blocked by one of the Land Rovers.

After five minutes the guard, who had been staring straight out towards Danny, turned to look back into the cave. Danny took his chance and disappeared back into the incline leading down from his OP. Then, keeping low, he ran back to the Hilux, where neither Caitlin nor the Imam had moved. He checked the time: 16.43 hours. Just over an hour till sunset. He needed to time this carefully. He had to give the Imam long enough to spin Al-Zafawi his story before encouraging them outside to pray, but not so long that he started thinking about ways of tipping off the militants.

Danny pulled the Imam to his feet. 'You understand what you have to do?' he said.

The Imam nodded.

'When you come out of the cave, you need to be walking on Al-Zafawi's right-hand side. That way we know who he is. Don't make a mistake about that or you'll find yourself in the line of fire. You understand I can hear every word you say, and that I can detonate that explosive at *any* moment?'

He nodded again.

'You understand what will happen to your family if you mess this up?'

And again.

'Okay. It's 16.45 hours. We move at 17.15. If you haven't led them out of the cave by sunset . . . we'll have our own little Tora Bora tribute.' And when the Imam looked like he didn't understand, Danny made an explosion shape with his palms and said, quietly, 'Boom.'

Seventeen-fifteen hours. The shadows were lengthening across the desert. Danny took the wheel and advanced towards the target, moving slowly to reduce the engine noise. When they reached the dip in the terrain that preceded the mountain face, he killed the engine. He and Caitlin alighted and removed their hardware from the back of the Hilux. Danny took the remote detonator to the cab, where the Imam was now sitting behind the wheel. He held it up as a reminder.

'Remember,' he said. 'You walk on Al-Zafawi's right. Now go.'

The gearbox of the Hilux barked as the Imam tried to put it into gear. Danny and Caitlin exchanged a look. It was important that Al-Zafawi believed his childhood confessor had made the journey here alone. He was relieved when the vehicle pulled away relatively smoothly. He and Caitlin picked up armfuls of hardware and followed the Hilux to the brow of the hill, bearing off slightly to the east towards the rocks that he'd identified as a firing position. As the Hilux trundled over the brow towards the cave, they laid their weaponry on the ground and took up surveillance positions, shielded by the rocks, immobile. Danny glanced up into the sky. He knew he wouldn't see a drone if it was up there, but there was always the chance that they were observed. All the more reason to get this done quickly.

But the Imam drove excruciatingly slowly. The guard at the cave mouth, flanked on either side by the two Land Rovers, had immediately spotted the vehicle. As expected, it clearly made him nervous: this was an unscheduled arrival. Danny just hoped the Imam had it in him to be convincing. The guard called back over his shoulder. Thirty seconds later, a second guy appeared. They stood side by side, their rifles engaged and pointing towards the approaching Hilux. The Imam negotiated the slope down to the open ground, then came to a halt a hundred metres from the cave mouth.

Twenty seconds passed. The vehicle remained stationary. The guards kept their weapons trained on it. One of them shouted something. The aggression in his voice drifted across the open ground.

'The fuck's he doing?' Caitlin breathed.

Before Danny could answer, the Hilux moved forward again. Even from a distance, Danny could hear the engine complaining as the Imam kept it in too low a gear. 'He's driving like a twelve-year-old,' Caitlin said. Danny agreed. It was a relief when the vehicle swerved off to the left and came to a halt thirty metres from the cave mouth.

Another pause. Ten seconds. Twenty. The guards looked twitchy, glancing nervously at each other as they kept their weapons on the vehicle.

Then the driver's door opened. The Imam stepped out. When the guards didn't lower their weapons, he raised his hands above his head and walked towards them. He looked very small from this distance. Bony. He was walking uncomfortably.

The guards allowed him to approach. He stopped again when he was about ten metres from them. There appeared to be an exchange. One of the guards disappeared back inside the cave, while the other kept the Imam at gunpoint. The first guard appeared two minutes later. There was another exchange. The Imam lowered his hands and walked out of sight into the cave, the two guards following him, leaving Danny and Caitlin unobserved.

They grabbed their chance. Danny took the rocket launcher and loaded up an RPG. Caitlin grabbed her assault rifle. They both put on their NV helmets, but kept the tubes raised for now. They took up firing positions behind the mound of rocks, Danny with the launcher resting over his right shoulder, Caitlin with her assault rifle primed. Neither of them knew how long they would need to keep this position, but when their targets emerged they needed to be ready.

Ten silent minutes passed. The sun was sinking fast towards the western horizon. Danny's left shoulder was pulsing with pain. He tried to put it from his mind.

'What the hell are they talking about in there?' Caitlin said.

'Who knows.'

'What if they don't come out?' Caitlin said.

'Then we hit them after dark. No other choice.'

'You think he's playing ball?'

'I don't know any better than you, Caitlin.'

Silence. Another five minutes passed. The sun hit the horizon. The sky turned a deep pink and the mountain face became darker.

'If we wait much longer,' Caitlin said, 'it's going to be tough to keep on target . . .'

But as she spoke, there was movement. Figures appearing at the cave mouth. The two guards were first. Their weapons were slung across their backs and they were carrying rolled-up prayer mats. A third guard followed them. He had no visible weapon but seemed to be carrying more than one mat. And after him, the Imam, walking to the right-hand side of a very tall man with a very black beard, wearing camouflage gear. No visible weapons.

The two armed guards scanned the area, but it seemed rather perfunctory. That was good. Danny had the sense that they'd bought the Imam's story.

The five targets moved as a unit, beyond the two parked Land Rovers to a patch of open ground approximately twenty metres from the cave mouth. Those carrying prayer mats laid them on the ground, facing south-west. They were in two rows: a solitary mat at the front, three mats in a line behind it. The Imam stood in front of them, his back to the setting sun, while the bearded man that Danny took to be Al-Zafawi knelt on the front mat. His three guys took the row behind.

'I'm going to hit the Land Rover on the left,' Danny said. 'The shock and awe should make them panic and run for cover. You take the nearest of the three guys. When we open up, they'll head back into the cave if they're smart, or to the other Land Rover if they're not. Be ready for that.'

They each made small adjustments to their line of sight as the Imam raised two hands and the others prostrated themselves before him. Danny focused the sights of his rocket launcher at the broad side of the Land Rover. He could just hear the Imam's chant drifting across the silent desert, flooded red by the setting sun.

'Are you on target?' he said.

'Roger that.'

'Take the shot.'

They fired in unison. The aimed round from Caitlin's assault rifle found its target instantly. The RPG took a couple of seconds longer. The double retort from the two weapons echoed violently against the mountainside. Danny lowered the launcher just in time to see the sudden devastation they had wreaked on Al-Zafawi's group. Caitlin's target was flat and motionless on the ground. The RPG fizzed towards the Land Rover and slammed accurately into its side. Danny saw the explosion before he heard it: a great cloud of black smoke burst from the vehicle, with a hot heart of orange flame somewhere at its centre.

It took the targets several seconds to realise what was happening, and to react. Al-Zafawi was the fastest. He rose to his feet and sprinted towards the cave mouth, past the Land Rover that was burning ferociously. He looked over his shoulder and seemed to shout an instruction at his two remaining guards. One of them ran towards the Imam, who had fallen to the ground from the impact of the blast. The second sprinted to the second Land Rover on which the comms satellite was mounted, to find cover. Caitlin released two rounds in quick succession, trying to put him down. She was unsuccessful. The guard covered the ten metres of open ground and hid himself behind the front of the Land Rover. His companion had the Imam on his feet now. He had pressed a handgun to the old man's head and was manoeuvring him towards the Land Rover.

'Put them both down!' Danny barked, as he rid himself of the rocket launcher and grabbed his own assault rifle. Before Caitlin could take another shot, however, there was a burst of automatic fire from the direction of the intact Land Rover. Shards of rock exploded from the front of their firing position, forcing them to take cover.

'*Get another RPG on target!*' Caitlin shouted. '*We need to take out the other Land Rover!*'

'You reload it,' Danny said. He had other plans. The shooter had their position. He knew he couldn't fire another RPG immediately without presenting himself as a target. Instead, he reached for the remote detonator. He peered through the rocks towards the targets. No sign of the shooter, but the other guard was still dragging the Imam towards the Land Rover. Distance: five metres.

Three.

The Imam's arms were flailing as the guard dragged him behind the cover of the Land Rover.

'Do it!' Caitlin shouted.

Danny flicked the switch on the remote detonator. Another explosion split the air. Danny didn't watch its effects. He knew the Imam would be dead, but he needed to be certain about the other two guards. 'Give me the launcher,' he said. He grabbed the reloaded weapon from Caitlin, mounted it on his good shoulder, breathed deeply and re-established his firing position. He saw tendrils of smoke drifting up from behind the Land Rover, which was clearly partially damaged because it was sinking towards the rear left-hand wheel. There was no sign of either militant, but that didn't mean they weren't there. He got the launcher on target and quickly released a second RPG, before ducking quickly back behind the firing position. He heard, rather than saw, the fizz of the projectile's trajectory and the sudden boom of its impact.

Then, silence. The desert air reeked of cordite and burning.

Danny was breathing heavily, and sweating. Caitlin too. They had their backs to the rocks.

'Al-Zafawi's still in the cave,' Caitlin said.

'Roger that.'

'What do we do? Wait till dark?'

Danny shook his head. 'That gives him a chance to regroup, hide, send for help, set up a firing position, whatever he wants. I'm going to advance to target. You'll have to lay down covering fire. You can do that?'

She gave him a look, then arranged several full magazines in a row and took up her firing position again. 'Try to stay alive, Danny Black. I don't want to be extracting from this shithole by myself.'

Danny discarded the launcher and grabbed his own rifle. 'Open up,' he said.

Caitlin fired two bursts of covering fire across the open ground in quick succession as Danny swung round the edge of the rocks and, crouching low to present a smaller target, ran thirty metres to his 10 o'clock towards the position where the late Imam had parked the Hilux. This gave him a moment's cover. It also meant that he could approach the cave mouth from an oblique angle, giving Caitlin a free line of fire towards it and ensuring that the first burning Land Rover presented an obstacle to anyone firing from the cave mouth.

It was almost dark now, but the two Land Rovers burned ferociously like beacons on either side of the cave mouth, the heat distorting the appearance of the space between them. There was a burst of automatic fire from Caitlin's position every five or ten seconds. Danny didn't linger in the cover or the Hilux, but altered his trajectory to close in on the cave mouth. As he ran, he could just make out explosions of dirt as the rounds hit the ground between the two burning vehicles.

He started to feel the heat of the nearer burning Land Rover from a distance of approximately twenty metres. A greasy diesel stench permeated the air, and the smoke and heat haze seriously compromised his vision. At ten metres – where the abandoned prayer mats lay, one of them covered by a bloodied corpse – it was too hot to get any closer, and the ferocious noise of the burning almost masked the distant bursts from Caitlin's assault rifle. Danny went to ground. He took a flashbang from his ops vest. Then he skirted round the back of the Land Rover. There was a gap of approximately five metres between the burning vehicle and the mountain face. Distance to the cave mouth: fifteen metres. Danny took a deep breath and followed the line of the mountain face, keeping as far from the heat source of the vehicle as possible. He reached the opening to the cave in five seconds. Stood with his back to the wall. Primed the flashbang and hurled it inside.

There was a three-second pause. Then, from inside the cave, a deafening, ear-splitting explosion and a sudden blinding flash of light. As it happened, Danny was engaging the NV tubes of his helmet. And the very moment the effect of the flashbang had subsided, he swung round into the cave, weapon engaged.

The cave was large and deep, but Danny couldn't establish its precise dimensions because his eyes were immediately drawn to another vehicle, parked about fifteen metres into the cave, facing out. In the green haze of the NV, he caught the outline of a figure behind the steering wheel, but a second later he was completely blinded as the headlamps switched on and the light burned into his NV goggles. Danny clamped his eyes shut just as he heard the roar of an engine starting up. He sensed the vehicle surging towards him. Instinctively he lowered his weapon a little. He fired a blind burst, panning left and right. Opening his eyes, he saw that he'd been on target. The headlamps were blown out. He could see again. But the vehicle was accelerating towards him. Distance, seven metres. The driver was going to run him over . . .

Quickly, Danny raised his weapon and released a single round into the centre of the windscreen. The retort echoed round the cave and the window shattered noisily. He jumped to the left, only just in time to avoid the impact from the vehicle. His wound shrieked with pain as he rolled on the ground, but he managed to put down two more rounds, each of them slamming into the front and rear right-hand tyres. The vehicle swerved heavily to the left and came to a sudden halt.

Danny advanced.

Distance to the driver's door: six metres. He crossed it with his weapon engaged and pointing directly through the side window. He could see the figure behind the wheel. He looked like he was desperately trying to knock the vehicle into reverse to straighten it up, but without success. As Danny reached his target, he lowered his weapon, opened the door and, gritting his teeth against the pain in his bad shoulder, manhandled the driver out of the vehicle and threw him heavily on to the ground. He landed on his back and for the first time Danny was able to positively identify Al-Zafawi, with his distinctive black beard and camo gear. He pressed one heel hard against his target's chest and aimed his rifle directly at his head.

'Your guys are dead,' Danny said. 'You and me – we're going to have a little talk.'

He bent down, pulled Al-Zafawi roughly to his feet again, then pushed him forcefully towards the cave exit, closely following with his rifle pointing at his target's back.

18

Al-Zafawi wasn't in the mood to come quietly. The Taliban leader was rigid and unyielding as Danny forced him out of the cave. The two vehicles were still burning ferociously. From this angle, Danny could see the remains of the Imam and the two guards. The guards' corpses had ignited. The Imam's body parts were scattered around the area. Looking through the heat haze back towards their firing point, Danny could see the refracted silhouette of Caitlin advancing across open ground. He turned his attention back to Al-Zafawi, who was having trouble keeping his eyes off the sight of his burning guards. Danny pushed him further in that direction, but didn't follow. When Al-Zafawi was about four metres from the blazing Land Rover, Danny shouted: 'Get to your knees.'

Al-Zafawi turned. He took a step in Danny's direction, obviously keen to get away from the intolerable heat of the blaze, but stopped when Danny raised his rifle a couple of inches as if about to shoot. '*To your knees!*' he repeated.

The Taliban leader did as he was told. He stared up at Danny with a look of absolute arrogance. Within seconds, however, his face contorted with pain. He raised his hands and tried to protect the back of his head from the heat, but it clearly scorched his hands too. Unable to bear the heat any longer, he curled himself up into a little ball, roaring with pain.

Danny let him sweat for another ten seconds. Then he approached, grabbed him by one arm, pulled him away from the blaze and threw him to the ground again. His clothes were almost too hot to touch, and there was a scent of singed hair.

Caitlin ran up to them. She was drenched in sweat. She took in the scene with one sweeping look. 'Should have brought some shrimps for the barbie?' she said.

Danny ignored her. He knelt down so that he was face to face with Al-Zafawi. The Taliban leader spat in his face. He was rewarded with a solid thump on his right cheek.

'Who are you?' the Taliban leader demanded fiercely. He had to speak loudly to be heard above the crackle of the flames.

Danny pointed at the burning bodies. 'I'm the guy who's going to do *that* to *you*,' he said, 'unless you tell me exactly what I want to know.'

Al-Zafawi gave him a look of absolute contempt. 'English?' he said.

'You don't need to know who I am. You just need to answer my questions unless you want to go the same way as your old mate the Imam.'

'You are English,' Al-Zafawi spat. 'I will not answer anything. I do not fear death.'

'It's the bit that comes just before you need to worry about.'

But before Danny could threaten him with his weapon, Al-Zafawi stood up and spread his arms wide. 'Go ahead!' he said. 'Torture me, shoot me, blow me up like you did my old friend – and answer to the Americans!'

Danny stared at him.

'Go on!' Al-Zafawi shouted. His English was very fluent. 'I said shoot me! Then we can wind back the clock by ten years. Your friends can kill my friends, my friends can kill your friends! We shall wipe out innocent families across Afghanistan! It will be back to the bad old days!'

He sounded to Danny like he was raving. Danny strode forward, intending to strike him again on the cheek with the butt of his rifle. But he felt Caitlin pulling him back.

'Wait,' she said sharply. Danny was going to argue, but her expression silenced him. 'You're in bed with the Americans?' she shouted over the crackle of the flames.

'British fool,' Al-Zafawi spat back.

'Aussie fool, actually.' She held a handgun to his head. 'Answer the question, fuckwit.'

Al-Zafawi clearly didn't like being addressed by a woman. His arrogant demeanour didn't leave him as he directed his reply to Danny. 'The Americans *need* me,' he spat. 'I am the only reason their men are not dying in Helmand Province by the thousand!'

'Why?' Danny demanded. And when Al-Zafawi didn't immediately reply, he grabbed him by the throat and started pushing him back towards the flames. '*Why!*'

'Because I distribute their bullion, British fool!' Al-Zafawi shrieked. His eyes were wild.

Danny yanked him away from the flames and pushed him to the ground again. 'What are you talking about?'

'Their bullion,' Al-Zafawi said. 'Their gold. How else do you think they stop Helmand descending into all-out war again? So go ahead! Shoot me, and answer to the Americans. You stupid British have already been stealing from me.'

'What do you mean?'

Al-Zafawi spat on the ground.

Danny hauled him to his feet again. This time he dragged him to where one of his guards lay burning. He forced him to kneel, grabbed him by the hair and pushed his head closer to the melting face. Al-Zafawi retched from the sickening stench. 'What do you mean?' Danny repeated.

'Last night,' Al-Zafawi rasped. 'Three soldiers. They killed my man. They stole my money.'

There was a pause, then Danny said: 'Do you still have the footage?'

If Al-Zafawi was surprised that Danny knew anything about any kind of footage, he was in no position to show it. His hair was smouldering, his skin burning. 'Yes,' he said. '*Yes!*'

Danny dragged him away again. 'Where is it?'

Al-Zafawi pointed towards the cave.

'Get in there,' Danny told him.

It was fully dark now, and the cave was only partly illuminated by the burning vehicles. As they entered, Caitlin raised a high-powered Maglite and shone it around. The cave was well equipped.

A thick cable ran in from the satellite dish, leading to a steel rack with two chunky laptops. There was military gear scattered all around: boxes of ammunition, firearms, body armour; the works. One area to the left was set aside for sleeping – a mess of blankets lay on the ground. To the right, there was an electrical generator. In the middle, a fire pit. An area deeper in the cave was for eating – there was a table with the remnants of a meal. Danny sensed that Al-Zafawi had been here for weeks, maybe months.

'There?' he demanded, pointing at the laptops.

Al-Zafawi didn't reply, but he staggered towards the laptops with Danny bearing down on him.

'Show me,' Danny instructed.

'Do it yourself,' Al-Zafawi rasped. He plainly hated being ordered around. But Danny only had to give him a dangerous look for him to back down. The Taliban leader powered up one of the laptops with obvious reluctance. It took nearly a minute to boot up. He navigated to a folder and double clicked on a video file. It opened up and started to play. Danny watched intently.

He recognised the scene. It was the room in Target Blue's compound, viewed from the covert camera in the air-con unit. The footage was grainy and monochrome, but with a degree of night-vision capability that showed Target Blue still alive but asleep in his bed. The wardrobe was in the centre of the screen, but closed.

'Get to the money shot,' Danny said.

'What are you talking about, British fool?'

'Move it on.'

The Taliban leader scrubbed forward. There was sudden movement in the recording as a dog burst into the room. It jumped on to the bed where Target Blue was lying and sank its teeth into the target's leg. Three men entered. Their heads and eyes were covered by helmets and NV goggles, but Danny instantly recognised them as Tony, Dexter and Cole. They moved swiftly, dragging Target Blue, who was naked, from his bed and on to the floor. Cole stuffed his mouth with a rag. Tony bent down to take a retina scan and DNA sample. Dexter aimed his rifle at the target's head while the dog took up position by the door.

Target Blue was writhing badly – worse than Target Red had done. He seemed to be pointing at something: the wardrobe.

Tony raised one hand, apparently to tell Dexter not to perform the execution. He moved to the wardrobe and tried to open it. It was locked, so he looked round the room, disappeared from the camera's field of view for a moment, and returned with an object Danny couldn't make out. He used it to force open the wardrobe. He looked inside and removed a small suitcase. It was obviously heavy. Leaning over the suitcase, with his back to the camera, he appeared to open it up. He examined the contents for about half a minute, then closed the suitcase and turned to his mates. He said something – Danny couldn't make out what – and there appeared to be a moment of hesitation among them. Tony spoke again. The two others nodded.

Tony looked around the room. His eyes obviously fell on the fake camera. He moved out of shot. When he came into view thirty seconds later he was carrying a tape. He said something to the others. Cole took up position above the prone Target Blue, weapon engaged. Tony and Dexter left, with the dog.

'I don't need to see any more,' Danny said. He turned his back on the screen.

Caitlin was just behind him. 'I don't get it,' she said. 'We should watch the rest. What the hell happened?'

'It's obvious. Target Blue was guarding a stash of Al-Zafawi's bullion. He's not going to keep it all in one place. When Tony and the boys turned up, he made the obvious call and offered them the bullion in return for his life. The guys decided to rip him off, but they didn't want me in on it.'

'Why not?'

Danny shrugged. 'Tony probably said I'd rat on them. Real reason? A three-way split's better than a four-way split. So they order me out of the compound, killed the family and make out that I'd lost it. Gives them an excuse to put me out of action, arrange a casualty evacuation, then pretend they're off chasing Target Blue. In fact they probably nailed him somewhere nearby, then went off and cached the bullion somewhere they can come back to and retrieve it in a year or five, when this has all died down.'

'Why didn't Tony just kill you? We know what he's like – he'd have done it.'

'Wrong call. If I come home in a body bag, the Regiment starts asking questions. This way, I'm the bad guy, Tony's the hero. He gets into bed with the RMPs. He knows they're looking for any excuse to pin one on the SAS so they're primed to believe him. And it's no skin off his nose if he discredits the Regiment, because he's got a stash of American bullion sitting in a hole somewhere in Afghanistan that he can come and collect whenever he needs it.'

'If I was Dexter or Cole,' Caitlin said, 'I'd watch my back.'

Danny nodded grimly, then turned back to Al-Zafawi who was still staring at the footage. The image hadn't changed: Cole was standing over Target Blue, occasionally looking towards the doorway. Danny pulled the Taliban leader away and threw him to his knees again. 'Do the Americans know about this? Do they know your bullion was stolen?'

'Of course not, British fool.'

That made sense to Danny. 'Because you don't want them to start thinking that they need to find someone else to do your job.'

Al-Zafawi spat on the floor. 'They will not need to, British fool. I intend to get my gold back.'

Danny snorted. 'Good luck with that,' he said. He turned to Caitlin. 'I'm going to make contact with Hereford. Give me the sat phone.'

'You sure that's the right call?' Caitlin said. 'We've got no hard evidence that you didn't do what Tony's accused you of. This whole thing's turning to shit. It would be convenient for Spearpoint if you disappeared. Me too, now I'm involved. I wouldn't put it past Cadogan to make that call. He's not just the pompous git he likes to pretend he is. He wouldn't think twice about shutting us down.'

Danny shook his head. 'Maybe. But I'm going to bypass Cadogan. Go straight to Hammond. Say what you like about him, he sticks by his guys. Throw me the sat phone and keep this charmer quiet.'

Caitlin removed the sat phone from her pack and threw it to Danny, who took it outside. The burning vehicles had subsided a little – more smoke now, than fire – and the corpses were shapeless, blackened forms. He positioned himself twenty metres clear of the cliff face to ensure the sat phone made a connection. Then he switched it on and dialled the emergency access number into Hereford.

The call was answered immediately. An emotionless, unrecognisable voice: 'Go ahead.'

Danny stated his identification codes. There was a brief silence, then a new voice came on the line. Danny instantly recognised Ray Hammond's voice. 'What the fuck ...' he blazed, 'what the actual *fuck*, is going on?'

Danny told him. Everything. Hammond let him speak. When Danny had finished there was a crackly silence on the line. Hammond broke it with two words: 'Cole's dead.'

'How?' Danny demanded.

'We're having trouble getting details out of Holroyd. From what we can tell, he topped himself this morning.'

Another silence.

'It was Tony, boss. You know that, right?'

'We can't be—'

'It was Tony. I'm telling you. Someone needs to warn Dexter. He's tying up loose ends ... boss, I *know* how he operates. He's a fucking psycho.'

'You *think* you know how he operates,' Hammond barked back. 'What's to say Al-Zafawi's telling you the truth?'

'I saw the footage,' Danny said.

'Did you see bullion, Black? Actual bullion, with your actual eyes? Did you see Tony and the others kill the family?'

A beat. 'No,' Danny conceded.

'Then right now, you're just a guy with a theory. Stay by your sat phone. I'm going to try to find out what the hell's going on.'

The line went dead. Danny swore. He looked back towards the cave. He could just discern the outline of Caitlin holding

211

Al-Zafawi at gunpoint. He looked around. The burning vehicles were a beacon in the thick darkness of the Helmand night. Staying here was dangerous.

'Get a fucking move on, Hammond,' he breathed.

Cadogan's personal mobile rang. He looked at the screen. Number withheld. He answered it anyway, without identifying himself. 'Who's this?'

'It's me. Hammond.'

Cadogan looked around the Spearpoint ops room, where his team were working hard as usual. 'My dear chap, you have a line direct into Spearpoint—'

'I have two operators in Helmand currently pressing gun barrels into the skull of a Taliban commander called Al-Zafawi. You sure you want to discuss this with all your Spearpoint team listening in?'

Cadogan fell silent.

'I'm waiting,' Hammond said.

'Hold on,' Cadogan said. He limped towards the exit, all eyes on him, the phone pressed to his ear with one hand, the other leaning heavily on his stick. He stepped out of the ops room into the reception area, where the young man with the blond beard covering his burned face, who seemed to be on duty at all hours of the night and day, watched him head to the main exit and step out into the open air. 'Tell me Al-Zafawi is still alive,' he said.

'You seem pretty concerned for the welfare of a Taliban leader,' Hammond said.

'Is this Caitlin Wallace? I gave that girl distinct instructions not to follow up her lead on Al-Zafawi.'

'Turns out she's got a mind of her own. That's why we put her in the field in the first place.'

'Who else?' Cadogan demanded.

'Danny Black.'

Cadogan fell silent. Stared towards the trees that surrounded the Spearpoint base. 'What the bloody hell,' he said, 'is Black doing with Al-Zafawi?'

Cadogan listened as Hammond explained. How Black had escaped Camp Shorabak. How he'd hooked up with Caitlin Wallace and moved on the Imam. How he'd suspected that Target Blue had a link to Al-Zafawi and that the Imam and Al-Zafawi had known each other back in the UK. How he'd laid siege to Al-Zafawi's hideout. How he'd worked out what had *really* gone down with the kill team two nights ago. 'Just tell me,' Cadogan said as Hammond drew to a close, 'that they haven't killed Al-Zafawi.'

'Is it true?' Hammond said. 'Have the Americans been paying off the Taliban?'

'It's a good deal more complicated than that,' Cadogan snapped.

'Since I have two operatives in the thick of it, why not take the time to explain?'

Cadogan hesitated. Gathered his thoughts. 'The American money goes to Al-Zafawi and people like him. They distribute it among the warlords and regional leaders however they see fit. The idea is that it keeps the warlords happy and more inclined to peaceful activities.'

'And you *trust* Al-Zafawi to do that?' Hammond said.

'Most certainly not. This is the Americans' strategy and it's a damned foolish one. Who knows where that money really ends up? In case you haven't noticed, we're following a different strat-egy, eliminating high-value targets and doing what we can to reduce the Taliban's power and influence. The Americans know what we're doing, we know what they're doing. There's tension. It's a messy, stinking compromise that somehow maintains the status quo. Neither of us like it. But it means that for us, certain targets are off limits. Al-Zafawi's one of them. If our people kill him, it'll cause a diplomatic incident between us and the CIA that'll take months to clear up. Black and Wallace *cannot* kill Al-Zafawi. If they do, we're all for the chop. Do you understand?'

It was Hammond's turn to fall silent.

Cadogan breathed deeply, trying to calm himself down. 'Do you believe Danny Black?' he said finally.

'I don't know,' Hammond said. 'That kind of work affects people in different ways. Maybe Black did crack on the job.

Maybe Cole did kill himself.' He paused. 'But on balance, yes, I believe him. However, we don't have a scrap of real evidence against Wiseman. Even if we did, in court it would involve us admitting we're party to illegal operations in Helmand Province. And we can't do that.'

'And in the meantime . . .'

'Holroyd's got Tony and Dexter in his pocket. He's going to use them to discredit the Regiment. It's what the RMPs have wanted for years, but it's personal for Holroyd. Some kind of crusade. If he plays it right, it could be the end of 22. And it'll suit Wiseman down to the ground. The RMPs will give him immunity, and he knows he's got his bullion stashed away.'

'Options?' Cadogan said.

'We have to get Caitlin back to Panjika,' Hammond said. 'If it gets out that she's had contact with Black, Holroyd will go in for the kill and then we'll have the Aussies to deal with too.'

'Agreed. What about Black himself?'

'He's wounded and ill equipped. He needs support. My team is in transit from Kabul to Helmand as we speak. We'll get them to coordinate so Black can stay under the radar for now.'

'Do we know Black's current location?' Cadogan asked.

'We have a lock on the sat phone he used. There's a village ten klicks to his south-east that took a basket of Hellfires a few years back. It's still a bombsite, and unoccupied. We'll get them to RV there. Right now, we need to make contact with Dexter.'

'Why?' Cadogan said.

'Because if Black's right, he's in danger.'

'It's too high risk. If Holroyd gets a sniff Wiseman's off the rails, it's more strength to his arm.'

'We can't afford not to,' Hammond stated. 'If we can make him see that Wiseman's a threat to him, maybe we can turn him.'

'And if he doesn't buy the Wiseman line?'

'There's leverage. Dexter has a family in Northern Ireland. Couple of kids. But all this is above my pay grade. I have to refer it up.'

A pause. 'Do it,' Cadogan said finally. 'And for Christ's sake get them away from Al-Zafawi.'

But he didn't know if Hammond had heard him. The phone line was already dead.

The sat phone rang. Danny answered it immediately. 'Go ahead.'

'Tell me Al-Zafawi's still alive,' Hammond's voice said.

'Last time I looked.' Danny glanced towards the cave mouth. He could still just see Caitlin holding their hostage at gunpoint. 'Not going to lie – he's probably felt better.'

'He stays that way.'

'Boss—'

'*He stays that way!*'

'That's insane, boss. You know who this guy is, right?'

'I know who he is.'

'Terrorist atrocities, hundreds dead, Red Unit—'

'I know who he is,' Hammond repeated.

'And you want me to turn my back on him and leave him here? He needs a bullet in his head for a hundred reasons – and one of them is so that he doesn't come after me and Caitlin.'

'Have you finished?'

'No I fucking haven't finished. What is this, hug a terrorist day?'

'That's enough, Black. I understand what you're saying. I want him dead too, but you have your orders. If we put Al-Zafawi out of play, we have the Yanks to answer to, and nobody needs that. Understood?'

Danny took a moment to calm himself. 'Understood,' he said.

'Good. Now listen: you need to destroy that footage of Tony taking the bullion.'

'Jesus, boss, that's my alibi.'

'You don't need an alibi. We know you're clean.'

'But does Cadogan? I don't trust him.'

'Cadogan isn't our biggest problem. That footage getting into the hands of the Americans is. I have a team en route from Kabul. They're heading to a derelict village ten miles to your south-east. RV with them there. Caitlin needs to head back to Panjika.'

215

'Boss—'

'Don't argue, Black. This is fluid and fast moving. Hook up with the team and keep a low profile. Am I clear?'

A beat. 'Clear, boss,' Danny said.

The line died.

Danny headed back into the cave. Caitlin gave him an enquiring look and Danny knew what it meant. *Shall I do him?* He shook his head imperceptibly.

'It's true?' Caitlin asked.

Danny nodded. Al-Zafawi spat at the ground in front of him. Bad move. His unshakable arrogance made Danny flip. He stepped forward, pulled Al-Zafawi up by the throat and smashed him across the cheek. The Taliban leader glazed over and collapsed, unconscious.

'Well that's one way to go about it,' Caitlin said. She lowered her weapon. 'So what's the crack?'

'We leave him here. Alive.'

'What the fuck?'

'I know. Hammond won't change his mind. Your orders are to head back to Panjika. I'm to RV with a Regiment unit coming in from Kabul. There's a derelict village ten klicks south-east.'

'I know it,' Caitlin said. 'I'll drive you there.'

'No. We get you back to Panjika first.'

'Spare me the fucking chivalry, Danny. Your unit will have vehicles. I want to keep the Hilux in case I need to get Tommy and Gabina out of town. Gabina especially. She's a good kid, I need to look after her. I'll drive you.'

Danny didn't argue. He strode up towards the laptops, unplugged them and tucked them under his arm. Then he looked round the cave one final time. Walking out of here with Al-Zafawi still alive felt like leaving a loose end, and he didn't like it.

But they had their orders. 'Let's go,' he said. He led Caitlin out of the cave. As he passed one of the smouldering Land Rovers, he chucked two laptops into the heat. Their cases instantly started to melt.

He and Caitlin scanned the area one final time, then jogged side by side to the Hilux.

19

It was 19.00. The sun had set. Dexter was still sleeping.

It was time for Tony to move.

He put on his ops vest. Double-checked its contents. Retrieved the spare pack of chicken curry from his rucksack, along with a pencil-thin torch, a pair of plastic SOCO gloves and a clear ziplock bag. He stepped outside the Portakabin.

The fierce daytime heat had subsided, but it was still warm and muggy. The base was lit with floodlights and vehicle headlamps. There was activity in the direction of the airfield, the medical centre and the accommodation blocks. But the path towards the dog enclosure was clear.

As expected.

Tony covered the ground unseen in the darkness. As he approached the gate to the enclosure, he ripped open the packet of chicken curry. Dexter's favourite. And the dog's favourite. Tony had seen his unit mate feed it to his animal enough times.

He entered the enclosure. As he crossed over to the dog crate that housed Baron he looked around for a suitable stone. He selected one about the size of a grapefruit with a sharp flinty edge, then proceeded to the crate. He couldn't immediately see the animal, which meant it was in the covered kennel area at the back.

He entered the crate. Shut the door behind him and dropped the stone. Almost immediately he could hear a low, throaty growl. A black shape appeared at the entrance to the kennel.

Tony grabbed a fistful of chicken curry. Held it low and approached the dog. The growling didn't die away. He stopped a metre from the entrance to the kennel. Better to let the dog come to him, than to encroach on its territory. He crouched, holding out the fistful of meat. Held his ground.

The dog emerged slowly. The growl was replaced by a snuffling sound. It approached Tony, its eyes fixed on the food. Its tongue was warm and sticky as it ate the curry and licked his hand clean.

Tony ripped open the remaining MRE. He put it on the ground in front of Baron. The dog, suddenly at its ease, continued eating.

Slowly, so he didn't spook the animal, Tony positioned himself by its side, facing in the same direction.

He attacked quickly. The slightest delay would give the dog a chance to fight back. If that happened there would only be one winner. Tony knew what it was capable of.

He curled his right arm tight around the dog's neck, squeezing hard. The animal went into a sudden seizure of panic. It bared its steel-capped teeth. Its legs went into a frenzy. It tried to bark, but Tony was throttling it hard enough to stop any noise. The dog was strong, though. Muscular and lithe. It wriggled like an angry snake. Tony knew he had to finish this quickly. He used his body weight, falling heavily on to the dog's barrel chest while keeping his arm firmly round the neck. He felt the dog's ribcage crack. Its movements became more panicked, but weaker. Tony tightened his grip around the neck while keeping the body smothered. Thirty seconds later, the dog was still.

Tony cautiously released his grip. The dog lay motionless on its side. He moved quickly. Dragging the heavy animal by its legs, he pulled it back into the kennel area. He positioned it with its legs pointing against the back wall, then moved to an opposite corner where he emptied the items from his ops vest. He pulled on the SOCO gloves, then stripped himself naked. He bundled his clothes and stowed them outside the kennel where they couldn't become contaminated by what was about to happen. Naked, he retrieved the stone he had dropped at the entrance and returned to the kennel. He lit his torch and approached the dog.

The stone was a good weight in his hand. He held it with the sharp edge down. Kneeling, he raised it about thirty centimetres above the dog's head and slammed it down hard. There was a flat, splintering sound as the skull cracked. Tony bludgeoned the head several more times. With each strike it became more disfigured and bloodied, until it was little more than a glistening, meaty mess. Tony moved back and examined his handiwork by the light of his torch. He was satisfied that anyone who saw it, especially if they had a strong emotional attachment to the dog, would be sufficiently distracted by the sight not to notice anything else untoward with its corpse.

He retrieved the explosives from the far corner of the kennel. Crouching back down by the dog, he unpacked the two blocks of C-4. He squeezed them together, then moulded the plastic explosive into a sausage about twenty centimetres long. He tucked this underneath the dog's ops vest, along the belly. Invisible, unless you were looking for it.

Next he turned his attention to the blasting cap. He removed the nine-volt battery, slid the prongs underneath the ops vest and inserted them into the plastic explosive. He traced the wire to the trip switch under and along the dog's body, resting the switch vertically but at a slight angle under the dog's head. It was out of sight, but as soon as anyone moved the head, it would slip to a horizontal position.

He breathed deeply and, with a steady hand, attached the battery to its terminal and tucked it under the head next to the switch.

Tony retreated carefully. It was a hair trigger. The smallest of vibrations could detonate his IED. He shone his torch down at his body. Apart from his covered hands, there was only the faintest spatter of dog blood on his chest. Outside the kennel he killed the torch, removed the bloodied SOCO gloves, put them in the ziplock bag and pulled his clothes back on. He would wash himself when he could, but for now he showed no sign of being bloodied. He picked up the remains of the MRE, stashed it with the SOCO gloves inside the ziplock bag, and was heading for the exit of the enclosure in less than a minute.

His instinct was to run. He suppressed that instinct as he moved through the darkness up towards the burn pit, which was smouldering as always by the northern perimeter. He had to remain the grey man. Unremarkable. Unnoticed. He threw the incriminating ziplock bag into the pit before returning, head down, towards the Portakabin. By the time he reached it, he had not come within fifty metres of anybody else in the camp. He slipped silently through the door.

His arrival made Dexter stir. He muttered something in his half-sleep.

'What's that, buddy?' Tony said.

Dexter's eyes opened. He looked left and right, as if momentarily disorientated. He sat up suddenly, then pulled a nauseous face. 'I feel like shit,' he said.

'You look like it,' Tony said. 'You've been asleep all day. Anyone ever told you you snore like a bastard.'

'What time is it?'

'Seven-thirty.'

'Have you dealt with Baron?'

'You fucking joking?' Tony said. 'Without his daddy there?'

Dexter got to his feet. He swayed slightly. He staggered over to his pack and rummaged inside, before pulling out a ziplock bag of dry dog food. 'I'm going to feed him,' he said.

'We'll have some scoff when you get back,' Tony said. 'Maybe see if we can put our hands on some grog . . .'

But Dexter had already left.

Tony stared at the closed door, his expression blank.

It would take Dexter ten minutes to get to the dog enclosure. Another minute to find Baron. He looked at his watch: 19.31 hours.

If anything went wrong, the spotlight would surely fall on one of the ANA soldiers.

But nothing would go wrong. Tony had a feel for these things. All he had to do was wait.

Five minutes passed.

The door burst open. Holroyd stood there. He was red-faced.

Out of breath. He looked round the Portakabin. 'Where's Dexter?' he said.

Tony hesitated. He instinctively wanted to lie, but he knew he couldn't. If the device was discovered or failed to work, and it turned out that Tony had misdirected the RMP man, he'd be in the frame. 'I think he went to deal with the dog.'

'Has he made contact with Spearpoint?'

'Why?'

'You don't need to know why. Just answer the question.'

'He's been asleep all day,' Tony said.

'How do you know?'

'Because I've been in here with him.' He paused. Maybe Holroyd had looked in on them at some point while Tony had been about his business. 'Well, I stretched my legs a couple of times ...'

'I've had Spearpoint on the line,' Holroyd said. 'They want a private communication with him.'

'Oh yeah?'

'They're going to try to turn him. Undue pressure. I need to make sure he's on board.'

'Oh, he's on board, mate. You don't need to worry about that.'

'I'll decide what I need to worry about.' Holroyd clicked his fingers twice in Tony's direction. 'Come on.'

Tony didn't move. 'He'll be back any minute,' he said quietly.

'I need to speak to him now. You're coming with me.' Holroyd stepped out of the Portakabin.

Tony checked his watch: 19.37 hours. He stood up very slowly. Moved to the exit. Outside, he saw that Holroyd was already striding in the direction of the dog enclosure.

'Mate!' he called. 'Wait up.' Holroyd stopped and looked back. Tony jogged very slowly towards him. 'Seriously, buddy,' Tony said. 'Save yourself a trip. He'll be back in ten minutes and the dog enclosure's a shithole.'

Holroyd didn't answer. He continued to walk briskly. Tony kept to his side. 'So I got some pretty evil atmospherics from those ANA boys who saw what Cole did,' he said. Anything to distract Holroyd and slow him down.

'Leave the ANA to me.' The RMP man was half walking, half jogging.

'Wouldn't put it past them to try something, is all,' Tony said.

'Just keep your heads down. We'll be out of here tomorrow.'

Nineteen thirty-eight hours. Distance to the enclosure: 300 metres. Tony scanned through the darkness. He thought he could just see Dexter's outline about 200 metres in front of them. He pointed to his right, across this deserted area of the base towards a brightly lit aircraft hangar about 250 metres away where several figures had congregated. 'Is that him?'

Holroyd stopped. Looked in the direction Tony was pointing. 'Where?'

'By the hangar.'

Holroyd squinted. 'What are you talking about? You can't see that far.'

'I just thought I saw him is all.' Tony shrugged. 'Maybe not.'

Holroyd gave him a suspicious look. Tony knew he had to ease off with the lame distractions. 'He's probably feeding the dog now. We'll run into him on his way back.'

Holroyd nodded. When he started walking again, he was slightly less brisk.

Distance: 200 metres.

'When we see him, I'll do the talking,' Holroyd said.

'Roger that.'

Distance: 100 metres.

Tony tried to pierce the darkness again. There was no sign of Dexter. Surely he was at the very least in the dog crate by now.

Distance: 50 metres.

They were getting dangerously close. It occurred to Tony that something was going wrong. Maybe he should abort. Shout out to Dexter. Make it look as if he was the guy who'd called his mate away from a potentially lethal situation.

And share the bullion.

They continued walking.

Twenty-five metres.

Ten.

As they approached the high wire fence of the dog enclosure, Tony positioned himself directly behind Holroyd. Cover.

'Don't go in there, mate,' he said.

'Why not?' Holroyd said.

'The dog gets jumpy when it's been cooped up. It's used to me and Dexter. I don't want him going for you.'

Holroyd stopped. He was a metre from the entrance to the enclosure. He hesitated for a moment. Then he shouted. 'Dexter! It's Mike Holroyd! Are you—'

The explosion, when it came, was bigger than Tony expected. An intense burst of orange light flashed from the entrance to the kennel on the far side of the enclosure. The noise, despite being contained by the kennel walls, was ear splitting. Tony and Holroyd both hit the ground instinctively, each man covering their heads. A couple of seconds later, a small shower of grit hit their backs. Tony stood up. Holroyd remained crouched.

'Stay where you are,' Tony hissed. 'There may be a secondary device.'

Holroyd nodded, clearly terrified. He was muttering something, and making the sign of the cross. Good luck with that, Tony thought as he entered the enclosure and, feigning a careful gait, approached the dog crate, and then the kennel.

The kennel's roof had collapsed inwards. Smoke was billowing from it. He was half aware of a siren approaching from the distance.

He knew the IED had done its job. There was a stench of burning flesh and the heat from inside the kennel was intense even at a couple of metres from the entrance. He had a part to play, though. Steeling himself against the heat, he pushed on into the kennel.

There were two burning bodies inside. The dog's was gutted and excoriated. Gobbets of burning dog meat were dotted around the interior like candles. As for Dexter, his face had taken the worst of the blast. It was scorched and unrecognisable. His clothes were aflame and as Tony looked down on him he could see the full sleeve of tattoos on his arm melt into an indistinguishable mess of burned flesh. Tony grabbed his ankles and dragged him out of the kennel and into the dog crate. 'Get a medic!' he shouted. 'Get a fucking medic now!'

But Holroyd was shouting too. 'Leave him! Get out of there! Now! It's an order!'

A vehicle with a siren and a flashing light was screaming towards them. Tony did as he was instructed, sprinting across the enclosure. When he reached Holroyd, the RMP man dragged him away by one arm. Tony let him do it. As the emergency vehicle pulled up by the entrance to the enclosure and three ANA guys emerged, shouting and bathed in flashing neon light, Holroyd grabbed him by both arms and spoke to him face to face. 'This is not a coincidence,' he said.

His eyes bored into Tony.

'First Cole,' Holroyd said. 'Then Dexter. This is *not* a coincidence.'

'What are you saying?' Tony asked. There was a dangerous edge to his voice. He glanced towards the ANA guys who were talking on radios and preparing to enter the enclosure. Could he take their vehicle? What would his next move be?

'Spearpoint,' Holroyd breathed.

'What do you mean?'

Holroyd looked over his shoulder. 'Don't you see? It's how they work. They know we're going to blow them wide open. They want you, Dexter and Cole out of the way.'

Tony narrowed his eyes. 'Cole did himself in.'

'Did you *see* him do it?' Holroyd demanded. 'Did you *see* it, with your own eyes? And Dexter gets taken out just a few hours later?'

Tony stared at him. He almost smiled. He pointed towards the dog enclosure. 'Mate,' he said, 'it was probably just one of those ANA cunts. I told you they were giving me the hate stares. The dog went for—'

'Don't be so naive. Look at what's happening. It's the easiest thing in the world to eliminate people on a military base in

Helmand Province. Once we get back to the UK, they've got problems. *Real* problems.' He prodded Tony on the chest. 'You're next, Tony. You're next on their hit list. We need to get you somewhere safe. You need sanctuary.'

Tony feigned a concerned expression. He looked around anxiously at the ANA guys who were investigating the dog enclosure. 'You'd better let me tool up,' he told Holroyd. 'I can take care of myself, but I need my personal weapons.'

If Holroyd had any doubts that this was a good move, he didn't show it. 'You got it,' he said. 'Stick with me.'

Tony nodded. 'I owe you one, buddy,' he said. He shook Holroyd's hand.

'I told you,' Holroyd said. 'You're my guy. Let's get out of here.'

He grabbed Tony by the arm again, and started moving back towards the centre of the camp. Tony allowed himself to be manoeuvred. Holroyd had got it all so wrong, but that suited Tony. He was entirely out of the frame.

He jogged alongside the RMP man, and didn't look back over his shoulder to watch the fallout of his hit.

Cadogan took the call within a second of his phone ringing. 'Who's this?'

'Hammond.'

'Do please tell me Al-Zafawi's still alive.'

'We've got a bigger problem.'

'Bigger than compromising Her Majesty's Government's entire diplomatic relationship with the Americans?'

'Dexter's dead.'

Cadogan fell silent. He looked around the ops room and realised all eyes were on him. For the second time that evening he limped out, through the reception area where the young man with the beard covering his burned face watched him hurry past, and into the open air. He stood with his back to the base. A blue Passat was parked ten metres in front of him, facing the exit. He stared over it, towards the wooded area that surrounded the base. 'How?' he said.

'Details are sketchy. We haven't managed to speak to anybody directly at the camp. I've tried to contact Holroyd to see if he knows anything. I can't get hold of him. But a report's come in through the MOD. There was an IED. One fatality, a British dog handler. That's Dexter.'

A moment's silence. 'It was Wiseman?' said Cadogan.

'I think we have to make that assumption.'

A pause.

'I think you and I know that there is now only one option available to us,' Cadogan said.

Another silence.

'You're suggesting a blue on blue?'

'I believe that's the euphemism.'

'You're a ruthless bastard,' Hammond said. 'That floppy-haired, public school act of yours is a fucking good disguise.'

'My dear chap,' Cadogan said very quietly, 'if you've a better suggestion, I'm all ears.'

Hammond didn't reply.

'You're a good egg, Ray. You want to look after your men, even the bad apples. I understand that. But if we don't do this, it's the end of Spearpoint and it could be the end of the SAS. If Tony testifies for Holroyd – I don't see how we can survive that.'

'Nor do I,' Hammond said.

'Well then?'

'We have an SAS team on the ground,' Hammond said with obvious reluctance. 'Black's hooking up with them now.'

'Splendid.' Cadogan stared into the middle distance. 'So for the avoidance of doubt,' he said, 'and so we can be clear that there are no crossed wires: you're agreeing that we give Danny Black and his team the order to hunt down and kill Tony Wiseman.'

Silence.

'Are we agreed?' Cadogan said.

'I'll give the order,' Hammond replied. The line went dead.

Cadogan didn't move at first. His bad leg ached. He needed to sit down, but he couldn't face the ops room. He turned slowly. As he did, he caught a reflection in the wing mirror of the Passat. A bearded face in the open doorway to the base. Burned skin. Cadogan turned more quickly. The door clicked shut.

His face hardened. He limped towards the door. Opened it. Approached the desk, where the young soldier with the disfigured face was sitting reading a paperback. The kid put the book down on the table as Cadogan limped up to him. 'What did you hear?'

The soldier blinked heavily. 'Sir?'

'Just now. What did you hear?'

'Nothing, sir.'

'You were at the door. I saw you.'

'Closing it, sir. For security. And there was a draft.'

'You're not Spearpoint cleared?'

'No, sir.'

'If you utter a word of anything you just heard me say, you're going to prison. Do you understand that.'

The young man looked chastened. 'I didn't hear anything, sir.'

Cadogan stared at him. 'Keep it that way, soldier,' he said.

'Yes, sir,' the young man said. He nodded earnestly. Cadogan turned his back on him and returned to the ops room.

The young man's name was Kenny Sterne. The burn on his face had been acquired in Iraq when the armoured vehicle in which he had been travelling to Basra had hit a roadside bomb. The word was that it had been installed by an American special-forces unit in an attempt to hit an insurgent's vehicle. Their act of road-side sabotage had gone very wrong.

Confined to a desk job, he had little option but to make the best of his remaining years in the army. But when a member of the Royal Military Police had approached him and asked for his help in curtailing the more excessive activities of the special forces, he was on board.

When he'd been posted to Spearpoint, the RMP had been delighted. Less so when it turned out his actual understanding of what went on in the base was extremely limited.

Now, though, he had some intel. Limited and fragmented, maybe. But intel all the same.

He stepped outside and made the call.

'McGuigan,' said a distant-sounding voice at the other end.

'It's Kenny Sterne.'

'What do you want, Kenny? We're busy.'

'Tell Holroyd I have something for him.'

'He's tied up at the moment. Give it to me.'

Kenny hesitated.

'Kenny, are you wasting our time?'

'No, sir. It's just—'

'Just what?'

Kenny licked his lips. 'I overheard Cadogan,' he said. 'He just gave the order for Danny Black to kill Tony Wiseman. I don't know if it means anything to you, or if it's helpful . . .'

Silence at the other end.

'Hello . . .'

'Get back to your post, Kenny,' McGuigan said quietly. 'Don't mention this to anyone else. Do you understand?'

'Yes, sir,' Kenny said. 'I understand.'

The line went dead.

Tony's weapons had been kept in a small hangar that had been set aside for the use of Holroyd and McGuigan. The magazine had been removed from the M4, but his Sig remained loaded. He checked over the assault rifle – definitely his, as it had the little Tipp-Ex kill marks on the stock – fed the magazine into the body and made it safe. Tony had felt naked ever since the moment it had been taken away from him. He felt better now.

Holroyd had been reluctant to leave him alone. Tony had managed to persuade him that an ANA guard at the hangar door was a bad idea.

'I can take care of myself,' he told him.

'Do what you need to do.' Holroyd had reluctantly left him alone for an hour now.

Tony was pleased to be rid of the stupid fucker. Typical RMP, adding two and two to get five. Not that it mattered to Tony. He was going to come out of this smelling of roses. When it had all died down, he could return to the Stan and pick up the bullion. It was safe enough where it was, dug into a featureless hillside in the Helmand desert. Now Cole and Dexter were out of the way, he was the only one who could ever think of looking for it there, let alone be able to find it.

Everything was sweet.

The hangar door opened. Holroyd entered. Tony could tell from the look on his face that he had news. And that it wasn't good.

'What is it?' he said.

Holroyd looked over his shoulder. 'I was right,' he said.

'What are you talking about?'

'I've got a mole at Spearpoint. He's just the kid on reception. He's never come up with anything till now. But he's just confirmed that Spearpoint are in contact with Danny Black. They've given him the order to take you out.'

Tony inclined his head. 'Say again?'

'They've given him the order to take you out.'

But Tony had heard Holroyd very well, and he'd understood even more. The RMP man's belief that Cole and Dexter had been picked off by Spearpoint was fanciful. A theory that fitted what he wanted to believe.

But if Cornwall had genuinely issued a kill order on him, it could mean only one thing.

They knew.

About the bullion. About Target Blue and his family. About Cole and Dexter.

Tony didn't know *how* they knew. But they knew.

'How certain are you?'

'My man overheard the order being given.' Holroyd gave him a grim smile. 'Someone's looking out for you, my friend.' He glanced towards the heavens.

Tony inhaled slowly. 'You sure it was Black?'

Holroyd nodded.

Think fast, Tony told himself. Step carefully.

He had to get out of camp. Into the desert where he could disappear and figure out his next move. But he was confined here. He needed Holroyd's help to get out.

'He's in camp,' he said.

Holroyd blinked. 'What?'

'Black's in camp.'

'I saw him leave—' Holroyd said.

'He's back. Cole ... Dexter ... If they were hits, they were sophisticated. I should have seen it before. They have Black's fingerprints all over them.'

For the first time since Tony had met him, Holroyd suddenly looked scared. 'They're giving him the chance to cover his tracks.'

Tony nodded. 'That means they want both of us out of the way. You as well as me. We need to get out of camp now. Trust me, I know Danny Black. I don't like the guy, but he's good. He'll find us.'

Holroyd looked sick. 'Surely we're safer here ...'

'Tell that to Dexter and Cole.' He grabbed his M4. Slung it across his body. Double-checked his handgun. 'Can you get us a vehicle?'

Holroyd nodded. 'I should tell McGuigan ...'

'Tell *nobody*. I can keep you safe out in the desert, but only if you do what I say. What vehicle do you have?'

'A Land Rover.'

'Where is it?'

'By the cookhouse.'

'Let's go.'

'Now?'

'Unless you want to hang around here for Black?'

Holroyd shook his head. 'I *should* tell McGuigan.'

'Don't be a fucking idiot. He'd stab you in the back as soon as look at you. We tell nobody. Move.'

He allowed Holroyd to lead the way. They exited the hangar and crossed the base. Tony glanced towards the dog enclosure. Bright floodlights had been set up there and a number of vehicles were active in the area. Holroyd half walked, half ran towards the cookhouse. It took about four minutes to get there. The Land Rover – beige, its windscreen plastered with red dust and with a crack across the rear window – was parked up alongside two other military vehicles. Five ANA soldiers were milling around. They eyed Tony and Holroyd with overt hostility as Tony got behind the wheel and Holroyd took the passenger seat. Tony started the engine, reversed in a narrow turning circle and headed towards the exit barrier at the south of the camp. He drove calmly, looking straight ahead, with no outward indication of the fast and panicked calculations going on in his head.

How did they know? Were they acting just on Danny Black's word? Or did they have more?

It took two minutes to reach the exit barrier. The Land Rover's headlamps illuminated five armed guards standing in front of the barrier. The place was clearly on high alert. Tony came to a halt ten metres from their position.

'I'll talk to them,' Holroyd said.

Without waiting for a reply he exited the vehicle and strode up to the armed guards. From behind the wheel Tony watched the RMP man clearly at his most officious, pointing back towards the interior of the camp, then forcefully out into the desert. The ANA guys looked unsure, but after a full minute of ear-bashing from Holroyd they stepped aside. Holroyd returned to the vehicle as the exit barrier opened. 'Get out of here,' he said, 'before they change their mind.'

Tony hit the accelerator. The Land Rover sped out of camp, its headlamps piercing the thick darkness of the Helmand desert.

They drove in silence, as the glow of Camp Shorabak faded in the rear-view mirror. Tony kept his speed low, his eyes on the road ahead, searching for inconsistencies that might indicate an IED. There was no sign of any other vehicle. After twenty minutes, he started looking to the side of the road. When they drew up alongside a deep ditch running parallel to it, he stopped.

'What are you doing?' Holroyd said. And when Tony didn't immediately reply: 'We need to find somewhere to bunk down for the night.'

'Get out,' Tony said.

An outraged look crossed Holroyd's face. He was about to say something, but Tony drew his handgun and Holroyd stayed silent.

'Get out,' Tony repeated, at half the volume.

Holroyd felt for the door latch. Scrambled out of the vehicle.

Tony got out too. 'Stand by the ditch,' he said.

Holroyd was a frightened animal. His eyes were darting around as he looked deep into the desert, plainly wondering whether to run, but too scared to do even that.

'What's ... what's going on, Tony?'

'Shut your fucking cake hole and do what I said. Don't force me to make you.'

Holroyd stepped around the Land Rover. He stood a metre from the ditch.

'Closer,' Tony said.

'Wiseman—'

'*Closer!*'

Holroyd did as he was told. He was less than half a metre from the ditch now.

'Face away from the car. *Do it!*'

Holroyd turned.

'Get on your knees. Like in church, hey?' And because Tony knew he wouldn't do it automatically, he kicked Holroyd in the back of his right kneecap so the RMP man sank to a kneeling position.

He aimed his handgun at the back of Holroyd's head.

'Tony,' Holroyd breathed. 'You're ... you're *my guy!*'

'Don't make me fucking laugh,' Tony said.

It crossed his mind to tell Holroyd everything. That he'd set Danny Black up. That he'd stolen and hidden a suitcase full of Taliban bullion. That he'd killed Cole and Dexter. That Holroyd had been backing the wrong horse all the time, and he still would be if Tony hadn't suspected that Spearpoint and Hereford knew the truth. That Holroyd had been useful to him right up to the point that they'd breached the Shorabak perimeter, but his usefulness had now come to an end.

But there was no point.

He could smell piss. It was coming from Holroyd.

'Please ...' the RMP man whispered. '*Oh Lord ... please ...*'

Tony fired. The nine-millimetre round pierced the back of Holroyd's skull with a small explosion of blood, bone and brain matter. Holroyd slumped forward, half in the ditch, half out. Tony holstered his weapon, then bent down, grabbed his victim's ankles and hauled the body round so that it fell wholly into the ditch, out of sight from anyone passing.

He spat on the corpse, then returned to the Land Rover. He sat behind the wheel for a minute, calculating his next move.

Then he started the engine and drove off.

20

The derelict village had clearly not been occupied for many years.

Danny surveyed it from the road through his night sight. Distance: approximately 750 metres. Craggy, mountainous hills formed a backdrop to the former habitation, half-obscuring a bright moon. In the magnified green haze, he saw the remnants of bomb-blasted buildings, and vast piles of rubble. There were no trees or other greenery – they were several klicks from the Helmand River or any of its tributaries. There was no movement. No vehicles. No overt sign of human habitation.

But that didn't mean there was nobody there. If the Regiment team from Kabul were *in situ*, Danny would fully expect them to be invisible.

He would also expect them to be watching.

'Give the sign,' he told Caitlin.

Caitlin was standing next to him. She held her torch above her right shoulder, facing the derelict village. On Danny's instruction, she gave five short pulses of light. Danny panned the night sight left and right, searching the rubble for signals.

'Go again,' he told Caitlin.

Caitlin repeated the signal. Danny panned left to right. Nothing. Until . . .

Something had caught his attention. He panned quickly left in time to see a distant light source – faint and green in the NV – mirroring their call.

He lowered his night sight. 'They're here,' he said.

Danny and Caitlin entered their vehicle – Caitlin behind the wheel – and pulled off the main road towards the derelict village.

They drove slowly and with their headlamps illuminated. Making a covert approach on an SAS position would have been unwise.

Danny's shoulder was bad. It sent a sinister ache down his arm and across his torso. He swallowed more painkillers as Caitlin drove. She glanced at him. 'The guys will be able to see to that.'

Danny ignored her. 'When you get back to Panjika, get your team ready to extract. My money's on Spearpoint pulling you out within twenty-four hours.'

She nodded. 'What about you?' she said.

Danny didn't reply. He could guess what his next order would be. He hoped he was wrong.

'Stop here,' he said.

They were thirty metres from the remnants of an old mud and straw wall. Beyond it was a dilapidated maze of former compounds, potholed streets and general debris.

'Kill the engine,' Danny said. 'Get out of the vehicle. No weapons. Hands visible.'

Caitlin was clearly reluctant, but she did as Danny said. They stood in front of the Land Rover and waited.

A minute passed.

Two.

The movement, when Danny noticed it, was directly ahead of them. Two figures emerged from the darkness fifty metres away. They walked a couple of metres apart and Danny could soon make out that they were armed. He looked down and noticed a dancing red dot on his chest. Caitlin had one too.

'I'm really hoping these are your good-time boys,' she muttered.

Danny knew they were, because he was still alive.

At a distance of fifteen metres, Danny could clearly see their military camo, their SF helmets and their rifles spray-painted in khaki. They were both bearded, and had their rifles engaged as they walked. At ten metres they stopped. Remained still for several seconds.

'Danny,' called a voice. 'How many times do I have to pick you up out of the shit?'

Danny narrowed his eyes. 'Brooker?'

The two men lowered their weapons. The guy on the left stepped forward. Now that his weapon was lowered, Danny recognised Ben Brooker's face: half British, half Nepalese and as tough as flint. He'd been called in to provide operational support for Danny on a previous mission and had shown his worth.

The two SAS men walked towards Danny and Caitlin. 'You know Jock Riley from D Squadron,' Brooker said, indicating his companion.

'Good to see you,' Danny said.

'Thanks for getting us pulled out of Kabul,' Riley said. 'What a dump.' He looked enquiringly at Caitlin.

'Caitlin Wallace,' Danny said. 'She's not staying.'

'I hear you've been crossing swords with your old mucker Tony Wiseman,' Brooker said. Sometimes, when Brooker spoke, his Nepalese ethnicity crept into his accent. Danny momentarily failed to understand the word 'mucker'. But then he did, and he knew there was no point denying it.

'You heard right,' he said.

'Hereford filled us in. Spearpoint, the kill team, everything that's happened. You'll be pleased to know Tony and the others fucked-up pretty bad.'

'What do you mean?'

'Your kill team had GPS trackers in their radio sets. Their story was that they headed north from the village of Gareshk to follow their target. But that's not what they were doing. They were heading north to—'

'To cache the bullion,' Danny said.

'Right. Spearpoint would have no reason to suspect anything out of the ordinary. But when you found out what was really happening—'

'Where's the cache?' Danny asked.

Brooker nodded at Riley, who took a map from his camo jacket. They walked over to the Hilux and spread it out on the bonnet.

'We're here,' Riley said, indicating an area about twenty klicks to the west of the Helmand River. 'Gareshk is here, Panjika here, Shorabak here.' He pointed north in the direction of the craggy mountain face that loomed over the derelict village. 'These peaks follow this line.' He indicated a region of dense east-west contour lines. 'According to Spearpoint's records, after the kill team left you, they headed north from Gareshk for approximately an hour and ended up here.' His finger followed the contour lines west, stopping at a point approximately thirty clicks north-west of their current location. 'They stayed here for forty-five minutes, then headed back towards Shorabak.'

Forty-five minutes. Time enough to dig a cache and secrete the bullion.

'What are our orders?' Danny asked.

'We're still waiting on Spearpoint,' Brooker said. He glanced at Caitlin as he spoke, but Danny didn't think she noticed.

'Well,' Caitlin said. 'My orders are to bug out of here. You gentlemen enjoy yourself. I'm heading back to Panjika.'

Danny nodded. 'Roger that.' And before Caitlin climbed back into the Hilux, he called to her. 'Hey, Caitlin?'

'What?'

'Go carefully.'

She winked at him. 'I always go carefully, Danny Black,' she said. 'Look after him, fellas. He's got a bullet wound on his left shoulder, looks and stinks like a ripe cheese.'

'You got it,' Brooker said.

Caitlin climbed behind the wheel, turned the engine over and reversed. Seconds later, she was heading back towards the empty main road, the rear lights of the Hilux disappearing into the distance. Danny felt her absence immediately. He tried not to let it show. When he turned back to Brooker and Riley, he saw that they were exchanging a look.

'What?' he said.

'Nothing,' Brooker said. 'We just need to get off the road is all.'

'Where are the rest of your guys?'

'There's the shell of an old compound a hundred metres up here,' Riley said. 'Gives us eyes on the surrounding area.' He spat on the ground. 'Jesus, I've seen some shitholes, but this one takes the cake.'

'You sure it's deserted?'

'We sent a nano-drone up with a thermal camera. Nothing. Even the animals stay clear of this place. Come on, let's get you some scran and water.'

None of the three men spoke as they entered the village. Despite Riley's promise that it was deserted, Danny was silently alert to his surroundings. This was a ghost town. Chunks of shrapnel were embedded in the ground and the whole area was pockmarked with ordnance craters. But it also showed the signs of a previous life. Burned-out car chassis. Old tyres on the ground. Sheets of corrugated iron that might once have been the roofs of the devastated buildings all around. Against the wall of the compound to which Brooker and Riley led them was a child's doll, its hair burned and one of its eyes missing. Danny found himself thinking about his own kid, back home. He quickly put that thought from his mind. It had no place there. Not right now.

He could see why the guys had chosen this shell of a compound. The walls were largely intact, but occasional cracks provided a vista on all four sides. Their two vehicles – sand-coloured Land Rovers – were inside the enclosure, parked facing a section of wall on the north-eastern corner that had been fully destroyed, offering an exit. There were two other guys in the unit. They were each positioned with their rifles poking through cracks in the southern wall, facing the direction from which Danny and the others had approached. Only when Brooker gave them the word did they stand down and greet Danny. Kit Hargreaves and Murray Jackson were bearded, broad-shouldered, silent, but not displeased to have been pulled out of Kabul to join him in the badlands of the south.

With Kit and Murray back on guard duty, Brooker threw Danny a packet of chocolate and a canteen of fresh water. 'I didn't tell you everything back there,' he said. 'Not in front of the chick.' The slang sounded slightly peculiar in his half-Nepalese accent.

Danny took a long draught of water and felt it soaking through his body. 'Go on,' he said.

'It's about Tony Wiseman and his team.'

'Or what's left of it.' He raised the canteen again for another pull.

'Nothing's left of it. There was an IED in Shorabak. Dexter bought it.'

Danny lowered the canteen. 'Tell me Tony's still in camp,' he said quietly.

Brooker shook his head. 'He was reported missing about an hour ago. Along with some RMP guy, name of Holroyd.'

Danny swore under his breath.

'You know him?'

'He had me under armed guard in Shorabak.'

'Then let's keep you under his radar.'

'No,' Danny said. He pointed towards one of the vehicles. 'Give me a set of keys,' he said.

Brooker shook his head.

Danny rounded on him. '*Give me a set of keys!*'

'You need to calm the fuck down, Danny.'

'You should have told me this before Caitlin left. What if Tony goes looking for her?'

'Why the hell would he? We're under orders, buddy. Spearpoint know that Caitlin and Tony used to be a thing.'

'Not any more. She fucking hates him.'

'Even so,' Brooker said, his tone measured. 'She might have a relapse. Tip him off.'

'What are you talking about?'

Brooker sniffed. Exchanged another glance with Riley. 'We've had a kill order on Tony Wiseman,' he said.

Danny fell silent. Looked from Brooker to Riley, then back again. Their expressions made it clear that the idea of taking out an SAS brother was not one they liked. But it was equally clear that they intended to carry out their orders.

'Spearpoint have given Caitlin's team the order to extract. They'll be ready for her when she gets there. Our job is to go after Tony.'

'He could be anywhere.'

'Sure. But at some point, we know where he's going to be.'

Danny stared at him. It took a moment to click. 'The bullion?'

'Right.'

'My money's on him heading straight there.'

'Maybe. He doesn't know we're on to him, remember.'

'If I know Tony, he'll twig. Say what you like about him, he's smart. Get that map out again.'

Riley opened it up on the bonnet of the nearest vehicle. Danny examined it closer. The cache location appeared to be on a slope heading up to a high peak. 'It's out of the way.'

'Exactly,' Brooker said. 'Chances of anyone coming across it by chance are insignificant.'

'What else do we know about the terrain?'

'It's green zone. We can expect rock, scree and trees. That's all we can guess till we put eyes on. But Spearpoint are adamant about one thing.'

'We IED the cache?'

Brooker nodded. It made sense. A covert assassination was one thing. Taking out your own guy? Quite another. It had to be plausibly deniable. Helmand was littered with IEDs. A British soldier being taken out by one was easy to explain away. An SF sniper round to the head? Not so much.

But it wasn't that straightforward. Danny checked the time. 21.59 hours. 'If he heads straight there, there's a chance we'll coincide. Then we'll have to do it however we can.'

'Either way, we need to move,' Brooker said. He gestured towards Danny's shoulder. 'You need med care?'

'There's no time.' He looked over towards Murray and Kit. 'Call your guys in. We head to the cache immediately. Let's get this sorted.'

Brooker nodded and gave a low whistle to the others.

Two minutes later they were on the move.

Caitlin was more anxious about the journey back to Panjika than she would ever have admitted in front of Danny and the other guys. A lone woman travelling the deserted highways of Helmand Province at night was not safe, no matter how much weaponry she had on her person and in the vehicle. If a group of armed Taliban hoods decided to erect a roadblock, her only option would be to fight her way through. So whenever she saw road lights in the distance, her pulse quickened and her eyes flickered to the handgun on her dashboard. Maybe she'd made the wrong call, splitting up from Danny Black.

She couldn't stop thinking about him. The dark hair and even darker look in his eye. It wasn't a romantic obsession. Caitlin had long ago learned that it was a bad idea to let your private life intrude on an op. No, it was something else. That grim, relentless nature of his. Danny Black was a guy who wouldn't take no for an answer. Caitlin had met soldiers like that before. Most of them had ended up dead, on ops. She couldn't help wondering if this was the fate that awaited Danny. She glanced around her as she drove. The moon silhouetted some craggy hilltops to her right. Would it be here, in the bleak wilderness of Helmand, that Danny's luck would run out?

Lights up ahead. She inhaled sharply and slowed down. A moment later she realised it was another vehicle approaching from the opposite direction. She relaxed slightly. She was just a couple of klicks from Panjika now. In a weird way, it felt like home. She was kind of looking forward to seeing Tommy, gruff and silent, and Gabina, wide-eyed and earnest. Familiar, friendly faces. A girl could miss her friends, in such an inhospitable location, so far from home.

Caitlin suppressed a shudder as she passed the location where the road bomb had exploded just four nights previously. She remembered the horrific sight of the kid with the flayed skin, and relived the scream of the young girl as Caitlin fitted a painful tourniquet to her life-threatening bleed. The wreck of the vehicle was still there, and the bitter smell of burning hung in the air. Caitlin didn't look back as she passed it.

She came off the road and parked up behind the treeline of a copse directly to the south of her compound. People seldom came here, and it was better for unfamiliar vehicles to remain unseen, if you didn't want to attract attention. She was about to turn off the lights when she noticed they were illuminating something through the trees. Another vehicle. She killed the lights and the engine, exited the Hilux and approached a beige Land Rover with a crack across the rear window.

An unfamiliar vehicle. Hidden, just like Caitlin's.

She stared at it for a moment in silence. A noise disturbed her. She spun round, scanning among the trees.

Nothing.

She returned to her vehicle and put on her robes, secreting her weapons underneath. She slung her rucksack over her shoulder. She looked around again, unable to shake the sensation that she was being observed. She saw nothing. Nobody. So she headed around the copse towards the compound.

As always, the village was silent, the streets deserted. Caitlin moved swiftly, keeping to the shadows, her eyes and ears fully alert. As she approached the compound, she saw that there was no light emanating from it. That figured. Tommy and Gabina would be asleep. Skirting around the southern wall to the entrance, she put one hand into her robes and withdrew the iron key that would unlock the door into the compound. Once she was there, she slid the key into the lock and tried to turn it.

The door was shut, but the lock was open.

Caitlin removed the key slowly and silently. She could feel a pulse in her neck. There was no way Tommy or Gabina would have failed to lock themselves in. Something was wrong.

She stowed the key and drew her handgun. Cocked it. Raised it. With her free hand she quietly opened the door.

And stepped inside.

Gabina's body was the first thing Caitlin saw.

The young woman was lying on her back in the middle of the courtyard. She was not wearing her usual burka, but a plain nightdress, demeaningly hitched up to expose between her legs. Her throat had been cut: a brutal, deep gash that had caused blood to flood on to her nightdress. There was a grotesque, rictus grin on her once-beautiful face. Those wide, innocent eyes of hers were open. The blood was fresh. It glistened in the moonlight.

Caitlin felt a mixture of nausea and raw, burning anger. A fog descended on her. Still brandishing her weapon, she stepped forward. She scanned around the compound. The doors to her room and to Gabina's were closed. But the door to Tommy's was ajar. Just a couple of inches. No light spill.

Caitlin advanced towards it.

She could smell excrement as she passed Gabina. The interpreter's body was undergoing its usual post-mortem procedures. But she kept her focus, and her weapon, trained on Tommy's door. When she reached it, she paused for a moment. Breathed deeply to steady herself. Then she hooked the door open with her right foot, weapon pointing directly into the room, finger on the trigger.

It was darker inside than out. Her eyes took a moment to adjust. The outline of Tommy's form appeared gradually over a period of twenty seconds. Each second revealed a detail more gruesome than the last.

He was dead, but that was not the most shocking thing. Whoever had done this to him had done it slowly. He was slumped against the far wall, his body limp and lifeless. A rag had been stuffed in his mouth to keep him quiet. Some of the material was sticking out from between his lips and, like his beard, the material was soaked with blood.

The blood came from his eyes. They had been gouged. Stabbed. Caitlin couldn't tell if the eyeballs were still in the skull. The eye sockets were just a bloodied, mushy mess.

She wanted to vomit. She wanted to cross the room to Tommy. At the very least to cover his brutalised form. In his gruff, military way he had been kind to her. They'd been friends. Tommy would have liked them to be more than that. Now look at him. Another wave of nausea flooded her body. She suppressed it. And she turned. Because she knew that Tommy had not only been murdered. He had been tortured first. And Caitlin had a good idea what his killer had been trying to locate.

Or rather, *who* his killer had been trying to locate.

Her.

She was sweating heavily as she turned. She exited Tommy's room. Scanned the compound. There was no sign of anybody. She fixed her attention on the exit. The door was slightly ajar. She ran towards it, past Gabina's stinking corpse. At the door she stopped. Breathed again. Readied her weapon. Prepared to make a sprint back towards the Hilux.

She stepped outside and immediately knew she'd made a catastrophic mistake.

Her attacker was waiting just to the right of the door. In her haste to leave the compound, she hadn't checked.

The first punch was a hammer fist straight to her face. Caitlin felt the bone in her nose crack and collapse. Blood flowed from her nostrils, over her lips.

The second punch was an action replay. It hurt more as it made contact with the broken bone.

She felt her handgun being ripped from her hand.

After that it was a blur. The blows to the face came in quick succession. To the nose, to the mouth, to the eyes, which she had to keep closed to protect them. She could feel her face bloodying up, her head spinning. An agonising punch hit her breasts. She doubled over, gasping for breath, and a knee jabbed her under the chin, knocking her back against the wall. A hand grabbed her hair tightly and the blows to the face started up again. Forceful. Relentless.

She tried to fight back. It was impossible. Her assailant was too strong. She knew it was a man, from the smell. But she had blood in her eyes and couldn't see him. When she raised one leg to knee him in the bollocks, it was swiped easily away. The gesture was rewarded by another agonising strike to the breasts.

She collapsed, trying to suck in a lungful of air. An elbow struck her in the side of the face.

She was unconscious before she hit the ground.

Mina was scared. But she was also in pain.

She had waited until her grandmother was asleep before crossing the village towards the compound where the female

British soldier stayed – the one who had given her painkillers and sanitary products before. She was in trouble with her grandmother. Mina had told the British soldier about Abu Manza and Abu Noor who lived in the village of Gareshk. And while she'd not admitted it to her grandmother, the old woman was wise. She knew Mina well. Her frowns and silence were eloquent.

To inform against the Taliban was dangerous. No wonder, then, that Mina's grandmother had refused to take her back to the soldier's compound for more medicine. That was why she was forced to do it alone, and in the dead of night.

Panjika was completely deserted, as it always was after dark. Wrapped in her blue robes and headdress, Mina kept to the shadows. She stopped and looked around frequently to check that she wasn't being observed and followed. Occasionally she winced from the cramping in her abdomen. Did the fear of being caught make it worse? She didn't know.

There was an old wooden bridge that crossed the dried-out river on the southern side of the village. The soldier's compound was directly opposite it on the other side of the main street. The bridge creaked as she crossed it. The noise made her cringe. Once she had forded the riverbed she stopped in the shadow of a tree and looked out towards the compound.

She froze. There was movement. A figure was approaching. It was skirting round the edge of the compound, towards the main door. The figure stopped there, its back to Mina. She had the impression that whoever it was, they were trying to unlock the gate. It only took a few seconds. The gate opened and the figure slipped inside.

Mina remained quite still. She didn't know who it was that she'd just seen entering the soldier's compound. She needed to be careful . . .

Thirty seconds passed. Then there was more movement.

It came from a different direction. There were five trees a few metres to the left of the compound. A second figure emerged. Mina could see that this person was male, and wearing military clothes. He moved quickly to the door and stood just to its left with his back to the wall.

Mina didn't like the look of him. She didn't know why. She wanted to run, but she was too scared to move. So she stayed where she was, an invisible, huddled mass beneath the tree, and watched.

Two silent minutes passed. Then the door opened again. The first figure appeared. She was carrying a gun. Mina could see her face now. It was her friend, the female soldier.

Mina was used to violence. In Helmand Province, you couldn't avoid it. But what she saw next still sickened her.

The male figure thumped her hard in the face. He ripped the gun from her hand, then continued to pound his fist into her face and then her breasts. It all happened silently. The woman doubled over and received a knee to the chin. Then more blows to the face.

She collapsed. Mina gasped involuntarily, then moved her hand over her mouth to silence herself. The man hauled the woman over his shoulder. He looked around once, failed to see Mina, then ran with his victim round the back of the compound, and out of sight.

When Caitlin regained consciousness, she was upside down and moving. With thickly blurred vision she could see the ground passing quickly underneath her. It took a few seconds for her to realise that she had been slung over her assailant's shoulder. Her mouth was stuffed with something to stop her shouting out. Her hands were bound behind her back. Her skin was sticky with blood and the pain in her face and upper body was debilitating.

Never agree to being moved. It was the first rule. She wriggled as violently as she could, trying to writhe herself off her assailant's shoulder. No good. He was too strong. Twenty seconds later he dumped her on the ground. She fell heavily. The world, still blurred through sticky, bloodied eyes, was spinning. She felt a hand round her throat, pulling her up from the ground and thrusting her hard against a tree.

Blurred features came close, face to face. She felt hot breath. She squinted, trying to make out her assailant's features, but her eyes were rolling in her head.

It was only when he spoke that she knew who it was. She'd recognise that voice anywhere, no matter what state she was in.

'Hello, sweetheart,' said Tony. 'Feeling rough? I'm going to be honest – you're *looking* pretty rough. Not as bad as you're going to look, though, if you don't tell me where the fuck Danny Black is, and what he's doing.'

21

He's bluffing.

It was the clearest thought Caitlin could manage. Surely Tony had no way of knowing Danny had made contact with her.

She could just make out colours in her peripheral vision. She was in an orchard of some description. Avocado trees, maybe, and vibrant flowers all around. It was unexpectedly lovely. There was a faint smell, like honeysuckle. In a corner of her mind, Caitlin wondered how she had managed to miss this place in all the time she'd been living here.

'You see what I did to your man Tommy?' Tony said. His harsh voice brought her back to the present.

Caitlin nodded.

'It was quite sweet, really. He didn't want to give you up. I took the first eye out when he told me you'd been called back to the UK. Second one when he refused to talk any more. That one killed him. I went a bit deep. My bad. I'll know better next time. Anyway . . .' Caitlin felt cold metal beneath her left eye. 'I'm going to take this rag out of your mouth. You know what'll happen if you make a noise.'

He inserted his fingers into her mouth and pulled out the rag. She gasped.

'Where is he?' Tony breathed.

He's bluffing.

'I don't know what you're talking about. I haven't seen him. I didn't even know he was in-country.'

Silence. Caitlin considered shouting out. But she could still feel the blade against her eye. Her vision was beginning to clear a little. Tony's face was more distinct. His eyes were red. Wide. He looked insane.

'You see,' Tony whispered, 'this is why I don't believe you. I'm thinking, here I am, Danny Black. I've been arrested by a member of the RMPs. I'm under armed guard in Camp Shorabak, waiting to be flown home to have all kinds of shit thrown at me. But I manage to escape. I'm injured. I'm alone in Helmand Province. I don't know a fucking soul, except one person – that's you, by the way – and I know where she is. So what am I going to do? Sit around playing with my dick until either the Taliban or the filth catch up with me? Or make contact?' He leaned in a little closer. 'That retard in the compound was one thing. You're quite another. Be a fucking shame to take *your* pretty little eyes out. Maybe I'd start somewhere else.' He moved the knife away from her face and pointed it between her legs. 'It's about time I put something up there again. Be quite romantic, wouldn't it, surrounded by all these flowers. So let's have another go, you stupid, stupid bitch. Where is he?'

Caitlin's body temperature had dropped. She was shaking. Her wrists hurt where they were bound behind her back. She knew Tony would carry out his threat. He was a desperate man. It was only a matter of time before she cracked. If she could just give him non-specific information for a little while longer . . .

'He's met up with a Regiment unit from Kabul,' she whispered. 'I don't know where they were headed. I think they're just going to get him out of—'

She didn't finish her sentence. Tony crashed his fist against her broken nose again. The back of her head slammed against the tree. She gasped in pain.

'I'm not fucking around, Caitlin.'

'I swear I don't—'

'He went absent from Shorabak twenty-four hours ago. He must have made contact with you soon after that. What have you been doing since then?' He leaned in closer. 'Word of advice,' he whispered. 'If you say nothing, I'm going to fuck you hard with this knife.'

Caitlin believed him. She knew she had no choice.

'We went to find Al–Zafawi,' she breathed.

There was a brief silence. 'The Red Unit guy? Why?'

Caitlin was finding it difficult to speak. Her words were slurred. 'We worked out he had a connection with your target in Panjika . . .'

'Did you find him?'

She nodded weakly. 'And the footage . . .'

'What footage?' He grabbed Caitlin's hair and squeezed. '*What footage?*'

'The footage of you,' she spat, 'stealing the American bullion.'

Another silence.

'What do you mean,' Tony breathed, 'the *American* bullion.'

Caitlin could feel her eyes rolling. 'They're giving it to Al–Zafawi,' she said. 'To distribute around the warlords in Helmand. Their way of trying to keep the peace.' She could feel blood pouring from her nose again. Her chin fell to her chest. 'That's what you found,' she said. 'His guy was guarding it, but there was a hidden camera.'

'What happened to the footage?' Tony said, his voice low and dangerous.

'Spearpoint told us to destroy it.'

'And did you?'

It was all she could do to nod.

He stared hard at her. 'How many guys in this unit?'

'Four, plus Danny.'

'What are they doing now? You lie to me again, I'll decide you're no fucking use to me any more and you know what that means.'

Caitlin hesitated. 'They know where the bullion is,' she said.

'What . . .' His eyes were momentarily panicked. He stared hard at her, as if trying to discern if she was lying, then appeared suddenly to have understood something. 'The radio GPS . . .' he said, almost to himself.

Caitlin nodded. Her vision was blurred but she could sense Tony's mind working. 'Did you kill Al–Zafawi?' he demanded.

She shook her head. 'Spearpoint told us not to. The Americans . . .' Her voice petered out.

'I bet Black loved that. So where is he?'

'Why do you want to know—'

Bang. He whacked his fist against her broken nose again. There was a flashing pain through her skull. She could barely talk. 'There's . . . there's a cave . . .'

She felt the knife move. Up from between her legs, back to her left eye. 'The next words you're going to say, Caitlin, will be Al-Zafawi's exact location.'

Caitlin inhaled deeply. Her chest rattled. She realised she'd been swallowing her own blood. 'You head north from here . . . hit the road heading east . . . follow it till you find a roadside shrine . . . head north towards the mountains . . .'

'Good.' Tony sniffed. 'I think that just about concludes our conversation, Caitlin. Leaves me with just one problem. What am I going to do with you?' He reached out and grabbed a fistful of flowers from nearby, then held them up to her. 'Maybe I should take you with me. We could go dig up my gold. Start a new life together, you and me.'

She nodded faintly.

'You'd like that, huh? You'd like to be rich? Well I'm sorry, darling. It's not going to happen.' He dropped the flowers in her lap. 'You're not coming with me. You're not going anywhere. I'm going to fuck you up just like I fucked up those muppets Dexter and Cole. And I'm going to fuck Danny Black up too, just as soon as I get my hands on him.'

Caitlin felt a moment of dizziness. When she regained her composure, she realised Tony had the blade of his knife held gently against her neck.

Mina felt paralysed. Fear had frozen her limbs.

The two soldiers, one slung over the other's shoulder, had been out of sight for nearly a minute before she was able to move. She eased herself to her feet. Her first instinct was to turn her back on the compound and head back home the way she came. She even took several steps in that direction.

But somehow she couldn't do it.

She turned.

Everything was silent. It was as if the violence she'd just witnessed had never happened.

She remembered the kindness the female soldier had shown her. It would be scant repayment to ignore her now.

There had been others in the compound, she remembered. An interpreter and another soldier, burly and bearded. She needed to alert them.

Mina looked around to check there was nobody about, then she ran towards the compound. She was a little out of breath by the time she reached the door. It was ajar. She gingerly pushed it open and stepped inside.

'Hello?' she whispered. It was the only word of English she knew. '*Hello?*'

She stopped. There was something in the middle of the courtyard. She could not tell what it was at first. Only when she took another few steps closer did she realise it was a body. Close up, she saw it was the kind interpreter from the other night, and that her throat had been brutally cut.

Mina doubled over and dry-retched. She couldn't look at the body. It was too much for her. She backed away, fully intending to run from the compound.

She couldn't. The image of the female soldier being beaten replayed itself in her head. She needed to find the man with the beard. She looked around the courtyard and saw that the door to one of the rooms was open. She headed towards it.

Stepped inside.

How she wished she hadn't.

The bearded soldier was slumped against the back wall. Not only dead, but brutally disfigured. Mina retched again, staggering back towards the door.

What sort of person would do that? she asked herself.

She realised she knew the answer.

Her hands trembled. The nausea returned. But although she wanted to run – every cell in her body shrieked at her to do it

– she didn't. She looked around the room. It was dark, but her eyes were getting used to it now. She couldn't find what she wanted and although she took pains not to let her gaze fall on the horrific sight of the blinded soldier, Mina knew instinctively that she would have to approach him at some point. Best to do it quickly.

She averted her eyes as she walked up to the corpse. And she kept them half closed as she patted down the body. It was already stiff and cold, and it felt wrong, touching a man like this, even a dead one. But she found what she was looking for within a few seconds. It was holstered under his camouflage jacket. She pulled the gun carefully from its holster.

Mina held it by the handle between her thumb and forefinger, but she immediately knew that would not do. She gripped the handle and forced her hand to stop shaking. She didn't know much about guns, but she had seen men in the village using them. She could tell that it was ready to fire. All she had to do was flick the switch on the side and squeeze the trigger.

The thought of doing that made her hand shake again.

Gripping the gun tightly, she hurried out into the courtyard and past the interpreter's body. At the door, she stopped and listened. All she could hear was her own panicked breathing. She told herself she was being foolish. That she should return home and forget what she had seen. No good could come of it.

But she knew she wouldn't. The female soldier had been kind. She had saved the life of Mina's friend. She did not deserve what was coming to her.

She stepped outside and hurried in the direction she had seen the two figures disappear.

'I'm going to fuck you up, just like I fucked up those muppets Dexter and Cole. And I'm going to fuck Danny Black up too, just as soon as I get my hands on him.'

With the knife still resting against Caitlin's throat, Tony picked up the rag he had used to shut the bitch up. He stuffed it back in her mouth.

253

He'd been ready to kill her the moment she'd admitted to helping Danny Black. But somehow that wasn't enough. The thought of them together had turned his blood hot. Caitlin had been Tony's once, for a brief time. To give herself to Black? That was a betrayal he couldn't forgive. She needed to know that. To be *shown* that. Then the bitch could die begging him.

He put one hand on her crotch. Grabbed it hard. Squeezed so it hurt. He spat in her face as he was doing it. 'You fucking whore,' he whispered. And when he spoke again, he emphasised each word with as painful a grope as he could manage. 'I should cut your fucking tongue out first, just for speaking to him.' He moved the knife to the edge of her mouth. 'Maybe I'll do that, hey?'

Her eyes widened in panic. She tried to say something but couldn't.

'Don't worry, love. When I catch up with Danny Black – and I *will* do that, with a little help from my friends – I'll tell him exactly what happened here. Then I'll do the same to him. You'll be just another couple of white dots on my M4. I'm getting quite the collection.'

He pressed the point of the blade into her lower lip. Blood trickled down it.

He angled the blade up, ready to stick it into her mouth.

Then he stopped.

Why wasn't she looking *at* him? Why was she looking over his shoulder? *Beyond* him.

He lowered his knife and slowly turned.

He didn't know whether to laugh or spit.

A girl was standing ten metres away. She wore blue robes and her headdress was unravelled to show her young face. She was slight. Her arms were outstretched, inexpertly holding a pistol. Her hands were shaking.

She said something in Pashto. Her voice wavered as she spoke. Whatever she said, she was clearly terrified.

Caitlin jerked violently, pushing herself up against Tony as she tried to shout out. Something snapped inside him. He didn't bother with the knife. He just elbowed Caitlin's bloodied face with all the angry force he could muster, crushing the back of her head against the tree trunk. She slumped, unconscious. Dead? Alive? He didn't fucking care either way.

He turned his attention back to the girl. She hadn't moved. She didn't know how to hold a gun. The chances of her accurately placing a round at that distance were almost zero. She probably didn't even know how to fire it.

He stood up slowly, knife in hand. It crossed his mind to throw the blade in her direction. He could probably hit her from here. Even if he missed, it would distract her and give him enough time to draw his own handgun.

She repeated herself. Her voice was cracked and harsh. Tony sneered at her. Maybe he wouldn't even bother with the knife. Maybe he'd just —

The girl fired as he moved his free hand.

The retort of the unsuppressed weapon was noisy, and the round was too close for comfort. Tony felt the air displacement as it whizzed past his right cheek and slammed into the tree behind, sending a shower of bark and splinters into the air.

The girl stepped forward two metres. She spoke again.

Suddenly Tony was less sure of himself. The girl had clearly known enough to set the weapon to semi-automatic. She was ready to take another shot.

He raised his hands and nodded towards his vehicle. It was ten metres to his two o'clock, parked at the edge of this flower-filled orchard.

The girl nodded. She kept her weapon trained on him.

Tony could taste his own hatred and anger. But he knew he was in danger. He sidestepped in the direction of the vehicle. The girl followed him with her weapon. He could see her eyes flicker occasionally towards Caitlin's motionless form. But her attention was on him, and her weapon followed him precisely.

He edged towards the vehicle. Five metres. Three. As he drew closer to it, the girl advanced, flattening flowers beneath her feet and keeping the distance between them to a constant eight metres. Opening the driver's door, he considered using it as a shield. If he did that, he could put her down. But there were other considerations. A loose round might put his vehicle out of action and he was going to need it. More gunfire would draw others from the village to this location. Not what he wanted.

No. The girl was reluctant to kill him. His best strategy was to take advantage of that, and get out of here.

He opened the vehicle. Got behind the wheel. It felt sticky. He realised that his hands were covered in blood. He turned the engine over. All the while, the girl stood with her weapon pointing directly at the driver's side window. Tony knocked the vehicle into gear and advanced to the south, out of the copse.

Before he cleared the trees he checked in his rear-view mirror. The girl was still pointing her weapon towards him. In his peripheral vision, he saw two more shadowy figures entering the copse. He had the impression that they were dressed in blue. Who the hell were they?

He wasn't sticking around to find out. He accelerated out of the treeline and up towards the road without looking back.

Mina waited until the vehicle was well out of sight. Only then did she lower the gun. Her legs were trembling. She felt as if they might give way beneath her. She took in a deep breath, then spun round to look at the soldier.

Only then did she see the two figures advancing out of the darkness into the orchard.

They were dressed like Mina, in blue robes, but their head-dresses were still wrapped around their heads. They stopped when they were a few metres away from her. Their eyes, visible through the slits in their headdresses, were wide and anxious.

'Your grandmother sent us to look for you,' one of them said in Pashto. 'We heard a gunshot. We thought—'

'You need to help me,' Mina said to her friend. She ran towards the female soldier, laid the handgun on the ground and knelt down next to her. Her face was covered in blood. Mina didn't even know if she was alive. She felt her neck for a pulse. It was weak, but it was there.

'Others are coming,' her friend whispered. 'Men . . .'

As if to confirm what her friend had just said, she shouted from the direction of the village. Somewhere, a dog barked.

'Help me with her,' she said. '*Come on, help me with her!*'

It took two of them to lift the unconscious soldier to her feet. The third girl went ahead, scouting in the shadows. With one arm over each shoulder, they dragged the casualty towards the village. Mina felt her heart pumping. If the men found them, she did not know what would happen.

But she knew this: she would do whatever it took to save the woman who had been so kind to her. If that meant risking the anger of the elders of the village, or the Taliban, or even her grandmother, then so be it.

22

Tony was sweating. Badly. Not just because of the heat. He'd messed up back there. He knew it. As the lights of his vehicle cut through the Afghan night, the tyres crunching on the rough road, he scowled as he relived the moment that stupid bitch of an Afghan girl held him at gunpoint. He should have done her. Driven the Land Rover straight into her body. It would have been easy.

Forget about it, he told himself. Caitlin was fucked-up anyway. Probably brain damaged. Maybe dead. He didn't need to worry about her.

But Danny Black? Danny Black he *did* need to worry about.

Because Caitlin hadn't told him everything.

Maybe she didn't know everything.

If Spearpoint and Hereford knew about the bullion, they'd have put two and two together regarding Dexter and Cole. Maybe they even knew he'd killed Holroyd.

So what was Black's real reason for hooking up with a Regiment unit from Kabul? What would they not want to tell that bitch with the broken nose? Tony thought he could guess. They knew she and Tony had been a thing. If a kill order had been issued, they'd keep it dark from Caitlin, in case she tipped him off.

He felt bile in the back of his throat. If Black had a kill order on Tony, he'd relish carrying it out. Tony would have to go off the grid. For a long time.

For that, he needed money.

His money. Safely cached, in the form of bullion, on the mountainside.

Tony, Dexter and Cole had positioned it well. Halfway up a

slope, well away from the nearest road, by a gulley among the trees. The slope was stony and boulder-strewn. Nobody would have any reason to climb it. Even if they did, the cache was well camouflaged. They had covered the freshly dug earth with stones from the surrounding area, and memorised its position: right next to an unmovable boulder with two sharp protuberances, like a V sign.

But now, Tony knew beyond doubt, a five-man Regiment unit would be advancing towards the cache. They'd set up firing positions in the hope that Tony showed. If he didn't, they'd confiscate the bullion.

That thought made Tony hit the brakes. The Land Rover jolted to a halt. In a sudden fury, he climbed down from the vehicle, walked to the rear nearside tyre and kicked it hard. 'Fuck. *Fuck!*' He spat on the floor.

Then he breathed deeply, clutched his hair and tried to think his way through this.

He couldn't take on a five-man unit. Not by himself. Back when he was questioning Caitlin a crazy idea had come to him. Could he really pull it off? Did he have any other option?

Suddenly, explosively, Tony slammed his fist against the Land Rover's chassis. He'd risked too much to let that bullion go. It wasn't going to happen.

He felt a wind on the back of his neck. He peered from the side of the road across the bleak, dark Afghan terrain. The wind was hot but brisk. It had picked up quickly. Tony knew what it meant. A sandstorm. Already he could feel grains of sand whipping his face. He hurried back into the vehicle.

What had Caitlin said? *There's a cave . . . You head north from here . . . hit the road heading east . . . follow it till you find a roadside shrine . . . head north towards the mountains . . .*

Caitlin had told him that she and Danny had received an order to leave Al-Zafawi alive. If he followed her directions, assuming Al-Zafawi had not yet had the chance to evacuate his cave, he would find the Taliban leader.

Tony checked the time: 00.15 hours. The night was passing quickly. The sandstorm was picking up. Visibility could be down to a few metres before he knew it. He knocked the vehicle into gear. Eased on to the accelerator.

You head north from here . . . hit the road heading east . . .

He headed north.

The five-man SAS team was heading cross-country when Brooker uttered a single word: 'Sandstorm.'

'All we fucking need,' Danny said.

They were driving slowly to keep full control of their Land Rovers over the rough, stony foothills of the mountain range they were following. And they drove unseen, without the benefit of headlamps, using NV goggles to scan the way ahead. But NV goggles couldn't see through sand. Their visibility was down to twenty metres. There was a sound like fine hail as the sand whipped against the metal chassis of the vehicles.

It would have been quicker, perhaps, to head up to the highway. But Danny had vetoed that idea. There was a high chance that their assault on Al-Zafawi had put the Taliban on high alert. If that was the case, there might be patrols and roadblocks on the main supply routes. Encountering one of those would not only slow them down, it could blow the whole operation.

Danny knew Tony. His first thought would be for the bullion. He'd killed to get his hands on it. It would be his priority now. Would he head straight there? Maybe he'd already got there and taken the gold. If that was the case they'd see the cache location dug up, and they'd have to rethink their strategy. Might they encounter him the moment they arrived? Or would he bide his time? Devise a strategy? He was, after all, alone and without backup.

The Regiment's ace card was that Tony didn't realise they were on to him, or that they knew about the bullion. But even so, they had to get to the cache quickly. There were no prizes for arriving second.

The two vehicles trundled on, their occupants silent. To take out one of their own was a bitter job, even if the target was a man like Tony Wiseman. There would be no bragging about this in the squadron hangars of Hereford. It was the kind of op you didn't ever talk about. You just left it to fester in a corner of your mind.

The unit trundled on. The howling of the wind grew louder outside. Danny scanned the parched, unforgiving landscape to their left, through the green haze of their NV. Already the stony, forbidding slopes to their right were invisible through the sand clouds.

Visibility: fifteen metres. The headlamps cut through the whipping sand like a torch through smoke. So Tony nearly missed it.

A roadside shrine.

He had imagined something ornate. This wasn't. It was a few old tyres, bound together with dirty bits of cloth and decorated with sticks that pointed out in all directions. Tony sneered at it, just as he sneered at everything in this shithole of a country.

He pulled off the road by the shrine and immediately saw, in the light of the headlamps, the indents of a vehicle's tyres almost covered by moving sand.

Head north towards the mountains.

He tried to penetrate the dry cloud all around him to see the mountain range to the north, but it was impossible.

By rights he should hunker down, wait for the storm to pass.

No chance. It could only last minutes, but it could also last for several hours. He didn't have that kind of time to waste.

Headlights on. Accelerator down.

Tony forced the vehicle north through the sandstorm for half an hour. He stopped only for a minute, when he was out of sight of the road, to check over his weapons. When half an hour was up, he took a risk, killing the lights and continuing in the darkness. He kept the engine slow and quiet. It was entirely drowned out by the noise of the sandstorm.

It was the smell that told him he was close. Something had been burning in this vicinity recently. Not an ordinary fire. This wasn't the smell of wood smoke. It was the stench of burning diesel and machinery. The stench of war.

He killed the engine. Grabbed his weapons. In the back of the vehicle he found an old blanket, which he wrapped round his head to protect him from the storm, with tiny gaps to see through. Then he advanced on foot.

The sand stung his hands and seemed to get into all the folds of his clothes within seconds. He didn't let that slow him down. The terrain undulated. He continued north for a hundred metres, up an incline that led to a neat brow. Here he crouched down on all fours and crawled. He knew he was almost on target, because the smell was getting stronger.

It was 01.15 hours when he peered over the brow of the hill and saw what he was looking for.

There was a patch of open ground ahead of him. Somewhere up above, the moon was bright, because he could see the swirling eddies of the sand, and could just make out that the ground was dotted with boulders and low gorse. It stretched for about 150 metres, beyond which the mountain face rose up dramatically. Ordinarily, he would not have been able to identify the cave – it would have been obscured by the sand clouds. But there was a light inside it – flickering, so probably a fire – which distinctly outlined the cave's opening. He could just make out two mounds on either side of the cave mouth. A dull orange glow emanated from one of them. They looked to Tony like burned vehicles, but he couldn't be sure at this distance.

There was no sign of personnel, armed or otherwise.

He rolled over the brow. He descended five metres on the other side before getting to his feet and priming his rifle. He advanced with the butt pressed firmly into his shoulder, the glowing cave magnified in his sights.

Tony moved forward at a brisk pace, his finger resting on his trigger guard, his eyes watering as grit entered the slits in his makeshift headdress. Twice, he saw a silhouette pass across the light source in the cave. It was occupied, but he couldn't tell how many people were there. Halfway across the open ground he quickly panned his weapon. He could now positively identify two vehicles. They had been hit by ordnance. There were bodies lying around them. And a comms satellite to his two o'clock.

Distance: fifty metres. He slowed his pace. Moved his finger from the trigger guard on to the trigger itself. He saw another vehicle just inside the cave mouth. Its headlamps and windscreen were shot out. The fire was burning just to the left of that, perhaps five metres back from the entrance. A figure was standing in front of it, his back to the entrance, head bowed.

Tony continued advancing to target.

Thirty metres.

Fifteen.

The figure hadn't moved. Tony could see that he was male, wearing camouflage gear, with black hair.

Ten metres out he stopped.

'Turn round!' he shouted over the howling of the sandstorm. 'Slowly!'

The figure didn't move.

'I said turn round.'

Nothing.

Tony pointed his weapon at the vehicle inside the cave. He released a single round. It ricocheted noisily off the chassis.

Only then did the figure turn.

Slowly.

He looked like shit. His face was battered and bloodied. His black beard was matted, his hair straggly over his forehead. The glow of the fire seemed to give his dark skin a red glow. His eyes burned. He looked like a man who wanted to kill.

'Al-Zafawi?' Tony shouted.

No response. Just that deadly stare.

'I'm the guy,' Tony shouted, 'who stole your gold.'

Tony didn't know what reaction to expect. Not this. Al-Zafawi didn't even seem to be looking at him. The Taliban leader was looking *past* Tony, into the distance.

Tony turned, looking back the way he had come. He saw four sets of headlamps burning through the midnight sandstorm. They were trundling down from the brow of the incline from which Tony had first viewed the cave. And they were moving fast.

Tony spun round. Directed his weapon back at Al-Zafawi and strode up to him. 'Get to your knees,' he screamed. '*Get to your fucking knees!*'

Al-Zafawi did nothing. Tony had to grab his neck with one big hand and throw him to the floor. Once he was down there, Tony aimed his weapon at Al-Zafawi's head.

'You move, I shoot. You got that? *Do you understand?*'

'I understand,' Al-Zafawi breathed.

The vehicles were halfway across the open ground. Already their headlamps had pierced the clouds of sand and were illuminating the inside of the cave, casting long interior shadows.

'Here's what I think,' Tony shouted. 'I think it's bullshit that you take the Americans' bullion. It think you keep it for yourself. And I think you use it to equip your guys. Your Red Unit or whatever the hell you call it. I know they've got serious gear. I've seen it. It costs money.'

The four vehicles had stopped twenty metres from the cave mouth. They were in a straight line, each five metres apart from the others. Their doors were opening.

'Here's what else I think. You want that bullion back.'

Figures emerged, two from each vehicle. They slammed their doors noisily and moved to the front of the convoy, the bright headlamps silhouetting them.

Eight guys.

'Here's the problem,' Tony shouted. 'The guy who was here earlier knows where I've hidden it. He's heading there now with a team of SAS. Your Red Unit guys – I'm guessing this is them, right? – they might be good. Eight of them, they *might* be able to force the bullion's location out of me. But trust me: they go to find it, the SAS will be waiting and they *will* slaughter them, and you. I don't care how much gear you have. They're dead men.'

As one, the silhouettes had moved down on to their knees. They raised their rifles and aimed them directly at Tony and Al-Zafawi.

'Your only hope of beating an SAS unit,' Tony said, 'is me.'

Silence.

The silhouettes remained in the firing position. Tony kept his rifle trained on Al-Zafawi's head. His grip was sweaty.

'You want your money back?' Tony said quietly, so only Al-Zafawi could hear. 'Never going to happen. Not if you work alone. But if we retrieve it together, we split it. Fifty-fifty. You supply the men, I tell you how to survive an SAS ambush. You can take the glory. You'll have pictures of a bunch of SAS corpses to stick on the net. You'll be the man of the moment and I'll help you do it. But first, you get your guys to stand down.'

Silence.

'Seriously, buster. If there's a firefight now, I can't guarantee I'll survive, but I can guarantee you won't.'

Silence.

Sweat dripped into Tony's eye. He blinked to clear it.

Suddenly Al-Zafawi barked an instruction. Nothing happened. Al-Zafawi shouted again. Then, with obvious reluctance, the silhouettes lowered their weapons. Tony watched them do it. Lowering his own was a risk. But it was one he had to take. He let the rifle fall to his side. 'Good call,' he muttered.

Al-Zafawi struggled to his feet. Tony grabbed him by the upper arm to steady him, but the Taliban leader brushed him away. 'I do not need your help to stand,' he hissed. 'Get off me.' He shouted something else to the silhouettes. They approached as a unit, the headlamps from their vehicles casting long shadows into the cave. They were military men. All wore camo, a few had bandoliers strapped round their bodies. Sturdy boots, khaki-sprayed weapons, sand collected in the folds of their clothes. They walked with the arrogant swagger of confident fighters.

Al-Zafawi approached them, leaving Tony by the fire. It was clear that the leader's authority over these men was not absolute. He started talking quickly, waving his arms, pointing back towards Tony, at the burned vehicle chassis outside the cave, and out into the desert. The men looked reluctant. They glanced over at Tony with aggressive looks. But Al-Zafawi was clearly persuasive. After a minute or two they were nodding. Some of them even looked at Tony with interest. A real SF guy, in their midst, prepared to show them what it would take to defeat an SAS unit. For a wannabe special forces team, this was something.

Tony moved away from the fire towards the Red Unit. 'We don't have much time,' he told Al-Zafawi. 'The SAS will be moving into position as we speak. The longer they have to bed in, the tougher it's going to be to take them out. We should get moving.'

The guys in the Taliban unit might have softened their attitude towards him, but there was no indication from Al-Zafawi that Tony was anything other than a necessary evil. His bruised, bleeding face had not lost its flinty, antagonistic expression. 'Where is it?' he demanded.

Tony knew he would have to give up the location of the cache at some point. But not yet. He had given Al-Zafawi good reason to work with him, but he didn't fully trust him to make the right decision. That said, he knew that these guys would know the terrain intimately. They would know the best routes and could likely command the main highway. At some point, he'd have to use their expertise. 'Does one of your guys have a map of the area?' he said.

'Of course. Not that they need it. Without us you will be lost.'

'For now we head west along the mountain range. When we get to the vicinity, I'll mark up our location on the map. Together we'll work out the best way to approach.'

Al-Zafawi looked like he was trying to find fault with the plan. The fact that he couldn't made him appear even more sour. He said something to one of his Red Unit guys. The militant stepped forward and handed Al-Zafawi his rifle. Al-Zafawi slung it expertly across his chest. He knew how to handle the weapon, no question. And he was a grisly sight, his face bloodied and his hair burned from his encounter with Black, his expression harsh, clad in camo gear and fully tooled up. Tony made a note not to underestimate him.

Al-Zafawi issued another instruction. The unit melted back

towards the vehicles. Al-Zafawi pointed at one of them, indicating that Tony should ride in it. Tony shook his head. 'Me and you, in the same one.'

The Taliban leader jutted out his chin arrogantly, but didn't dissent. Tony followed him to the nearest vehicle. He saw now that they were all Land Rovers. Sand was drifting up against their tyres, but Tony at least trusted the militants to make their way through these conditions. Instinctively, he took the back seat position behind the driver. The safest place to be. Or, at least, the place where he could most easily put the driver out of action if he needed to. Al-Zafawi took the seat next to him. Another Red Unit guy sat up front. The stench of sweat and death hung in the air.

Al-Zafawi rapped on the dashboard. The driver took it as an instruction to move off. Their Land Rover took the lead in the convoy that headed back across the open ground in the direction of the main highway. The vehicle's suspension was poor and they jolted roughly across the uneven ground, the light from the five vehicles illuminating the swirls of sand ahead. Tony stared out of the window. His thoughts turned to Danny Black. What was he doing now? Was he caught in this sandstorm? What was his strategy?

And how were Tony and his scratch band of Taliban militants going to get the better of him?

Mina's grandmother was unimpressed. The sound of the sandstorm outside was rising. They all wanted to be shut up and safe. But even the old lady could tell that the female soldier needed help, and that she wouldn't get it anywhere else.

The woman was lying on Mina's thin mattress. Mina had used a cooking knife to cut the plastic ties that had bound her patient's wrist. The horrible wounds on her face glistened in the candlelight. She didn't move. There was barely a sign of breathing.

'Is she even alive?' the old woman had said as Mina and her friends carried the unconscious woman into their poor dwelling place on the western side of the river that bisected Panjika. And then a question that was plainly of more immediate importance to her: 'Did anybody see you?'

Mina shook her head. 'We were careful, Grandmother,' she said.

Her two friends loitered by the door, blue-robed shapes in the candlelight. They were obviously keen to be away. Mina nodded at them and they left silently. Mina turned back to her grandmother.

'Her ... her friends have been killed,' she stuttered. 'Tortured and killed. A man was going to kill her too. Another soldier. Not an Afghan. I stopped him. He ran away, but first he slammed the back of her head against the tree—'

'You stupid child,' her grandmother whispered. 'The Imam has disappeared. The Taliban will be asking questions. What are you doing, involving yourself in the affairs of men at a time like this? Do you want to get yourself killed?'

'What do you mean, the affairs of men?' Mina hissed at the old lady. '*She* is not a man?' She pointed at the soldier.

'She thinks she is, doing men's work. Look where it has got her.'

Mina's eyes flashed in the candlelight. She was tired of doing nothing. Of being just a faceless shape in the background while the men ruined her country all over again. She was tired of doing what she was told, instead of what was right. 'She helped us,' she said, 'so we should help her. And if you won't, I will do it alone.'

Granddaughter and grandmother stood, locked in a fierce stare. It was the grandmother who turned away first. 'Fetch water,' she muttered. 'We should clean her face and give her something to drink, if she will take it.'

'Thank you, Grandmother,' Mina said. She looked over at their patient. The woman was like a corpse. Maybe she would be, soon.

That thought was enough to send Mina scurrying into the other room where there was a clay jug of fresh water sitting on an old wooden table. She found a bowl and a cup, filled them and carried them back to her patient. Mina's grandmother was crouching by the woman's side, muttering a prayer. She had a cloth in one hand. Mina placed the bowl of water by her side. Her grandmother dipped her cloth into the water and started dabbing their patient's facial wounds. Each time she rinsed the cloth, the water turned a slightly darker shade of pink. The patient's face didn't look any better.

'Let me give her a drink,' Mina said.

Her grandmother nodded, moved back and allowed Mina to shuffle along so she was crouching by the woman's head with the cup of water. She put one hand behind the head and gently raised it. Placing the cup to her patient's lips, she gently moistened them. She didn't know why. It just seemed like the right thing to do.

The soldier coughed weakly. Mina almost laughed with relief. It was the first sign of life she had seen. 'How are you feeling?' she asked in Pashto. It didn't matter that the patient wouldn't understand her. Mina just wanted her to hear a friendly human voice.

The patient exhaled. It was a painful, rasping noise. It didn't sound good. Anxious, Mina put the cup of water to her patient's lips again. This time, she seemed to drink. Just a tiny sip. And when she had swallowed it, she spoke.

Mina had no English. The word her patient weakly uttered had no meaning to her. It sounded like: 'Tony . . .'

'Are you okay? Can you sit up?'

She didn't sit up. She spoke again. 'Danny . . .'

'You need to rest. We will be safe here. We will look after you.'

'The Red Unit . . .'

'Hush now. Rest.'

The patient started to shake her head. 'They're coming . . .' she whispered, every word clearly an effort. *'They're coming . . .'*

23

Time check: 01.58 hours. According to the map, Danny and his team were approaching the point where the GPS trackers on Tony, Dexter and Cole's radios precisely indicated that they had stopped for half an hour on the night of the hit. In other words: the cache location. The two-vehicle convoy stopped. There was a lull in the sandstorm, though it was still swirling enough to compromise their vision. They wrapped shemaghs round their heads for protection, and tried to survey the terrain through a night sight.

They had followed the line of the mountain slope. They could just make it out, rising into darkness on their right. If their intel was correct, they were approximately 750 metres from the cache. But that didn't tell the full story.

This area was more fertile than the terrain they had crossed to get here. More fertile than any terrain Danny had yet seen in Helmand. The mountainside was covered in the pointed outline of tree silhouettes. He supposed that in wintertime water drained down gullies and ravines from the peak, irrigating the slope and the ground at its foot. Close up, the slope was a series of verdant peaks and gullies. Scanning the area, Danny realised he had no line of sight towards the cache's location: it was blocked by a hill, about fifty metres high, covered with conifers, low dry gorse and large flat boulders. This terrain repeated itself all the way up the mountainside and as far as Danny could scan to the west. A vast forest of tree, rock and scree sprouting up from the desert floor, with the sandstorm swirling all around it.

A good place to hide something. And a good place for an ambush.

The ground at the foot of the mountainside was far from level, but a rough path led through it from the south. It was dotted with copses and areas of vigorous bush growth. Tony and the others had cached their bullion quickly. They'd have taken the most direct route. To return there, Danny reckoned, it would be most efficient for Tony to take the same path. He would want to recognise his route. He'd approach covertly, but most likely from that direction.

The unit needed to approach the cache and set up OPs and firing points. They had to do it quickly. Tony could arrive at any moment, but they also needed to be prepared for the possibility that he was already there. They would need to approach very cautiously and be ready to take him out if they saw him. First, though, they needed to ditch their vehicles. Brooker identified a dip in the terrain thirty metres to their south-east. The guys removed all their gear and drove the vehicles into the dip. They covered them with loose branches and gorse, then used more branches to dust away any imprint the tyre marks had made on the dusty ground – though this was barely necessary on account of the swirling sand. They supplied Danny with a boom mike and earpiece and performed a quick comms check. When Danny was linked into their personal radio network, they shouldered their gear and their weapons. Then they moved at a north-westerly bearing up the slope.

As they climbed, they emerged above the sandstorm and encountered an eerie silence beneath the shadow of the conifers when they hit the treeline. They moved with the aid of NV goggles. Patrol formation: Brooker in the lead, Danny second, the guys snaking out behind him. Danny stepped carefully. The ground was littered with rocks, loose branches and scree. Careless footing could lead to a twisted ankle or worse. But the bulk of Danny's attention was focused on the surroundings and searching for movement. Tony probably didn't know they were on to him, but if he was in the vicinity and they stumbled across him . . .

Put it this way. Two Regiment guys were dead already by his hand. It wouldn't bother Tony to add to the tally.

Brooker had a GPS unit on his wrist. Every fifty paces or so he would stop, consult it and adjust their bearing. The going became steep. Danny had to use his hands to clamber over several sections of the terrain. Not easy with the wound in his left shoulder sending stinging pains through his torso every time he tensed those muscles. He forced himself to focus on his objective, not on his injury. It was the only way.

After half an hour of climbing he was sweating heavily. He was aware that his body was not functioning at a hundred per cent. Five metres up ahead, Brooker raised one hand to indicate a halt. Danny moved up to join him. They had emerged from a wooded area and were now looking out over a deep gully, almost a ravine, rocky and unforgiving, that led from about fifty metres lower than their current altitude in a straight line up the mountainside to a false peak – about 150 metres. There was a slight kink in the ravine about twenty metres to their one o'clock.

'I think that's it,' Brooker said quietly.

Danny scanned the area carefully. No sign of Tony. No sign that the cache area had been recently disturbed. 'We're in time,' he said, relieved. 'It doesn't look like he's been here.'

'You think it's booby trapped?' Brooker said.

Danny shook his head. 'Tony and the guys had some C-4 that we picked up at one of our target's compounds, but I don't think he'd risk priming the cache with that. An animal could set it off, anything. His bullion would be worthless.'

'I'll get Kit to scout it out anyway. He's our explosives guy. Assuming it's clean, we'll dig in our own IED.'

'We could always do a Tony,' Riley said. 'Dig out the cache, replace it somewhere else, come back in a few years and reclaim our treasure.' And when no one replied he raised his hands defensively. 'Joke, fellas. Joke!'

Danny was almost certain it was.

The guys took up firing positions on the edge of the treeline. Murray faced south, down the gulley. Riley faced north, uphill. Brooker faced back the way they'd come. Danny covered Kit, who advanced carefully towards the gulley, his weapon across his chest, Brooker's GPS on his wrist. A faint breeze blew occasionally through the hot night air, rustling the trees. Apart from that, dead silence. Kit reached the gulley. He climbed down into it and Danny momentarily lost sight of him. When he emerged at the other side, he was on all fours. Danny held his breath as Kit examined the ground. The location was marked, Danny now saw, by a distinctive boulder. It was flat and weathered on the side closest to the gulley, but with two sharp spikes protruding on the far side, like a victory sign. If Danny was looking for a place he would remember in the days, weeks or even years to come, he'd have chosen that boulder. He was quietly certain that Tony and the others had done the same.

Silence. Then Kit's voice over the radio. 'It's clean. You can tell something's been dug in here. They must have been in a hurry. It'll take me about ten minutes to get a pressure plate in and a couple of blocks of C-4. I'll dig in now.'

'Roger that,' Danny said. 'Can you work things so that it doesn't destroy the gold?'

'I'll pack it so the blast goes upward.'

Danny remained immobile, weapon primed, watching Kit remove a small camera from his ops vest and take a photograph of the cache area. He then unpacked an entrenching tool and got to work. Occasionally he heard a sound of scraping from where his unit mate was digging in the explosive.

Danny used the time to survey the area for suitable firing positions. If the IED didn't do its job on Tony, one of them would have to open up. There was a thick bush of thorny gorse about thirty metres west of the cache. It looked unpleasant and inhospitable – the kind of location most people would avoid, which made it perfect for a shooter. Several metres to his right, the treeline was very thick. A second guy could take up position there and be completely hidden. Thirty metres down the gulley was another copse where two guys could be positioned and have line of sight on the cache. Danny turned his attention up the gulley. There was a further inhospitable thicket at a distance of thirty-five metres, from which one guy could keep line of sight on the northern side of the boulder marking the cache. He was convinced that they could install themselves in positions where nobody would see them, especially in their camo gear.

Kit lay the entrenching tool to one side and removed some other items from his bag. He spent five minutes fitting them into the hole he'd made, and then covered it up again. When this was done, he gingerly moved around the cache, heading away from the gulley. When he returned he had a conifer branch, which he used to brush away footprints and loose dirt. He double-checked the cache against the picture on his camera. 'Okay,' he said over comms. 'We're done here.'

'Get back to the treeline,' Danny said. 'I've identified firing positions.'

The guys congregated around Danny, who pointed out the positions. 'Kit, Murray, get behind that treeline.' He pointed to the copse thirty metres down the gulley. 'That's position one. Murray, you have the comms gear?'

'Roger that.'

'Try to make contact with Hereford. Tell them we're in position and we're waiting for Tony to put in an appearance. Brooker, you and me are going to take those gorse bushes.' Danny pointed them out. 'You take cover the northern side of the marker boulder, I'll cover the cache side. Riley, you take this treeline. Will you all recognise Tony Wiseman?'

The unit nodded. Tony was known.

'Hopefully, if he turns up, the IED will take him out. If not . . .' Danny looked at each of the guys in turn. Their reluctance to shoot another Regiment guy was plain in their faces. 'If not, I'll take the shot. Understood?'

Understood.

The unit separated. Danny jogged towards the gulley, negotiated its loose, rocky sides and emerged on the other side about five metres south of the booby-trapped cache. He edged carefully around it, then ran to the gorse bush. It was about four metres by four, a couple of metres high. Danny entered it from the far side, cursing silently as the thorns tore the skin on his face and snagged his clothes. It took a couple of minutes to position himself correctly. He lay on his front, his weapon engaged, the cross hairs of his sights precisely pointing towards the cache.

There was no sign of the others. They were all installed in their respective OPs. Danny spoke into his comms. 'Do we have contact with Hereford?'

'Negative,' Murray replied. 'We're in a comms dip. I'll keep trying.'

'Do it quietly,' Danny said, and he turned his attention back to the cache.

Had they made the right call? Would Tony be along to retrieve his money? Or would he make the smarter decision and lie low?

No. Danny was certain. Tony's greed, and his unshakable faith in his own skills, would lead him here.

All they had to do was wait.

The Taliban convoy moved fast. They were used to these conditions. The sandstorm was a minor irritation to them, and they could travel without fear of interruption. In the occasional lull of the storm, Tony saw the mountain range looming on their right. They were getting close.

'Who's your weakest guy?' Tony said. He was confident that Al-Zafawi was the only other person in the vehicle who understood English.

Al-Zafawi stared at him. 'What do you mean?'

'You know what I mean.'

Something passed between the two men. Al-Zafawi's flinty eyes narrowed. He looked back, as if towards the car behind them.

'Is he the same sort of size and build as me?' Tony said.

'Smaller.'

'Then choose someone my size. Just so long as you know he'll have his seventy-two virgins before the rest of you.' He looked out of the window again. 'Or whatever the fuck it is you believe,' he muttered.

'What do we tell him?' Al-Zafawi asked.

Tony gave it a moment's thought. He needed to control the amount of information Al-Zafawi possessed. Too much, and the Taliban leader might start to think Tony was surplus to requirements. But he couldn't hold back everything.

'The SAS will try to ambush us,' he said.

'How do you know?'

'Because it's what I would do. They know about the bullion. They know where it is. They're going to expect me to rock up and claim it. That's when they'll hit.'

Al-Zafawi's eyes lit up. 'Then all we have to do is find their positions and attack.'

'Forget it. You won't see them. They're the SAS.'

'You underestimate us. My men are very—'

'You won't see them, buster. I *might* be able to spot a couple of them, but . . .'

'Why you and not us?'

'Because you haven't spent months sweating your bollocks off in the jungles of Brunei training for this shit. You think all you need to be an SF unit is the expensive gear? That's the *least* important thing. It's the training.' He shook his head. 'Never mind. Trust me when I say you won't see them. We have to make sure they show themselves. Then we hit.'

Al-Zafawi looked confused. 'But how—'

'I think the SAS want to kill me. So we're going to let them do just that.' He smiled. 'Except it won't really be me.'

The light of understanding dawned in Al-Zafawi's eyes.

'When we stop,' Tony said, 'I'm going to ask you in front of the others who's your best guy. You point him out. I'm going to give him my weapon. I'm also going to give him my camo gear, because my pattern is slightly different to yours and the team will definitely clock that. You tell him it's what British soldiers do – a sign of respect because he's doing the most dangerous job. Plus, he gets a better firearm. You think he'll buy it?'

Al-Zafawi thought for a moment. 'He will do what I say.'

'We tell him we need someone to scout the path to the bullion from the south. Just him, no one else is up to the job. Meanwhile, we're going to approach the location from above which means we'll have the advantage of height. We'll put a shemagh round your guy's head. When he approaches the cache, the team will make a false positive ID by his clothes and weapon. Once he's down, they'll emerge from their covert firing points. That's when we hit them.' Tony smiled again. 'You like the idea, buster? I can tell from the look on your face.'

'The two who attacked me in the cave. They will be there?'

'Not the chick,' Tony said. Al-Zafawi looked confused. 'The girl. Not the girl. But the guy ...' Tony nodded.

'He is mine,' Al-Zafawi said.

''Fraid not, Buster. Your guys can have the rest of them. But there's only one person in this unit who's going to nail Danny Black, and you're fucking looking at him.'

He stared out of the window again. There was a brief lull in the sandstorm and by the light of the moon he could see the outline of conifer trees on the ridge line of the mountain range. That more verdant terrain told him they were surely close. The sandstorm whipped up again and the view was lost. 'Stop the convoy,' he said. 'We need to look at the map.'

'There is a place further on where we can shelter,' Al-Zafawi said.

It took five minutes to get there: a deserted stone barn on the roadside. It had no roof, but the walls were enough to protect them from the sand. It was large enough to fit the entire convoy. Once in, one of the men had spread out a dog-eared map on the bonnet of Tony and Al-Zafawi's vehicle. They were examining it by the light of a torch as the storm howled above them, depositing grains of sand into the folds of the paper. The map was clearly old. Tony didn't trust its accuracy. But it was all they had. He located the village of Gareshk and traced the road north towards the mountains that he, Dexter and Cole had followed with the bullion. Some rudimentary contour lines indicated a ravine leading up the mountain face. By Tony's estimation it was in roughly the correct place. He took a pen from his camo jacket and circled the area. He could sense Al-Zafawi examining it closely, but the area was intentionally too general for the Taliban leader to work out the exact location of the cache. Tony drew an arrow towards the gulley from the south, then two arrows from the north-east over the mountain ridge.

'Our guy goes in this way,' he said quietly, pointing at the single arrow. He indicated the double arrows. 'Do you know a route that will take us up to the high ground?'

'My men know the area well. They will get us into position.'

Tony nodded. 'Gather them together. Let's get our guy sorted.'

Al-Zafawi barked an instruction. The unit lined up. If Tony marshalled them well, from the high ground and with the element of surprise, they'd have a chance. He'd lose a few of them, of course, but that hardly mattered.

Al-Zafawi walked up and down the line like a tin-pot general, instructing his troops in Pashto. He stopped by one of the younger-looking men. He probably wasn't more than seventeen. His beard was wispy and only half grown. But he had a kind of arrogance to him. Tony could tell he would believe that Al-Zafawi thought he was his best guy.

As Al-Zafawi spoke, the young man stepped forward. He was preening. He gave Al-Zafawi his AK-47, and Tony handed him his own M4 with the little white kill dots Tip-Exed on to the side. The young man clutched it, holding it up slightly with a greedy look in his eyes. Al-Zafawi continued to speak in Pashto, while Tony removed his camo jacket and handed it over. The young man took off his jacket – awkwardly, because he didn't want to let go of the M4 – and swapped.

'Trousers too,' Tony said.

Al-Zafawi translated. The young man looked coy. Tony pulled off his own camo trousers and handed them over. He had to wait for the young man to move behind one of the vehicles and make the swap in privacy, before returning fully clad and handing Tony his trousers.

'Tell him he must wear a shemagh.'

'He would wear it anyway, in the storm.'

'Just tell him. He needs to keep it on, even when he gets above the storm line. Explain that we don't want the SAS team photographing him. Tell him he'll become a high-value target if things go wrong.'

Al-Zafawi explained this. The young man went to his vehicle and returned with his head wrapped in a shemagh. Tony looked him up and down. They were almost exactly the same height. The Taliban fighter was wearing Tony's clothes. Holding his weapon. If Danny Black was lying in wait, he would certainly mistake this patsy for Tony.

'You need to head north from Gareshk,' Tony said, Al-Zafawi translating as he spoke. 'When the road stops, leave your vehicle and keep heading directly north towards the mountains. It will take you half an hour to climb the foothills, then you'll see a gulley heading up the mountain. You've got your phone?'

The young man shook his head and pointed at Tony's jacket. Tony felt in the pocket and took out an old mobile with a stubby aerial. He turned to Al-Zafawi. 'This thing works up there?'

'Of course.'

'When you see the gulley, stay hidden and wait for the word from us that we're in position. It's 03.00 hours now – I'm guessing you won't hear from us until after sunrise. When you do, follow that gulley uphill. You'll be safe while you're doing that. But when the gulley enters the treeline again, that's when you need to be careful. Scout the area carefully. Use all your skills. If you see any movement of personnel, alert us by phone. You understand?'

The young man nodded as Al-Zafawi translated for Tony.

'Then go.' Tony put one arm on his shoulder. 'You're a brave guy. You're looking out for your brothers. When we've finished this, we'll all owe you.'

The young man looked round at the others. For a moment, Tony thought he was having second thoughts. But then he bowed his head and moved towards his vehicle, still clutching Tony's M4. Half a minute later, his red tail lights were disappearing out of the barn and into the storm.

The remaining Taliban were muttering to each other, some of

them casting glances at Tony. It was clear that they were suspicious of him. Tony didn't care. They'd find out what he was doing sooner or later. Just so long as Al–Zafawi had enough authority to keep them moving.

Which he did. The Taliban leader issued a single command and his team moved back into their vehicles. Tony folded up the map that was still spread out over the bonnet.

'It's over to you now, buster,' he said. 'Get us to the high ground. Let's hunt some SAS.'

The convoy didn't return to the road. Instead, they headed north across bumpy open terrain, battered by the sandstorm, but with the ridge line of the mountain ahead occasionally appearing, illuminated by the bright Afghan moon.

24

There were shapes.

Caitlin didn't know what they were. They hovered above her like ghosts. All she knew was the pain in her head, face and torso. Her lips and nose felt twice their usual size, and throbbed agonisingly. Her head was split. It hurt to breathe.

She certainly didn't know where she was.

At first, she wondered if she was back in Australia. Maybe the shapes hovering over her were her mum and dad.

But her mum and dad were long dead. She had nothing to be back in Australia for.

One of the shapes spoke. It sounded distant, as if the voice was in another room. The language sounded guttural.

Pashto.

Caitlin inhaled noisily as awareness flooded back. Danny Black. Tommy and Gabina.

Tony.

She saw him in her mind. His crazed, deadly expression.

She felt his fist in her face.

Water. Someone was putting a cup to her lips. It was only as the fresh liquid flooded her mouth that she realised she could taste blood.

She tried to sit up. Water spilled down her chin. Her torso shrieked with pain. Two voices started jabbering and a hand forced her back into a lying position.

'No,' she tried to say. 'I have to go . . .'

The shapes above her became more distinct. Women's faces. One young, one old.

'Mina,' she whispered.

Mina started to talk. She sounded half anxious, half relieved. Caitlin had another go at sitting up. It hurt, badly, but she managed it this time. She became aware of another sound: a howling, outdoors. Her vision was clearing. She was in a dark room, lit only by candles. Mina was standing above her, staring in wide-eyed concern. There were bowls of water on the floor. Bloodied cloths. They had clearly been tending her.

Wincing, Caitlin got to her feet. She had to grab hold of Mina's shoulder to steady herself. The grandmother looked on from the corner of the room in stony-faced disapproval. Mina started to speak again. Caitlin understood the gist of what she was saying: lie down, don't move, stay here.

But that was impossible. It wasn't just that her presence here compromised the women. Danny and the others were in danger. She had to move.

She took Mina's hands in hers. Looked her in the eye. 'Thank you, Mina,' she said. '*Thank you.*'

Silenced, Mina gave a helpless smile as Caitlin released her and nodded at the grandmother, who would plainly not be sorry to see her go. She headed towards the exit of their poor house.

'Hello!' Mina spoke the single word of English, perhaps the only word she knew. Caitlin turned. Mina was holding up a fresh set of blue robes. Caitlin looked down at herself. Camo trousers, bloodied T-shirt. She accepted the robes gratefully, put them on and covered her head. Then Mina handed over a handgun. Caitlin recognised it as Tommy's – the young girl must have taken it from her compound. She was a brave kid. With a final thank you, she stepped outside.

She realised now what the howling was. A sandstorm raged around Panjika. At least that meant nobody else would be outside. She checked her watch. 03.15 hours. A couple of hours till dawn. She wrapped her headdress more tightly. It was a struggle just to move. Her whole body ached. But she forced herself forward. She was on the opposite side of the village to her own compound. She hurried through the storm to the little wooden bridge that forded the riverbed, keeping to the shadows, her head down. As she crossed it, she could see her compound fifty metres away, the door flapping open in the wind. It was the last thing she wanted to do: to revisit the corpses of Tommy and Gabina. But she had no option. By morning, the compound would be overrun. ANP, ANA, Taliban, all wanting to know what had happened in there. By then, she had to be gone.

But first, she needed something.

The door to the compound creaked open.

The courtyard was empty, apart from the grotesque form of Gabina's body dead on the ground. The walls offered some protection from the storm, but there was still a little sand drifting against the corpse. Caitlin averted her eyes as she passed the young woman – though she couldn't help noticing that the body was already starting to smell in the warm night air. She approached Tommy's room. The smell was worse in here. Tommy's bloodied eyes had clotted over, giving him the full horror show look. Caitlin forced herself to look elsewhere. Tommy's comms equipment was in the far corner of the room. Danny had taken Caitlin's sat phone, but she knew Tommy had a spare here somewhere. She needed it, because she *had* to get in touch with Spearpoint. As she rummaged through Tommy's stuff in the dark, Tony's words echoed in her head. *When I catch up with Danny Black – and I will do that, with a little help from my friends – I'll tell him exactly what happened here.*

What friends did he mean? Dexter and Cole? They were dead. Tony had admitted that. There was nobody else.

The next words you're going to say, Caitlin, will be Al-Zafawi's exact location.

Why would Tony need to know that?

There was only one reason, so far as Caitlin could tell.

Spearpoint would surely know by now that Tony was AWOL. Danny and the team would have been tasked to hunt him down. But they would be expecting Tony to be alone. Whereas Tony, she knew, had other plans. Spearpoint needed to know about them.

She found Tommy's spare sat phone. Took it out into the storm and powered it up. Dialled the access number.

Nothing. The link was down.

She cursed. Perhaps it was something to do with the storm. She tried again.

No signal.

She felt dizzy. Like she was going to pass out again. She steadied herself with one hand against the wall.

Tried to think.

With great difficulty, she pictured the map that Brooker had shown them outside the deserted village. He had pinpointed the cache location. That was where Tony would be, eventually. And if Tony was there, Danny surely wouldn't be far behind.

Clutching the sat phone, blasted by the swirling sand, she stumbled as fast as her agonised body would allow, out of the compound and towards the copse where Tony had laid into her and where she had left her Hilux. Minutes later, she was burning out of Panjika, visibility massively compromised by the sandstorm and her blurred sight, her body aching, the anxiety in her mind as sharp as the pain in her broken ribs.

03.30 hours.

The Taliban convoy came to a halt.

They were still in the foothills. Tony estimated that, as the crow flew, they were a klick from the cache. That klick would lead them through densely forested, steeply undulating terrain. But they were taking the long way round. At the base of a scree slope they parked their vehicles in a dried-out wadi where sand was drifting up against the western side. The Taliban team started tooling up. Al-Zafawi threw Tony a shemagh to protect himself from the sand. He pointed up the slope.

'That way,' he shouted. 'The ground is difficult at first, but then there is a path that heads west.'

'How long till we get to the top of the ravine?' Tony bellowed back as he wrapped the shemagh round his head.

Al-Zafawi thought for a moment as he too wrapped his head. 'Two hours.' He looked Tony up and down. 'My men are used to this terrain,' he said, 'and to these conditions. Maybe you will find it too difficult.'

Tony sneered. 'One of these days, you and me can do the fan dance.'

'I do not understand.'

'It doesn't matter. Tell your men to get ready. We head up there right now.'

Al-Zafawi inclined his head in acknowledgement. But before he turned to give the order, Tony grabbed him by the arm. The Taliban leader clearly didn't like being touched. His hissed something in Pashto, and struggled. That was fine by Tony.

'I know what you're thinking, buster,' he shouted over the storm. 'That once we get on target, you can do away with me. You can't. You'll never find that bullion if I don't show you where it is. You got that?'

They locked gazes for a full ten seconds through the gaps in their shemaghs. Al-Zafawi shook Tony off and shouted the move order to his men.

Caitlin had to stop more than once.

It wasn't the pain in her body that was the problem. It wasn't the storm. It was her head. She guessed she was concussed. Every twenty minutes or so the world would spin, her eyes would roll and nausea would flood over her. The swirling sand outside seemed to be in her head at the same time. She had to pull over on the side of the road. Take deep breaths. Hold her head in her hands until the nausea passed and she could operate the vehicle without taking it off-road in a moment of dizziness. Whenever she stopped, she tried to make sat phone contact with Spearpoint. Occasionally there was a distorted sound of electrical interference. Mostly, there was nothing. So she would drive again, until the next time her faculties let her down. The going was very slow. The panic in her gut was rising.

★   ★   ★

Tony and the Taliban team trudged in single file through the storm. There were four guys ahead of Tony. Looking up at them, he was reminded of old pictures of Antarctic explorers forcing their way through life-sapping blizzards. Here, the blizzard was the sandstorm blasting them from all sides. The scree, though, was just as slippery underfoot as snow. Even though he was fully clad and wrapped in his shemagh, Tony felt as though sand had contaminated every part of his body. His tongue was leathery, his eyes watered. The wind howled deafeningly around him.

He kept going. He could almost taste the prize. Sure, once Danny Black was out of the way he would have to deal with Al-Zafawi and his men. There was no way they intended to let him disappear with half the bullion. But if Tony had learned anything over the past few days it was this: he had a gift for getting people out of the way. This bunch of Taliban SF wannabes would hardly present a problem.

And then what? Once he had his bullion, where would he go? The UK was out of the question of course. Maybe central Africa. There were a thousand places where a former SAS guy could live comfortably and go the full Lord Lucan while everyone forgot all about him.

He snapped his attention back to the job in hand. There was work to do before he could consider his next move. Namely: Danny Black. Tony felt a keen tang of anticipation at the idea of putting that cunt out of action permanently. It was just a shame he'd been disturbed before he could do the same to Caitlin.

Talk about a missed opportunity.

There was a shout from one of the guys above him. Tony peered up. The lead Taliban appeared to have cleared the storm line. Tony quickened his pace and soon he, too, was clear of it. He removed his shemagh and breathed a lungful of sand-free air. It was cooler here than down on the desert floor. As the remaining Taliban congregated, he saw that they were on the edge of the treeline. A path led into it, heading west just as Al-Zafawi had said.

As Tony was looking towards the trees, he was aware of the Taliban surrounding him. He turned to face them. They had murder on their minds, no doubt about it. But not yet. Tony was still useful to them, and so they were holding back. More fool them.

'Move,' Tony said. 'The sun will be up in forty-five minutes. We need to get into position.'

Al-Zafawi clearly didn't like being ordered around, but gave the instruction. The Taliban patrol moved west. Tony trod carefully in more ways than one.

05.00 hours.

Dawn arrived slowly. Danny and his team were protected from the rising sun by the peaks and forests on all sides of their position, so the transition from darkness to steely grey was almost imperceptible. Danny wondered if the storm was still blowing beneath them. Up here, in the hills, he had no way of knowing.

Since installing himself in the harsh thicket of his OP, Danny hadn't moved. Nor had there been any sign of the others. The four armed men, their weapons trained on the booby-trapped cache, were completely invisible even when you knew they were there. For Danny, the only evidence of their existence was the occasional whispered acknowledgement over comms. After fifteen minutes, Murray had confirmed that he'd successfully made contact with Spearpoint, who were aware of their situation. Apart from that, a half-hourly check-in to confirm all was well.

But there had been too many of those half-hourly check-ins for Danny's liking. Doubts had started to creep into his thinking. Where was their target? Danny had been so sure that Tony's priority would be to get to the cache and, like any self-respecting Regiment man, he would want to take advantage of the SAS's best friend: the cover of darkness. But darkness had left them. Did that mean Tony had something else in mind? Had Danny got it wrong?

The pain in his left shoulder was worse than ever. The whole of one side of his torso had gone numb. He had a bad feeling it was infected. In this heat, without proper medical care, that could be dangerous. But he couldn't tend to it now. All he could do was lie and wait until the man who'd given him the wound in the first place arrived.

Suck it up, Danny, he told himself. Suck it up.

Brooker's voice came over the comms. 'How long do we give it?'

Danny panned up and down the ravine with his weapon's sights. Nothing but grey rock, slate-coloured scree and deep green conifers. 'As long as it takes,' he said, with more confidence than he felt.

Spearpoint.

The ops room was silent. The unit had made contact two hours previously, but since then: nothing. Cadogan sat in a chair, staring up at the screen on the wall, which gave him none of the information he wanted to know: what was happening on the ground, and was Tony Wiseman still alive? The rest of the Spearpoint personnel did the same. Nobody spoke or even moved. Twelve men, anxiously waiting for intel.

Cadogan's phone rang. Almost everyone in the room started. He answered it quickly.

'It's me,' said Ray Hammond. 'What news?'

'Nothing.'

'Have you been able to raise the Panjika team?'

'Negative.'

'Caitlin hasn't phoned in?'

'What do you want from me, my dear chap? I said I haven't heard from them.'

A pause.

'Black and his men will pull this off,' Hammond said. 'They're the best we have.'

'I certainly hope so,' Cadogan said. 'For all our sakes.'

He killed the line and went back to waiting.

The rocky path through the conifers was treacherous. There were fissures in the ground, often camouflaged by dead wood. Two of the Taliban team had twisted their ankles and were limping their

288

way through the mountainside forest. They were quiet enough, and moved more deftly than Tony had expected, but it helped when dawn crept through the trees, lighting their way a little. But dawn was also a warning. They needed to get into position.

05.35 hours. The lead Taliban guy held up one hand. Tony and Al-Zafawi approached him. He was standing by a fallen tree trunk. As they approached, he pointed south, down the hill. Tony saw that they were on the edge of the treeline. And peering down, he saw scenery he recognised.

The gulley that marked the position of the cache looked steeper from the top. When he, Dexter and Cole had dug in the bullion, it had been dark. Maybe that was it. In the dim half-light, his gaze traced the length of the gulley until he saw what he was looking for: a boulder, weathered on one side, with two sharp spikes pointing up on the other. It was on the far side of the gulley, maybe seventy-five metres down from their current position. There were forested areas on the eastern and the southern sides of the gulley. On the far side of the boulder itself were several patches of gorse, maybe a metre high. Each one could easily hide a man.

'Okay,' Tony breathed, sufficiently quietly that only Al-Zafawi could hear him. 'Nobody moves beyond the treeline. If they do, we're blown. We're going to place one man at ten-metre intervals.' He indicated the treeline, which curved north, circling the top of the ravine. 'When the targets show themselves, it'll mean we'll fire on them from several angles and from good high ground. We'll have the advantage of surprise, numbers, height and trajectory. We ambush the ambushers. You understand? My shot will be the go order. Your guys need to open up on automatic immediately they hear it. There isn't much cover down there. The SAS team will want to head back into the trees when they're under fire. They'll be pinned down, but I estimate we'll have approximately ten seconds to put them out of action before they can either coordinate a response or organise a retreat. Have you got all that?'

'It is what I would have done anyway,' Al-Zafawi said.

'Yeah, if you say so.' Tony gave Al-Zafawi a piercing look. 'One more thing. You stay with me. All the time. You leave my sight, the deal's off.'

Al-Zafawi gave him a look of contempt, but he nodded silently.

'Position your men,' Tony said. 'Quietly. Stay behind the tree-line. If the SAS see movement, it's over.'

Al-Zafawi turned to his guys. He spoke to them in low, urgent tones. Tony could tell from his arm movements that he was reliably translating his instructions. He watched as the Taliban unit disappeared silently into the trees. After a couple of minutes there was no sign of them. Tony and Al-Zafawi were alone, camouflaged by the treeline, looking down the gulley. Tony picked out the boulder again, then scanned the surrounding area. Nothing. No sign of movement. No sign of personnel.

No sign of Danny Black.

Not yet.

But he was down there. Tony could sense it.

He got down on one knee and aimed the AK-47 he had exchanged with his Taliban patsy towards the cache location. He'd have much preferred his M4 to this hunk of junk, but that wasn't possible.

'Okay, buster,' he told Al-Zafawi. 'Let's get your guy walking up the gulley. Make the call.'

25

Time check: 06.00.

Danny and the team had been in position for more than three hours.

And still there was no sign of Tony.

Danny felt cold exhaustion creeping over him. He tried to work out when he had last slept. It had been nearly twenty-four hours and his wound was sapping his remaining energy. Concentrating was hard. He'd managed it up till now. But at some point, he would have to sleep. A sinister numbness spread up his arm. He wasn't sure he'd be able to use it. If only he could rest. That would make things better ...

He put that thought from his mind. Sleep wasn't possible. Not now.

'We've got movement.' Brooker's voice was quiet and tense in Danny's earpiece.

'Where?' Danny breathed.

'Coming up the gulley from the south. Someone's emerging from the treeline.'

'Can you make a positive ID?'

There was a pause. Danny could hear his own pulse. He realised he was holding his breath. He forced himself to exhale slowly.

'That's a negative,' said Brooker. 'Our guy's in camo gear and he's carrying a rifle – M4 – but his head's wrapped.'

Danny cursed silently. He wanted to see Tony's face. To be certain he had his guy. Sure, Tony would identify himself by going straight to the cache, the location of which only he knew. But still, Danny wanted the satisfaction of knowing.

He allowed himself to move slightly so that he could see down the gulley. It took him a moment to pick out the figure, whose clothes camouflaged him well against the rock. But his eyes zoned in after ten seconds. The figure was scrambling carefully up the ravine. Distance: 100 metres. He was moving slowly. Every five or ten metres, he stopped and looked around.

Danny had a moment of uncertainty. That figure was not moving like an SAS operator. He was out in the open. There was no attempt at a covert approach. He looked . . . unfit.

He reassured himself. Tony had no reason to approach covertly. He wasn't expecting company. It was dawn, and this was an unpopulated area. And what if he *did* look unfit. He was probably exhausted. Like Danny.

'You thinking what I'm thinking . . .' Brooker's voice came over the comms, tense and quiet.

'Wait,' Danny said. 'Keep eyes on. He'll identify himself by going straight to the cache.'

'And if he doesn't?'

'Just wait,' Danny said, to mask his own uncertainty.

Silence.

Tony had the patsy in his sights. Fucking muppet looked liked he was half dead already, the way he struggled up the hill. He congratulated himself for taking extra precautions.

'What if they are not there?' Al-Zafawi said. He sounded brash, but Tony could tell that it masked deep uncertainty.

'They're there,' Tony said without taking his eye from the sight. 'Trust me, buster. They're there.'

Distance: 55 metres. The figure stopped for what felt like the hundredth time.

The cross hairs of Danny's sights were trained precisely on his head. Even though his weapon wasn't properly zeroed, he reckoned he could take Tony now, so long as his numb arm didn't let him down. He felt his trigger finger moving. A single shot would do it. The world would certainly be a better place without Tony Wiseman in it.

Danny wondered if he was being honest with himself. Had Tony outsmarted him every step of the way until now? Was he the better soldier?

He stayed his hand. He would take the shot if necessary, but their original strategy remained the best: an IED strike. As common as sand in Helmand Province. Easily explained away.

'I don't think it's him.' Brooker sounded uneasy. 'Look at the way he's moving. Like a fucking rookie.'

Danny carried on following him with his rifle. The target had reached a particularly deep section of the gulley. His shemagh-covered head was bobbing in and out of sight. Each time it reappeared, Danny adjusted his aim to keep it trained on the head.

A minute passed. The target advanced another ten metres.

'He's wheezing like a fat boy,' Riley said over comms. 'I could take this cunt out with a pea-shooter.'

'Hold your fire,' Danny warned. 'Let the booby trap do its thing.'

Another minute. Distance to target: thirty metres. The gulley had become shallower. Danny could see the top three-quarters of the target's body.

Something caught his eye. The figure's rifle was slung across his shoulder. Danny focused in on it. It was a M4, spray painted in khaki colours. And painted on the stock was a series of tiny white dots. Tipp-Ex marks.

Danny felt a surge of relief.

'Okay, fellas,' he said over comms. 'I have a positive ID.'

'You sure?' Brooker didn't sound convinced.

'A hundred per cent. That's Tony's weapon. I saw him with it. He's marked his kill tally on the stock. I have eyes on. It's Tony.'

A pause. Then, Murray's voice: 'Roger that,' he said. 'I'll update Spearpoint.'

Cadogan nearly jumped out of his seat when the communication came through. It was as if everyone in the ops room exhaled at once.

'This is Kestrel One,' came a grainy and indistinct voice over the secure radio. 'We have a positive ID on Tony Wiseman. Repeat, we have a positive ID on Tony Wiseman.'

'Is it just him?' Cadogan demanded. 'Does he have any backup?'

'That's a negative,' said the voice. 'It's just him. It won't be long now.'

Danny followed Tony with his rifle. He could taste the anticipation. He thought of all the times that Tony had wronged him. On a blazing oil rig in the Persian Gulf. On a migrant boat in the Mediterranean. In the forests of Sandringham. In the badlands of Helmand. If their situations were reversed, Danny knew for sure that Tony would already have taken the shot. The rest of the unit were turned off by the idea of taking out another Regiment guy. Danny was honest enough to admit to himself that his trigger finger was itching.

He didn't scratch that itch. He just allowed Tony to get closer and closer to the cache. He was ten metres away now, his upper half visible above the edge of the gulley.

He had stopped.

He was looking in Danny's direction, but Danny felt certain he wasn't observed. He had Tony directly in his sights, the cross hairs central on his target's chest.

They stayed in that position for a full ten seconds.

'What the fuck's happening?' Brooker said over the comms.

'I don't know,' Danny said.

'He's avoiding the cache.'

'He's scouting the area,' Danny said.

'I think he's waiting for someone,' Brooker replied.

'Who the hell would he be waiting for?'

'I don't know, Danny. But he's avoiding the cache. So what do we do?'

Danny gave it twenty seconds' thought. He tried to separate his own desire to nail Tony from the necessity of making the right call. Was he really waiting for backup? If so, who from? Did they really want to get into a fight, if they could avoid it?

Danny narrowed his eyes. Tried to ignore the awful numbness creeping down his arm. Kept the target in his sights. 'I think I need to take the shot,' he said.

'Any second now,' Tony breathed, his weapon engaged and the cache area in his sights. 'They'll take him out, then they'll approach the target. That's when we open up.'

Al-Zafawi said nothing. He was staring intently down the gulley.

'Any second now,' Tony repeated. Damn, he hoped Black was the first of these idiots to approach the body.

'The cache is by that strange rock,' Al-Zafawi said. 'Am I right?'

'Don't you worry about the cache, buster. As soon as we've put these fuckers down, we'll open it up.' He sniffed. 'Any second now,' he said for a third time.

And to himself, he said: *Come on, Black. Show yourself.*

Caitlin had lost count of how many times she had tried to raise Spearpoint on the sat phone. Ten? Twenty? The whole journey from Panjika was blurred in her concussed mind. She didn't know how long it had taken. All she knew was that the sun was coming up, and that she had arrived at the place where she needed to ditch her vehicle and head north, if she was going to have any chance of warning Danny.

She staggered out of the vehicle, making no attempt to hide it. The sandstorm had subsided a little, but the clouds of sand still blasted her face and body. She peered north. She could just make out a rough path over undulating ground towards the mountain-side looming ahead. It seemed to lead towards a forested slope.

Thirty klicks north of Gareshk, dug into the mountainside where Al-Zafawi will never find it . . .

Was this the place? She couldn't know for sure. But she had no time to doubt herself.

She headed north, clutching her sat phone. Her attention was fixed on the path, but almost by reflex she dialled the access number into Spearpoint as she stumbled forward. Expecting nothing but electrical interference, she put the handset to her ear.

'Go ahead,' said a distant, crackly voice.

Caitlin stopped. For a moment she couldn't speak as she tried to get her head in order.

'*Go ahead.*'

'This is asset Charlie Foxtrot Niner,' she shouted above the noise of the storm. Her voice was weak and rasping. 'Get me Cadogan!'

'Say again?'

'*Get me Cadogan!*'

She turned as she waited, surveying the area around the path. She was exposed. What was she thinking? She crouched to the ground to make a smaller target.

'Cadogan.' The Spearpoint controller's voice was abrupt.

There was no time for wasted words. Caitlin screamed over the storm. '*Tell Danny . . .*' she started to stay, but then she coughed, and couldn't stop coughing.

'Tell him what?'

'*Tell him . . . Tony and Al-Zafawi . . . working together . . . he's not alone . . . he's got a team . . . hello . . . hello?*'

The electrical interference had returned. There was no one at the other end of the line. Caitlin cursed, pushed herself painfully to her feet and almost tripped as she pushed on through the storm, heading for the protection of the forested slope, and whatever lay beyond.

Danny's breathing was slow and measured. His finger rested lightly on the trigger. The cross hairs were squarely on Tony's chest.

One shot, he told himself. You have to put him down with one shot. Otherwise you give him a chance.

He stopped breathing so there was no movement to screw up his aim.

Prepared to take the shot.

'*Hold your fire!*' Murray's whispered voice over comms was urgent. '*Hold your fire!*'

Danny quelled a kick of disappointment in his gut. He didn't move his weapon, but he returned his finger to the edge of the trigger guard.

'Go ahead,' he breathed.

'Spearpoint are on. They've had a communication from Caitlin Wallace. She says Tony's hooked up with Al–Zafawi.'

'Bullshit,' said Riley. 'What's she on? Al–Zafawi would cut Tony's head off and stick the footage on YouTube half an hour later.'

But Danny said nothing. He felt like something had clicked in his brain. Instantly, he understood Tony's play. And he knew beyond question that Brooker had been right. The guy Danny had in his sights now was *not* Tony.

'Nobody move a fucking muscle,' he breathed into comms. 'It's an ambush.'

'Course it's a bloody ambush,' Riley said. 'We're the ones who set it up.'

'No,' Danny said. 'Tony's the one who set it up.' He paused. 'He's in the high ground. He's got Al–Zafawi's team. We fire on this guy, nothing's going to happen. But when we show ourselves, they open up. Nobody fucking move.'

Silence. The target looked around a little, evidently unsure of himself. Then, quite clearly, he looked up the hill, as if searching for something, or someone.

'What's our next play, Danny?' Brooker whispered. 'What the fuck do we do?'

'We stay put,' Danny said. 'They don't know where we are, otherwise they wouldn't need to draw us out. That means they don't know for sure that we're here. If we stay put, they'll advance on the cache.'

A pause.

'Roger that,' came the reply.

'What is happening?' Al–Zafawi spat.

The Taliban patsy in the gulley was looking up towards them.

'Fuck's *sake*,' Tony hissed.

'There is nobody there, you fool,' Al-Zafawi said, making zero attempt to hide the accusation in his voice.

'Keep your fucking voice down,' Tony said. 'They'll show themselves eventually. They'll have to. We just have to wait—'

'I will not,' Al-Zafawi said. 'There is nobody there. We must take the bullion while we can.' He called over his shoulder in Pashto.

Tony turned, pointing his weapon towards the Taliban leader. 'What did you just say?' he demanded. '*What did you just say?*'

They stared at each other, hate crackling between each man. Seconds later, three Taliban militants emerged through the trees, weapons engaged, pointing towards Tony.

'Don't be an idiot, Al-Zafawi,' Tony said. 'I'm the only one who knows—'

'Put down your weapon,' Al-Zafawi said.

Tony kept his AK trained on the Taliban leader. Sweat dripped down his brow. The three gunmen, sneering and clearly pleased to have the British soldier where they wanted him, kept their weapons on him.

'We release a single round,' Tony breathed, 'we give away our position and we're fucked.'

'Put down your weapon,' Al-Zafawi repeated.

Tony's brain was making minute calculations. Could he switch his weapon to automatic without them noticing? Could he take all four men out in a burst before one of them fired on him? Could he disappear into the forest without the Red Unit finding him?

None of these calculations gave him the answer he wanted. He lowered his weapon. There was no other choice. He laid it on the ground. 'Look, guys,' he said in his most reasonable tone of voice, 'if we're going to get past that team—'

'*There is no team!*' Al-Zafawi said. 'Only us!' His eyes flashed. He nodded at his men and said something in Pashto. They advanced on Tony, stopping when they were about three metres away. 'Get on your knees,' the Taliban leader said. '*Now!*'

Tony knelt. His weapon was still close. Half a metre. He could grab it if he needed to. He knew Al-Zafawi wouldn't give the kill order yet. Not till he had his hands on his bullion.

Al–Zafawi spat on him. He felt the gobbet of saliva on his left cheek. 'I am going to get my money,' Al–Zafawi said.

Tony forced himself to breathe slowly and keep his heart rate down. 'Don't go,' he said. 'You'll fuck the whole thing up.'

But Al–Zafawi was already stepping out from the treeline. In seconds, he was in full view of anybody surveying the gulley.

Tony waited for the shot. It didn't come. The three gunmen grinned at him.

Tony sweated, and kept one eye on his weapon.

'Movement to the north.' Brooker's voice, low and urgent.

Danny twisted his head to look up the gulley. A figure had emerged from the treeline. Male. Afghan. Distance: eighty to eighty-five metres. Danny squinted. He recognised the bruised, black-bearded face.

Al–Zafawi.

The figure in the gulley shouted something in Pashto: final proof that it wasn't Tony. Al–Zafawi didn't reply. He was sliding clumsily down the slope, his arms sticking out to keep his balance.

'Hold your fire,' Danny warned as the Taliban leader approached. 'Don't give away your positions. Tony's up there somewhere.' He tried to identify the point up above where Al–Zafawi had emerged from the treeline.

'Can you see anyone?' Riley asked.

'Negative,' said Danny.

Instinctively, he wanted to change the trajectory of his weapon so that it was pointing uphill. But that would involve too much movement. He would risk being seen. For now, he had to bide his time.

And watch.

Al–Zafawi was halfway to the cache. He had a fierce, greedy look on his face. The Tony substitute shouted to him again, but received no reply. Now Danny could see that all his attention was on the strangely shaped boulder that marked the cache. Danny moved his gaze from Al–Zafawi to the treeline and back again.

Any moment now, he knew, it was going to go noisy.

Al-Zafawi was ten metres from the boulder.

Five.

He shouted something aggressive at the Tony substitute, who backed off a little so that he was maybe six or seven metres from the cache. Al-Zafawi reached the boulder. He held on to one of the protruding spikes to steady himself. Then he started scanning the ground, his eyes keen and wide.

Danny watched. The comms was silent. He was holding his breath. Jesus, the pain in his arm.

'Fucker's going to set it off,' Kit breathed.

Danny remembered Hammond's urgent question when they'd spoken outside the cave. *Tell me Al-Zafawi's alive . . .*

Not for long. This was out of Danny's hands now. The Yanks could scream about it all they liked.

Al-Zafawi stepped round the boulder. Danny could see his face directly. He was clearly looking for disturbed earth.

He found it. A slow smile spread across his face. He took a step towards it.

The final step of his life.

The volume of the explosion told Danny that Kit had been heavy on the C-4. Its crack and boom echoed across the mountainside. The explosion itself immediately rendered Al-Zafawi and the Tony substitute invisible, hidden by a huge cloud of dust and earth blown skywards. Danny caught a flash of red in the cloud, and he knew that both men would have been instantly killed. Dust and tiny pebbles rained down on the bush where he was hiding. He tried to look through the cloud, up the hill towards the treeline. He was searching for movement.

He saw it.

Tony saw the explosion a fraction of a second before he heard it. He saw earth and rock and dust spit into the air. He saw body parts flung up the ravine.

But most of all, he saw his bullion cache, destroyed by a device that was evidently meant to take him with it. A fierce burning sensation pulsed through him. He had to suppress the desire to scream a curse at the top of his voice. His money. His *fucking* money. After everything he'd done to win it. After all the graft . . .

He saw Danny Black's face in his mind's eye and his own face contorted. He would do anything to nail that cunt right now. If Black was in front of him, he'd do it without hesitation.

But Black wasn't in front of him, and Tony had his own skin to save.

The three gunmen, shocked by the sudden explosion, moved to the treeline and stared down the gulley. No longer at gunpoint, Tony grabbed his weapon from the ground. He was on the point of raising it to take out the three Taliban when they moved beyond the treeline and he stayed his hand. There was an SAS team down there. Their attention now would be fully on the Taliban – not just these three muppets, but the other four too. Looking through the trees, Tony could see them emerging from their positions. He guessed their anger at seeing Al-Zafawi blown sky high was trumping whatever tactical ability they had. Well, that was fine with Tony. The Regiment could slog it out with the Red Unit. It would give Tony the opportunity to make his escape.

The Taliban seemed to have forgotten about him. They had their weapons raised. It was going to be a rout. Tony knew he should turn and run. But something stopped him. He moved slightly closer to the treeline, watching as the Taliban fighters advanced. And further down the hill, finally, he saw movement. The explosion had subsided and his eye was suddenly drawn to a thicket, about thirty metres west of the cache boulder. The thorny foliage shuddered just a little. Tony stared at it. The movement subsided, but he knew someone was hiding there. Was it Danny Black? Instinctively, he raised his rifle, ready to fire a burst directly into the bush.

But then he lowered it again. He wasn't going to give away his position as easily as that.

He stepped backwards. Then he turned. By the time he started running back into the forest, the first gunshot had been fired.

* * *

Movement of enemy personnel.

Danny saw three guys emerge from the treeline. Distance eighty metres. He adjusted his rifle. He knew that the movement might give away his position, but that was too bad. He needed to prepare to fire towards the oncoming threat. He viewed the three militants through his sight, but something else caught his attention. Movement, just beyond them, behind the treeline. The powerful sight picked out a fourth figure. It was raising its rifle, pointing directly towards Danny's firing point. But then the figure lowered its rifle and Danny saw his face.

Tony.

For a moment, it was as though Tony was staring directly at him. Danny prepared to take the shot.

Too late. Tony had melted back into the forest.

But Danny knew his position.

'Okay, fellas.' Brooker's voice over comms was calmer than it had been all morning. 'We've got seven targets advancing in line down the hill. Distance between each target, approximately ten metres. I'm assigning numbers one to seven from left to right. Tell me who've you've got in your sights.'

Danny aimed directly at the figure at the right-hand side of the line. 'Seven,' he said clearly.

Murray, Kit and Riley spoke in turn.

'Two.'

'Five.'

'Six.'

'I have three. On my word, take the shot.' There was a two-second pause. Danny kept his cross hairs squarely on the chest of his guy. Held his breath to ensure accuracy. Brooker gave the word. 'Go.'

Danny fired. Even though his weapon wasn't zeroed, the aim was good. The round hit his target in the chest and the man went down with a heavy, leaden finality. Four more rounds split the air in unison. Danny knew he didn't even need to check that his unit mates had made their targets. There would only be two Taliban fighters left.

He turned to get the others in his sights just as a burst of automatic fire rent the air. Rounds fell metres from his position. He caught sight of one of the fighters down on his knee in the firing position, aiming directly towards him. Instinctively, he pressed himself into the earth, covering his head with his hands.

Voices came over his comms. Completely calm.

'One.'

'Three.'

Another burst of automatic fire. The rounds fell closer this time. Just a metre or two from Danny's position.

'Take the shot.'

Danny heard the retort of two single rounds. Then silence.

'Targets down,' Brooker said.

Danny looked up again. He panned around the area. All seven Taliban were immobile corpses on the slope.

'Not a bad day at the office,' Riley's laconic drawl came over the comms.

'Not over yet,' Danny said. 'There might be others, and we haven't taken Tony.'

'May not be there, mucker,' Brooker said.

'He's there. I saw him.' A pause. 'I'm going after him. I need covering fire while I get up to the treeline.'

'Roger that,' said Brooker. 'Lads, you know what to do.'

From his firing position, Danny plotted his route up to the treeline where he had seen Tony. He would make use of the gulley, he decided. It would give him extra cover. He spoke over comms. 'Moving in three, two, one, go.'

The covering fire from his unit mates started the moment he emerged, scratched and sore, from the thicket. Single shots, from the various directions of their positions, one every four or five seconds. Danny sprinted, head bowed and wincing from the pain in his shoulder, towards the gulley. He passed the marker boulder. A crater the depth of a man had been blown out of the ground by Kit's booby trap. There were gobbets of molten gold scattered around.

'You weren't supposed to blow the bloody gold,' Danny muttered over the comms.

'Yeah,' Kit said. 'Sorry about that.'

Al-Zafawi's torso smouldered at the edge of the gulley. Danny couldn't see the Tony substitute, but there were body parts and gristle littered over the area. He scrambled up the gulley, keeping his head and body low. The unit's rounds crossed just a couple of metres above him as he powered over rock and scree and foliage. He felt none of his previous exhaustion and he even managed to compartmentalise the shoulder pain. His mind and body were finely tuned to his objective: catching Tony, and putting him down.

Fifty metres up the gulley he spoke into comms. 'I'm moving out on a north-easterly trajectory towards the treeline.'

'Roger that,' came the four-way reply.

Danny pushed himself out of the gulley. Distance to the treeline: twenty metres. He engaged his weapon and advanced towards it, releasing single shots into the trees as he advanced at a jog. The unit's covering fire continued behind him, but it stopped as soon as he hit the treeline.

Silence.

Danny panned his weapon left and right, hyper alert for any sign of movement. He saw none. He was certain this was where Tony had been. But where had he run? His best move would be to head further into the forested area. There he could find cover, maybe a concealed firing point. Danny looked at the ground. It was too dry for footprints, but he immediately noticed a stone, about the size of his fist, that had been turned over to reveal a less dusty underside. It was about three metres from his position in a north-east-east direction. There was a faint imprint in the ground next to it, on Danny's side. It had clearly been kicked as somebody retreated in that direction. Danny had his trajectory.

Finger on trigger, weapon raised, he advanced. He made no noise. In an instant he was on exercises back in the jungles of Belize. He could almost hear his training officer whispering in his ear: 'Don't look *at* the trees. Look *through* them.' Danny did just that, piercing the forest with his gaze so that he was aware of what was twenty metres ahead, despite the obstructions.

He was aware of other things too. A cracked twig on the ground ahead. The thin, sun-starved, shoulder-height limb of a tree bent in the direction that someone had recently passed. He knew he was on track. He knew that any moment –

There was a sound to his right. A sudden, massive crash as a figure hurtled himself towards Danny. Danny twisted his body to try to make the shot, but he wasn't fast enough. He saw the briefest glimpse of Tony's face – the anger on his lips and the madness in his eyes – before he was thrown to the ground, his opponent's heavy body crushing him.

Danny's immediate thought was to make a distress signal over comms. But that was clearly Tony's first thought too. He ripped away Danny's boom mike and yanked the comms earpiece from his head. Then, with one hand on Danny's throat and the weight of his body against his weapon, he started to punch. He knew where Danny's wound was, of course, because he had inflicted it. He pounded his fist against Danny's shoulder several times, putting all of his bodyweight behind the blow. The pain was indescribable. With each strike, Danny felt his eyes roll and an electric flash clouded his sight. He sensed a thin line of dribble drip from the right of his mouth. He didn't know if it was blood or spit. Retaliation was impossible. He could do nothing but endure the pain. Above it all, he could hear Tony's hate-filled, whispered hiss.

'I'm sick of you fucking things up for me, Black. It ends now.'

Tony's anger was clearly such that he wanted Danny to suffer some more before putting a bullet in his skull. He yanked Danny's left arm up and pinned it down with one knee. Danny caught a glimpse of his mad eyes as he held his rifle upside down in two hands, almost gently touched the butt to the wound area, then lifted it high and brought it smashing down with all his force.

Danny tried to scream, but his throat wouldn't work. He couldn't feel his arm. A sodden patch of blood oozed through his camo jacket. His limb felt alien, like it belonged to someone else. When Tony raised his weapon for a second time, Danny closed his eyes before he smashed it down again. Held his breath and endured the excruciating agony of the impact when it came.

When he opened his eyes again, Tony was standing up. He pressed his right foot on top of Danny's weapon, which was still slung across his chest, to stop him using it. Tony's own weapon was the right way round now. Its barrel was pointing directly at Danny's face, and Tony's finger was on the trigger.

'Nailed by a Taliban AK-47,' Tony said. 'Of all the ways to go. Those twats at Hereford will probably chalk you up as a hero. Shame it's only me who knows you're a cunt.'

Everything was spinning. Danny tried to roll away, but he had no energy. He couldn't move. He closed his eyes and waited for it to happen.

The gunshot was loud. It made his whole body start. He gasped for breath.

Why hadn't he felt anything. Had Tony shot him in his numb arm?

He opened his eyes.

Tony was looking down at himself in horror. He had dropped his weapon and there was a patch of blood oozing through his clothes, at exactly the same point on his left shoulder where Danny was wounded. Tony looked up, staring beyond Danny into the trees. There was no doubting it. He was scared.

Tony staggered back, one hand over the shoulder wound. It was pissing blood.

Ignoring the screaming pain in his own wound, Danny found the strength to grab his weapon with his good hand and swing it up to point towards Tony. But he didn't fire. A figure moved past him to the left, bearing down on Tony, brandishing a pistol with two hands.

It was Caitlin, and she was moving with purpose.

Tony continued to stagger backwards, but Caitlin was almost on top of him. She didn't fire. She kicked out with her right foot and struck him squarely in the right knee.

Tony collapsed. Caitlin stood over him, her weapon aimed precisely at his skull. Blood poured through the fingers of his hand as it pressed against his shoulder wound.

Danny forced himself to his feet. His bad arm hung limply by his side, but he brandished his weapon with his good arm, pointing it at Tony. In his peripheral vision he was aware of movement to his right. More Taliban? No. He glimpsed Brooker through the trees, about fifteen metres away, well camouflaged and weapon engaged. He looked to his left. Riley, ready to attack.

But they were hesitating. Danny could sense it. None of them really wanted to be the one to nail another Regiment guy.

Danny looked at Caitlin. She was a mess. Her face was bruised, swollen and scabbed. Her nose broken and bloodied. She looked as though she was having trouble standing. But she was managing it, and she had her right arm stretched out, a handgun pointing at the back of Tony's head.

Tony looked at Danny. 'Just fucking do it,' he said.

Danny didn't reply. He just kept staring, first at Tony, then at Caitlin. Her gun arm was trembling, but she still had the handgun pointed at Tony's head.

Thoughts jostled in Danny's mind. Flashes of bad memory. So many of them involved Tony. 'He did this to you?' he asked Caitlin.

Caitlin nodded.

'He was going to kill you?'

'Of course.' Caitlin's voice was hoarse. It hardly sounded like her.

'He was going to kill me too.'

'Just do it!' Tony hissed. There was a frightened waver in his voice. Danny was pleased to hear it.

He looked around at the others. Their reluctance to fire hung among the trees like a mist. Maybe, he thought, they could bind Tony. Take him back to Camp Shorabak. Bundle him on to a C-130 and let the RMPs have their fun with him.

But Danny knew that wasn't an option. Tony was a liability to the Regiment. His crimes had to be covered up. Hereford and Spearpoint had made their decision and passed their sentence. All that remained was to carry it out.

'They won't put *you* down as a hero,' he told Tony. 'They'll write you out of the history books. Good thing too.'

Tony spat at his feet.

Silence.

Danny looked at Caitlin. 'He's all yours,' he said. 'Do it quickly.' He turned his back on them.

As he walked away, he heard the retort of Caitlin's handgun. Then the unmistakable sound of a body slumping to the ground.

Three more shots. Danny didn't stop and he didn't look round.

'Burn him,' he called to the others in a blunt voice. 'No identifying features. Tony was never here.'

The rest of the unit moved into the clearing. They had lowered their weapons now. There was no need for them.

Danny stopped by the nearest tree. He collapsed to his knees and slumped against the trunk. He sensed Caitlin looking down on him but no longer had the energy to speak. The job was done. The Regiment would live to fight another day.

The question was: would he?

EPILOGUE

Hereford, one week later

Jacko McGuigan, newly promoted since the unexplained disappearance of his former boss Mike Holroyd, gave the MOD police officer at the entrance to RAF Credenhill a superior look. He was proud of his recent promotion, and didn't mind showing it. The officer checked his accreditation, nodded as he handed it back and waved Jacko through.

It was raining hard, but Jacko was glad of it after his stint in Helmand. He didn't want to see sand or sun for a while. And he didn't much want to see a member of 22 SAS. Some character by the name of Ray Hammond had summoned him here, however, and although Jacko was under no obligation to respond, he was curious. Holroyd had been right about the Regiment. They were out of control and Jacko felt he had enough to continue his predecessor's work and bring these liabilities down. In his view, there was no place for them in the modern military. But if they had something to say, he wanted to hear it.

He was led into the main building by a broad-shouldered, bearded guy in civvies who had done no more than ask his name. He emanated disdain as he took Jacko along a network of corridors into a section at the heart of the building that was guarded by two armed men in camouflage gear. They stopped outside a plain, wooden door. Jacko's guide knocked three times then opened the door and indicated that he should enter. Jacko did. The door closed behind him.

It was a plain room with one desk and one chair. A man in fatigues sat behind the desk. He had a mournful expression, and very dark rings around his eyes, almost as if they'd been painted on. He uttered no word of welcome. He just stared at Jacko.

'Hammond?' Jacko said, making his voice as authoritative as possible.

No reply.

Jacko wondered whether to stand or sit. He decided to sit and instantly regretted it. Standing, he could look down on this man. Sitting, they appeared to be equals.

The man behind the desk still said nothing. The silence ballooned. Jacko felt uncomfortable.

'Your men are out of control,' he said finally.

Silence.

'I saw their handiwork in Helmand Province. I've been making my inquiries. You can expect arrests very soon, starting with Danny Black.'

Silence.

'The word is that Spearpoint's been dismantled. Cadogan's gone to ground, surrounded by a protective barrier ten lawyers thick – hardly a sign of innocence, to my mind.'

Silence.

'God damn it, man, *you* invited *me* here. Don't you have anything to say for yourself?'

Silence.

Jacko felt his anger rising. 'I've had enough of this. I'm a busy man.' He stood up. 'I don't have time for your games.' He made for the door, but then turned again. 'As for Tony Wiseman ... We haven't found him yet, but we will. And I should tell you that the rumours aren't pretty. I have several sources stating that he had a direct association with a known Taliban militant.' He narrowed his eyes and circled one forefinger. 'All this,' he said, 'is going the way of the dodo. There's no place for it. Mark my words.'

He headed for the door again and was just about to open it when –

'You're right.'

Jacko inhaled slowly as he turned. 'What?'

'Well,' Hammond said. 'You're half right. You *won't* find Tony Wiseman. But yeah, he got together with Al-Zafawi. He also killed two Regiment men, and frankly that's just the beginning.'

Jacko moved back towards the desk. He knew he had to play this carefully. It sounded like a confession. Like Hammond was blowing the whistle, just like Wiseman had before him. No wonder he had been reluctant to speak at first. 'Go on,' he said.

'Tony Wiseman was a bad apple.' Hammond sniffed. 'He's been removed from the barrel. End of story.'

Jacko smiled. 'I'm afraid,' he said, 'that's nowhere near the end of the—'

'Shut the fuck up, McGuigan, and look at this.' He passed a sealed A4 envelope across the table. McGuigan stared at it for a moment, then picked it up and opened it.

It contained a photograph. CCTV maybe, or taken from a smartphone. It showed a Land Rover, front on. Through the windscreen two faces were visible: driver and passenger. The image was blurred, but there was no doubt who the people in the photograph were. Tony Wiseman and Mike Holroyd.

'You've been making inquiries? *We've* been making inquiries.'

'What is this?' Jacko said.

'That photograph was taken about half an hour before Wiseman and Holroyd were reported missing. We have an interview with an ANA guard at Shorabak who recalls both men leaving the camp together. They appeared to be working side by side. That's certainly the impression most people would have, looking at the evidence.'

Now it was Jacko's turn to be silent. He looked from the picture to Hammond and back again. 'Are you trying to suggest—'

'You were working directly for Holroyd, isn't that right? It's a terrible thing, really, but I can't guarantee you won't be dragged into all this, if it's made public. Embarrassing for you, and your family. A boy and a girl, isn't it? Seven and nine?'

Jacko stared at him.

Hammond got up, walked round the desk and stood right by him, looking down at him with his hangdog expression. He took

311

the photo back. 'Probably best if I look after that,' he said. He bent down so that they were at eye level and continued to talk in a very quiet, very calm voice. 'If I hear that Danny Black, or any of my men, are getting any kind of hassle from you or anyone else at Fareham, I will drag you through the shit. Am I clear?'

Jacko clenched his jaw.

'*Am I clear?*'

'Clear,' Jacko said.

'Good. Now get the hell out of my office and get the hell out of Hereford. Now.'

Jacko stood up. His pulse was racing. He headed for the door for a third time.

'And McGuigan.'

'What?'

'The Regiment sorts out its own problems. Tell your mates. Don't fuck with the SAS.'

McGuigan felt his nostrils flaring. He locked eyes with Hammond, but he couldn't withstand that black-ringed stare for long. He bowed his head and left the room, closing the door quietly behind him.

AUTHOR'S NOTE

Fact: in recent years, a large quantity of American gold bullion has found its way into the pockets of warlords and militants in Afghanistan.

Fact: the Royal Military Police have been investigating the activities of British special forces in Helmand Province and elsewhere.

Fact: at the time of writing, the Taliban are on the rise.

You have to **survive it**
To **write it**

NEVER MISS OUT AGAIN
ON ALL THE LATEST NEWS FROM

CHRIS
RYAN

**Be the first to find out
about new releases**

**Find out about events with
Chris near you**

Exclusive competitions

And much, much more …

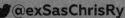